THE HUNTSMAN

Whitney Terrell

THE

HUNTSMAN

VIKING

FIC
TERRELL

VIKING
Published by the Penguin Group
Penguin Putnam Inc., 375 Hudson Street,
New York, New York 10014, U.S.A.
Penguin Books Ltd, 27 Wrights Lane,
London W8 5TZ, England
Penguin Books Australia Ltd, Ringwood,
Victoria, Australia
Penguin Books Canada Ltd, 10 Alcorn Avenue,
Toronto, Ontario, Canada M4V 3B2
Penguin Books (N.Z.) Ltd, 182–190 Wairau Road,
Auckland 10, New Zealand

Penguin Books Ltd, Registered Offices:
Harmondsworth, Middlesex, England

First published in 2001 by Viking Penguin,
a member of Penguin Putnam Inc.

10 9 8 7 6 5 4 3 2 1

PUBLISHER'S NOTE
This is a work of fiction. Names, characters, places, and incidents either
are the product of the author's imagination or are used fictitiously,
and any resemblance to actual persons, living or dead, business
establishments, events, or locales is entirely coincidental.

LIBRARY OF CONGRESS CATALOGING IN PUBLICATION DATA
Terrell, Whitney.
The Huntsman / Whitney Terrell.
    p.   cm.
    ISBN 0-670-89465-6
    I. Title.
    PS3570.E692 R44 2001
    813'.6—dc21   00-043946

This book is printed on acid-free paper. ∞

Printed in the United States of America
Set in Electra
Designed by Francesca Belanger

For the Sloans and Terrells

THE HUNTSMAN

1

FOR TWO GENERATIONS in the city's life there had not been much comment about its river. The populace moved southward from its banks into rolling hills and finally board-flat prairie, easily corralled, paved, and developed into suburban plots. Iron-gray and sinuous, banks heaped with deadfall and bright flecks of plastic trash, fish poisoned, docks crumbling, stinking of loam and rot, the river seemed an uncomfortable reminder of a gothic past when life had not been so clean. Bums lived along the river within sight of the mayor's office, a paper mill and several chemical companies rimmed the levee, and on the east side, the river flowed past housing projects for the poor. Most Kansas Citians never saw these things. Once every three years or so, some young reporter at the *Star* would get spring fever and spend the day riding upriver on an empty grain barge. In the morning, citizens at their breakfast tables held up bright color photos of the river's wide expanse and read a breathless article invoking Twain and explaining, to everyone's amazement, that barge traffic still existed. In fact, barges (this year's article read) transport one and a half million tons of cargo annually and are cheaper than trucks or rail.

"Now *there's* some decent reporting!" Mercury Chapman exclaimed, tapping the article with his fork. "Tells you how things work, instead of just writing up the next moronic car wreck. It's not that I don't have sympathy for any poor bastard has to die like that, but what good's the sympathy of a stranger? When I die . . . Lilly, what's the plan around here for when I die?" he shouted, suddenly rearing from his seat.

"The plan is, you do it after three o'clock." Lilly Washington glided through the porch door and retrieved the pitcher of milk so it wouldn't spoil. She had cooked for Mercury for thirty years, the last ten since his wife's death, and in the mornings she had business to administer. "At three o'clock the roof man's coming about that leak, and you've got to be here to show him around. Wednesdays are when I get my hair done."

"Ha!" Mercury said, sitting down.

"You've got shaving cream in your ear." Lilly's crisp lemon pantsuit darted, finchlike, into the kitchen's gloom.

"Ha!" Mercury said, rearing again for effect. The small comedy pleased him. He had talked to himself for most of his adult life, preferring to communicate by way of competing monologues rather than formal conversation, wielding the non sequitur and selective deafness like a surgeon's blade. His wife had been a formidable competitor in this running gag—in talk he found most men lugubrious—and it had been the boon of his widowerhood to discover Lilly's abilities in the field. Chattering to himself in an empty house, he would've taken his life by his own hand. "Decent reporting!" he repeated. "How much gloom is in the paper, and how much wonder all around? What about phones? You can call China by a machine on the wall, have been able to for thirty years, but who knows how it works? Or where clean water comes from, or how the TV signal goes out? How does beef get to market? Who built the Broadway Bridge? All Henry puts in here is sports, death, and politics: nothing for the common man. That's what I'm going to tell him, and watch the look on his fat Texas face. . . ." Henry Latham was the president of the *Kansas City Star*, and Mercury often invited him bass fishing on weekends. He shook the paper

2

and gazed past his Wolferman's English muffin at a photograph of the river's broad and muddy flow, a scalloped line of cottonwoods in the background.

"I like to hear that river's got a use still yet," he said, raising his voice so Lilly could hear him in the kitchen. "Booker and I went goose hunting once right along her banks, down near old Pete Martin's place. We laid out in a muddy field."

A snort of disapproval disturbed the pantry. The words "That's one way to camouflage a boy that black" reached Mercury's ears.

"Maybe he built a raft and went downriver," Mercury answered sadly, as if he had not heard a thing. "Floated clean away."

That same morning, sixty miles east of Mercury's cool, porch-flanked house on the 500 block of Highland Drive, Stan Granger headed out to check his lines. Dredging, dikes, and levees had transformed the Missouri River from a wandering, swampy titan a mile or two in width to little more than a drainage ditch (nostalgics said), at best a half mile from bank to bank. People believed that the Mighty Mo would never flood again, her mythic connection with great rivers from Abraham's time forward removed, like a stinger, by the Corps of Engineers. Still, outside Kansas City, the river flowed somnolent and muscular, centuryless, churning on without the permission of man's belief. At thirty-three, Stan Granger had acquired the habits of a much older man, a loner who fished more by habit than for useful trade. He had lost the necessity of words. Days passed in bundles when he did not speak, and as he hauled his trot line outside Waterloo, the town where he lived, his mind brooded with the same glinting, continuous flow as the river, its steady and unbroken stream of action unappended to so flimsy a vehicle as speech. So when he saw the trot line bellied far too deeply between the oak trunk and the anchor buoy a hundred yards offshore, he did not think it. He quartered his skiff against the current, set the line over his oarlock, and slid along it patiently, lifting and rebaiting the hooks that hung from steel-tipped leaders. He had caught a drum and two small catfish, and he broke their backs along the gunwales and dropped them on the skiff's floor. The closer he got to the trot line's middle, the harder the work became: the line hitched and popped jerkily along the galvanized oarlock, the weight pulled his gunwale down, and the river entered in a thin, gruel-like stream. Stan shifted his body away, grunting, to keep the gunwale up. He still did not think it but merely followed from one action to the next, each determining perfectly its successor, and when the weight and current grew too strong, he freed the line from the oarlock and played it by hand. The river darkened the flannel arms of his shirt. At the height of this ballet, his elbows bent and he thrust his chin beyond the gunwale, appearing from a distance to be ready to spring a handstand in the long, bright scarf of river, and then he set his back and tumbled a dead woman's body into his boat. Leaders trailed after it like roots, and Stan cut them one by one with his knife, just past the steel.

The corpse's head rested against the skiff's middle seat, her legs jumbled stiffly in the bow. A windbreaker had shifted rudely off her shoulders, pulling back her arms, and her breasts pressed dark aureoles against a golf shirt emblazoned with a country club's burgundy crest. She wore a khaki skirt, a needlepoint belt, and a two-toned, spiked golf shoe on her right foot, a tee stuck through the lacing flap; her left foot was bare. Her sable hair fanned the skiff's bench between Stan's knees, and her pupils, in death, had rolled backward in her head so she stared white-eyed at a cloud of starlings angling in unison against a glowing field of blue. He bent over the dead young woman without repulsion and reached beneath her shirt for a charm, which he silently unclasped. One of his hooks had caught her by the neck, and he removed it with a deft twist, leaving a glossy and bloodless wound.

Stan finished running his line. He had difficulty untangling his bait pot from the dead woman's legs, but he managed. He pulled in

4

two carp and one more catfish and, reaching his anchored buoy, judged that if the river rose two feet more, the buoy would be submerged. None of this he put into words, but firing the skiff's outboard and heading back toward town, the dead woman's bare, finely arched foot jutting into his line of sight, he felt the need of them. He could see the small town of Waterloo banked steeply on the bluff, clapboard buildings screened by cottonwoods and willows, the railroad grade, and above everything the white spire of the church steeple. "And on a Wednesday," were the words he found. "Right on a Wednesday morning, too."

At the landing, he tossed the fish in a bucket of water and left it in the shade and walked into town wearing overalls and a dirty shirt. At the church, early choir practice had begun, and organ music drifted through the still, gnat-laden streets, and when Stan arrived at the sheriff's house—a split-level ranch along a gulley on the edge of town—the tan patrol car shimmered in the drive. The sheriff stepped out onto his balding lawn with the city paper's sports page in his hand.

"I got one," Stan said.

The sheriff glanced at him quickly and then looked back at his box score. "Dead body, you mean."

"Yeah."

"That's the first one in a year. Black fella?" Sheriff Wade Crapple was forty-five and stood a full head shorter than Stan. He had played second base both in high school and for his company team in the marines and conveyed, even while reading, a laconic preparedness for the imagined, well-struck ball. "Go on, tell me," he said. "I can do two things at once."

"She's white," Stan said. "Young. My dad used to talk about the Italians came down in the forties, but not nobody white. Not a lady."

The sheriff sniffed. "That's not what's bothering you."

"Why wouldn't it be?" Stan said. He chafed his broad hands, the necessary evasion stretching before him like a desert. "You throw a person in the river in Kansas City, and this is where they'll beach.

Currents. City pitches her trash out, and it floats up at our door. I've took fifteen bodies out of that water, and that's how I looked at it— cleaning up trash—but this is the first time I've seen a face like that. Clean, young-looking. Been out golfing, I think."

"A debutante, eh?" the sheriff said. "They'll have the reporters out for that."

Stan Granger had expected a different body, if he'd expected one at all. The two were intimately connected in his memory—the dead girl, Booker Short's thin silhouette—and as the sheriff's patrol car wheeled him forward, his mind went in reverse, calling up the shadowed figure he'd seen outside old Pete Martin's cabin, two years ago last spring. Blacks of any sort were a rarity in Chapman County, and so Stan had punched his brakes, fishtailing on the gravel road, until he recognized Mercury Chapman's more familiar, whiter face, following the black one with a shovel and a rake.

He'd left them alone for a couple of days. He could not have said why, since he was caretaker of the place, except for the fleeting sense, garnered across a hundred yards of upturned soybeans, that some transaction was being conducted in which he did not care to participate. On the third day, he'd brought the water truck. The cabin stood at the end of a raised and rutted drive that split the soybean field like a dike. Beyond the cabin, a curtain of elms and pin oaks hid five hundred acres of prime duck fields bordered by a creek that, with luck, would flood them when the rains commenced. Stan had pulled the tanker in a half circle before the unshaded cabin, the screw mounts for its rain gauge blazing hot.

Seeing nobody, he'd stepped down.

"I didn't do it any," a voice said.

Wheeling, Stan had seen an empty soybean field and a washing machine colandered by target practice, and when he turned back the boy was slouched before his truck grille, head tilted, as though leaning back against a post where none in fact existed. His skin rose

6

smooth and intensely black from the zip-collared neck of his orange shirt, though when he moved, Stan could see glimmerings of yellow in the tone and a fine, adolescent mustache on his lip. The boy glanced off toward the duck fields, sucking hard on a cigarette, and then stamped out the butt. He lifted his eyes to Stan.

"Just so's you know."

Stan's nostrils caught the distinct reek of pot, wafting in the breeze.

Then Mercury Chapman splintered through the treeline below, talking and grunting dyspeptically, as was his habit: "And so the psychiatrist tells the priest, 'I know one thing they forgot to mention in the Bible, and that's PMS.'" He labored up a short hill of thigh-deep swale, a machete dangling from his wrist. "'Hell, no, they didn't!' this preacher says. 'What about the part where Mary rides Joseph's ass clear to Bethlehem?' Hello, Stan. Why haven't you gentlemen introduced yourselves? There's goddamn enough lack of manners in the city without we start it out in the sticks. I'm of the idea we should dig this clubhouse a permanent latrine." With this he marched between them and, turning on his heel, disappeared around the cabin's corner, where Stan heard him open the door.

"Stan Granger," Stan said, holding out his hand.

The boy leaned forward from his imaginary post and gripped Stan's fingers, smiling. It was a smile of reserve, blurred in meaning, and Stan believed he'd just been invited to share amusement at the eccentricities of his employer. He closed his face.

"Booker Short is my name," the boy said when they were no longer touching. "So you work for the man?"

"I look after the club."

"Is that 'man' singular or plural?" Mercury said, rounding the cabin again. He'd exchanged the machete for the key to the water tank. "Booker is teaching me a whole nother language, Stan. All these years, and I never learned to speak jive. 'Man' means white people in general, right?"

The boy whistled. He lifted his cap and looked bleakly over the gray, long-stretching fields and the dust-streaked water truck.

"I have just heard a living person say 'jive,'" he said.

Mercury sucked the spittle off his lip. "I tell ya what, kid," he said. "Me and this old boy are gonna teach you how to fill a country water tank and work a piece-of-crap pump like Stan's got here. And you cut us some slack on vocabulary." His words were friendly, but irritation whined through his gray-tufted nose, and, as he headed for the tank, Stan saw the boy staring at him with what he judged to be (at the time, of course, before he knew Booker—though even now he did not know for sure) a look of hate.

This confusion had always troubled Stan about Booker Short—both now, as he rode in Sheriff Crapple's cruiser, and in the past. Click, like the aperture of a camera, and Booker changed from one thing to the next. His first words to Stan, "I didn't do it any," had been spoken in what Stan would have called street talk, familiar from shouting black singers on TV and pretty much how Stan expected him to speak. But later, when he said his name, the voice had been rich and melodious, each consonant savored and pronounced in the manner of black preachers or older actors, and still later, when he'd become upset over the word *jive* (or was it what Mercury had said about "the man," or had he even been upset at all? In retrospect, Stan still could not be sure), he'd spoken with a parodic English burr.

One person could not be so many different things before somebody decided one of them was wrong, Stan's thinking went. And furthermore, what *didn't* he do? Stan hadn't even known what the boy *was* doing out in that cabin with Mercury Chapman, a wealthy and well-connected man. Uncertainties like these made Stan's broad hands squeeze and loosen against the patrol car's polished vinyl seat. Had he in fact seen hatred in the boy's gaze? And if so, why? He still didn't know the answer to that. Nor could he say for sure what Mercury had meant when he drove with Stan to the front gate and folded

8

three hundred dollars into his palm, saying, "It's not the job you've done. The kid needs a chance to work, so I'm going to have him look after the place. I'd appreciate it if you'd look in on him time to time." It was the first time in fifteen years that Stan had ever heard Mercury plead for anything. The older man wore a faded pink handkerchief around his head, clamped beneath a straw hat and soaked with sweat, rubber muck boots, and a tarnished service revolver on his hip. His pale-blue eyes watered in their sunburned sockets.

"I can't promise more than twice a week," Stan had told him.

"If I wanted you to baby-sit him," Mercury said, "I'd have offered more."

That had been the beginning of it: the first appearance of mystery to a man not prone to surmise. He could not remember when he had first seen his father unhook a body from his trot line or utter a low "Hep, hep" as their skiff nudged the deliquescent skull of a Mexican, snagged by his belt loop on a submerged limb. He had never puzzled over the origins of the bodies that he ferried to the river's shore, any more than he had wondered about Mercury Chapman's regular life in the city, sixty miles away. There had been, perhaps, grander times for bodies back in his father's youth: soft-fingered bookies with their heads wrapped in pillowcases, gangsters awash in tailored wool suits, their vests like corsets around their corruption, front men murdered with piano wire or lawyers punctured cleanly in the temple by a bullet. Until his own death, Stan's father had kept a set of brass knuckles as a paperweight, salvaged from a bouncer's full-length cashmere coat. But it was Stan who'd remained as witness to the river's decline, both in the fish that surfaced tumored and deformed by poison and in the increasing tawdriness of its dead. They arrived now barefoot, bony, and half starved, or wearing gaudy basketball sneakers and bright-red warm-up suits, their teeth inlaid farcically with gold. He had seen or heard tell of Vietnamese, Filipinos, Mexicans, and Chileans, but mostly there were the blacks, drug dealers, he guessed, participants in some trade violent and illegal enough to get them shot. Beyond that, however, he had avoided any curiosity about their lives. The terrors and strivings, the bereaved relatives and yellowed Polaroids stashed in cupboards of the hopeful children these corpses once had been—all the things implicit in the dead he retrieved—had never managed to disturb his peace of mind.

The truth was, until he met Booker, he'd never known a black man alive.

That spring Mercury had stayed with the boy for a week. There was a second building on the place, a converted boat shed, which had for a period of time housed a succession of itinerant farm hands who squatted there rent-free in exchange for keeping an eye on things during the off-season. This had been some fifteen years prior, before Stan was hired to do that work, and the shed had since fallen into disrepair—windows broken, raccoons and possums filling its corners with hard, white turds. Mercury and Booker worked on it by day and in the evening retired to the cabin, a strange, fanciful couple whose figures appeared matchlike across the milo fields when Stan passed by in his truck. One day, the Volvo disappeared, leaving the grounds preternaturally still. When on the second day it did not return, Stan waited until late afternoon and then parked before the driveway gate, unlocked it, and drove on in.

The sound of his truck announced him, and as he strode through the mudroom, past racks of hip waders hanging by their heels, he heard the scrape of furniture, sudden and concealed. When he entered the cabin itself, Booker sat facing him, shirtless, in a ladder-backed chair. "Hello, Stan," the boy said, his accent this time smooth and rootless.

"Why, howdy," Stan said. His greeting died when he noticed Booker's unnatural posture, his chair pulled away from the long, wax-dribbled dining table so the boy faced the door directly, his feet together and his naked shoulders braced. Stan had once felt the same uneasiness visiting a widowed farmer that he knew, and had stepped out on the back porch to find the man's hunting dog, its throat slit,

10

wrapped in a bloodstained sheet. "Wouldn't stop barking," said the widower sanely. But Stan had sensed within that house the passage of loneliness and unreason, like a solitary summer cloud, and he felt the same presence now. "I suppose you're getting along fine," he said.

"Mmmm," the boy said, looking not at Stan but out the door.

"Doing work down at the shack?"

"Oh, yeah, lots of work."

Stan watched the boy's hands flutter and expire in his lap. The cabin had no electricity, only a portable generator run at intervals to prime the water pump, and he noticed that the gas lamps along the rafters were all lit and glowing despite the afternoon sun. The floor and kitchen were methodically neat. "I reckon we've got time to take a look down there," Stan said.

"'Time'?" Booker's teeth flashed, and he covered his mouth with his hand. "Did you say 'time'?"

"That's what I said."

"'Cause that's a good one, man—time. That's one thing Booker Short's got in spades, a lifetime supply with warranty. No deposit, no return. Everlasting flavor for your everfresh breath. The old man said you were slow, but you are an outrageously funny man . . . Stan."

"Do you want to go look at it or not?" Stan said.

"Let me see if I can, um . . . *pencil you in*."

The gossamer strands of spider webs that laddered the path down to the shack told Stan what he already suspected: Booker hadn't been down it since Mercury left. The boy sauntered after him with a pair of yellow earphones curled about his head, humming lightly. Stan had been certain of his impression of loneliness and fear, of some crisis that he'd interrupted, and yet Booker's response to his sympathy was ridicule. Why waste my time with that? Stan thought angrily as he pushed his way down the faded path and around the copse of evergreens that hid the shack.

At first sight, the "rehabilitation" of that structure seemed nearly complete, a surprise to Stan, who had known Mercury Chapman to

11

be an energetic but wholly ineffectual carpenter. A new roof had been laid in and covered with rolled shingle, the window screens replaced, the stooped doorjamb torn out and roughed in square. While Stan examined these things, Booker stumbled about the piles of lumber and stacked paint cans as if he did not exist. When Stan looked again, Booker had squatted beside the warped porch with a square and a tape measure and was writing numbers on a block of pine.

"Planning to build something?" Stan asked, grinning.

The boy plucked out one earphone and laid it against his scalp. "How's that?" he asked.

"I said, are you gonna fabricate something today?" It was the same tone Stan used with Mercury, physical labor being one topic on which he presumed to condescend.

"Got to shore up the joist for this porch," Booker said. "Whole thing's rotted out underneath. I figure we can sister in the new joists beside the old, through-bolt the two together, but I'm gonna need a couple jacks to hold the thing in place. Don't feel like having a porch fall on me, out here alone."

Stan tugged up the thighs of his overalls. He said, "Let's see."

"You got a flashlight?"

"Little one on my keychain."

"Well, shimmy on underneath."

When Stan crawled out from beneath the porch, he handed Booker the tape measure. "Thirty-seven and a quarter, the joist I looked at. They might not all be the same."

Booker was sketching deftly on the woodblock, his earphones replaced. Stan set the tape on the porch. The boy seemed scrawny from growth, and his collarbone bulged awkwardly beneath his skin, too large for the slender child's biceps and sunken chest that hung below it, loose, like cloth on a rack. Sweat glistened on the small pooch of stomach above his jeans. "I guess you did most of this work yourself," Stan said.

12

"How's that?"

"I said I was wondering where you learned your carpentry."

Booker put down his pencil and stared levelly at Stan. "I took shop in jail."

He picked up the pencil again.

"That right?" Stan asked.

"Yep."

The porch and the small, beaten circle of grass where the two men squatted were covered, at that time of day, by the purple umbra of the nearby firs; beyond them the land fell away in shades of broken gold to a still slough overhung by cottonwoods, the figures of the two men vibrant against the cool russet of the larger trees.

"How long was you in jail for?" Stan asked.

"Sentenced to five years, served two, supposed to do the last three on parole," Booker said. "Only I'm not on parole."

"How come you're not on parole?"

"Because I jumped it," Booker said.

Stan was not aware that they had struck a bargain until some weeks later, when he was buying groceries in town. For years he'd purchased canned tins of soup, bags of rice, and sandwich meat in something like a trance, ambling through the aisles and grabbing whatever came to hand, and so it was with an obscure sense of self-deceit that he found himself at the counter not with his regular arm-basket, but pushing a cart. "Understand you've got a new neighbor," the grocer said, "got himself some trouble with the law."

"What neighbor is that?" Stan said, browsing the gum rack.

"That black boy out on Pete Martin's place."

"Didn't have any troubles when Mr. Chapman brought him down. Maybe you've seen him do something wrong since then."

"Just thought maybe you'd know about it." The grocer balanced a watermelon on his scale and grinned at the pale-blue numbered lights.

13

"I didn't want that," Stan said.

"No? You mean somebody else put it in your cart."

"I mean I don't want it," Stan said. "You just hand it to me, and I'll put it back."

It hadn't really been friendship, or at least Stan would not have called it that; in fact, he did not know what to call it. When he brought Booker the groceries, it was as though the boy had known that they would come, if not from Stan then from somewhere else, despite the fact that he had no car or money and lived five miles of gravel road from town. The same sense applied to the hydraulic jacks Stan had carted out from the mechanic's shop to prop up the porch: not ungratefulness, but calm acceptance without admission of debt, as though the boy had expected that if Stan didn't bring the jacks, they would just materialize somehow out of the club's five hundred acres of smartweed, sumac, and willows. Perhaps it had been the sheer conundrum of Booker Short himself. Stan's own trailer stood on four hundred feet of riverfront land due north of the cabin, fully wired, supplied with running water and a satellite dish for TV, and in the hot nights of late summer, he'd lain beneath a single sheet, the fan blowing on him from the dresser, and found himself thinking of the boy. He would have no electric fan. He would have no television to provide voices against the night. He would have no phone (though Stan, admittedly, rarely used his own). Stan himself was well acquainted with the dangers of a solitary life, had worked hard to adjust himself—he accepted, yes, the rigors of it, the barren necessity of taking himself in hand before the kitchen sink and washing his own seed down afterward with a sponge, accepted the poverty of averting his eyes from his own embarrassment. And yet he had the sense that Booker had not accepted this at all, out of either ignorance or some better quality: he was waiting for something. Perhaps it was this quality of waiting that attracted Stan. *That poor kid acts like something's going to happen out here,* he would think, staring at the same

14

acoustic-tiled ceiling he had stared at for the past fifteen years. Then his heart would quicken as he thought, *By God, what if it did?*

An implicit moment of change had been approaching then, because in November the club members would come to hunt. The cabin was known as old Pete Martin's place by habit more than accuracy. It was supposed to have been a ski chalet. The company that invented the prefabricated chalets had gone broke selling them in Kansas City, so Dr. Martin had bought one for two hundred dollars and shipped it to Waterloo on a truck. That had been forty years ago, the wheeled conveyance of a two-story, triangular cabin into the duck flats causing such a stir that Peter Martin's name had lingered with the structure long after he'd grown too old to visit it. A club of eight dues-paying members now maintained the grounds, men in their seventies like Mercury and a few younger, satellite members sprinkled in with an eye toward the future. The older men had hunted all their lives, and for them the care and upkeep of some drafty, mouse-infected hunting lodge between the months of November and January were a ritual of unquestioned propriety. Their young manhoods had been formed in such environs, and in the fall they returned achingly to the bachelor bunks, the liquor and gun oil, and the taut gray winter skies to steal back some portion of what was gone. The cabin, decorated with antlers and bartending signs and plat-book maps, its bathroom cabinet stocked with an ancient bottle of hair tonic, seemed to them over time a place of classical permanence, not prefabricated in the least.

Stan thought about this as he stood on the Waterloo boat landing and watched the sheriff, knees shaking for balance, examine the corpse laid out in his narrow skiff. He had enjoyed a relatively private summer with Booker that first year, teaching the boy—again without Booker's asking or showing any sense of debt—how to run a trot line and handle the river from that same skiff, how to shoot squirrels, even drinking with him solemnly in the evenings, missing his regular shows at home; but the first day of the season had changed all that. This date had worried Mercury like little else Stan had ever seen. It had lain behind his desire for Booker to fix up the shack, and his decision to drive out every other week to volunteer his busy and bumbling aid. Stan had been present one day in mid-October, the three of them digging the shack a "water-saving" latrine, when Mercury leaned on his shovel and said, "In two weeks, Booker, the members who run this club are going to start showing up. They know you're living here, and the deal is, you work for all of them, not just for me."

Booker, slight and shirtless as usual, continued to dig.

"Hell and damn," Mercury said. Beneath the old man's sternum, Stan could hear the dyspepsia start to work. "I don't mean you work for me, but that's the way we've got to play it. Hell and damn. Don't get touchy with me on this, Booker; it isn't like your grandfather wrote ahead and told me I needed a hunting cabin all my own. You got any other family I'm gonna have to put up?"

Booker had stepped into the hole by now, standing nearly to his waist in the black soil, and he spoke without varying his stroke: "My grandfather knew what kind of shack this is."

"What's that?" cried Mercury. "I'd be damned interested—"

"Why, this here's a nigger shack, Mr. Chapman," Booker said, his voice curling with the bogus tones of the South. "A li'l ol' *sharecropper's* kind of place."

"Hell *and* damn!" Mercury was digging now, too, a furious paddling motion along the edges of the hole that did no more than slough dirt back in. "Son, we've had a tabernacle choir's worth of sorry humanity pass through this shack, with a whole helluva lot less promising bloodlines than you, and every last one of them white. It wasn't a matter of what their skin—"

"So that's what you do in the country," Booker said, coolly now, hardly moving his lips. "If there aren't any regular niggers around, you get them from your own kind."

"We never got them from anywhere." Stan watched the old man's

16

high, patrician face blanch beneath his hat. *He ain't seen this good an argument in years,* Stan thought with admiration. *Might have got hisself out of shape.* "Never got them from anywhere," Mercury repeated, "but what they came looking for a place. Free to go, free to stay, free to do the work that's offered. You can piss on those that give the work, but it's not ever going to change."

The two men shoveled for a while, Booker patiently clearing out the dirt that Mercury knocked back in. Then Booker stopped and leaned on his shovel haft. "You vote Republican, Mr. Chapman?" he asked.

"I vote my interest at the box."

"And the residents of this here shack?"

"I don't like this arrangement any more than you," Mercury said. "But instead of arguing fucking politics when those old boys get down here, just try being quiet for a change."

The members convened the afternoon before opening day, thickset and hale old men with their canvas jackets and their calls packed in the same leather bags they had been left in on closing day the year before, their guns the same cheap and well-made fowling pieces they had purchased as young men, oiled and stored in inexpensive sheepskin sleeves. None was anything less than a millionaire, and they took a private, languid pleasure in every possible concealment of this fact, arriving in Buick station wagons and Oldsmobile sedans that younger, less established Kansas City men would consider fitting only for their wives. They sipped discount bourbon from plastic cups and, when they stopped at the local gun shop in Waterloo, inquired intelligently after the clerk's kin. All subscribed to the *Waterloo Free Press* and read it with more sentimentality than contempt. The country to them was a necessary source of stasis, a permanency that they preferred to see no one add to or subtract from, and so it was really only a matter of keeping Booker out of sight and giving them the chance to realize that nothing would change by having him there. With some embarrassment, Mercury had sent Booker to the shack at noon, and by three o'clock the lot was double-parked with cars, their doors propped open for the broadcast of the Kansas-Nebraska game. Stan found himself holding a paper cup of raw whiskey that made his throat expand, then contract. He could see, down the faded path, the pines that hid Booker's shack, and sensed among the men—Podge McGee and Hugh Singleman, busy driving stakes for the skeet machine, as well as Mercury—an uneasiness. They avoided looking that way.

Podge McGee's ancestors had run the first tavern in Kansas City, and he had continued in their taste for irregularity, never having a job, exactly, but trading in land, development rights, restaurant equipment, car parts, brass pipe, landfill, sand—anything of transient brightness and high yield. Skin cancer had gotten him twenty years back (Podge farmed his own ancestral lands south of town and had spent too many summers in open tractors). His nose had been excised, and what they had put back did not resemble a nose at all but putty spackled unevenly around two blowholes in the center of his face. With his yellow eyes blazing over this appendage, he looked like some terrible, scavenging bird. Hugh Singleman was senior vice president at Woolcombe & Lee, a foot taller and a hundred pounds heavier than Podge, whom he'd followed around since grade school commenting on the sprier man's profligate ways. In the kitchen, Edwin Coole fixed a steak marinade. He was president of Alderman, Hadley Insurance and an artist manqué whose hand-lettered signs dotted the property and whose watercolors of old Pete Martin's A-frame hung in each man's home. He was dying of prostate cancer, unbeknownst to his fellow members, but that didn't bother him so much as the fact that Mercury, his best friend, hadn't taken him into his confidence on the subject of Booker Short.

In fact, the men seemed incapable of commenting on Booker Short or anything else. They believed in the power of the final word, and so no one wanted to utter the first, a situation Mercury encouraged contentedly, his chatter diverting their attention as softly as canvas baffles on a stream: "Say, Eddie boy, you and I got to talk about this electricity problem. I think it's worth us getting wired in, rid of this dangerous gas and such, but I want to hear your ideas first—privately, see."

At four, Remy Westbrook arrived in his Oldsmobile coupe. In the name of Westbrook Lumber, Remy's ancestors had felled entire forests across the state, and their legacy was the closest thing to actual royalty that the city possessed. Remy, a hump-shouldered man with boiled-looking jowls and neck, knew this, and he estimated its worth by the niceties it allowed him to forget. "You all been out?" he asked, stepping from the car.

"Not yet today," Mercury said.

"Ah." Sighting through black bifocals, Remy unbuttoned his pants, rested one elbow on the car roof, and peed luxuriantly in the dead grass. "Heard Mercury's brought in a Negro fella, gonna put you out of business, Stan."

Hugh Singleman's stake driving stopped, and Stan felt the men listening around the yard. "I don't mind," he said.

Remy raised his eyebrows. "*I* would," he said. "But I ain't you. I wonder if it's too much trouble for a fella like that to come up and say hi. . . ."

"You better put that up, Remy," Hugh Singleman said.

"What? What's that?" But then Remy—and Stan with him—followed Hugh's line of vision to the tangerine English sports car idling up the drive and Clarissa Sayers's face squinted against the white dust, leaning eagerly out the passenger side.

"Maybe it's wrong to get a group of fellas to accept something they might dislike by distracting them with something they dislike for sure," Mercury had said that night to Stan, "but that's the first time I was ever *glad* to see Thornton Sayers." And though two years later he would revise that statement, adding, "I should've known you can't trade one trouble for the next," it seemed at the time that the judge's arrival put Booker out of harm's way.

Thornton Sayers was then fifty-two, some twenty years the junior of the club's other men, who'd invited him to join both out of respect for his position on the federal bench and because his father, Ezra (whom the current members recalled with distaste), had been Pete Martin's closest friend. In fact, his invitation could hardly have been avoided, an open-and-shut case, and yet the instinctual resistance of the members had been proved right. There was something off about Judge Sayers's style. First the car, an outrageous contraption for hunting, whose presence in Waterloo subjected the other members to unsubtle digs about "fanciness" that they would have preferred to make about other men in other clubs—the air-conditioned, new-money lodges in Mound City, for instance—but now were forced to accept as reflecting on themselves. The car often died in cold weather, and when Judge Sayers was hunting alone, this required a trip to the filling station in Waterloo, another thing the members would eventually hear about. He had an obsession with fancy shotguns, too, had separate and expensive firearms for geese and ducks, muzzle extensions, locking waterproof cases, even a specially crafted over-and-under for shooting trap, which he refused to take into the field: the ultimate folly, in the other members' opinion, trap shooting being an activity designed to give a man practice in shooting ducks, with the same weapon that he used to shoot ducks. The business with the guns, though, would have been less irritating, even laughable, had Judge Sayers not been such a good shot. Each of them, Stan included, had survived the unpleasant experience of missing a bird that Thornton Sayers had subsequently hit, and of hearing the undisguised vanity in his voice as he said, "I believe that one's mine." And then watching as he flapped hand signals to his Labrador retriever (none of the other men bothered with dogs, the duck fields being shallow enough to

20

wade) and offered comments like, "You know, it's amazing how much you have to lead a bird in a wind like this. I must've been a foot and a half in front."

Still, they might have forgiven the rest of it had it not been for the girl. They had established no written rules against women hunting at the club, having never known a woman, whether wife, daughter, or mistress, who had had the slightest desire to spend three days in an unelectrified cabin with an unreliable toilet, to sleep on a musty cot, and to discharge a shotgun in the woods. So they had no answer when, two years after the judge joined, Clarissa appeared with him on opening day. That night Mercury casually walked the judge outside to explain. "Is it in the charter?" Thornton asked, loudly enough to be heard inside, where the other men sat over a meal of pork chops, smiling in horrified, red-faced embarrassment at the girl. "If it is written in the charter that there can be no women, I accept it. Otherwise, such a stipulation was not presented to me when I paid my dues. It holds no weight."

"You know as well as I do that we don't have a charter," Mercury said. "It's just our custom, what we do."

"She can shoot as well as any man here," the judge replied, his tone not dissimilar to the one he used when describing his dog. "I taught her myself. A good eye, steady hand. She took two birds today, and the second was the prettiest overhead. . . . Wait a minute, I see: you're jealous of her."

"I have two grown children and six grandchildren," Mercury said. "The idea is absurd."

"Of course, yes," the judge said, not listening. "For a woman to shoot things and still be afterward a woman: it is attractive, I am aware of it. It has been that way with Clarissa since she was eight—schoolteachers, janitors, shoe salesmen, always older, as though the younger ones were afraid, as though that quality in her were so advanced it would take an older man to understand . . ."

"What quality?" Mercury was stuttering. "How . . . ?"

But the judge leaned in close to him, his hazel eyes oddly exhilarated. "We had her in four schools growing up, until finally I had to send her to Saint Mary's and the nuns. In the last one, the headmaster himself made a pass at her. Can you believe it? The headmaster himself. Here, there would be the difficulty of showers and the drying of underthings in close quarters. . . ." Suddenly he was formal again, upright, the moonlight playing off his cropped and barbered hair, so dark it gleamed with the blueness of a gun. "I'm sure we can reach a reasonable accommodation. For instance, you men don't hunt here every day, so the cabin is sometimes vacant. That's when Clarissa and I will come."

Clarissa had been sixteen then, just budding, though they had not known then that that would be her permanent state: small-breasted and straight-hipped like a boy, seemingly without self-consciousness or sentiment, with the habit of running the base of her thumb against her teeth. She had kept eating straight through her father's conversation with Mercury, finally chewing the bones oblivious to the table's embarrassment, and just as her father's exultant exclamation "The headmaster himself!" drifted clearly through the cabin's thin walls, she had asked Edwin Coole, "Could I have Daddy's piece?" She was wearing one of her father's sleeveless undershirts, knotted at her stomach, and a pair of cast-off hunting pants slung low enough that her hip blades showed, and her expression as she rose and wiped her lips with the butt of her hand was one of pity and mockery for the gathered men—an admission of her last word's meanings in their world, followed by the giggle of a girl.

For the next four years the men had sedulously avoided learning anything more about that glance, failing to notice when they arrived at the cabin after the judge and Clarissa had been there which beds had been slept in, refusing to admit that the idea might even occur to them. The same went for the bowers of handpicked wildflowers that would be left arranged with a man's awkwardness in a cup, or the forty-dollar bottles of wine left draining on the sideboard, or the ridiculous gilt birthday cards they found covered from corner to corner in the judge's tight, obsessive script, which they would not read. It had become a game, in which the men attempted not to see what the judge did not even seem to think it necessary to hide. They would even use that in his favor, thinking (for it was a game that no one spoke openly about, though each knew the others played), *He would not talk and act like that in public if he noticed it himself, and if he doesn't notice, then he has not acted on it, and so it's nothing, it is still okay.*

And so, as the tangerine sports car approached, a general mutter rose among the men: most significantly from Remy Westbrook, who stood struggling with his fly as the judge's car parked two yards behind him and Clarissa Sayers stepped out onto the dusty grass. "When a man can't pee in hissown yard," Remy said, stalking past Stan with his pants front clenched in his fist, "that truly is a black and ugly day."

Mercury was the only one to greet the pair, removing his straw hat and draping his arm over the judge's shoulder: "Always a fine surprise to see the best marksman on the federal bench. Never mind Remy: he has crabs." He guided him to Podge and Hugh, his voice facile, mellifluent, broken only by the steady report of his dyspepsia, which he contrived to make sound like welcoming laughter. "Podge, whaddya think we can make space for the judge tonight? I told him we'd trade our room for two bottles of his Château *La Toor*. . . . I thought that girl of yours was out east, Judge."

"Clarissa is finished with school," the judge said. "She's decided to come back."

She was twenty by then, Stan guessed, though her physical appearance remained unchanged from sixteen, or even thirteen: the same lithe, boyish figure, the same pale, unblemished skin that reddened appealingly in the chill November air—the palms of her hands, two splotches on her cheeks—the innocence of being on the cusp, of not yet having reached the fullness and thus decline of womanhood, coupled with the blank stare of experience that had felled the headmaster of her school. It was the juxtaposition of the two, the choirboy's body and the uninterest, even impatience, of the mind inside as to its possible attractions or the manner of its use. She still wore her father's cast-off hunting pants and jacket, tailored at the sleeves, and had opened the English car's hatchback, methodically unpacking and jointing an Orvis twelve-gauge, when she noticed the shack. She did so without comment, registering the new paint that showed through the pines, the faint smoke from the stove, and then returning to her work, culling brass-rimmed shells from a hunting bag and fitting them into the webbed pockets of her coat. The judge's dog whined in his kennel, and she silenced him with a single word.

"Is there water in the fields yet, Stan?" she asked when she was through.

"Puddles," Stan said. "There's enough around blinds two and three to not be embarrassed about sitting there, and there's good water in the woods." The club's land lay on a creek that fed the Missouri River, and the members relied on fall rains to swell the creek, backing its dark waters into the fields. Often, this failed to occur.

Clarissa made a face. "At Bert Gauss's club they have pumps, and if it doesn't rain, they flood it anyway."

"All right," Stan said.

"Bert says he honestly doesn't understand the point of a hunting club where you can't hunt half the time."

Stan had a mortal dislike of pumps, preferring the mysterious completion of the creek, the water lipping its bank and spilling through the trees, but he did not take the comment personally. It would be like accusing her of insulting a water faucet or a stool. "Who's Bert Gauss?" he said.

"A lawyer my father doesn't like."

"Is that so?"

"He hates seeing me with him, says if we keep it up he's going to talk to Henry Latham and spike Bert's career. Nice, huh? But if there's no hunting here this weekend, that's where I'm going to go."

24

"How come your father doesn't like him?"

"Because Bert's hunting club has pumps and electric heating in the blinds and cable TV," Clarissa said. "My father doesn't like not having better things."

It was the most interest Stan had ever seen her display about a man other than her father, and he asked, "Do you like him?"

"Mr. Pumps?" Clarissa laughed. "I've never been so bored."

For dinner, they gathered at the same wax-spattered table where Stan had found Booker alone four months ago, all marks of loneliness and fear now dispelled. Candles glowed in wrought-iron holders; the shadows of the men's heads arced against the cabin walls. The back of the cabin was glass and mirrored the entire scene, creating a double image, the reflections of the dinner party imposed upon the black humps of the duck fields and the pricks of stars above the trees. "There's a light on at the old shack," Clarissa said unexpectedly.

"New hand," Mercury said. "Fixed the place up himself."

"Mercury's got himself a protégé," Remy Westbrook said, smiling, his sentences punctuated by mouthfuls of steak. "He is attempting to improve the lot of our darker brothers step by step. Up from the ghetto and into the woods—better than playing midnight basketball with the mayor, I say. I read an article the other day, Judge, said that for every four black boys in Kansas City, three will end up in court."

"That's the juvenile system," said the judge, staring at his daughter with disquieting precision. "I don't see them unless they're charged with a federal offense."

"Do you mean he can't eat with us because he's black?" Clarissa said.

"What you may not know, little lady," Remy Westbrook said, leaning his chin across his plate, "is that Mercury commanded an entire company of black troops in the war. A civil rights leader before they even had that for a word, isn't that right?" His voice was as genial as Mercury's but hard underneath, emphasizing the language of the press to men uncomfortable with any association, good or ill, with such abstract terms. "Hell, he got along so good with those fellas driving his jeeps and all—what was the name of that driver you had, Merc?"

"Gettysburg Jackson," Mercury said quietly.

"That's right," Remy said, laughing now, but without mirth. "Craziest old name. And there was the time they wouldn't let him into the whorehouse—excuse me, Judge—in Paris. Mercury here not only ate with his men, he slept with them, said their prayers at night, and buried them, to hear him tell it. And that was nearly fifty years ago. Fifty years. And to think of all that's happened since then: riots and school reforms and Senator Danforth putting a black justice on the Court. Jack Danforth—I knew his father at school. Yes, so why not now, why not here?" He held Mercury's eyes as he said this. "Tell us the one about the train in Deauville. Just for the girl."

Mercury had put on a corduroy jacket for dinner and sat watching his friend speak with his blue eyes alight, the ghost of that young officer still extant despite his worn and sunburned eye sockets, the freckled dome of his bald head. He acknowledged Remy with a nod, their eyes communicating, but before he could answer, the judge's dog—he had left it kenneled in his car—began to bark and Clarissa excused herself to quiet it.

"Some other time, gentlemen," Mercury said as she left. He smiled shyly. "I'm a little too tired for telling stories anyway, tonight."

"Maybe you can do it when Booker comes up," Remy said.

"Ah," Mercury said, nodding again and then widening his eyes. "Maybe I will at that."

Clarissa returned some time later, the flow of conversation uninterrupted, and so it was not until the end of dinner that Stan noticed her again. He had by then ceased to pay attention to the voices of the old men, the slow, soporific exchange whose topic remained unstated, oblique, like an argument over a chess game whose pieces had already been cleared away. Instead he watched his own reflection in the window behind Remy Westbrook's head, fussy over some detail that he could not name. Then he noticed that Clarissa was watching, too, not his reflection but the window itself, placid, aware of her father's precise attention two places to her right. It was like in the comics where an artist might have drawn a dotted line from the judge's eyes to his daughter and from Clarissa's to the window and from the window . . . at this point he rose so quickly that he had to catch his chair, his understanding still below the level of words but complete, it seemed now, in all its possibilities, as if that very moment had held within itself the preformed seed of everything to come, down even to Clarissa's neck jerking against his trot line as the river's current sifted across her lips. At the time, however, he disturbed the party only briefly, muttering, "I got to get on," and bolted out the mudroom door and around to the back window, where he found Booker sitting in the grass.

"I figured you'd be out," the boy said.

"What are you doing?" Stan whispered.

"Listening to the gentlemen speak," Booker said, raising a bottle toward the broad, lighted glass, the dinner party viewed in bright tableau, the haloed candles and the men's hot and satiated faces and Clarissa gazing straight out past them with a choirboy's half smile. Remy Westbrook's voice sounded clearly through the cracked panes.

"But how did . . . what if . . . ?"

"I dunno," Booker answered. He looked half drunk in the moonlight, celebratory, tilting the bottle to his lips. "It was like she knew I was coming, was already standing there with the beer. Well, well, well," he continued, inspecting Stan as though he'd caught him out somehow. "You gentlemen certainly do have interesting things to say."

"Are you planning to watch me clear dead ladies out of your skiff," asked the sheriff, who'd nearly fallen twice during his examination of the girl, "or might I trouble you to help?" The river frightened him, the way it tugged restlessly on the skiff's painter, the way its broad expanse slid and welled: despite his vaunted balance on land, the truth was that the sheriff could not swim.

"I'm coming," Stan said.

"Well, get on it." The sheriff had suddenly felt the need to kneel and grasp the skiff's gunwale with both rubber-gloved hands. He had imagined the gunwale would be cool, but when he touched it with his forehead it was hot as a griddle iron, and when he leaned over the river, it seemed hot, too.

"Are you feeling poorly?"

The sheriff looked up directly into Stan Granger's eyes. Stan was waist-deep in the river, arms crossed to keep them dry. "What are you doing?" the sheriff said.

Stan shrugged. "Gonna tote her up onshore."

One of the deerflies that had been on the body landed on the sheriff's face, and he scooped up a palmful of water to splash it away. The rubber glove did it—its sweet, suffocating smell, with its suggestion of things doctors did to the dead. In his peripheral vision, he saw Stan backpedaling against the current; then he was sick.

Stan carried Clarissa Sayers up from the river alone. Her backflesh and her thighs where they pressed his arms had the gelatinate ripeness of the drowned. Her armpits and the open cavity of her mouth strongly stank. He had intended to lay her on the hood of the patrol car, but instead he discovered that he had carried her to the shade tree where he'd left his fish, and stretched her out in the summer grass. Removed from smell and touch, the grass hiding the wound Stan's hook had left in her neck, she appeared grotesquely beautiful, her bare foot's arch and ankle marbled with fine blue veins, the swelling of corruption bringing forth curves that alive her body, slim and breastless as an adolescent's, had not possessed. Mercury had once said her eyes were dry as a snake's, but that, too, had disappeared, leaving only the innocence of death. Squatting, Stan imagined how it would look to any member of the law, much less the press.

Through the wet fabric of his pocket, the charm he'd taken from her felt cold against his thigh, and as he watched the sheriff stumble up from the skiff, pissed off and dabbing a handkerchief against his mouth, he realized that he was already committed to telling that man a lie. As with most of the lies he'd told for Booker, he had no recollection of having made the choice.

The sheriff's tennis shoes stopped beside him in the grass. "You'd think I would remember seeing a face like that," he said. "I'm starting to wonder if I do."

"I got to get on home," Stan said.

"How many times you and I done this, Stan—five, six?" the sheriff said. "And before that you done it, what, ten times with Sheriff Phipps? I don't recall you ever refusing to talk with city law." Below them the river folded upon itself soundlessly, tectonic, as though inhabiting a different time frame than the static bank and sky, and at the far corner of their vision, five linked barges pivoted around the bend like some medieval warship ventured inland from the sea.

"I'm not avoiding any law," Stan said.

"Good," the sheriff said.

2

STAN GRANGER had unclasped his buck knife and was halfway through cleaning his fish. He sat with his back against the shade tree where the body lay, a driftwood plank between his knees, his bloody hands poised in silent astonishment as the slope-nosed Crown Victoria bounded over the railroad crossing on the hill above, all four tires airborne, and poured into a curving skid through the landing's gravel lot, the engine dopplering to nothing precisely as the car came to a halt. The sheriff lifted his head from the picnic bench where he had been asleep. "Somebody's been watching tee-vee," he said.

The car rested at an angle to them in the eddies of its own dust. The far door opened, but nobody got out. That is, nobody above the vehicle's tinted windows who might be connected to the pair of tiny, spit-shined boots visible beneath its frame. "Sheriff Wade Crapple?"

"Yeah."

"I've come in reference to your Jane Doe. Could you escort me to the body, please?"

It was a voice almost comically adapted to the male idea of female, lush and slightly hoarse, linked by its very intonations to the throat and tongue and lip, an effect that the official cadence of its speaker served only to enhance. The sound evoked in the sheriff a conspiratorial male grin. "Why don't you step out from behind that big ol' car, honey?" he said. "This here drowned person's not going anywhere."

But she already had: a starched, nondescript figure striding across the lot in black, a forty-five athwart her hip. She passed the sheriff without a glance—his grin undergoing the first of several transformations Stan would see, molting from genial condescension to uncertainty—snapped two rubber gloves about her wrists, and swung the picnic blanket from the girl's parted knees. From this position she appraised Stan, her gaze ticking from his face to the half-filleted catfish carcass in his lap and back again with barely perceptible amusement. "I guess this must have come as a surprise, Mr.—"

"Granger," Stan said. He stood up as though startled, the board pitching from his knees and, hopping, tried to clear away the fish and wash himself simultaneously. "Stan Granger," he said finally, holding out a dripping hand.

"Marcy Keegan." She had knelt beside Clarissa Sayers's head and was examining her temple. "There may have been some trauma, Mr. Granger. Did you find her?"

"No, ma'am." Stan retrieved his hand and wiped it on his pants. "I mean, yes, ma'am. I found her, but it wasn't no surprise. This is, not her specifically, not like I expected . . . why, shoot, I'd be as surprised as the next guy to haul in a girl like that off my line. I mean, bodies in general. Regular ones. It's not a real surprise to find bodies in this river is what I mean." Then he saw the woman's eyes watching him, as inert and inexpressive as pond water but fully alert.

"Don't touch anything else, please," she said.

She was forty, he guessed, or possibly more—at any rate older than him by a fixed amount measured in something other than time. She was not beautiful. Rather, it seemed as if everything about her were designed to be in rebellion against the prodigality of her own voice: the chapped and roughened skin, the unpainted lips, the faded strands of once-red hair that escaped a bun of bobby pins. She wore her clothes like a man, as a replacement for her physical body, the thick folds of serge (not a uniform, but imitating one) offering no invitation to speculate on what lay beneath. And so her voice, husky, almost wanton—which apparently she no longer even heard or paid attention to—could not have seemed more outrageous had she begun speaking Chinese. She slipped paper bags over Clarissa's hands and secured their necks with rubber bands.

"See here, now," said the sheriff. "That girl there is drownt."

"That's what I'm hoping to find out."

"Don't seem to need much detective work to me."

But she did not listen to the sheriff. It was as though from the moment he had first spoken she had judged that he no longer needed to exist. "Okay, Mr. Granger," she said, handing him a pair of rubber gloves. "I just need a couple of photographs."

She removed a Polaroid camera from a small black bag and squatted around the body, photographing its position, the matted hole above the ear, pausing only to write in a notebook she produced from the pocket of her pants. It was a troubling still life, the dead girl's skirt hiked up over her bluish flanks, her panties disarranged, and when ants began to crawl across her face, Keegan slid a plastic sheet beneath the body, her gloved hands working with a fierce impartiality while the sheriff cursed from a distance of ten feet. He had examined other bodies in this way, but never one from a class higher than his own, never a young woman, and when Keegan knelt between the dead girl's legs, the flash suddenly revealing the black tangle of her privates, he said, "All right, by Jesus, that's enough," and whipped the plastic sheet around the body. "If you want to do that, you don't do it here."

"She might have been raped," the detective said.

"We don't got to take pictures of it, do we? Out here on a public boat landing, for all the world to see?" The sheriff was breathless, trying to fix the too-short flaps of plastic so they would not blow open in the wind. "Stan, go get my jacket from the car."

"The pictures are just procedure—the fewer steps we miss, the less chance the perpetrator has of staying free," Keegan said. She was not angry, merely factual, patient. "Provided that there was one, Sheriff. Semen can stay in the body for weeks."

"Can it? Can it?" the sheriff said with a false, harried grin of outrage, teeth bared, still struggling with the sheet.

"Yes," Keegan said.

"Go get my jacket, Stan," he repeated. "Or are you getting your jollies off this, too?"

Stan didn't move. The sheriff, trying now to close the girl's legs without seeing what lay between them and to cast a backward glance of condemnation, bleated through his nose.

"It's all right," Keegan said. "Go and get it."

Obediently, he went.

A city ambulance came for the body, a small crowd clustered in its wake. The sheriff hovered around the paramedics as they slipped Clarissa Sayers into a bag, covering the spaces between their shoulders with his jacket and his hat. "We'll have to wait for positive ID," Keegan said as the stretcher was carried away. "But we had a missing-person's come in for a Caucasian woman, same general specs. Clarissa Sayers. Any chance you boys might know about that?"

"Laying a girl out on a boat landing and taking pictures of her crotch," the sheriff said. Stan worried that he'd recognized the name. "Imagine what her pa would say."

"Do you know her father?" Keegan asked. She had her notebook out.

"I'd be embarrassed if I did."

"Please answer yes or no."

"I'll answer you something, little missy," the sheriff said, wheeling on her, conscious of the local faces gathered out of earshot, the same ones that had watched the sandlot games of his youth. "I'll answer you to go on home with your nice notebook and all and send me back Lieutenant Miller or Charlie Schiff. Somebody who knows how to conduct decent business and ain't working on their first case. I might remember a helluva lot better then."

"Thank you, Sheriff," Keegan said, studying him as she wrote. Then she walked over to Stan and crouched at the water's edge while he loaded the bucket of half-cleaned fish into his skiff. She even smelled like a man, the neutral odor of coffee and deodorant spray, but it was the voice that he responded to, at once guttural and soft, calling up impossible and indecorous images of the apparatus of love, of silk, elastic straps, and humid sheets: a sound to which he saw with complete foreknowledge he would gladly surrender all he knew. He had seen Booker Short and Clarissa Sayers together in the shack at Pete Martin's place as recently as March, and knew that at any time in the past eighteen months, except during hunting season, one stood a decent chance of finding them there, Clarissa's car hidden in the pine copse, the two of them tending house not like lovers but in a union Stan did not fully understand, heatless, more like two widowers whose relations were founded not on sex but on convenience and the acceptance of fault. They had welcomed him, fed him, entertained him, requesting in exchange only simple privacy, and he believed that what mysteries had lain between them should remain theirs. But only a virgin's resistance kept him from revealing this to Marcy Keegan, knowing without admitting that if he told it now, there would be no reason for her pursuit—that being the price that any maiden would demand.

"Was there anything else you wanted to say?" Keegan asked. "Anything you remember about the body—jewelry, maybe? Or any kind of charm?"

"You seen that ring and watch," Stan said.

"Yes, I did."

"Then you seen what I seen." He held her gaze, staring back at the stagnant-pond-colored eyes, the lined face and the stapled hair that had not moved since she'd arrived, and thinking: *You could say it was like an opera singer, but that wouldn't be right. An opera singer's*

34

not dangerous. But I can't think of anything else that is so different be-tween how it looks and how it sounds.

"I thought maybe there would be one more thing," she said. "A girl like that would wear something around her neck, don't you think?"

"I never paid much attention to girls like that," he said, thinking joyously, *A wolf, a wolf's call is that way.*

"Maybe you don't remember it now, but you'll remember it later," Keegan said. "We'll trade: I give you my card, and you write down for me where you live."

He accepted the newly printed card and then the pen and note-book, still warm from her hands, and ecstatically wrote his address and his name.

It is Wednesday evening now. Traveling the two-lane road west from Waterloo, you pass through country that seems removed from the press of any particular decade or even century. It is bottomland, black and rich and rimmed with fire, for it is the time of year before plant-ing when farmers burn their fields. The twisted bluffs that protect the bottoms are resistant to roads; the river is bridgeless, and so the vil-lages built at intervals along the single thread of blacktop possess the same haggard, paintless defiance as Basque towns in the Pyrenees. Even the profiteers that franchise snack shops and gas stations in small towns have ignored this place, and what signs exist are painted on whitewashed plywood, or erected by the state. It is isolated by the cause of its fecundity: the river, its loamed floodplain, the impassable, female-curving bluffs. Vines spring from the soil to choke phone lines and sunder porch balustrades. Here is a town where, over dinner, remnants of the kaiser's German can be heard, and the residents of the graveyard were born on the Black Sea. Here is a clapboard Baptist church overlooking a lonely cliff and beside it the weathered rector's residence, which seems abandoned until one sees the pastor hanging his laundry out back. The houses of wealthy farmers, surrounded by elms, sit like green oases amid miles of their own scorched and smoking fields. The land is warped, bony, fragrant, and there is little trade or commerce save what it allows, and then the valley ends like a dream or wrinkle in time, and you round a bend in the river and reach the city. It simply appears, circled with highways, reasonless, a sudden forest of signs.

The city has its oases and isolated vales too, only of a different kind. In its heart, more than sixty streets (and double that number of actual blocks, counting terraces) from the river, Clyde Wilkins looked out the broad bay window of the Colonial Country Club bar at such a view. It recalled, as though by tribal memory, the hill country it had once been: knolled and humped, fat with ancient elms and willows, cut by limestone-shelved streams. But it was a controlled illusion, as Clyde knew, with every tree break, undulant fairway, and razored green representing not the absence of man's wealth and will but their apotheosis. There were times when he saw the pins and their crest-emblazoned flags as the bloody standard of the city's conquerors, and the leather seats of his bar as their thrones. But he did not like to feel this way and happily did not feel so now, enjoying the cool, grass-scented optimism of early summer and the soft breeze that blew through the half-opened window onto his arms, and watching a fox pad through the twilight of the first fairway. Buddy Acheson, dressed in lemon shorts and a seersucker English motoring cap, was stealing from tree to tree beside it in the rough. Mr. Acheson had been a member since 1947 and played the course every evening carrying a five-iron, a wedge, a putter, and a cheesecloth bag of balls salvaged from the water hazards. Clyde sympathized with the old man's style. He would have done it the same way, strolling in solitude through the course's nether parts, a place in his imagination as mysterious as the Taj Mahal or Borneo, because he would never see any of them: save for the rare tournament caddie, no black man had ever so much as bent a blade of grass on the Colonial Country Club's first tee. So the irony was not lost on Clyde that Mr. Acheson could not bear sharing the acreage with a fox. He had hunted the animal since its first appearance at the base of the sixth tee five years before, setting out iron traps in secret along the creeks. This lasted until the night watchman heard young Shelley Mann, her ankle cut to the bone above her black prom pump, loudly demanding medical attention while Harris Walford carried her down the dogleg seventh, trying to reach his car. The roughs were searched with metal detectors and, after a severe reprimand from the board, his petition for one sweet evening with a gun refused, Mr. Acheson now waged a nightly ballet of impotence through firefly-lit dales. As Clyde watched, he stole into the fairway behind the fox, set down three balls, and without pausing to check his stance, lifted an arcing hook across the club's front drive. Over his shoulder, the fox watched his huntsman top his second shot and then squarely meet his third, a stroke of implacable fury that plopped softly on the first green, the fox not consenting to move until Mr. Acheson ran after him, firing by hand. When their twinned figures disappeared, Clyde left the window and began washing ashtrays.

"Why, Chester, you can't close now!" Ms. Hargreavey was clasping the brass rail of the waitresses' station like a swimmer rising up the ladder of a pool.

"It's eight o'clock, ma'am," he said. "That's when I always close."

"Oh, you don't, either," Ms. Hargreavey said gaily. "You close at nine o'clock, Chester. You can't fool me."

"The rule book says eight."

"Nonsense." Ms. Hargreavey sat on a stool. "I will have a Manhattan, and you can make Bobby a gin martini over shaved ice. Bobby is my date."

Clyde looked up from the sink to find that Ms. Hargreavey was wearing what he called the mask: a dry narrowing of the pupils against which Clyde ceased to exist. "Don't ignore me, Chester," Ms. Hargreavey said, producing from her handbag the slender nail of a cigarette. "I've been waiting for this all day." He placed a clean ashtray before her, and she touched it disapprovingly with her thumb. "It's wet," she said.

It was eleven o'clock when Clyde, with the help of a kitchen boy, finally loaded Ms. Hargreavey into a waiting cab. Bobby had never arrived, and Ms. Hargreavey had drunk her first Manhattan and then a second while his martini slowly dissolved in a pool of sweat. She drank that, too, and then spoke bitterly of her divorce and her only son, who had run away at age sixteen and worked his way through Yale, never so much as sending a postcard back, until Clyde was obliged to lead her forcefully outside, outraged by the pointless tawdriness of the scene and by the fact that twice Ms. Hargreavey had given him boxes of her lost son's clothes (Clyde had a son of his own), and he'd accepted them like a friend. His last image of Ms. Hargreavey was of a single bloodshot and mascaraed eye peering out from the cab's cavernous backseat, and the slurred words "Don't you ever lay hands on me again, buddy. I know exactly who you are." He walked then through the soft June darkness from the club's side portico to the employee parking lot in back, slowly divesting himself of his apron, his tie, and his starched linen shirt which stank of Ms. Hargreavey's smoke: a large and still well-proportioned man in his fifties with an athlete's rolling gait (he'd been a lineman and a shot-putter in his youth) and a prematurely white, close-cropped Afro that lent him a distinguished air. He got into his car and drove. He drove without seeing the road, or the statued parks, or the mansions that he passed and had passed now for fifteen years, the car seeming to guide itself automatically, his mind opaque with rage. He was forced to listen, as he had known he would be, to the familiar voice inside his head that told him that the job he had accepted was a devil's deal, and the salary he'd drawn for fifteen years nothing more than blood money that had stripped him of his rights as a man. He whispered to the voice and pleaded with it to stop, but it did not, and so he drove on desperately through the last white neighborhood to the east and crossed Troost Avenue and entered the ripe, walnut-scented alleys of the black side of town. Still it would not be quiet, and so he passed the relatively prosperous street where he lived and continued farther east into the poorer neighborhoods he had surpassed, the low, dark, filthy houses and the trash-strewn lots, the street corners where young men emerged from the shadows of locust trees with the sibilant cry of "Smoke, smoke?" and their women swaggered to the package stores in housedresses, with gaudy plastic scandals on their feet, whispering to himself now, "See? Don't you see?" with violent triumph until it was over and his mind was empty and he returned westward, pulling onto his own street, beside his own neatly fenced yard, which he had bought and paid for at the price of nights like these, and where nothing could happen that he did not will to be.

"Clyde Wilkins, I need your help." The voice caught him as he was unlatching his gate, nasal, arrhythmic, and for an awful moment he thought his employers had discovered a way to order their drinks clear across the city. Then he saw a man in a rumpled tan suit, mopping his forehead in the street. "I know it's a terrible thing to bother a man this late, and just off work—"

"*Off* is the key word," Clyde said. He turned his back to the man and pushed through his gate and closed it, intending to mount his stairs and go through his porch door and close it, too, because it was his right to do so, bought and paid for in a deal whose terms he had not even invented, and thinking this way, ran headlong into his wife.

"He's been waiting for you since eight o'clock," she said.

"Who?" he said, trying to step past her to the door.

"That man," she said. "All he had for supper was a peach."

"I don't see no man." He had reached the doorlatch around her waist and, brushing his lips beside her ear, opened it gently past her rump. "We don't want any," Clyde said. "Good night." And it was only when the screen had closed with a slap and he was inside with his wife's soft giggling that the voice came again and he placed it.

"It's Mercury Chapman," the man said. "There's a boy in trouble for his life."

They sat catty-corner to each other on the narrow screened porch that fronted the house, Mercury's bony haunches perched on the foot of a deck lounge against which he would not permit himself to recline, and Clyde, hammocked in a soft canvas chair, deciding he'd let the old man stay that way. They knew each other intimately, though neither acknowledged it, not merely from the club or from the checks Mercury routinely sent to the "outreach" program run by Clyde Wilkins's church, but from a shared past and the memory of their own ancestry, a relationship as paradoxical as the city itself, where few black matrons died without the attendance at their gravesites of the middle-aged or older white men who had been their erstwhile sons, some traveling from as far as New York or California, even if for twenty years these same families had not spoken. Mercury had been raised by Clyde's paternal grandmother, Eve, who had been employed by the Chapman family since she turned eighteen. He remembered her scent's mixture of wet wool and chive cut from the garden, her voice, the emery texture of her fingers, more clearly than he did the details of his own mother. They had struggled fiercely, like equals, and it had not been uncommon for Eve Wilkins to lock Mercury in the coal room for hours at a time, a punishment he never mentioned to his parents, who had no jurisdiction in their world. She had beaten him, removed thorns from his hands, and once with a water hose driven off a wild raccoon that had trapped him in a tree. Leaving for war at age twenty-seven, he had watched "Miss Evie" serve his dying mother a martini through a tube in her throat. It so happened that at that very same moment Clyde Wilkins had been in the Chapmans' basement, watching his mother iron the stiff, brass-buttoned wool of a captain's tunic. He had invested that tunic and its owner, Mercury Chapman, with the shining halo of glamour that soldiers wear for boys.

That had been the old city. It was gone now, the races having separated against all plan or reason *after* the laws that kept them apart were abolished, the customs and habits that had intertwined families for generations suddenly appearing unseemly to both sides, embarrassing. It was an unspeakable rift. No one would argue that the

40

change had not been just, necessary, and yet it was also true that when Troost had been the legal line of segregation, Mercury had crossed it often and with pleasure—there being five or six houses open to him for a meal and, later, clubs he would attend—but now, save for funerals, he and others like him did not return. As for Clyde, he could not remember ever receiving a white man in his home socially, not in fifteen years, and would have endured torture to preserve his son from ever seeing the laundry rooms of the white.

"The first time they met was a year and a half ago," Mercury said. "I had—or we, the fellows in the club, anyway—had this extra cabin on our land nobody used and so Booker and I fixed it up for him. You know, a free place to stay and maybe earn a little money keeping an eye out on the place. And I guess you're familiar with the other men who go out there, Remy Westbrook and Podge McGee and Eddie Coole, and the main thing I was worried about was how they'd get along. Not so much because of color"—he glanced anxiously at Clyde Wilkins's face—"but because that could make it easier to start off on the wrong foot, easy for them to say something Booker would take wrong, and easy for him to do the reverse. The point was gentling everybody along, and so I never even noticed what was happening with the girl." He mopped his forehead with a balled handkerchief and smiled ruefully, his teeth pinching his lower lip. "Hell, this is the modern world and all, but I would've told him to pick just about any other woman in the state."

"So they dated," Clyde said. "A young black man and the daughter of a judge. If I took a walk in Loose Park tomorrow, I'd have a good chance of seeing that. I know you've got a better reason to come sit on my porch at eleven-thirty at night."

"I never said it was dating," Mercury said. "I don't know what it was, only I wouldn't have recommended it to anyone—black, white, or Cherokee—for the exact reason that I don't think she cared who it was so long as it made her father mad. But that's not what I'm trying to tell."

41

The younger man was laughing now, behind pursed lips. "'School Bus' Sayers don't like how his own pudding tastes—"

"What I'm trying to tell," Mercury interrupted, "is that they were doing whatever it was they did for a while before they let anyone find out. I guess at first she used to drive down to the cabin and stay there when the place was free, and then later on she convinced him to get a place in town. Because I don't think it was him. I don't think he was looking for any more trouble than he'd already found when he got here . . . how long did he stay working at your church?"

"He quit six weeks ago."

"Six weeks," Mercury said, his right knee jogging in agitation. "Six weeks, and I never even bothered to call and check. That's my failure. Last year, when he asked me about a city job, he wanted something where he wouldn't have to fill out any forms or get asked too many questions. I made that clear to you in my letter, I think: that he might've had some trouble in his past."

"The church fixes up houses for poor people," Clyde said. "It pays three hundred a month and the ones that take the work do it because they can't get a job someplace else. Booker was the best carpenter I had. He was also unreliable as hell."

Mercury widened his eyes: "Go on."

"He'd come and work five or six days straight, and I mean straight—sleeping on the site, already on the ladder at six when the gang showed up, like if he just hammered fast enough he'd scare away whatever it was he didn't want to go home to. Then just as quick, he'd be gone for two or three days, maybe a week. I didn't fire him, I just docked his pay. He could've been doing any number of things on the side, most of them wrong, and none of which concern me."

"Could he have been doing enough of it to afford a Stingray coupe?"

Clyde Wilkins liked to imagine himself as a captain on his small, maple-shrouded porch with the humped and perfectly weeded lawn leading down beyond it like a prow. He enjoyed this sense of protec-

42

tion, the sound of his wife reheating dinner in the kitchen and the presence of his son somewhere inside, and he examined the rumpled, hatchet-faced figure before him as he might a mutineer. "Are you trying to ask me about this boy selling drugs?"

"I don't know."

"You've come to the wrong place to find sympathy for that."

"He's a good kid," Mercury said.

"Do you believe that?"

"I don't know," the old man said. And then he told Clyde about the car and how the previous summer it had been parked outside the clubs all over town and outside the judge's own house when he was at his office. How, in fact, there were few places in the city it had not been seen (the car being difficult to ignore and lacking even a roof for privacy) and how it had frequented most often those neighborhoods where a red Stingray coupe carrying a young black man and the daughter of a federal judge would be an occasion for comment, if not offense. "It's almost like he was trying to make up for what he'd missed," Mercury said, "being twenty already and never having had a chance to drive a good-looking girl around in a car." They hadn't just gone to clubs, but had attended football games at Pemberton Academy, and picnic lunches for the Friends of Art, and the maypole dance at Briarwood Day School. They had appeared together at the Republican Women's luncheon in Rozelle Court—a shocking event in itself, given Judge Sayers's long-standing repudiation of the "provincial" right—where Booker had been introduced to Senator Hawklet's wife as an eye surgeon from Washington, D.C. Clyde allowed himself to smile at this uneasily, and seeing him, Mercury pressed on: "It's like they were on a spree," he said, "or more like she was, and he just went along because he'd never done it before. That's the point I'm trying to get across about her father: the places she picked were places he'd be damn certain to know." And he told how only four days earlier, the car had been spotted at the Nelson Gallery, on the night of the Founders Ball.

"She invited him to the ball," Clyde said. He had stopped smiling and his face was alert and still.

Mercury was not smiling either, his rumpled officer's frame hitched over his steadily jogging knee like a weaver trundling a loom, as he continued the same nasal and persistent narration that was his only way of making sense of the world. This time Booker had gone alone. The Founders Ball, ostensibly a benefit for the museum, was in fact the sanctioned and publicly celebrated attempt on the part of white society to repeal time, an effort both mythic and bizarre in scale. The fathers of the debutantes would stand with red sashes across their tuxedos amid suits of armor and the violent crests of medieval fiefdoms in the museum's main hall, and old women raised from hospital beds and homes for the infirm would file in wearing lace, their faces painted and their eyes glittering with the feverish excitement of hunters scenting again the blood and powder of the field. There would be the laconic young men, drunk and in rut, wearing their grandfathers' wool tails and satin gloves that smelled of mothballs, understanding like the old women that the event was a ritual in blood, and that when the fathers presented their daughters to the city, they were really offering up their flesh to them. He did not need to tell Clyde that the Founders Ball had never had a debutante who was black, nor that for several years the organizing committee had sent the city's first black mayor an invitation without embarrassment (by tradition, it was the mayor who opened the event), accepting his unequivocal refusal as a measure of his tact. Everybody knew this, just as everybody knew that Thornton Sayers wrote a yearly essay in the *Star* deploring the provincialism of the event, which he always then attended anyway. People still spoke of how he had cried movingly the year Clarissa was presented, during the final, father-daughter waltz. Instead, Mercury told how the red Stingray had stopped at the bottom of the museum steps and Booker had climbed out and walked straight up among these people, the feverish old women and the red-sashed men and youths, wearing a new tux. "I guess people would've had a hard enough time figuring out who he was," Mercury said, "since by then some of them would think he was an eye specialist from D.C., and others that he was Clarissa Sayers's chauffeur, and the rest of them would assume he'd been sent by the mayor. So he might have bluffed himself in any number of ways, but I'm not even sure that was his plan. It is possible that he thought Clarissa was inside, and he was jealous; that's the argument a prosecutor would use. But the fact is that she was eating dinner with Bert Gauss at the Hilton, and I don't think Booker was jealous of Bert Gauss. He hadn't any reason to be. . . ."

Mercury's voice had taken on a tone that Clyde found disturbing, a conspiratorial mix of enthusiasm and pride, and the younger man clapped his hand over his own sympathetically bouncing leg. "I think it was the judge he wanted," Mercury continued, "because when he got to the door and Guy Sturges asked for his ticket, he didn't even hesitate. 'I'm Judge Sayers's guest,' he says. 'He's holding my ticket.' So they fetch the judge. And this starts to cause a problem, because people stop wanting to go in. They've all read the judge's editorials, and they want to see what he'll do. So Guy Sturges finds the judge and he comes up joking and holding his father's top hat, but when he sees Booker, his face goes blank. Not like he doesn't recognize him, but like he's trying to pretend he doesn't exist. 'There's no one I recognize,' he says. 'There must be some mistake.' And Guy Sturges grabs Booker's shoulder and says, 'It's this guy here,' and without looking, the judge says, 'He's lying. I do not know the man.'"

The talking had made him hungry, and with the intestinal divinity of the aged, Mercury felt the peach he'd eaten for dinner turning over in his gut. Then, for the first time that evening, the dyspepsia started up. Checking it, he looked through the open first-floor window into the Wilkinses' living room and saw Clyde's son. The room was like many others he had seen, arranged with far more precision and formality than a white's, the sofa backs covered with mantillas, the top of the television an obsessive shrine of photographs and

45

framed news clips, and the boy sat in the front corner, where in former days the piano would have been. He even sat in the same formal posture of recital, arms raised and wrists slack, the difference being that his face—with the same acutely curious expression that he remembered Clyde wearing nearly fifty years ago, when he himself went off to war—was bathed in the blue light of a computer screen. He realized that the sound he had been listening to, without identifying it, was the tapping of plastic keys.

"After dinner, I let him write letters on the thing," Clyde said. "Sends them all around the world."

"Yes," Mercury said. "We've got them at my plant."

"Let a kid learn the computer, and in ten years people will line up to work for him."

"I don't see why not," Mercury said, and yet something in the fixed attention of the boy's features left him curiously without hope. The scene felt repetitive: the tidy, immaculate house, the steady throbbing of the locusts, the threadbare expressions of optimism and pride. He had once watched Clyde take apart a vacuum-tube radio while his mother said much the same thing. Then he decided that he had avoided for as long as possible what he'd come for.

"The ball doesn't matter so much as where Booker got the money," he said, calculating in the air. "To pay for the car and to pay rent wherever he stayed. I never hunted him down and I should've. I never asked about the car, either, because I thought he paid for it by working for you. Money is a good motive in any trial, and it's the one thing we can't explain. Either it came from her, or she found some way for him to make it without actual work, and I don't know which is worse."

"What trial?" Clyde said. "Motive to do what?"

"The key point is that it came from someplace other than the church," Mercury said, "and they'll know that as soon as they talk to you. I'm not going to ask you to lie, only not to tell them right away. We'll talk to the lawyer and see how long you can wait, and then—"

"What do you mean, *we?*" Clyde said it loudly enough to stop the

46

locusts. His close-cropped white hair floated like the mark of some affliction above his muscled shoulders, and for the first time Mercury realized that he might have made a mistake.

"There's no reason you would've heard," Mercury said.

"Let's cut the shit and tell me, then."

Then he knew he'd made a mistake, because the affliction was in Clyde Wilkins's eyes, very close to his own as he leaned forward in his chair, and filled with the defiant fearfulness of a much older man. He told him anyway. "They found Thornton Sayers's girl dead in the river this morning, about sixty miles downstream," he said. "Henry Latham called me this afternoon from the *Star*. She was still dressed up to go golfing."

Clyde Wilkins continued to stare at him after he spoke, not blinking even when the high beams of a passing car rose up his torso and crossed his face, his eyes shining with the steady, glaucous whiteness of the blind. "Go on home, Mercury," he said.

"I can't," Mercury said. "Henry called me because he thought the police had a suspect, and that the suspect might be someone I knew. It was like fair warning: neither one of us mentioned names, but it had to be Booker that he meant. He said they'd already found one possible witness and gotten some kind of anonymous tip."

"Go on home," Clyde repeated.

"You know exactly what it's going to be like," Mercury said. "Front page of the paper and a composite drawing on all the news shows. That kid is going to be running for his life—hell, he was probably running from something when he *came* here. We've got to find him, see what we can do."

Clyde stood and in a single fluid motion closed the living-room window with the flat of his hand. He sat again, his bulk settling among the shadowed porch furnishings, a light gloss of sweat on his cheeks and neck. "And you want me to help?"

"How would I know where to look?" Mercury asked.

"You seem to assume I would."

"You've worked with him," Mercury said. He found that he was whispering now, a harsh hiss between his teeth. "For Chrissakes, Clyde—*he's one of your own.*"

Clyde Wilkins normally moved with the courteous care of a big man, not wanting to frighten people with his size, but when he slammed his fist on the table next to him, the hurricane lamp atop it broke. "That," he said, "is the stupidest thing I've heard a white man say in years."

"I just meant—"

"No," Clyde said. "You're in my house now, and you listen to me. I am no more responsible for every Chicago-born pusher who shows up on the East Side than you are for the members of your club. Or at least no more than you think you should be. And secondly, I am tired of people trotting across the line once a year—or once every twenty years—and swearing they're going to save our bad kids. Nothing gets you more excited than a chance to kneel down in the gutter with some real bad, nasty black. But what about the good ones, the ones who want to take your children's jobs and go to your children's schools? I'll tell you what: the good ones don't get shit." He had leaned close again, and Mercury could smell what he did not know was the reek of Ms. Hargreavey's cigarettes. "So let me ask you something, old man," Clyde said. "After all these years, why would you care about this kid?"

"It's the war," Mercury said, not meeting his eyes.

"What?"

"The war," Mercury repeated stubbornly. "His grandfather fought under me in France."

"And so you—" But Clyde was laughing now, not from humor, he realized, but rage. "And so he—well, ain't *that* fancy. What did you do, sign an oath in blood?"

"I made some promises, that's all." The old man rose, the bitter taste of peach in his throat. "I can't believe he did it, Clyde."

"Go on home," Clyde said harshly. "If Lilly Washington's not too mad at you for missing dinner, she'll say the same thing: dead white women are not anything old men and us Negroes have any business going near."

He was still lingering at the screen door when his wife called him in to the dinner for which she'd set two places, thinking he'd invite Mercury. She'd been born in Oakland, and even after a dozen years, the baroque protocols of her husband's city (she had met him while visiting an aunt) seemed to her befitting more an equatorial republic than a city on the edge of the Great Plains. But she had heard him shout—a rarity—and heard the hurricane crack, and so she let him stand awhile, clearing away the second table mat and set of utensils and putting their son to bed. For a long time, Clyde merely listened to the rapidity of his own breathing, waiting for it to slow and smelling the staleness of the wire mesh. He had screened in the porch himself, not so much to keep insects out as for the privacy it brought and the way it seemed to cast, as now, a gauzy veil between himself and the dead street, the lamp and fire hydrant, his neighbors' beaten cars. The Chapmans' old house had had two porches that they chose between depending on the wind, huge affairs with latticework and rolled canvas awnings for the rain, which Mercury had once taught him how to work. He had been seven then, and Mercury twenty-seven: the summer before he left for war. A sudden thunderstorm rolled in, violent, booming, and the rain that slashed sideways through the screen and billowed the thick green canvas sheets lent the porch the exhilarating air of a ship at sea, wind-beaten and precarious, a place for the hearty to make safe. Mercury had seemed to him then the epitome of such a being. He hauled on the thick cotton cords and battened the flapping awnings by their brass eyelets, barking instructions through the thunderclaps, and when they stood panting in the safety of the salvaged porch (suddenly prosaic with its upholstered lounges and lamp-lit wicker seats), Mercury had thrilled him by saying, "Now, if a storm comes while I'm gone, you'll have to be the man of the house." He remembered this with bitterness because years later—trading on

49

those memories—he had turned to Mercury for help. He had started a radio repair shop on Thirty-ninth and Standard Avenue and over a period of five years had watched it slowly die for lack of capital and because whites would not cross Troost to get their stereos fixed. Although not yet thirty, he had known, sitting at the empty register and gazing at the reversed letters on the storefront's glass—Iᖷ-IH 'ƧᴎIꓘ⅃IW—that this failure would mark his life. In the horrible loneliness of the shop, he had daydreamed of Mercury recognizing its name in the phone book and suddenly offering to invest, saving him from submersion with the terse confidence that Clyde remembered from his boyhood (surely Mercury had money to spare). In the last stages of his desperation, he had drafted a letter to this effect and mailed it to Mercury's address. No response had come, the business had failed, and later, when Clyde had been forced to take the job at the Colonial Club, he and Mercury had pretended not to know each other, in order to avoid discussing his disgrace. The phrase *he's one of your own* had particularly outraged Clyde because he'd once believed Mercury would think that way about *him*. Instead, he was out hiring lawyers for some punk twenty-three years too late.

3

ON THURSDAY MORNING the story broke, and what had previously been the disordered impressions of a very few were now codified according to a formula no less rigorous than the hexameters of the Greeks. The intern Wallace Evenrake had spent his lunch break beside the *Star*'s police scanner the day before, an assignment he did not mind because the hour lost listening to burglar-alarm reports and traffic accidents would allow his resume to claim that he had covered "cops." Also, being a newcomer to the city, he had nothing better to do than to savor the scene of his young life's greatest triumph: the humming, fluorescent-lit newsroom where on every desk and in stacks piled waist-high were copies of Wednesday's paper, whose front page trumpeted, complete with pictures, his story about the miraculous longevity of barge traffic on the Missouri River. He couldn't look at it too much. So when the dispatcher announced in her dispassionate voice: "Detective Keegan . . . [*static*] . . . returning a body from the river," he felt that he had reached the moment of his creation as a journalist: the call had been the voice of fate.

Unfortunately for Wallace Evenrake, this was not true. He knew nothing about reporting on cops and had to ask the lone editor on duty for directions to Headquarters downtown. Once there, he was so enthralled by the dingy secrecy of the homicide waiting room, its smoke-stained blue walls and pedal-worked water fountain, the three bolted doors stenciled *Sex crimes*, *Robbery*, and *Homicide*, with peep-holes leading to who knew what kinds of interrogation rooms, and the presence of a breed of humanity (some discreetly hustled past in handcuffs) to which he suspected the term "stool pigeon" might actually be applied, that he forgot why he'd come and began jotting down notes for a story that dispensed with the usual conventions of the police beat and celebrated the true atmosphere of the place. Consequently, he missed what would have been the scoop of the day: the urbanely haggard arrival of Judge Thornton Sayers, in an open-necked tennis shirt and black blazer of mourning. The judge stayed only long enough to nod to the secretary posted behind a window of wire mesh, and then glided, accompanied by a buzzing sound, through the electronically unbolted door. But even a rookie would have noticed that the judge, who had never been known to smoke in public, had three quarters of a Winston clamped between his lips, and that, even though the news of his daughter's death had reached him only that afternoon, he was unshaven. A pro would have known that people aren't normally invited in to the homicide unit after their children die: the judge had a tight furrow of skin between his hazel eyes, not sure yet if he should be pissed.

Not long after the judge had disappeared through the bolted door, Detective Marcy Keegan stepped out. She spoke to Wallace, whose muse was struck dumb by that miraculous voice. "Yes," he said, "yes," while his pen hovered above a blank page.

"There's no comment at this time," Detective Keegan said, and closed the door in his face.

Thornton Sayers had not slept in three days. It had not troubled him at first because he had never slept well, even as a young man, and so associated the relentless persistence of consciousness with the triumphs of his youth: he had played twenty consecutive games of chess with Preston Gibbard the night before they were admitted into Skull and Bones at Yale, and had, with the calm conviction of success, watched the first rays of dawn steep the Charles River on the morning of his final contracts exam at Harvard Law. Usually he liked to walk. The house he owned stood forty feet from the state line, still legally in Missouri, where he'd been appointed to preside, but within sight of the sculpted lawns and gated clubs of Mission Hills, Kansas, whose occupants formed the nucleus of his private life. There were few streetlights there, and over the long, cool lawns and dew-bright tennis courts, the stars shone clear and the city would hold for him the same innocent propriety that he'd envied as a boy. Sometimes he would carry three clubs with him to the golf course and play with profound exhilaration by the light of the moon. The transgressive nature of these walks, his illicit passage among the birdbaths and pool patios of the haut monde, where he would stop on gardenia-scented evenings and enjoy a smoke, was directly connected to the pleasure that he took in them. His father had owned drugstores. A salesman and a gambler with the bristled hair of a shoe-shine brush and a foul red mouth, Ezra Sayers had (to Thornton's embarrassment) charged shamelessly through the various scandals of his past in an effort to achieve the very respectability that his son now grasped. At first, no impropriety had seemed to stick: price-fixing, political malfeasance, charges of bribery or outright theft, not even the fact that Thornton himself had been the product of the second of three wives and had the privilege at age thirteen of watching his own mother be replaced with the same brusque eye toward advancement that other men displayed when buying cars. "If you've got money," his father said, "the best they can do is curse you through their teeth." This rule was proved by the enactment of its reverse. Thornton had been with his father the day he was thrown, quite literally spitting with rage, off the Colonial Country Club course. He had speculated wildly on expanding his chain of stores, the same bank presidents and loan officers who ridiculed him at cocktail parties having agreed in private (and with the full expectation of a quiet, tidy profit) to advance him a minor fortune in unsecured loans. The saying went that when Sayers Drug finally admitted to bankruptcy, half the residents of Mission Hills mortgaged their homes. The fathers of two of Thornton's classmates lost their jobs thanks to loans they'd tendered to Ezra Sayers. Although Thornton humiliated himself by making a public apology in the Pemberton Academy cafeteria, neither the boys nor anyone in their families—including their mothers—ever spoke to him again.

"You bastards treat risks like you do dirty books," his father had shouted as he was ejected from the Colonial Country Club golf course and thus from society itself. "You like to read 'em, all right, only you're too scared to jerk off!" It was a valiant blow for simile, but this disaster left Ezra Sayers more disconsolate than his son realized, and in three years he was dead. From that moment on, Thornton Sayers's life could be understood as a series of acceptances that were in fact erasures of the past: Yale College; Skull and Bones; Harvard Law; the Missouri bar; partnership at Morrison, Thackery, Sitwell; a seat on the Children's Hospital board; the sanctity of the federal bench; membership in the Colonial Country Club itself. He had for so long directed the coarse passions of his father's blood toward clearing the hurdles of gentility that once he reached the bench, he hardly knew what to do with himself. For a time he could publicly endure the surrender of Clarissa's mother to ovarian cancer, accepting congratulations for his bravery when secretly the death of that meek woman filled him with relief. After that there was nothing left to accept, and thus commenced the pleasure of trespassing: he violated his neighbors' lanes and gardens with the wakefulness of a man who'd courted darker truths.

The first night Clarissa was gone, he had forced himself to walk out of habit, which he had declared at many dinner parties was the best cure for grief. Wearing a dark jogging suit and tennis shoes, he visited the Filmores and the Ebersons by way of their backyards and was greeted with the usual familiarity by the Marquands' retriever, who wore an electric collar programmed to shock him if he left the

54

family lawn. Sometimes Thornton removed this collar and invited the dog with him on his walks, but tonight he merely caressed his muzzle and continued down the steep hill of Drury Lane, crossing the stone footbridge that led to his father's old estate. It was still known as the Sayers House, though his father had sold it immediately after his crash, and its twenty-two rooms, five baths, seven fireplaces, and fully appointed servants' quarters were now occupied by Cecelia Lofton, the widow of a diplomat. Mr. Sayers had built the house in 1948 (Thornton had been nine) and it remained a sadly gaudy, useless affair—for reasons the judge did not understand, his father had installed a full pipe organ in the front hall—but he still enjoyed the sanctuary of its pool. The pool stood on a pavilioned patio to the south, sheltered by hulking elms, and though Mrs. Lofton suffered from pleurisy and rarely left the house, she maintained it out of form.

He kicked the elastic waistband of his jogging pants from his ankles, unzipped the top, and dove naked into the water, chlorine burning in his eyes. He swam twenty laps without setting down a foot, his mind emptying with the silent repetition of the pool's pale-blue floor, broken by eddies of helicopter seeds. He finished with a sprint, his lungs pumping and blood pleasantly tightening the muscles of his arms, retrieved his clothes, and pulled a lounge chair to a shadowed corner of the patio, where he lay down to dry. The exercise seemed to have done the trick and when he gazed up into the clear summer dark, it was without foreboding: what he saw was just the sky. He was so intent on maintaining this state that he didn't notice he had company until he heard the pool hoppers giggling at the deep end. Teenagers, a boy and a girl—and as he watched, the boy unfastened the front of his partner's brassiere and cupped one breast, coyly pointed in the moonlight, against his lips. Stricken, the judge listened to her clear, foal-like cry: the same note of triumph that might have accompanied the discovery of a lost barrette. A tremor gripped his heart, his limbs went cold, and he felt what seemed to him the lewd touch of death as the boy finished caressing her and slid his underwear down his skinny flanks. He offered himself to her as she dangled her ankles in the pool, and when she lifted her hand to greet him (she still wore a leather bracelet of the sort that marked friendship between young girls), the judge sprang foward with the groan of a wounded animal, upsetting his chair.

As he watched the young lovers shriek down the purple bowl of Mrs. Lofton's lawn, Thornton Sayers remembered that he, too, was naked, and imagining himself through the eyes of the fleeing girl, he saw a body ravaged by age: gray hair drooping from his nipples and sparse as corn silk about his pubes. He was suet-colored from a lifetime of inside work, and time had atrophied his calves and thighs and surmounted his hips with a merciless roll of fat. Pronated toes, hemorrhoids, fallen arches . . . shivering with disgust and fright, he dressed and went directly home. Fortunately, it was almost morning by then, and he did not have to wait long before he could watch the early news, but the following night he could not bring himself to make his normal rounds, haunted as they were by memories of his daughter. He tried walking east, across Ward Parkway and among the tidy settlements of the middle class, but these only reminded him that the city's residents were as banal as he had always feared. Finally, sleeplessness became a battle not unlike fever, fought in the confines of his own bed. He would snap his eyes open with the conviction that he'd been unconscious for hours, glance at the clock on the bed table, and discover that ten minutes had passed. It was an obsession, a grotesque, harried fugue, and he stopped shaving or even changing clothes when he realized that there was no longer a difference in his life between the nighttime and the day. The vagueness of this existence racked his normally ordered soul, and so when the call came from Detective Keegan, he secretly rejoiced: the recovery of the body provided some sort of concrete close. And the fact that she had summoned him to the station made it even better, suspicion being something he knew how to fight.

"I have a right to see my daughter's body." The judge interlocked his fingers against his chest, thumbs pointing toward the sky. "At least, that's how I would rule."

"That's not procedure, Mr. Sayers," Keegan said.

"You know me better than that."

"Procedure is procedure," Keegan said in a way she knew would be irritating, but looking up into Thornton Sayers's hazel eyes, she faltered, adding, "Judge."

"Was she raped?"

Keegan held his gaze. "I don't yet know."

"Beaten, shot, dismembered?" The judge had bent forward now across the table, one hand splayed flat. "What clothes was she wearing? My daughter did not accidentally fall into the river, Marcy, so I'm curious what you think happened instead. Also, you can't legally prevent me from seeing her: you know that, so let's cut the shit."

"When did you last see your daughter?"

"Do we have an understanding?"

"The autopsy is scheduled at five," Keegan said. "If we get this over with, you'll still have time."

The judge relaxed, withdrew his hand. The room in no way resembled the bare interrogation chambers he'd expected from TV: vacuumed carpet, a long Formica table ringed by watermarks, ten vinyl chairs. A blue and white candy wrapper had been left on a chair, and he read the name of one ingredient, *lectin*, repeating this meaningless word inside his mind as he stared past the surprisingly dull face of Marcy Keegan, who was clicking a tape into a recording machine. *Lectin you sow*, he thought, but she could not hear it. "So, this is your lair," he said, pretending to look now that he already had. "I'd imagined it would be more severe: the dregs of the city, that kind of thing. Is that a one-way mirror?" He nodded to the dark band of glass that split the room's narrow end.

"Yeah," Keegan said.

"Do I need to be observed?"

Keegan smiled. "We look through it *from* this room."

Most homicide detectives appeared in Judge Sayers's courtroom as witnesses, but Marcy Keegan had first entered as a defendant, a beat cop accused of shooting an unarmed Mexican who'd resisted arrest. He'd sorted through the basics of the case on his way downtown: Keegan had responded to an early-morning disturbance call at the victim's address; she had found a girl there, beaten, underage, and (as the girl claimed) raped. Both the girl and the victim were high on coke. Keegan had chased the victim, Carlos Ramirez, into the backyard, where he had turned on her, she said, despite repeated commands to freeze. She shot him through the neck. The trial convened in winter, ice floes grinding along the river day and night, dirty furrows of snow along the streets, and something wintery flickered in Keegan, bereft and ugly in her wool cap and rubber overshoes. The family pressed charges, while Councilman Hernandez blatantly trumpeted the issue of race, but the case hinged on the claim that Keegan had known the victim—perhaps, as the prosecution implied in chambers, romantically. She had been jealous, not racist.

Judge Sayers had refused to admit charges of a romantic link, and his decision had killed the case. Relative justice: when he watched Keegan in the courtroom, he'd felt sure that her cold hands (she had seemed perpetually cold, frozen somehow from the start) had pulled the trigger for reasons she did not care to reveal. But her victim had been a sociopath, a drug dealer, and a rapist, while Keegan herself was an honest cop, or so he believed: a gut decision that had salvaged her career. The gratitude of the acquitted toward her judge, as toward the captain of a long and deadly voyage, still lived inside her now.

"I'm sorry about your daughter," Keegan said, quickly shuffling her papers. "I called you in because it's faster this way."

"I'm glad to have someone serious on the case," the judge said. "The reason should be clear. I last saw my daughter Saturday evening at the Founders Ball, where she was escorted by Bert Gauss. Have you spoken to him?"

Keegan shook her head. "Have you?"

"I called him Sunday when Clarissa wouldn't answer her phone," the judge said. "I got worried. Clarissa has often made it clear to me that, at age twenty-two, she can sleep where she wants, but I tried Bert anyway, and he was very polite: he said that after the ball she'd gone to meet a young black named Booker Short."

"Tell me about him," Keegan said.

"Booker Short murdered my little girl." The words surfaced of their own accord, triumphant, venal, and he felt the same wetness in his mouth that accompanied the forbidden words of sex.

With two fingers, Keegan keyed her tape machine. "Start at the beginning," she said, "and tell me why you think Booker Short would have killed your daughter."

But he regained control after that. It was like the moment of ignition of a shell, the sullen stench of nitrate and scorched brass, the jet of smoke, in which a potential only formerly imagined—even cherished, just as he had since childhood enjoyed the weight and texture of the brass itself, holding the dense lead nub between his fingertips and picturing how someday it might pierce a moving heart—became real and separate from the chamber, engaged in its own irrevocable arc. "I'm sorry," he said. "That was over the line. Your turf. That they were friends is all I know for sure." And so he spoke to Keegan about the rest with the mechanical simplicity he would have accorded a child who could not possibly be expected to understand the deeper laws at play.

"Excuse me," said Keegan. "But if you'd known Booker Short for almost two years, why ignore him at the ball?"

"Because Clarissa didn't want to see him."

"Even if she went out with him later." It was not a question but a statement, and the judge looked with incredulity at the face he had until then not cared to notice—bovine, slightly mustached, shaped generally like the reverse imprint of a spade.

"Detective Keegan," he said, his palm brushing the note he had

59

stuffed inside his jacket four days before, and whose text he remembered with the engulfing whiteness of an atomic blast, "what father does not wish he could read his daughter's heart?"

Only in the city, Mercury Chapman had once observed to Henry Latham of the *Star, can there be such a thing as death by words.* The two men had been sitting in Mercury's bass boat, surrounded by the jungled channel of a flooded strip-mining pit (this was his fishing club, some miles distant from the hunting one), and Henry waited to answer until he'd finished retrieving his lure. *Or absolution,* he had said.

If Alvin Bailey had heard his boss, he would have laughed. Alvin believed in two kinds of words: those that were facts and those that weren't. A fact was defined not as what actually happened, but as what could legally be published according to specific rules: confirmation by three sources, attribution to a source by name (a detective, for instance), or presence in a document signed by persons of worth. Facts could not be expected to represent the true spirit of an event. Murderers failed to give Alvin advance notice of their crimes, and even if they had allowed him to lie in their beds for six months and take notes on family history, motivation, and scene, the paper had no room to print that kind of crap. No, facts were self-incarnated, unhinged from the vanished past—the paper's archives *replaced* the past—and Alvin often despaired at how the white community understood this so much more readily than the black. His friends always called to say how one story or another wasn't true, they'd seen how it went down, to which Alvin would respond, "You going on the record with that?" and when they inevitably refused, he would say, "Then it's not a fact."

Consequently, he had very little patience for the rhapsodic intentions of Wallace Evenrake, a guy who'd grown up in one of those small Kansas towns that were the very definition of white, who had studied journalism with a professor (Alvin had started as a mailboy at

60

the *Star*), and who had been stupid enough to wear a glen plaid suit and wingtips to the homicide waiting room. Alvin expressed impatience by smiling, and by the time Wallace used the term "stool pigeon," his mouth hurt. "That's cool," he said. "You find out anything about who died?"

Wallace had found out that Detective Keegan had a voice like Marlene Dietrich's.

"You go on and write that down," Alvin advised. Before Wallace had executed his first sentence, Alvin had called five people. He wore a secretary's headset, which, together with his normal office uniform—khakis, denim shirt, and the kind of ugly knit tie that put homicide detectives at their ease—made him look like a sports announcer, except that he stared at the support column before his desk. He appeared to be doing play-by-play for a purely imaginary game. First he called the homicide sergeant, who refused to confirm or deny anything. Optimistic, he called Detective Keegan's line, got her voice mail, and then rang Charlie Schiff, whose desk was next to hers and who patronized an escort service that Alvin knew about but had not exposed. Playing a game of Twenty Questions, he discovered that a body had been found in the river, that it had happened in Waterloo (an easy guess, since all the bodies washed up there), that it had been someone famous—no, a relation of someone *locally* famous—not mafia, not a politician, not a businessman or a cop. "Thank legal," said Charlie, who'd grown up in Tulsa and who proceeded to hiss in Alvin's ear. "What the fuck is that?" Alvin asked. "That's the first letter," Charlie said. "Judge Sssss." "Federal?" Alvin said.

He found Sayers in the green book and called the clip library upstairs, gratified to get a human voice. Ten minutes later a bell rang, and he walked around the post that fronted his desk, opened a door in its far side, and removed a manila folder of clips from an electric dumbwaiter. The clips said Judge Sayers's wife was dead, but he had a daughter named Clarissa, age twenty-two. He then phoned the Truman Hospital morgue and asked the medical examiner about the body of a Clarissa Sayers, whose presence he confirmed, along with age and name, cause of death not yet known. By then Alvin had broken a sweat, and he fetched a sheaf of paper towels from the bathroom to swab his neck. He could by now feel the story emerging from what he grandiosely referred to as the "realm of the unseen," the kingdom of minor gunplay, knifings, rapes, arsons, holdups, car thefts, deaths by lightning, boating accident, or highway wreck, extortion, prostitution, larceny, etc.—everything that wasn't worthy of a story and that thus, beyond its moment of execution, ceased in Alvin's eyes to be real. He copied Thornton Sayers's home number from the court reporter's Rolodex and left a message on his machine. Finally he called the police department's officer of media relations, who was both an idiot and never there. At four o'clock he headed for the station house, stopping by the Metro editor's desk to tell him that Judge Sayers's daughter was dead.

"What about Carl Sandburg?" the Metro editor said, nodding down the long double line of editorial computers mounted on wheeled carts, their shells humped like cicadas, to the general-assignment bullpen. Wallace sat typing with his heels hooked on his chair rung.

"Hey Wallace," Alvin said. "Let's go downtown."

Wallace trotted over fast.

"Alvin's taking you to the cop shop," the Metro editor said. "He offered to."

Wallace's eyes shifted from the editor to Alvin and back again. "I was kind of working on something," he said.

"You're working on something."

"Kind of, I was."

Alvin wore a tremendous smile.

"He's working on something," the editor reported, swiveling in his chair.

Wallace had chewed the butt off a pen while thinking, and blue ink streaked his hair. Finger-dabs to his upper lip left a small azure mustache. "I'll do whatever's fair," he said, "but if Alvin goes to the police station with me, we'll both be doing the same thing. Don't you think, Al?"

"Please don't touch me," Alvin said.

Deep into the age of information, Clarissa Sayers's death became news by the most traditional means: a sweating beat reporter hoofing the nine blocks from his office to police HQ, a fresh notebook at his hip. There would be no cameras until Thursday afternoon because the television stations stole all their stories from the *Star*. The paper's federal court reporter was visiting cousins in Belton for the week. Instead, there was only the odd silence that Alvin Bailey often noticed before a good murder broke, correspondent to the apogee of Judge Sayers's imaginary shell, the moment when something existed before it had a telling, an audible sound. Alvin already knew what the telling would be and so felt like he'd moved forward in time, cresting Twelfth Street and heading right between the henna-lit faces of City Hall and the Jackson County courthouse, their upper stories bare, clean stone black-lined against the sky and their lowers parts ornamented with chiseled foils and grape leaves. The buildings seemed injected like brass studs into a landscape of crumbled brick, bail-bond offices, and coin-operated parking lots, their corners swollen with bums and sullen commuters, and yet Alvin saw tomorrow the hushed, excited buzz of secretaries, councilmen, bureaucrats knowing what they did not know before, the buzz of its own accord starting to move things, calls being made, confidences exchanged, the story faxed, warrants issued, and then later the news vans gathered at the federal courthouse a few blocks away, and the reporters waiting with cameras outside Judge Sayers's chambers, and the hot, bright floodlights of curiosity—none of these people, nor this space, these buildings, knowing yet what tomorrow it was now predecided they would do. The whole business filled Alvin with a pleasurable sense of control.

Upstairs at police headquarters, Judge Sayers leaned his forehead against the long black strip of one-way glass while Marcy Keegan threw a switch. Halogen lamps lit the room beyond a blaring white.

"So you really do lineups," he said, unable to control the eager twitch of his lip. "Just like on TV." Going down, he rode the elevator while Alvin Bailey walked up the steps.

Twenty blocks away, at Truman Hospital, the medical examiner (spurred to action by a reporter's call) lifted a scalpel and opened Clarissa Sayers's body from her pelvis to her neck. He intended to check her lungs for water to determine if she'd been breathing when she went down—a formality because in his opinion she'd been killed by the "blow of a blunt object to the head," as he'd tell police.

Sixty miles downriver, Stan Granger stood tortured by doubt in the shack that Booker Short had left. He held a pair of World War II dog tags and Detective Keegan's business card, one in either hand, as if offering them to anyone in the empty room.

"What I want to know is the suspect's name," Alvin Bailey said inside police headquarters. "If you've got one, we should know."

"He's not a suspect yet," Detective Keegan said.

"Tell me how to phrase it."

In the *Star* newsroom, Wallace Evenrake wrote his first line: *There is an office in this city that traffics in the industry of death . . .*

"Authorities are interested in questioning a young African American male, last seen in the victim's company Saturday night," said Detective Keegan.

Stool pigeons, junkies, and new widows sit indifferently in plastic chairs . . .

"He was driving a red nineteen sixty-seven Stingray."

After nearly a half hour of argument and threat, Judge Thornton Sayers gained admittance to the chilled holding room of Truman Hospital's morgue. Bodies lay on gurneys, covered with sheets. An attendant checked the toe tags and found Clarissa. His daughter's torso had been closed with metal staples, like a zipper, and he prodded them with his finger one by one. "She is . . ." He looked at the attendant. "She has decayed."

"Sorry," the attendant said.

64

4

HE READ THE STORY while sitting in a McDonald's on Forty-seventh and Troost, where he had gone, out of perversity, to make obeisance to the great white corporation that had taught more *Nee-groes*, as his grandfather would have said, to say please and thank you and keep their shirts tucked in and generally *know their place* than all the leg irons, auction blocks, and devilish TV-movie slave drivers of the old plantation South. Or so he estimated vaguely, not having the figures right at hand. He had come to stand before Ray Kroc's bronze visage, hung appropriately by the cash registers (was that Kroc as in Krocodile? Or maybe Kroc-o-shit?), and say that he'd learned his lesson, oh yes: he knew where he belonged, Mr. Kroc, and what's more, he was afraid.

"An Egg McMuffin, orange juice, and a small coffee," he said politely.

"You want hash brow'?"

"Are they extra?"

"No char'." The young girl behind the plastic-covered register spoke with the slurring musicality he'd thought confined to the deepest South; she tapped inch-long false fingernails on the keys. "They included in the McMuffin meal."

Ah, Kroc: what genius! Who would've thought to buy the very language in which we speak!

The girl pointed with her lavender prostheses to a plastic square on the board behind her head. There, illuminated by a light bulb from behind, glowed a photograph of his order and the words

EGG MCMUFFIN MEAL™

The food arrived almost immediately, hot and clipped in foam. The paper place mat underneath offered a maze of linked yellow arches and a crossword puzzle whose answers were the names of sandwiches. He chewed over it absently for a moment and then thought, *It's enough to eat here; I don't actually have to read this shit.* The newspaper vending machine was chained to a streetlight outside. The headline ran below the fold, so he didn't see it until the spring-loaded door slammed and he flipped the paper against the inside of his forearm, reading, conscious of the other patrons behind the tinted glass, and forcing himself to walk calmly through the crowded restaurant and sit down at his place. *You're clean. There's nothing here that can touch you.* That was not how he felt. Kroc's eggs and sausage simmered in his stomach; his hash browns tasted like burned cork. He read the headline again—JUDGE'S DAUGHTER PULLED FROM RIVER; SUSPECTED FOUL PLAY—and the front-page body, setting the paper flat on the table when his hands began noticeably to shake and then scanning with trembling fingers through the jump section on page eight until he found, in the final paragraph, the most frightening of all murder story phrases . . . *interested in questioning a young African American male* . . . and then the year and model of Clarissa's car outside.

He rose and walked calmly past the counter and down the short back hall to the false-wood-paneled door emblazoned MEN. And there, in the white stall of Mr. Kroc's white toilet, he retched.

He felt better afterward. Washing his face, he even managed to think, *there's one communion that didn't take,* preserving some small glimmer of his own voice against the underground babble that now welled from the base of his skull. He studied himself in the mirror (zip-front sweatshirt, white T, jeans: his most anonymous rags), but when the eyes of his reflection met his own, his knees caved and he braced himself against the Formica bowl. Overlaid like a morph on his water-glistened features were the sallow cheekbones and fish-hook grin of his father, the same hunted loser's stare. He shitcanned a handtowel and, though visibly walking, spiritually ran.

Most of what he knew about his father he'd invented: a talented mimic of others, Carothers Short had rarely spoken about himself. He'd been a con man (this more a state of being than a profession), band manager, and gambler and—during the period of "straightness" that coincided with his marriage—had run a makeshift recording studio out of a shotgun shack on Beech Street, in East Tulsa. Booker remembered him best this way. The walls and windows of the shack's rear anteroom had been carpeted to keep out sound. No air conditioning or even fans were allowed, and his father would sit in colored silk underwear before the chrome and matte-black machines, sweating like a boxer on his stool. "Wouldst it violate you unneedfully," he'd say into the microphone, "to make my shitty song sound sweet?"

Sometimes Booker didn't catch the source of his father's imitations, but Richard Burton had played Hamlet on television the night before, and the accent was unmistakable. His father turned his head to wink. "Darling?" he added. Although he could hear his father conversationally from outside the studio door, the microphone was wired to the hall closet, also carpet-walled, which served as the isolation booth where his mother, Illyria, sang. The door opened and she stuck her head out, earphones about her neck. "It's crap," she said.

"But it could be such *nice* crap."

"A song about a robot?"

"Here's an idea," said his father, grinning. "Try singing it neutrally."

The door slammed. His father, motions fluid, cued the track. The music was inaudible to Booker, playing only through the headphones that now both his parents wore, its only evidence a rhythmic ticking in his father's heel. But Illyria Short's voice was there. It emerged from the closet muffled, like singing heard from a different street, full-throated, swollen with the heat, and leaving an almond taste of bitterness in its wake. His father popped his earphones off and listened a cappella, too.

"Your mother's singing always makes me ache," he said. "The problem is, aching don't sell that much today."

He'd left when Booker was seven, slipping literally out the backdoor, as all men did in the Tulsa blues songs his mother liked to sing (and which Carothers considered horribly out of date). It was August, sultry, mulberry-scented, and Booker had surreptitiously spent his vacation exploring the secrets of the studio's equipment. He'd mastered the mikes and mixing board, but the magic of Carothers's four-track recorder had eluded him: how was it that his father could record his mother at a different time from, say, the drummer, and yet their sounds blended on the machine? For several weeks he'd eliminated, in quiet, intense hours, false leads, resisting the temptation simply to ask (he wanted to present his father with a fait accompli), until he'd solved it and listened with the shallow breathing of success as the black ribbon fed through the heads and he heard himself talking and whistling all at once. He was rewinding to listen again when he heard footsteps in the forward room and froze above the button of the machine. A voice spoke that he did not recognize: "Five thousand dollars, professor," it said, "is one hell of a gambling debt."

"I'm not a professor," his father said, doing Cagney even then.

"I won't argue with that." A sound made Booker rub his teeth. "Sit down, Short," the voice said.

"Fuck you." His father slurred his words as though he'd been asleep, and then a groan escaped the front room, onrushing through the hall to Booker's ears, followed by a squealing noise, and he looked up in horror at the loose unspooling of the tape. When his father teetered in, Booker was standing on a chair Chaplinesque, arms filled with the black spaghetti of the unreeling spool. The hair above his father's ear was wet and his lips were misshapen, and he held one fin-

68

ger up for silence as he stepped out of his platform shoes, his purple slacks ballooning about his ankles. Something seemed to amuse him as he peeled back a neatly razored flap of carpet and unlatched the door behind, his eyes flickering to the bunched curls of tape, as if discovering at this last moment the secret emulation of his son (that was what Booker later hoped, prayed was true), and then he was gone, running sock-footed through the dog fennel and clematis, across the creek, and into the backyard lots of Tulsa, where they lived. The studio's windows being carpeted, Booker could not see him go.

Booker was rewinding the tape by hand when the lawman came in. He wore a sheriff's stare beneath a nameplate that read "Timpson," and he stepped forward to grab the tape, examining it like the ticker of a stock machine. "I'll be damned if this little shit might've recorded me," he said.

A black man entered, holding a cut length of garden hose with duct tape over its ends. "You gonna just let him run?" he said.

Timpson was busy wadding up balls of Booker's recording.

"I thought that's what my payments covered," the black man said. "Collecting debts."

The skin around Timpson's eyes was cracked and shiny, and he had bright-red hair dusted with peelings from his scalp. He unclasped a penknife and cut Booker's tape at either end. "If I was a bookie, I'd not compromise myself by talking crap," he said. "Besides, it appears to me that this here's some valuable propery, just waiting to be repossessed."

When his mother returned from her Saturday bridge game, Booker simply refused to speak. Illyria milled with frantic repetition through the empty and now heavily footprinted anteroom and outside to the grass-divided driveway where her husband's Lincoln usually sat, and back again. She touched as though for warmth the undusted rectangles left atop the folding tables and packing crates and clattered to their bedroom, where Booker found her sobbing, arms buried in a drawer of her husband's gaudy silk shirts. He put his face in the hollow of her neck. "Tell Mama what happened," she said. Her fingers grabbed his beltloop and drew him against the opened bureau. "You saw it," his mother said. She was kneeling and shook him rhythmically. "You saw it," she repeated. "Don't you dare come at me with no lie. That's a sickness, don't you see? A sickness—"

His head snapped against the bureau lid, and his mother's eyes rolled white. "I didn't see it, any," he said, voice hopping. "I was playing down at the creek." She struck him a hard, flat blow, orange flares and vivid sunbursts blossoming inside his skull.

He believed that if he told her what had happened, his father would never return.

Years later, lying with Clarissa at the hunting club, he'd tried to re-create how his mother and father had met: whether or not they'd been in love, how they'd known. But having finally developed a practical interest in his parents' history, he had no parents left to ask.

In Ray Kroc's dining area, he meticulously gathered up each section of his paper—ROYALS FADE 3–2; MONTGOMERY BLOWS 10TH SAVE— dumped his Styrofoam into the Thank You bin, and strolled into the parking lot, where, reaching for the Stingray's keys, he froze in mid-stride. The Stingray blazed against the blue-black asphalt in full view of the street, and forcing himself *not* to look around, he eased alongside its glossy flank, the top mercifully down, snagged his duffel from the back, and tucked the keys under the floor mat. He walked north, past a pom-pommed used-car lot, the Epicurean Adult Bookstore, and Brownback's Rubber Stamps. Clarissa had once indignantly explained how Troost marked the boundary line between black and white (as if such an arrangement would surprise him in any way), but the avenue seemed less a boundary than the site of some colonial exodus. Every third building front was boarded over, every fourth transmuted into a "thrift store" with junk gilt-and-ebony lampstands jumbled outside (JIMMY'S CRACKCORN CURIOS; BIG CITY SURPLUS; TOP

70

METAL RECYCLING: WE BUY COPPER, BRASS, LEAD), though the pediments above were of intricately cut stone, often inlaid with tile, and the burned-out brick apartments boasted three-story fluted columns and beveled glass, evidence of a fine civilization that once had been. He had a dangerous feeling about Clarissa's death, dangerous because it was not fear, and passing the J&G Troost Market, the bubbling began again inside his head: *I said, it still is stealing and she said, not if what you're taking has already been stolen and I said, so that's why you give it to him, because you've already been took.* As he skirted wilted racks of lettuce, a slouched and sweatshirt-hooded boy released a stream of urine that angled steaming across his path. He crossed it. Clarissa's voice kept repeating, *you don't know anything about what I do* and holding his mind still against this, he continued toward the river, heading north.

Three days after his father left, he had watched rain jerk in upward rivulets against a taxi window as the cab crested a long hill. "Look," Illyria said. "Look there, now. Can you read it?" He squinted through the drizzle at the plain below and at the house that appeared to him little more than a ruin, stark, its windows like eyeless sockets unlit against the gray day. The writing outlined on its roof was illegible, BF NTI ΛM, but his mother seemed not to notice, humming tunefully, searching for a compact in her purse. So he did not ask why.

She had dressed him in a starched, short-sleeved shirt and necktie, so he expected some variation on the tedium of Sunday service, followed by his return home and release. The taxi stopped on the dirt apron beneath the carport, and Illyria told the driver to wait, a hopeful sign. Through the side door, they entered what once had been the dining room. A chandelier hung from the ceiling, its dusty crystals barely clearing a butte of furniture that monopolized the room. Settees mounted bureaus and chiffoniers tilted atop wingbacked chairs. There were gilded lampstands, spindles, chamber pots, and cider presses. Sideboards and rolltop desks lined the walls. A narrow oval track ran around the central summit, and Illyria led him along this without a second glance.

The next room smelled of horsehair. Sofas stood in sheet-covered rows like church pews, and Booker followed his mother down the middle aisle, haunted on both sides by their reflections in a gallery of warped and smoky mirrors. "Well," Illyria said in the only moment of unsteadiness he recalled during this final encounter. "This collecting bug seems literally to have bought the farm."

She did not call out for anyone until they reached a door whose crevices had been stuffed with pot holders that rained down on their shoulders when they opened it. This led to the cramped and notice-ably warmer rear of the house. "Hello?" Illyria ventured. A scuffling sounded ahead, then ceased. "It's your daughter, Illyria. Don't shoot." She meant this as a joke, but it sounded less than convincing.

They sat in the steam-dampened kitchen with Mrs. Bentham, who had greeted them with a claw hammer in her hand. Isaac was down at the shop, and Booker, after several minutes, began to worry about the cab. He did not like his grandmother. Her eyes flittered like a chipmunk's, looking at the wall clock, at the shadowy figures on her portable TV, at her boiling potatoes, and out the kitchen's steam-thick windows, without actually seeing any of those things. Illyria sat calmly on a step stool and ignored her. All three of them watched Isaac cross the farm's backyard and enter the mudroom, where he stamped off his boots. He came in wearing crisp gym socks over what could have been a dancer's feet, gave the room a single, sweeping glance, and sat down at the place setting his wife had nervously pre-pared. She served him in silence, and he ate with his back to them, the room fragrant with soup broth.

When he finished, he pushed the bowl away. "All right, what is it?" he said.

"Carothers left me," Illyria said.

"The music man?" Isaac grunted through his nose.

72

"If you want me to say that you were right, I will," Illyria said. "But I didn't come for pity: I came to make a deal."

Isaac pivoted his chair to face his daughter. It angered Booker how closely this unpleasant stranger—the title "grandfather" carried no emotional weight for him—resembled his mother: the coppery skin, the high, bruised-apple cheekbones, the obstinate angle of the chin. "It's all or nothing," Isaac said. "I won't run a grazing service: if I pay room and board for something, I want to know it wears my mark."

"At sixteen, he gets to choose."

"Eighteen," Isaac said. "That's the law."

They both spoke in such ruthless shorthand that Booker didn't immediately realize they were discussing him. But by the time father and daughter shook hands—touching for the first time since their running, upstairs battle eight years before, when Carothers had brought her out to get her things—he'd disappeared. They searched for him through the three shabby rooms Isaac and his wife occupied in what would have been called the servants' quarters, and then they branched out through the cobwebbed provinces of Isaac's antiques. Mrs. Bentham rattled an open bag of ginger snaps as she went, embarrassed that she hadn't offered to feed the boy. Illyria discovered a possum nursing in the base of a cherrywood water closet and snapped the lid shut in irritation. The cabbie was enlisted in the hunt. Isaac himself did not start looking right away but instead sat finishing his crackers, wearing an expression at once dreamy and sharp. After a time he pulled on his boots in the mudroom and crossed the back lot, brick-colored chickens squawking in his wake. He reached what looked like a half-buried woodshed, its angles askew with age, surrounded by chicken wire. The gate whanged on a leather hinge. He stooped beneath the door frame and waited for his eyes to adjust to the dark, smelling the rot of termites. Booker sat in the corner of the gnomic structure with a nickel-plated pistol between his knees. "This is the homestead my great-grandfather built in eighteen thirty-eight,"

Isaac said. "For one hundred and forty-two years Benthams have kept it up. You must have taken that revolver from my collection by mistake."

"Nossir," Booker said.

"You're fixing to use it, huh?" The high-hipped figure of Isaac Bentham filled the door like an inverted guitar case, stray beams of light shafting about his shoulders and knees. The way Booker held the pistol, it pointed at his grandfather's groin.

"Lemme alone."

"You got to pull the hammer back first," Isaac said. "And after that, watch out: trigger's got such a feather touch, it'll go off if you sneeze." He could make out the white field of Booker's shirt, bisected by his red tie. "That pistol belonged to a Union colonel named David Houseman, family lives near here. Bought it off them. He fired it charging a rebel picket during the Battle of Woolly Creek. Got the papers on it, too."

Booker cared nothing about his ancestors' original homestead or the pistol, which he'd happened upon by chance. Instead, he listened to his mother calling from the house: the bitterness had lifted from her voice entirely, and the warbled melody with which she summoned him—*Booker! Hey-lo Booker Short come here!*—was stolen from one of his father's songs.

"You can have the gun back," he told Isaac. "But first get her to go away."

5

WHEN BOOKER TURNED FOURTEEN, Isaac decided that he should learn to drive the combine. Fall harvest had started, and like many of his classmates at Consolidated School No. 5 (among whom Booker's face resembled an anomalous fleck of chert), he received two weeks off to work. Isaac had hired a white itinerant to drive his combine that season, a Texan who'd trailed the harvest north. White hands worked for Isaac only as a last resort, so Booker assumed some tragedy had come his way.

Isaac woke him at five, as had become his habit, and they drove the four hundred yards from the carport to the tractor shed in the back lot. Nobody was there. The air smelled of iron and the isopropyl residue of Isaac's shaving cream, and they waited a half hour in silence, the truck's lamps dull against the red clay drive. Booker had never been out with his grandfather before a harvest and was surprised to find him restive, silently intense. Isaac shifted in his seat. "You got to kick their asses every morning," he said to himself aloud. "Otherwise they'll forget your name by noon."

At precisely quarter to six, Isaac got out and stood with his back against the truck grille. Headlights appeared on the distant hill above the house, feathered through roadside willows, and bounced up the drive in a flurry of white moths. Three Mexicans descended. Two other trucks followed at intervals, the first carrying the Haitian who lived in a rental house nearby, and the last—wheel wells rusted, sock stuck in the gas tank—disgorging a boy who seemed no older than Booker himself, towheaded, with a broken cigarette in his mouth. Isaac leaned forward from the grille and said, "You're late." He proceeded to harangue the gathered hands with such harsh, impious contempt that Booker worried they would either fight him in the still-unlit lot or quit. At sixty-five, Isaac still bought the same cut jeans he'd worn at thirty, the fabric perfectly faded and molded to his boot tops like the drop-forged legs of a toy soldier. In the false dawn, he looked fifty. He didn't believe in vices among men, only habits that he would or would not tolerate, and he listed these in a hard, flat bass. "Fucking don't make no never-mind to me," he said. "I know you spic Don Juans aren't worth shit without you get some *coño* and a good night's sleep. Don't care if you beat your kids, grow marijuana in your basement, gamble, or poach deer, so long as it's not on my place. Don't even care if you're a legal resident of this country, which some of you ain't. What I do care about is excuses, mistakes, laziness, and being late." He walked inside the ragged circle of men and stopped before the young Texan. "And if you have trouble taking orders from a colored farmer, as the newspapers used to say," he continued, staring directly at him, "my advice is to remember that the Bentham family—that is to say, *me*—is the oldest landowning family in the county, if not the state."

The Texan's jaw opened and closed silently, as if operated by a spring.

"My grandson's learning the combine this season," Isaac said. "Some of you know him already. Make nice."

Hot-cheeked, Booker offered each his hand. The Mexicans responded with a loose-limbed, coy respect, commenting in their own language about his slenderness. "*Su padre era musico,*" Isaac said, as if this explained it. The Haitian was eating an egg wrapped in a corn tortilla and wiped his massive fingers delicately. Booker had never dealt with a white who owed him anything, and when the Texan drew the broken cigarette from his mouth and jerked his chin, he accepted this as fit.

"He'll shake your hand," Isaac said.

"I drive farm equipment," the Texan said.

"So?"

"Baby-sitting ain't part of the deal." His skin was so badly acned that his chin worked without definition into his throatflesh. He spat nervously. "I don't mind you *colored farmers* so much as I cain't tolerate kids."

The Mexicans hid their faces in their hats.

"It's my combine," Isaac said. "I say who rides."

"A man works better if he gets respect," the Texan said.

"And you need this job more than I need you." Isaac waited. The Texan stood up from the truck, shook Booker's hand limply—they were the same height—and retreated. He smelled of kerosene. "Good," Isaac said. "You're cutting the southwest field. Booker, show him where it is."

Booker was already heading for the tractor shed when he heard the Mexicans laugh. He turned and saw the Texan crossing the lot with four telephone books tucked like luggage beneath his armpits. "Go on and giggle with the wetbacks all you want," the Texan said, catching up to him. "But I lay twenty dollars that by lunchtime you'll wish you had some, too."

The cab of Isaac's International Harvester sat twelve feet off the ground, and to reach it, Booker climbed the ridges of its rear tire like stairs. Inside, he found the Texan seated on a double layer of Houston directories. He was strapping wooden blocks to the bottoms of his tennis shoes, and Booker noticed in the glow of the dome light that his ears burned red. If Isaac had any qualms about his new driver's talent (and in a half century of farming he'd seen stranger things), they were eased by the Texan's fluid and apparently offhand negotiation of the front drive, his stubby arms pulling the walking stick–length levers and his wood blocks punching the clutch and gas with the familiarity of a church organist during Friday Mass. He glided neatly around the carport, lit a cigarette as they processed down the drive, and, following Booker's instructions, swerved left onto the roadway in a vast exhalation of smoke. "You never told your name," Booker said.

The Texan opened the door to ash his cigarette and closed it again. He hunted intently over the combine's immense console and felt with a backturned palm the cab wall behind his head. "They cain't not have a radio in this thing," he said loudly, as though addressing the driver of a passing car.

"You shouldn't take it personal about him yelling," Booker said. "He does everyone like that."

"Let's you and me get something straight." The Texan wrinkled his forehead and perused a row of gauges, eyes wide. "Don't get any funny ideas just 'cause I'm working here. I'm not a *mixer*, see? If your grampa wants to wipe his ass with me, fine. Soon as I get a real job, he'll have to find himself a darker rag."

"We had a Dominican who was afraid of lightning," Booker said. "Every time it rained, he'd get a hundred yards away from anything metal: a tractor, a fence, even a box of nails. Stood in the middle of the field. One time, it rained three days and the guys had to carry food out 'cause he wouldn't leave. Finally Isaac comes down in this truck. This Dominican sees that steel Dodge heading his way, and he lights out. Pisses Grampa off even more. He starts trying to run the guy down, only it's so muddy the truck can't keep up. The guy zigzags. Then he jumps a drainage ditch, and Isaac roars right after him and gets stuck, nose first."

"I bet your grampa was fried!"

"He was pretty mad, all right, but he controlled it. He took off everything metal he had on, even his watch, and walked out to the Dominican with his hands up. 'Thomas,' he said, 'watch out, 'cause that lightning's straight behind you.' And when the Dominican turned to look, he knocked him out."

"So he's a tough guy," said the Texan.

78

"Oh, yeah," Booker said. "When he was only five years older than I am now, he invaded France."

"All by himself? Well, I'll be very damned."

"No," Booker said. "He went over with some of the first black soldiers in the war—Truck Company Four-nine-seven-one. They came in right after the invasion and fought all the way across France, in the Ardennes Forest and on the Somme. He killed seventy-five Germans. I've seen their sabers and their guns."

"I guess maybe he liked killing white people."

Booker shrugged. "That was the only kind they had," he said. "His captain was a white guy—Mercury Chapman of Kansas City, Missouri. He was rich, too. The story is that he owes us big time, because Isaac saved his life."

"My, my, my—rich white people," said the Texan, looking at Booker out of one blood-rimmed eye. "Maybe I should've dressed more nice."

The southwest field was planted with feed corn and they entered it across a dirt bridge. The thresher blades wove before them like a reversed paddle wheel, and the sun beat through the cab's bubbled glass, and the air vent on the floor blew hazy with corn dust and bits of chaff. One of the Mexicans shadowed them with a tractor and rice buggy and at intervals the Texan waved his hat out the window, pulled a jointed lever, and the corn spilled liked gold pennies out the combine's grain chute and into the buggy alongside. He did everything on the fly. A coyote squirted into the open field, and he jumped from the cab, rolled beyond the tires, and ran to the tractor, where he grabbed the Mexican's rifle off his seat. He knelt and fired twice, squeezing the trigger slowly. When the animal veered out of range, he cursed, chest-passed the rifle to the Mexican, and ran back to the cab, where Booker sat in utter terror, clutching the steering wheel but afraid to actually turn it. Seeing him, the Texan gave a whooping cheer.

At noon they squatted in the new-cut stubble and ate the lunches

79

Mrs. Bentham had packed. "My name's Batson Putz," the Texan said, squinting forlornly at a hand-cupped match. "I'll take it kindly if you gentlemen don't laugh."

But Booker paid no attention to the oddity of his name. He'd been watching the coolness with which Batson struck a wooden match along the inseam of his jeans.

Isaac Bentham owned four thousand acres of hill and floodplain along the Verdigris River, east of Tulsa. Booker had lived there seven years. At first, his mother had written him postcards from Detroit, promising to send for him as soon as she got "set up" (ignoring, he knew, her deal with Isaac), but then the postmark changed to Fort Wayne, Indiana, and she informed him, in a letter whose prose became increasingly illegible, that she'd married another man. He'd ached to see her, unreasonably, in spite of his churning certainty that she'd injure him again. But when Isaac told him he hadn't been invited to the wedding, he felt relief: at least the message was clear.

Isaac ran his farm like a general abandoned by his troops, as if the survival of his crops depended, seasonally, on his sheer expense of will. He took pleasure in describing how he'd acquired each field, stories that usually involved the Bentham family's defeating someone white. "Eddie Masterson's hay pasture," he'd say, pointing out his truck window. "Drank. Said he'd never sell his land to Negroes; my father just waited till he went bankrupt and bought it from the bank." History was his passion. His most prized annexation was a bean field purchased from the grandson of a lieutenant in the Confederate guard, who (the grandson) had never liked farming and used Isaac's payment to buy a condo in St. Petersburg. Nearly all the things that crammed the Bentham household's front rooms and lay beached, like flotsam at low tide, on the stairs had similar pedigrees: a humidor said to have been the property of General Arbuckle, who oversaw the Cherokee relocation at Fort Gibson; brass tapers from the county's first Episcopal church; a collection of local settlers' andirons, washtubs, spinning wheels, and butter churns. And of course Isaac's collection of guns. Booker learned more about local history from his grandfather than he ever did in class, and he even wrote a paper, with Isaac's enthusiastic aid, about his great-great-great-great-grandmother, a Cherokee who'd walked to Oklahoma along the Trail of Tears. She'd married a black drover named Horace Bentham, and together they'd built the farm's original shack, predating the land rush by some sixty years. The paper got an A, but Booker felt something troubling in Isaac's fixation on the past, and in his uneasiness glimpsed, for the first time, a possible motive for his mother's escape.

There were good things, too. His grandmother emerged as far more interesting than he'd first thought. Her name was Maggie, and she'd grown up in St. Louis, where Isaac had met her at a Knights of Columbus social before the war. She'd left him during their engagement (looking at the hoary portraits of Isaac's father and older brother, now dead, Booker sympathized with her cold feet), married a brakeman on the St. Louis–Alamogordo railroad line, and when their union ended in violence six months later, begged Isaac to take her back. In this way, both she and Booker were in his debt. Maggie seemed to love her life mostly in comparison to the disaster it might have been: in an effort to be indispensable, she had welded her personality to Isaac's needs, worrying that rain would fall, that food would be prepared on time, jeans washed, floors swept, dishes cleaned, so that only when he was safely distant in the field could she be herself. Booker enjoyed her then. She appreciated, in ways Isaac couldn't, the gift for impersonation he'd inherited from his father, and would laugh until her eyes watered as Booker shouted the slogans of Jimmie Walker or cussed potatoes in the voice of Flip Wilson's Geraldine—actors whom Isaac abhorred because he considered it debasing to play Negro for an audience of whites.

She taught Booker by subtle example to hunt for decency in his grandfather beyond an outward stubbornness that could turn as rank and bitter as the hedge apples that littered the front drive. He was fair. He never asked his hands to do more work than he did himself, never

81

punished Booker unreasonably or spoke of his father with disrespect (though it was often implied). He was exacting in his accounts, however, and his rages sprouted from the conviction that his own family had left him shortchanged. By running off with a "musician," Illyria had cheated him, and though Booker saw Isaac writhe with sorrow and regret when her letters arrived, he never responded: *She knew how I felt after she took off. Why didn't she write then?*

Booker took pride in his grandfather's tough reputation, the way he could walk into the coffee shop in Flora (the nearest town) and stop conversation dead. In school, he himself received the same silent, grudging respect, which was the opposite of actual membership. No one harassed them, but neither did anyone come to borrow tools or sell Girl Scout cookies at the door. If a wounded deer strayed onto Bentham property, hunters let it go. It was as if a spell of exclusion had been cast around the borders of Isaac's land: not until Batson Putz showed up did Booker realize how intensely lonely he had been.

The snow had been down long enough for its surface to melt and freeze slick. A new flurry had dusted it that morning, coning about the stubble rows, its dry granules dappled with fresh, blue-shadowed tracks. Booker's boots broke through the crust, and he stumbled, while the tan beagle out ahead cantered eagerly on top.

"She's got one," Batson said.

The rabbit flushed from a clump of swale. He saw its gray, immediate streak and was fumbling with the safety on his twenty-two when Batson put his hand atop the gun. "Jes' watch her," he whispered. The beagle had leapt after her quarry, her progress mapped by an intermittent rooster tail of snow, only to return several seconds later to the original site of the flush. Booker's spirits fell. The rabbit had disappeared, but Batson kept his hand atop his rifle—*Jes' watch!*—and then he saw the gray streak again. It ran directly at the beagle, who steadied, then dove. When the snow cleared, the dog held the carcass by its broken neck. "*Sayo-nara*," shouted Batson, "is how the Japs say *Adios!*"

They killed three more that day and dangled the carcasses from their belts with loops of twine. Booker was exceptionally proud of the dog. His grandfather had purchased her as a present, but only Batson had recognized her ability to hunt. "Rabbits run in a circle," he explained as they walked. "A regular dog keeps chasing till he loses it. But a beagle—a damn na-too-rel hunter like you got there—she'll skip out on the circle and cut that rabbit off. Outsmart the fuckers, see?"

Booker had managed to keep Batson on after harvest. During its second week, rain had left the fields impassable, and Isaac had sent them to clean up the shop. Batson showed up feverish and pale. At midmorning Booker called to him and, receiving no answer, found him twitching in the paint closet, knees drawn up to his chest. "What's up with this damn workhouse?" Batson said. "Can't a man go someplace private and rest?"

"You're sick," Booker said.

"Get outta here," he grunted. "What's a rich fuck know about being sick?"

Booker roused Theo and Fernando, two of the Mexicans, from the woodpile, and together they carried a struggling Batson to the house, where Maggie unlaced his tennis shoes and coated his pimply chest with Vick's. Isaac had gone to town, and when he returned, Maggie was waiting on the kitchen step. "Nobody leaves this house with a temperature of a hundred and two," she said, brandishing a thermometer. "Not until I know he's got someplace dry to stay."

It was exactly what Booker had hoped she'd say. Batson made a pathetic patient, his face poked above the ticking of Maggie's blanket with the angular helplessness of a drowned rat's. "I'm not sick," he protested when Isaac strode in. "I never took sick a day in my life. Ripe as a . . ." Only when Isaac promised not to fire him did he admit to living in his truck. Two days later (with a slight nudge from Booker), the old man gave him the keys to a vacant rental house, the home of a pig farmer he'd bought out.

Returning from the rabbit hunt, Booker felt exultant. Even the lonely hulk of the Bentham house looked appealing as they approached it over the final ridge, Maggie's kitchen light casting bright squares on the snow in back, and he found himself chattering, not noticing that his partner—and the cause of his good mood—had dropped several steps behind. "The next thing we oughta figure out is whether she'll hunt birds," he said. "Wouldn't that knock Grampa out? I mean, rabbits are fun, but they're not much for eating, not like quail."

"You can do whatever you want, bud," Batson said. "She's your dog."

"She's both of ours," he said expansively.

"No, she ain't."

"You're the one found out she could hunt."

When he looked again, Batson was removing his two rabbits from the twine loops around his belt. "Want these?" he said.

"They're yours, we split 'em up."

"I wasn't brought up to eat rabbits," Batson said, "any more than I'd eat coon or skunk." He tossed them at Booker's feet.

A year later, Booker faced his grandfather in the butane-sweetened air of the shop, Isaac dressed in the stiff canvas jumpsuit he wore ubiquitously in winter, twirling a joint between his forefinger and thumb. He dropped it on the bandsaw table. "It's only squealing if I intend to hurt those who gave it to you. I don't. I only want their names."

The paper cylinder sat among the oily clots of sawdust like a shard of bone. Booker's stomach cramped. "It's not mine," he said.

Isaac's glove squarely met his ear. More a swat than a full blow, it still popped the tendons in his neck. "Maggie found it in your drawer," he said. "Names."

"I don't know."

Isaac tucked his gloves beneath his armpits and blew into his fist. "It might be okay for them," he said. "Cops are nicer, judges more lenient: they get a second chance, maybe a third. You'll get one. That's all. If you waste it"—he opened his empty, callused fingers—"I don't own anything out there."

It was a Saturday in winter and the hands did not check in until ten. He'd already been standing beside the bandsaw for three hours when they arrived. He could hear Isaac barking at them in the lot, the cold wicking from the concrete floor through his bootsoles. He was supposed to play basketball that night: both he and Isaac knew it, just as they both knew that if he did not make the game, he'd be cut from the team. A flat winter light glowed through the high, chinked windows of the shop, and he watched it pool on the icy floor, unshifting, as though the sun itself had stopped. Around noon, Batson stuck his head in the door.

"What's he keeping you for, bud?"

"Your pot," Booked said loudly.

"Jeez! What the—" Batson hustled through the door, caught his jacket on the lock, freed it, and high-stepped across the floor in a ludicrous pantomime of quiet. He examined the joint. "I never give you that," he said.

Booker watched him patiently.

"Never seen it before in my life." Batson pinched the joint as one might a fishing lure and squinted at its underside. "Nope," he said. "Don't reckon it's mine."

"I'm not going to tell him," Booker said.

"Aren't ya?"

"No."

Batson lifted his cap and scratched his wildly parted hair. He'd set the joint back on the table and together they observed it like a museum piece. "How come you didn't smoke the thing?" he asked.

"Not interested, I guess."

"Why keep it, then?"

"'Cause you gave it to me," Booker said. "It was a gift."

Batson smiled at this. His hair was straw-colored, but his beard had grown in dark, and the stubble, coupled with his cratered skin, made him look like the victim of a shotgun blast. "You're crazier than batshit, ain't ya?" he said.

"You're my friend."

"You figger?" He regarded Booker in cockeyed analysis. "Well, fuck it all," he said, sticking out his hand. "Okay."

"I still got to tell him something."

"All right, all right." Batson paced quickly to the shop door and looked outside. "First of all, they never should've gone through your shit. Always make that perfectly clear. And if he wants to know where it come from, just say some peckerhead at school."

"School?"

"Sure." Batson put his cap on and smoothed the brim. "What's the worst thing can happen? He's not gonna take you out of school."

He spoke with his grandfather that night in the unheated front room of the Bentham house, its broad, uncurtained window glossy with frost. Isaac often spent his evenings there, sorting through the cluttered compilations of his neighbors' pasts. Booker found him seated in a small clearing amid the stacked furniture and rat-gnawed steamer trunks, contemplating a framed photograph. He held it out: "You ever seen this?"

A single porcelain lamp had been plugged into an orange extension cord that ran down the hall to the kitchen. Booker held the photo in its circled light. A slanted limestone abutment bordered a sky that was entirely blank, void, the same hue and texture as the photograph paper itself. The men stood in four ascending rows beneath what appeared to be an open garage or shed, the wool caps of the topmost row grazing the flat eaves. The soldiers were black. They wore greatcoats, each of a different cut and shade, and boots laced around their pants. Puddles broke a muddy foreground still dimpled with long-spent drops of rain. "Yours truly," Isaac said, "is number forty-two."

On the surface of the photograph, someone had painted a white number over each man's chest, and he traced along the rows until he reached Isaac's smooth and unlined face. "Damn," he said. "What were you, twenty?"

"Twenty-three," Isaac said.

"*Damn.*"

"Outside Bastogne."

"Was that in France?"

"No, Belgium," Isaac said.

"*Damn.*" The place names meant little to him, serving only to increase the exoticism of seeing his grandfather—the man who sat across from him—standing in the mud of a foreign land. His finger stopped beside the sole white face in the picture, just to the right and in front of the other men. Pale ears stuck out enormously beneath his visored officer's cap. "And that's the guy . . ."

"Mercury Chapman."

"The guy whose ass you saved."

"Yes," Isaac said. His face in the half-light appeared in stark contrast to that of the glossy young man outside Bastogne: creased, wind-stung, hard. "That's what I wanted to talk about."

"What about?"

"Mercury Chapman," Isaac said, "cured me of the dangerous idea that a white man could be my friend."

6

THEY BEGAN to meet in secret after Booker was kicked off the basketball team. Isaac still allowed him to attend the games, and he would wait to see the taillights of his grandfather's pickup leave the school drive before he walked past the lit gymnasium to the service entrance, where Batson waited in his truck. It had started innocently enough. The town of Flora existed mainly as a backdrop for the grain bins that vaulted in corrugated magnificence beside the train tracks, the tallest structures for miles. Neither of the two bars would admit them, so they cruised with aimless deliberation along the six blocks of storefronts, the parchment-shaded second-floor apartments and mossy lintels, the garage with its sweet reek of oil; bought cigarettes at the convenience store; and tacked through streets whose cobbles bore the imprint of a foundry sixty years bankrupt, heading for the cemetery, the reservoir levee, the boat landing on the Verdigris.

A formerly respectable hotel and boardinghouse survived on the main street, and the wan tongue of light that spilled outward from its lobby, the frosted rococo facade of the cigarette machine, the obvious dishonesty of its pamphlet rack enticed them. The Whitmore's days were numbered in the face of the brightly lit and anonymous motels that lined the highway into Tulsa, and they associated its air of obsolescence with sin. One February evening, Batson saw a woman dressed in black smoking on the hotel's porch and scouted out where she was staying. That night they climbed the fire escape and crouched on its grating as she entered her paltry, water-stained room. Her face was pinched, her nose slanted to the right. She kicked her shoes off and unzipped her dress so the fabric fell from her shoulders, and they could see red half-moons where her shoes had rubbed raw her heels and bony buttocks through her slip. She sat at the small vanity and with a convulsive gesture pulled a plaited coil of hair out of her bag: a gray-white human braid, long and thick as a horse's tail. They watched dry-mouthed as she buried her face in the dead hair and breathed its smell, rubbing its length against her neck and breasts, until a man in a tweed jacket came in. He held a water glass full of whiskey, and seeing her, he cursed and yanked the braid away.

"You shouldn't do that, Morton," the woman said. "You shouldn't do that to my mother's hair."

The man carried the braid between two fingers, like a dead rat, and with a sickened expression dropped it in the trash. "You shouldn't do that," the woman repeated. "I know this is a terrible place, and I should feel lucky that you took me away from here, but you shouldn't do that to my mother's hair. I've always done what you wanted, haven't I? I've always gone on vacations with your family, and I've always had Christmas in the Bahamas, where you can't even have a tree. I don't know why you never wanted a tree, but I didn't mind. I didn't even mind pretending that I didn't have a poor mother and leaving her in a terrible, awful, muddy town like this where she could die and rot in that awful house for two whole days. Can't you see? I'll do anything you want, Morton. I'll do anything right now. Do you want me to do something right now? Is that it?" She rose from the vanity and stripped off her slip. Her mouth was crooked and her mascara had run and the man backed away from her against the window, so close they could see the stitching of his coat.

"All right, then. If that's what you want," the man said, and when he fumbled for the window shade, they scrambled away.

They drove that evening to a rocky sandbar beneath the railroad trestle outside town and fought. Neither remembered later what words had caused this dispute: there probably had been none. They battled silently, stumbling over the frozen stones and rolling over piles of driftwood, and when they were both exhausted they squatted in the ice-crusted shallows and washed their wounds. Driving back to town, Batson said, "I don't know about you, but I'm getting out of here someday."

He began stealing: bread, milk, eggs, frozen cuts of meat. Isaac kept a stand-up freezer in the mudroom and filled it yearly with a side of beef butchered from one of his own steers, the waxed paper labeled in grease pencil. Booker copped the lesser cuts from the bottom of the pile and hung them from a dead cottonwood behind the house whose branches were sheltered by a copse of pines. Once, Maggie found him bent over the freezer. They evaluated each other. "I left this house once over a man," she said. "Don't expect I'll go that far again."

Booker tucked a round steak under his jacket.

"I wouldn't," he said.

This marked the second stage of his relationship with the words *Mercury Chapman*. The first stage had not extended much past the boilerplate sentiments of a Veterans Day parade: the white man whose ass his grandfather had *saved*. The second cast him as the evil incarnate in the Anglo-Saxon race, the ubiquitous referent of every black's "they," and a bogeyman in whom Booker chose not to believe. According to Isaac, Mercury Chapman had hanged his best friend. It was not this that Booker disbelieved (though he did wonder how, within the strictness of the army, such lawlessness could exist, or how a solitary white captain might execute such a judgment amid a company of 140 healthy, Mississippi-trained blacks. "He lynched Reggie Hammonds," Isaac had said. "And he enjoyed it, too. I was there: I *saw his face!*" The language allowed, technically, room for metaphor, but Isaac's blunt anger, his glazed, inward-looking eyes, and the spittle that dusted Booker's face left him with the standard cinematic image of the scene: the bare tree limb, the coiled noose, and a black man, head bent before a frothing sea of white), but rather that such an action, occurring on a different continent and lost in a dead, insoluble past, should have any application to him.

So he rebelled, not against the story so much as against the past itself, his grandfather's ridiculous mirrors, guns, and butter churns— "the Bentham junk store," as Batson said. He considered it justified to steal. Isaac paid his hands four dollars an hour, a full two dollars less than other farmers, banking on the fact that the hands who approached him had nowhere else to go. In winter, when Isaac needed Batson only two or three days a week, his rent far outstripped his pay. He ate beans, cabbage soup. The rabbits he'd refused the year before had represented a feast, and Booker took care not to offend his pride again. The dead cottonwood was equidistant from the Bentham house and Batson's rental, on the opposite side of the section, and they used it as a meeting place. Booker tied his frozen packages of meat to its limbs with twine, safe from coyotes and raccoons (sometimes adding a fresh pullet or, with almost motherly concern, a bar of soap or roll of toilet paper) and did not return until the gifts were gone. Neither mentioned them.

On the night of his sixteenth birthday, he found Batson waiting for him at the cottonwood. Isaac had brawled through dinner with awkward good cheer that served only to underline (in Booker's eyes) the solitude of the house. As his heart had sunk, he'd peeked up at his grandmother and seen compassion on her face—not for him, whose rotten birthday this was, but for an old man. He'd headed for the pine copse as soon as he finished his cake, stealing a steak on the way.

"How's life in the big house?" The voice startled him as he fumbled with the lengths of twine, and Batson's scrawny figure appeared from behind the tree.

"It was just . . . ," he stuttered. "I didn't . . ."

"Birthday, huh?" Batson sat against the tree trunk, pulling a cigarette from the front pocket of his shirt. "So what's it feel like turning sixteen?"

"Not like much."

"No?"

"No." Booker awkwardly held the zip-locked bag of meat. "I would've invited you if I could."

"Yeah? Well, I don't think the old man looks on that stuff too kindly, fraternizing with the hands."

"It's not right."

"It is what it is." Batson spat. "You want a shot at inheriting this place, you got to suck it up."

It was early spring. The thawing earth filled the pine copse with a scent that seemed to Booker charged with longing, directionless, without intent. "I don't ever want to get stuck out here," he said.

"No?" Batson's face was a blur of white, offset by a single, centered coal. "Tell you what: I've got a proposal you might like."

Batson Putz grew marijuana in the back corners of Isaac Bentham's fields. He was particular about it. He'd ferried the seeds of *Cannabis indica* from Afghanistan by way of Amarillo and never gossiped about his work. What mongrel forms of ditch weed bred naturally in Isaac's wooded creeks and among the viney belts of timber that embroidered the Verdigris's floodplain he methodically pulled and burned to ensure that his stands stayed pure. He limited patches to fifteen plants each so as to provide them with the plausible alibi of growing wild. The joint he'd given to Booker (foolishly, he admitted, to see how he might act) had been the product of his first harvest, an experiment of sorts. "It's a felony," he said to Booker now. "Just so's you know."

"What's a felony?"

"Worse than a misdemeanor."

"You ever get caught?"

Batson hitched his belt and led him to the back edge of the pines.

92

An unplanted bean field stretched beyond them, ashen beneath the darker night. The land folded to a grove of oaks that grew westward, hiding a creek. "Had a patch there all last year," he said. "Way people feel about your grampa, nobody ever walks across the place. No deer hunters, mink trappers, nothing."

"What about Isaac?"

Batson spat. "When your grampa wants shit done in the boonies, he usually sends me."

"He'd never think of it."

"That's right."

Booker still cradled the bag of meat.

"I been appreciating this little trick of yours," Batson said, patting it. "But just selling my stuff small time, the last few months, I'm taking in a hundred a week."

They forded a root-banked stream, the earth mottled with a coat of winter leaves, and marched through knee-high plots of marsh violets that spread beneath the blooming maples like banks of gas-blue flame. The beagle danced in front, sniffing beneath a fallen log (Booker was ostensibly hunting), and the sun shafted through the treetops as through a nylon tent. "Be vewy, vewy quiet," Booker told the dog, trying to relieve his own nervousness. "Uncle Batson is—"

"Cut it," Batson said.

The small stream joined a larger creek, and along the low peninsula they met a solid wall of horse nettles and thornbushes shot through with red stalks of burrs. Batson crawled wordlessly through a low opening. A peculiar greasy twang rose from the opening, and as Booker attempted to follow his partner, his elbows locked with fear. The fear was somehow connected to the banality of the day, which seemed to beckon with an enviable calm, the wind-twitched arcade of trees containing an offer he'd always intended to accept: go home, put the dog up, and go to sleep unchanged. Instead, he crawled ahead.

"Damn," Batson said as he emerged, arms clawing.

"What?"

"Those cockleburs got a liking for you."

They'd arrived in a horseshoe-shaped clearing, open toward the confluence of stream and creek. Batson, suddenly solicitous, plucked the burrs out of his hair. Booker endured it for a moment (at school, he hated the fascination white students harbored for his hair, sometimes reaching out to pat him during a conversation, like an animal on display), then knocked his hand away. "All right," he said, "where are these things?"

Batson looked at him, smiling.

"Get off the James Bond crap."

"If you spit," said Batson, "you're liable to get one wet."

The plants were mere sprouts, not much more than ankle-high, a dark and waxy green. They blended with the local ragweed and only after several minutes of scrutiny did Booker discover evidence of human intent. Narrow holes had been bored for the seeds, and along the creek Batson had camouflaged a tin pail. "At the very least, you got to water them every other day," Batson explained as he dipped the pail. "Between this one and two more patches by the river, I don't hardly get to sleep. That's why I cut you in."

He dribbled water tenderly at each plant's base, lecturing as he went, "And once these babies get a little older, we got to pull out all the males. That's the sinsemilla technique."

"Sinsa-what?"

"Sinsemilla. The idea is, see, that you keep the males from pollinating the females; that way the females' buds get real big and fat. Then you got to watch out for your hermaphrodites, your mealy worms, your deer chewing up the patch. Oh, yeah, all *kinds* of things, you know. When I was down in Texas"—Batson paused with the tin bucket cradled in both arms and gave a bedraggled leer—"I ever tell you about Texas? My foster parents? Now, first of all, old Joe and Betty (that's their names. Aw, goddamn *Betty Putz*, it's just too much!) they run a retard farm down in Amarillo. Don't laugh! Adopted all kinds of retards and cashed their disability checks from the state. (Would you look at this sweet Afghani weed!) Anyways, I started my own little pot patch down by the pond, dried the stuff way up in the hayloft where Joe wouldn't see, and the seeds fell down in the hay. Well, shit, man: that hay goes everywhere! Cows eat it and crap it out, Joe spreads it in the farrow house, dumps it on the lawn, and by next spring we got marijuana coming up everywhere, thick as lily pads in a cesspool, *goddamn*! And Joe didn't know what it was, going around with these little shears, cussing, carrying on, and the retards, man, they start to *eat* it. . . ." Batson shook his head in amazement and stared up at the sky where a curtain of sparrows swirled, his blue eyes focused on the faded shred of memory. "Yep. When the retards start eating your marijuana, it's time to hit the road."

"So how'd . . ." Booker's lips trembled as he forced them around the words. "What'd . . . how come they adopted you?"

"Looks," Batson said.

The late-spring light had fallen, and they recamouflaged the pail and called the beagle from where she rolled contentedly in a pile of scat. They crawled out of the thicket and left, at Batson's insistence, by a haphazardly looping path. Booker's fear had receded, calmed by the innocuous appearance of the plants, their matter-of-factness, and by Batson's unhinged soliloquy. Although sober, he felt different: the fear had changed to a liquid coolness, a sliding sensation in his chest, and the leaves and cool night air that brushed his cheeks seemed to be touching skin that was, in a peculiar way, no longer his. The feeling gave him strength. When Batson suddenly faced him and said, "You swear you won't narc, right?" he answered, in a dead-on mockery of Isaac Bentham's bass:

"Putz, you white-trash bastard—have you been growing locoweed? I mean, have you been spreading your honkie nastiness over my ancestral lands?"

Batson stopped. His smile was edgy, and he appraised Booker

95

through squinted eyes. "That's funny," he said, clapping Booker on the arm. "Yeah, that's real good. I never heard you do the old man before."

Booker walked twenty paces before he discovered that his face was still frozen, blank, and that he'd never matched the Texan's grin.

Batson expected to harvest six pounds of indica and sell them for eight grand. He offered Booker three. Since Isaac didn't pay Booker wages for his farm work, this was a sum large enough to be almost meaningless, entirely abstract. He did not need it. He knew by then that he would not run away, not that year, perhaps not any year, finding that the very agent of his escape had finally created conditions ripe for him to stay. For the first time in his life, he seemed to be coming into his own. It was not the money that did it, but the tending of the plants, the possession of a knowledge that was forbidden to others; he represented in his mocking diction, in the wooden and (as he imagined it) superior detachment of his expression, a physical version of that unknown. Batson had about twenty ounces left over from the year before, and they salted this with oregano and sold individual joints. Their customers were Booker's classmates, cheerleaders and Future Farmers in their crepe-soled town shoes, the front line of the Flora Hornets basketball team, carloads of tight-assed farmer's daughters headed for Phi Delt parties at Oklahoma State: the red-bloodedest, as Batson put it, dopers you could ever hope to meet.

They worked out of Batson's truck, the former aimlessness of their evenings having some purpose now, a goal. Booker brooded in the passenger's seat, expressionless, staring ahead while his classmates dealt with Batson (seated on two phone books) through the window, waiting for that silent moment of recognition mixed with awe. "Hey, Book—" some would say, peering hopefully inside. And others, "Well, I was kinda hoping you guys might have something, see, 'cause Booker and me here"—bending now to direct their voices across the static cab—"we go way back. Don't we, Book?" He took a staid pleasure in this kind of courting, shifting his head slowly to view the supplicant, white-blurred face, the eyebrows fawning, and assessing it with reservation as Batson said, "You know this guy?" He would wait another beat before answering, "I never seen him, and he's never seen me," the face immediately changing, apologetic now, beset by tics: "Oh, sure, fellas, you don't gotta worry about me. This never happened. I get it. I never seen you, right? Sure, that's right."

He would let them maunder on as long as they wanted, fixing each in his bland gaze. "Cold—oh, man, I'm telling you," Batson would giggle, after the customer paid and left. "You worked some ice up on that guy."

He discovered, paradoxically, that having something to hide made life easier at home. He did not drink, and at quarter to eleven on the nights when they went out, Batson would drop him on a residential street and he'd walk past the neatly manicured, asbestos-shingled bungalows and into the school lot, where Isaac would be waiting in his truck. The old man smelled his breath without pretense, saying, "I'd feel better about it if I knew you went out to drink. That would be doing something, anyway. Seems like you just go to town and stand on a street corner. What's the point?" He answered that he went to the movies, and when necessary, he invented for Isaac a list of made-up friends, describing for him the banalities of their adventures with an intoxicating, triumphant glee. The truck Isaac drove was the following year's model: seats sheepskin-covered, acrid with newness, it served primarily as a public expression of Bentham will. When planting season ended, Isaac presented him with a spare set of keys. He returned late from disking the last field, having stopped at sundown to water and check the plants, and he found the old man waiting for him in the lot. "Leave it," Isaac said as he unhooked the disker's linkage. "Tomorrow's good enough." He'd set two plastic cups of whiskey on the hood of the new truck. "I don't trust much in town," he said. "But as a representative of the Benthams, you might as well drive something decent there. Curfew is the same."

He lost his virginity in July. She gave her age as thirty-five but was, in fact, closer to fifty, a product of the piedmont farms of North Carolina who had gone to San Francisco to find love and become a whore instead. The man who owned the house had scrutinized Booker across a calico kitchen tablecloth matted with wax paper and marijuana leaves. "Lucy services our black brothers, don't she?" he called over his shoulder. "Being from California and all?"

"I'd sure think so." The second man had an apron strapped around his jeans and was tending chili on the stove.

"Dandy," said the first. He'd returned his gaze to Booker with a smile that appeared genuine. "No offense," the second said. Without removing his eyes from Booker's face, the seated man placed a salt-cellar in the other's outstretched hand.

She was watching television when he walked in. Unlike the kitchen, the second-floor rooms were bare, coldish, and she had draped the unpapered plaster with bandanna-print sheets held up by pins. "Just one minute, hon," she said, poised in slack-jawed meditation before the colored screen, and then rose at the precise ending of the credits to cheerfully reverse the sheets. She was heavy, even matronly, and wore black socks to bed, returning from the bathroom with a towel and a bottle of Johnson's oil. "I'm going to massage you," she informed him, "then you can massage me." He neither expected nor desired any particular warmth, viewing his virginity as something to be defeated, an ignorance that left him weak. But as he lay on his back and felt the cold oil rivulet his loins, he'd desired her to talk. "About me?" she'd said. "Why, there isn't very much to know about a girl like me," proceeding to list the states where she'd practiced her trade, evaluate their receptiveness or lack thereof, and inject an interlude about her travels with the Grateful Dead. "Interesting," he said. They chatted also about her life in Tulsa, where she worked in a massage parlor and made summer trips to this house in the country—her vacation, so to speak. "Everybody in Tulsa," she said as he examined her sagging breasts, "they're real nice about what I do. People in the grocery store and down at the dry cleaner's, they're all real polite. To each his own, don't you think. That's kind of like my creed."

It was like it had been in the forest, when he'd first learned to separate from himself. He knelt above her without trembling and entered with the guidance of her practiced hand. In movies and Batson's dirty magazines he'd already seen the general geometry. Gently, she'd closed her eyes, the lids painted a Kabuki blue beneath which he could see the oblique swell of pupil. He felt the insides of his thighs press tight against the warm smoothness of her rump, hitched thrice, and released. When he removed himself, she opened her eyes and began, vaguely, pleasantly, to watch the TV. "It was my first time," he told her as he dressed.

"Honest?" she said, pulling on her sweatpants. "Well, honey, I never would have guessed."

The men in the kitchen were buyers. Their house sat on a bluff overlooking the Verdigris, halfway between Flora and Tulsa, and when he and Batson pulled up the drive on moonlit evenings, something shimmered in his memory. One night he noticed the snout of a sheriff's cruiser gleaming in the mouth of the barn, and his back went chill. A card game was in progress. Entering the front hall, they could hear the men betting in the kitchen—Davis, other regulars, the usual desultory patter—interrupted by a voice as harsh as broken shells: "What kind of croaking game is this, a man don't win with a queen-high straight?" He recognized it and spun Batson by the shoulder, hissing, "This is who your buyers are? You intend to do business with . . . ?"

Batson clapped his arms against his side and held him, jerking. "Whoa there, bud. Slow up."

"You expect—!"

"You gotta tell me who you're talking about," Batson whispered. "Is it Timpson? You know Timpson?"

Then Booker struggled again, and they wove dancelike on the bare floor, bumping against a rack of coats. Batson pinned him there. "You gonna take it easy?" Booker nodded, his head enveloped in a red-checked mackinaw. "I'll be damn if I know how you know Timpson," Batson said, backing away with one arm stretched forward, as from a felled deer. "But he's not our contact, see? He's just here, around—you know, kind of got a finger into everything. That's what sheriffs do, see?"

"I'm all right," Booker said.

"We're not even here on business," said the Texan. "This is supposed to be a pleasure trip."

Entering the kitchen, he saw the players with the bizarre soundlessness of aquarium exhibits, as if separated from them by thick glass. His ears rang; his steps seemed oddly to float. Timpson looked out of phase, appearing both as the foreshortened giant who had (was it nine years ago? ten?) driven his own father from their house, and the man who sat before him now, drunk, his sheriff's tunic unbuttoned beneath a wattled throat, dandruff dusting a red tonsure of hair. When his mouth opened, Booker waited for a bubble to appear. Halfway through the third hand, Booker raised him. He looked across the calico-covered table, eyes suddenly alert. "Do I know you?" he asked.

"Why would you?" Booker said.

"Why?" Timpson chuckled. "Why? Bcause some of your people are my best customers." The table broke into laughter, sustained, nervous, and hard. "And friends!" Timpson was insisting, his pinky finger raised. "And friends!"

Booker felt Batson kick him in the shin. "I'm out," he said.

"Aw, shoot," said Timpson. "Tell him not to worry about me, fellas. I always throw the small ones back!"

After the game they went to the sandbar where they'd fought among ice-encrusted stones the winter before. It was warm now, humid; banks of caddis flies moiled in the truck's headlights, the river coruscant with their dead. They waded toward the train trestle, bumping elbows when they slipped. "Timpson ran my father off," Booker said. He discovered in the story (which he'd never told before) not the shame that he'd expected but a kind of pride. "Having the cops bust in like that," he said, embellishing slightly, "would've scared the piss out of me. But he offers Timpson a drink, *then* tells him to fuck off." When he'd finished telling it, he dove beneath the current and rose twenty yards downstream. Batson was shouting for him, smacking a bottle of Southern Comfort against the water, and he watched him silently, nose just above the flow. His face was settled then. The water's coolness pressed his lips, and when Batson had gone hoarse, he stood and said, "Excuse me, Mr. Redneck—you sharing that bottle with me?"

Harvest began and he had no time to think of Timpson or anything else. Isaac had decided to instruct him on being a landowner, especially the need for developing a hardened attitude toward one's help. Batson provided a natural target. He needed only to shuffle his feet during the morning address and Isaac would be on him, jaw to jaw, the black spikes of his mustache aquiver. "Is there a problem, Putz?"

Batson would toe the dirt, face puckered in absurd coquetry. "Thinking about soybeans, I guess," he'd allow. "The ones you want to cut in Tinker's field."

"Well?"

"I guess if I was farming—which I ain't," he added quickly, drawing sunflower seeds from his pockets and sorting away the lint, "I might not do that."

By this time Isaac was bleating through his nose like a steam valve. "DO . . . YOU . . . HAVE . . . A . . . REASON?" he asked.

Batson spat a sunflower shell against his employer's denim chest with a satisfying *phhht!* "Too wet," he said.

This final outrage set off a tremor in the older man's swollen knuckles that seemed to travel by stages through his torso, followed by a monsoon of abuse, Isaac citing the entire precipitational history of Tinker's field, its camber, its excellent drainage (improved by Isaac's

101

father, no less). After his fury subsided and the meeting ended, Batson would deliver a final, stubborn shot: "I'm of a mind it was wet last year, too."

Most of these eruptions remained comical in some way, farces that even Isaac knew gave pleasure to the other hands. And Booker noticed that through his undertone of prodding—and by drawing Isaac's fire—Batson had contrived to keep the fields around their patches unharvested (sometimes achieving this goal by recommending that they be harvested *first*, allowing Isaac righteously to refuse). But there were other times when he sensed a cold and dangerous hatred in the curl of his grandfather's lip. For two entire weeks, with cutting halted due to wet weather, and the other hands sent home, Isaac ordered Batson to repair a fence line in what amounted to a swamp. Heading off to school, Booker would see him shuffle from his truck, his pants, his shirt, even his face covered with a patina of the previous day's mud. In the afternoons, Isaac forced Booker to accompany him to the site, where he cheerfully discussed plans for drying out the slough—repairing the fence was only a stopgap, it would have to be torn up again next year—while below them Batson dug postholes in a bog. When the rain ended, Booker found a slip of paper in his lunchbox, also mud-stained, bearing a single word written in child-like, almost imbecilic script: *NOW!*

7

THERE WERE TIMES when Isaac Bentham could not sleep. He believed sleeping, like any other necessary task, to be essentially a function of will, and so hid the embarrassment of his failure from his wife, yawning at the bedside and stilling his breathing as he lay beside her, eyes open, until he felt the loosening moment when her consciousness was released. Then he tenderly separated himself from her flank and crept from the bedroom on silent, callused feet. On breezy nights, the plastic sheets that insulated the upstairs windows flapped like a playing card stuck in a fan, a sound whose mournfulness (it was a crime to close windows with the night still warm) he resisted. The truth was that he'd tacked the plastic up himself two days after his daughter's birth, furious at the news that there had been problems with his wife's delivery and that these problems had left her unable to conceive again. But he strove not to connect these two events, attempting to view the aimless flapping that haunted him from room to room as a practical problem to be practically endured. The second floor simply had no use.

He put on his insulated Carharts, uncoiled the orange extension cord from its hook, and embarked like a miner into the front rooms. He returned for Maggie's portable TV, hoping to get a weather report. He had assigned himself the project of entering all his acquisitions into four black-and-white schoolboy's notebooks he had purchased with furtive embarrassment at the Flora drugstore. The last entry read: *.22 caliber Derringer, or "pocket rocket," carried by my great-uncle William Morris Bentham. Worked as a roofer. Claimed he rode with Teddy Roosevelt during invasion of Cuba, though Father said this not true. Who knows? Not many aware that black soldiers accompanied Rough Riders there. Cannon-fodder. Little expense. No need to report deaths.* The words blended with the network anchor on Maggie's portable TV: *In San Diego, folks can break out the suntan oil,* and suddenly he saw a clear picture of Reggie Hammonds's face. He had been a private from the Louisiana delta, barely literate, with a gray cast to his left eye. They had driven the same truck. That was all his company had done, drive trucks: none of the romance you saw in movies, no firefights, no exploding tanks. He and Hammonds had once driven 120 straight hours, spelling each other at the wheel. In winter they heated water on the muffler; in summer they washed in gasoline for lice. He wasn't even sure he would've liked Hammonds on the outside: the man was frivolous, a pleasure hunter. On night runs, he would describe for Isaac the women he had known, categorized by the shape of their rear ends: "You got your basic southern teardrop; that's my type. If it gets flat on the bottom, it's a Hershey's kiss. There's butter boxes, tubas, *footlockers*—what kind of asses do the Okies have, Bentham?" In the shuttling light of the truck's cab, his face would be visible: thin, eager, its jaw peppered with razor bumps. "What do they got in Oklahoma, Bentham, some kinda *tornado* ass?" But Hammonds's frivolousness had gotten him through the war: he'd added something that Isaac didn't possess and without which he would have broken, dried out, like dead wood. Once, alone, he'd dragged a dead cow forty miles behind their truck so the camp could have fresh meat. But what Isaac remembered now was Hammonds's face the day they took him to the stockade. A French-woman had accused him of rape, and there was evidence of a scuffle in the cabbage patch behind their camp. Word spread that Ham-

104

monds's helmet liner had been found. Isaac had been sitting with him in their tent, Hammonds laughing softly out of fear.

"They gonna hang me, don't you think?" he asked.

"Did you do it?"

"If I'd've raped that French lady"—Hammonds's hands were trembling violently, and he steadied them on his fatigues—"she w-wouldn't be up shouting like she is now."

"They can't kill you if you didn't do it," Isaac said.

Hammonds cocked his head so the cast eye wobbled at him, blindly. "Man, you really did grow up in the boondocks. Who's coming to save me, Pecos Bill?"

"Chapman," he'd answered. "He at least owes us that."

Now Isaac rose and opened the broad front window, feeling the inrush of the still-warm fall air. The memory seemed absurdly disconnected from the present of the well-dressed announcer, also black, whose image flickered on the TV screen. He felt a tearing sensation, as if his innards were being separated from his body, as casually as a child might rip a picture from a magazine. He kicked the television off and leaned slantwise out the window. His daughter was gone; his grandson, he had no feel for, and as he descended into this, the darkest and most feared of his nighttime depressions—the specter of the Bentham house gone to seed, empty, and all its gathered contents sold on the auction block—the grinding of truck gears reached his eardrums with sonorous immediacy.

He went out the backdoor and saw the truck's empty space. He had not bothered with shoes, and so he crossed the drive sock-footed, hobbling gently on the sides of his feet, and paused beside the twinned sets of bootprints that accompanied its tracks, air bubbles still rising from the pressed clay. He appeared calm, his lank figure stooped beneath the stars like a beachcomber wandering familiar flats. The reddish glow of brake lights lipped a distant ridge, and the sound of truck engines drifted to him on the breeze. He checked his watch. Satisfied, he removed his stained white socks in the mudroom, replaced them with an identical pair from the laundry hamper, embraced his wife, and fell asleep.

They had started cutting down the plants at night. The buds were the size of pinecones, and the plants themselves had grown six feet tall, their scent so resinous and powerful that Booker had to change clothes before going home. They began with the two patches by the river, felling the plants with machetes and hauling them gingerly through the brush to Batson's truck, returning to his house by a tortuous combination of unpaved section roads and open fields, headlightless, the Chevy crouching like an ancient roebuck at the intersections of blacktop roads that ribboned barrenly into the distance and then roaring across them in a burst of gas. On the third night they drove the paved roads with the truck bed battened by a tarp. On the fourth they didn't even bother with the tarp, and the truck wove from lane to lane as they slapped their own cheeks to stay awake. They dried the plants in Batson's attic. The house Isaac rented him was entirely too large, too vacant, for a boy of eighteen, and he'd parceled out his meager belongings with royal wastefulness: his flannels, long johns, and silk-embroidered town shirts dangled from a single clothesline strung between two light fixtures; a walk-in closet held nothing but cigarette packages ("A hundred more and I send for a dirtbike"); a children's room was completely empty save for a stack of X-Men comic books and a Styrofoam pad where Batson apparently lay to read. Booker imagined his friend pacing through these threadbare chambers, visions at once hilarious and sad. They reached the attic hatchway through a room that contained a single, hand-built desk, an ashtray made of an overturned skeet target, and a yellow legal pad on which Batson had scrawled the salutation: *Dear Joe and Betty, Life in Okieland not half bad.* The paper was curled and flyspecked; it appeared to have been sitting there for years. On the first night, Batson had set a chair atop the table and they'd climbed up through the

106

hatch. He'd clamped heat lamps to the ceiling joists and they'd hung the plants head-down from the rafters so they'd dry. By the fourth night the smell was fierce, and Booker squatted in the vaulted attic space, head pounding from lack of sleep. "We've got enough," he said.

Batson grinned. His face was raw from brush clawings, and his chapped lips oozed blood. "What about the patch you been tending?"

"What about it?"

"The way I had it figured," Batson said, "that patch was, uh, *representational* of your share."

The two of them were panting, balanced on a ceiling joist. Seeing his partner's loopy grin, Booker smiled involuntarily. "Texans," he said.

"Hate to see good work go to waste."

Batson dropped him off before the Bentham house at four o'clock, and he walked up the drive by starlight, entering the same side door he'd entered with his mother a full nine years before. The legitimate harvest had resumed, so Isaac woke him at five and he tottered like a drunk to join the other hands in the windswept lot. Batson engineered a breakdown of the combine around midmorning, and in a distant field, they sprawled beneath the machine, half asleep. "Where're we gonna go?" Booker asked.

Batson sighed. "Alaska, I expect."

"Fuck off!"

"Alaska allows its citizens to possess up to five ounces of weed," Batson said. "Legal and everything."

Booker studied the gritted undercarriage of the combine, its U-joints, axles, and springs. In the silence, he heard Batson adjust his hat. "We've had a real nice run, the two of us," the Texan said, "so let's not spoil it by you talking shit."

"Whaddya mean?"

"I mean you're not planning to go anywhere with me."

They rested for a long time without speaking. Batson reached up with a lug wrench and aimlessly tightened a strut. "We both could stay," Booker said.

"Yeah?" Batson grunted, heaving on the wrench.

"Yeah, I mean, it's like you always said: Isaac's not gonna live forever, and after that . . ."

"After that what?" Batson looked at him across his flexed bicep. "You gonna offer me a job, wipe the dirt out of my ass?" He loosened the wrench and cleaned it on his shirtfront, staring at Booker with what he would realize, years later, had been not hate so much as a refusal of and contempt for pity, dangerous in its own way.

"That's not how I mean it."

"Then maybe it shouldn't have been said."

It rained again around sunset, a brief, ozone-scented thunderstorm that left puddles standing in the low grounds. The old truck's tires were nearly bald, and though Batson had thrown two sandbags in the bed, it began to slip as they crossed the mown bean field that night. Both sat in utter silence. The ground immediately behind Batson's house had drained, but the middle part was soup, and the truck approached suddenly and without warning a point of no return. They urged it forward in wordless unison, calibrating each reduction in momentum against the distance that remained. The engine's whine increased while the truck itself slowed steadily, inexorably, both of them upright now, fists clenched against the door panels, heads stuck out the window slots like jockeys, their mount progressing with the dreamlike slowness of a barge until finally they were moving not forward at all but to the side. When it stopped, they continued to crouch like figureheads, frame shaking, wheels spinning, and Batson leaning on the gas. Booker got out to push. He pushed first from the door frame and then from the rear, his feet and the tires engaged in a spurious imitation of motion, neither going anywhere. They were in the middle of the field. The treeline that concealed their pot patch was half a mile away. They spread their jackets beneath the tires and Batson returned to the wheel while Booker, wedged against the bumper,

108

watched the tires turn at first slowly and then suddenly quite fast. The truck jerked two feet. They hunted briefly in the brake lights for the jackets, but they had disappeared. For a time they tried gathering bean stalks and chaff to dry the ground and then, cursing now in earnest, remembered the rolled tarp. This seemed to work, and they advanced the truck by tarp lengths, no longer aiming for the treeline but executing a slow circle that would return them to Batson's house. They checked their watches now and the reeling stars, the truck lurching over the oozing length of canvas and the two mud-covered figures retrieving it on their knees and spreading it again beneath the frame and running to their posts. The field seemed by then as featureless as the open sea, the treeline gone, all markers faded, and they steered for a swell of high ground that loomed above them like a frozen wave. On the incline, the canvas tore, and both shouted for the first time, Booker diving from the bumper as the truck slid backward twenty feet. They picked through the mud for scraps, their breathing ragged now, animal-like, yarding lengths of mudclotted fabric up from between the furrows with strange, impatient peeps. The canvas disintegrated after that. The truck lurched and sank to its axles, the tailpipe submerging with a muted snore. Booker walked the mere fifty yards to the drier high ground and sat with head in hands. Batson arrived clutching a scrap of impastoed material no larger than a notebook. They could see the Bentham house from there, the floodlit lot and paddock fences, the shiny shape of Isaac's new truck.

"It's four-wheel drive," said Booker.

"Yeah?" They sat there, breathing. "You got the keys?" Batson asked.

"I do indeed."

It was three-thirty when they reached the house. They had tried to run, but the mud had layered about their boots until they seemed to be wearing snowshoes, the two of them falling, springing up, and falling again with the spraddled gait of clowns. They went immediately to the truck (they would have noticed Isaac's light had they

109

walked around in front; the house's back was dark) and rolled it down the driveway and through the clay back lot, each jumping onto the running board as it picked up steam, not firing the engine until they had reached the unlit field. The truck had a winch on its front grille, and they hauled Batson's truck to the high ground and Booker followed it back to the rental house and continued without stopping through the driveway, onto the gravel section road, and toward the Bentham home, covering in five minutes the length and width of the field that had imprisoned him all night. He parked the truck at four o'clock and ran to the house, stopping only when he saw the viscous smear of his handprint against the whitewashed door. He whimpered and turned back to the truck, then to the door, and pulled his hand away as though it had been burned. Isaac's truck stood in the colorless glare of the floodlight with mud flared to its door handles and piled in dollops on its roof. He walked numbly to its mottled window and peeked in. The sheepskin seat covers held two clear and crisply shaded imprints, like blots of ink, and turf clung to the steering wheel and gearshift, mixed with drooping beans.

He could not remember later with any clarity what he'd done to get it clean, or how much noise he'd made. His actions played out at some distance, telescoped, with the antic quality of a sporting event viewed from the gondola of a blimp. He remembered trying to scrub the seats with a currycomb from the barn, and that the more he scrubbed, the dirtier they became, stained by the mud on his own clothes. He remembered turning the garden hose on himself, the shriveling coldness of the water and the absurd fear that overcame him at the noisy squelching of his shoes. He hosed the truck down, too—this worked, actually—and washed the seats after a fashion with a rag and a bucket of soap that came from who knew where. It was daylight when he quit, sneaking into the house naked, his wet clothes in a ball. His own body seemed to have no more respect for his urgency than the muddy field. He did not remember falling asleep, and he woke with an aching erection, naked atop the coverlet, clawing

110

immediately at the electric clock whose metal stem he'd forgotten to pull out. It was eight A.M. He ejected from the bedstead as if propelled by jets, chest flung forward and arms flailing behind, and entangled himself with a rocking chair at the far end. It was one of Isaac's, and a white tag wired around one leg identified it as former goods of the Larson family, circa 1873. A pale blond varnish crumbled off the seat. He caught himself among the back spindles, stepped on a rocker, the chair flinching and catching his hip, and then hopped when the other rocker pressed his toe (still naked, still embarrassingly erect and conscious of the embarrassment), and all at once he grabbed the creaking chair and hurled it against the wall. It exploded in a burst of tinder, and by the time the sticks stopped rattling, he had his jeans on and was scrambling hurriedly out the door.

He had in mind to burn the patch that still remained. He made no judgment as to the idea's reasonableness; it was merely there, springing to his mind fully formed, and he entered the kitchen still buttoning his pants. Maggie was packing lunches at the counter. As he shouldered past her to the mudroom, her hand rose to adjust a knot of graying, straightened hair. He hesitated long enough to notice the gesture, the solid lump of hair, wondering, *Have I ever seen it down? Was there a time . . . ?* and then fumbled with his boots, still bricked with mud. When he finished, she was standing at the door. "Don't think you're too smart to make a deal," she said. "He won't fight if people want to leave, but why should he take them back? Who in this family has given anything to him?"

He was putting on his jacket by then, still glancing at her curiously. *She even wears it that way in bed,* he thought. *I wonder how long it is, I wonder*—and then his eyes widened and he asked her, "Could you put your hair down in a braid, Gram? Did you ever . . . is it long enough, you think?"

"What?" she said, blinking.

"Down in a braid," he said. He was stamping and pulling his sleeves out of his jacket cuffs. "I saw this woman once had a beautiful braid. Batson and I did. She was dead, and her daughter came clear up from some island just to fetch it. Maybe that would be nice if it happened to you. Not dying, I mean, but having Mother come . . ."

His grandmother froze, separating herself from the conversation like a record needle lifted from its groove. "Don't," she said.

"I always thought you should try it," he said.

He stepped behind her, removing first her reading glasses and then the wooden pick that held the bun, together with its leather thong. She had taken one of his arms by the wrist, at first resisting and then—the bun was tight, the hair bound on itself—beginning to help. It loosened all at once, the hair unraveling about his elbows and falling thickly down her back. He pulled it sideways so she could see. "Pretty," he said.

"Your friend left something out back," she said. "He said you'd know what to do."

But he was already running by then. He skidded into the sparse, lemon-thatched yard and pivoted quickly in each direction in a glazed attempt to remember why he'd come. He was still thinking with amusement about the hair. He picked up with a hollow crinkle the red can that sat in the drive, marked with the diagonal letters GASOLINE, and the box of blue-tip matches laid beside it (remarking on the luck that someone had left them there, a chance reminder of his plan) and continued on into the bean field, still thinking of it as the cut stubble snapped beneath his feet: *I guess it would be older on the ends, not in the middle, like a tree. I wonder*—switching the sloshing can from his right hand to his left, telling himself in one brief, automatic sentence that he should not be thinking this—*if some of it was there when Mom was born. Like if she never cut it, we maybe touched the same . . .* He lumbered oddly with the can braced against his thigh. He halted and looked back at his footprints and cut immediately into the grass draw that led down to the stream and the leafless copse of trees. Crows stood in the bare field to eat, chuckling in his wake. When he'd gone half a mile, he slowed. His pupils bled into

112

their irises like a stain and he lifted the can and studied it, one leg bent in midstride. A dull roar sounded both inside his head and out, meeting at his eardrums like an echo and its source. He began to run, first down the grassy draw and then recklessly across the field, dropping the can and heading for the high ground where they'd winched out Batson's truck. The roar switched from inside his head into the distance, and a plume of smoke condensed ahead of him, snapping forward from the September sky. From the rise, he saw his grandfather and the other hands wearing kerchief masks and watching the window frames and gutters of Batson's house blacken like a melting movie still from orange, up-welling flames.

He stole a three-wheeled ATV from Isaac's shop. It was the only vehicle he could find, and he rode it across the bean field, bursting through the line of bushes that surrounded the burning house. The Mexicans scattered like quail. As he wheeled through the side yard and—the machine going airborne for one thrusting beat—over the storm cellar's frame, Isaac's face flashed in front of him, shouting, smoke-wreathed, his arm outstretched like a traffic cop's. When it disappeared, he felt a bump. Without pausing he made another circuit, the Mexicans scattering again, and found Isaac sitting in the middle of the front walk. His hat was crooked, his kneecap at an awkward angle to his boot, and Booker rode straight at him, skidding to a stop. "Where is he?" he said. Isaac's face was smeared with soot, and he gestured at something Booker could not see. "NOW DO YOU BE-LIEVE ME?" he shouted, his voice triumphant, hoarse. "NOW DO YOU SEE?"

Then Booker noticed the empty driveway where Batson's truck should have been. He chunked the three-wheeler into gear. "WAIT!" Isaac yelled, scrabbling at Booker's jeans. "YOU IDIOT! PAY AT-TENTION TO ME!"

Booker knocked his hand away. "Shut up, old man," he said.

When the Mexicans reached him, Isaac was shouting curses they'd never heard before. "QUANTRILL," he shouted. "PICKETT

JACKSON!" He scooted in the direction the boy had disappeared. "YOU . . . DON'T . . . KNOW . . . SHIT!"

Four miles outside Flora, Booker ran out of gas. Sitting on the squat, balloon-wheeled machine, he remembered the gas can he'd dropped in Isaac's bean field, its Day-Glo print enlarging to a single, yellow O. He went cross-country, navigating by the sun through late cornfields and then emerging into a barren, treeless development. A man caulked his bass boat outside a brick ranch home; children played on an aluminum swing set beside a bulldozed heap of stumps. Uneasy, he followed new curbing through pointless turns until he found the railroad tracks and crossed them into town. He phoned a Tulsa cab from the lot outside the grocery and took it to the buyers' house. The fare ran to fourteen dollars; he had nine. As the cabbie swerved cursing down the gravel drive, the Texan leaned out a cracked dormer, flanked by Lucy's pillow-wrinkled forehead. "Well, I'll be titty-whipped," said Batson. "Next he'll be asking me for a ride."

Lucy fixed them breakfast in the kitchen (no one else was home). "You hit him," Batson whinnied, lips pulling back along his gumline. "You actually went and run down the damn old fart? I'm purely blowed away. And he didn't pull out General Custer's gun or nothing? How'd you do it?"

"It was an accident," Booker said.

"Bullshit an accident!" Batson shouted. He'd been chain-smoking since Booker's arrival, lighting one thin cigarette off the consumed filter of the last. "An accident my ass! Couldn't've done better myself."

"It was an accident," Booker repeated. "I went down there on the three-wheeler to find out what he did to you: the house was on fire, Bat. I thought maybe you'd got hurt. I couldn't see him at first 'cause of the smoke, and so I went around the house, and he jumped out at me. Must've laid up on the porch, waiting for when I turned the corner, only he didn't jump far enough. I think I caught his leg."

114

"What's this?" Lucy said. "What house?"

"Caught his leg." Batson chuckled, the smoke exiting his nose in parallel blue streams. "Caught his leg."

"I don't like this kind of talk," said Lucy. She wore a kimono and turned two vitiated strips of bacon in a cast-iron pan, her eyes painted like a cerulean raccoon's. "About houses blowing up and whatall. You're supposed to be bringing something in. That's why I'm standing here cooking breakfast, is 'cause you're supposed to be bringing something in, and now you've run somebody over on a bike. Davis won't—"

"Did I say we weren't?" Batson's nostrils were rimmed with white. He stood, holding a butter knife underhand. "Did I?"

Lucy crossed to the far side of the stove in an elephantine cringe. Her kimono had loosened, and the shirt beneath bore a silkscreen of a drooling tongue and lips.

"What about these bacons?" she asked.

"Eat 'em yourself," Batson said. "Booker and I got to make a trip."

They drove Batson's truck out of the farmhouse drive and through the pallid half-world of freeway, industrial park, and patchwork field that lapped the eastern border of Tulsa. Easing onto the interstate, Booker said, "Lucy's right. How are we supposed to get anywhere with both of us being broke?" Batson looked at him. "Broke's an attitude," he said. "I got the perfect fix." The old truck knuckled like a whiffle ball at highway speed. They had less than a quarter tank of gas, and Booker's eyes moved between the falling gauge and the flat, on-ramped city, catching a glimpse of a broad green sign on a different highway whose letters read BEECH STREET 1½—his parents' former street. They pulled over when the truck began to cough and lurch. There were gas stations on every exit in this place, together with outlet malls and car lots beneath fluttering, triangular flags. They coasted up beside a roofed flotilla of pumps, and the truck expired with a hiss. "I got you a present," Batson said. When he slid a

115

vinyl booklet from his pocket, Booker felt relief: he'd half expected a gun. "Pinched it off Timpson," Batson said. "Thought you might like to get him back."

"What?"

"It's a checkbook, stupid." Batson fished again through his breast pocket and produced a yellow carbon and a bank card embossed with Timpson's name. "Here's how he signs it. Usually they'll take this other for ID."

He sat there holding the laminate booklet while Batson pumped the gas. The checks were banknote green, with a scalloped border and the name Edwin Timpson printed in stately letters, upper left. The register, in contrast, was a vortex of ink. The scrawls of Timpson's expenditures repulsed him—$6.50 for foot powder, $19.75 for the ominously titled "videos," lettuce, cigarettes, "bar-b-que." It was like thumbing through someone's underwear drawer. He rolled the window down. "What's our other option?"

"I write it," Batson said.

"That's it? That's our other option?"

"If we wanna pay for this gas, it is."

Booker got out of the truck. He set the checkbook on the hood and handed Batson a pen he'd found on the floorboard. "Write me a check for thirty bucks," he said.

Batson took up the pen. His face wore the misplaced intensity of a man trying to split a diamond with a hammer. He wrote the words *thirty bucks* in the right-hand box and filled the other lines with the statement *This check payed to Texaco Oil Company for services rendered.* Booker tore the check up and threw it in the trash.

"Shit's not so bad," Batson said. "What's it gonna matter a little twenty-dollar check here and there? All you gotta do in a big place like this is wait till the cashier's busy, walk in real seriouslike, bang your check down on the counter, say, 'Twenty dollars on pump four,' and walk out before they start pestering you for ID. Here's a deal: I'll do that part if you just write it out."

116

"You really don't have any other money?"

"Not on me," Batson said.

The Tulsa Texaco accepted their bogus check, and they more confidently tried the McDonald's in El Reno around dinnertime. "All's the closest you need to get is the drive-through," Batson explained. "Hand 'em the check, flash the bank card, and scat." As they left with their fries and milkshakes, the window clerk held Booker's forged signature beneath her nose. She was seventy-eight and lived in a retirement villa down the road, where, though the place had a perfect security record, she reported prowlers twice a year. "Something's not right about them," she said. "That one wrote the check was . . . funny. I got a shiver, you know." "Black kid?" said the manager. The window clerk licked her lips. "I thought maybe I'd seen him on the TV," she offered, "on that *Wanted* show."

"If you feel that way," said the manager, "our policy is to call the check in."

The state troopers picked them up at the Elk City Holiday Inn, where they'd registered under Timpson's name. "Hell," Batson had said as they went to sleep. "Isaac's been talking about razing that house since I moved in. I made it easier for him, is all."

Booker sat up, his elbow propped atop the cheap bedspread, his eyes depthless, like balls of shot. "You mean he didn't . . . ?" he said. "You mean you were the one . . . ?"

"He knew about it," Batson said. "What else was there to do?"

Afterward, Booker stretched out on the formless mattress, his head filled for the second time that day with an ominous, mounting roar. The room had a popcorn-plaster ceiling and champagne drapes; the window heater jolted like the transmission of a car, and he thought of Hammonds lying in his tent and staring up at the mildewed canvas, pacing, humming snatches of song. He attempted to imagine that the dark outside was the dark of France, and how Hammonds must have known he was too far from home to run, in too foreign a place. When the state trooper's knock boomed through the hollow

117

door that morning, it seemed the very thing he'd been waiting for, the fulfillment of his long night's dream. "Don't you—," Batson whispered. "Don't you—" But Booker undid the wall chain and opened the door with a smile, the troopers lunging forward with their gun muzzles lifted in attitudes of prayer, two snagging Batson as he sprinted for the bathroom with the languid deliberation of hawks, and the other telling Booker how to move his arms and legs: "Get *down*— as in the opposite of *up*, homeboy." And, "When I say spread your legs, that means apart." Booker wanted to explain that such instructions weren't necessary, that he was all too ready to comply, preferring the trooper's knee against his spine to the night's suspense. He imagined, face pressed against the cheap carpet, the relief his father must have felt when Timpson finally came for him. In the bathroom, he could hear Batson's high-pitched voice saying, "I don't know nothing about any bad checks, Mr. Officer. He said they were his."

8

A DEPUTY LOCKED HIM in a holding cell. On one bench a man lay drunk, his trousers dark where he'd fouled them, and when Booker entered, he began to moan. Another man rose and kicked the first one in the back, his motions silent, vacuous, the impact of his tennis shoe like that of an eraser on slate. He sat again. "Next time," he said to Booker, "you shut him up yourself."

For a long time he stood at the entrance to the cage without looking back. At one point he discovered he'd curled his fingers around the bars, the metal smoothed and polished by other flesh, and he pulled his hands quickly away. He kept them in his pockets after that. The others spoke behind him fitfully, and he listened to their movements, afraid to let them see his face. Outside was a cinder-block wall painted glossy orange. The passage curved, and he could see the slanted shadow of the deputy approach along the wall, and then the deputy himself, who ignored him, and then the slanted shadow of his retreat. The man on the bench moaned again. He listened to him as a child might listen to the creak of floorboards outside his darkened room. He could sense the other men's gazes against his back. "Hey, fuckstick," one said. Then he walked over to the injured man. He walked with his face averted, as if from rain, and rolled the man by the shoulder and looked at him. He was white, but only barely. His face was streaked with grime, his lips a gelid mass of blood, like congealed fat. "He's not drunk," Booker said.

He'd not expected to say anything, and glanced up with surprise at the other men in the cell. They'd kept their distance from the beaten one, lounging on the opposite bench or on the floor. The man began to moan again, fumbling at Booker's sleeve.

"That fella there's a noisemaker." It was the same man who'd done the kicking earlier. "I can't stand a noisemaker."

There was no other explanation, but Booker felt something curdle in the air. It was the first time he'd ever felt it, the sudden, metallic sourness of violence, and he could feel it gathering, connected to the pleading of the beaten man. One of the prisoners made an unintelligible remark, another shifted on his heels, and Booker rolled the beaten man onto the floor and slapped him in the face, forehand and backhand, and he could hear one of the onlookers saying lightly, *Ah-ah-ah-ah!*

He would recoil long afterward from the memory of the pouchy feeling of the man's face, like decayed fruit. But at the time he felt relief: he had done what was expected, and that nameless thing implied within the violence—that thing which would cause a man to soil himself—had not yet occurred to him.

He was sentenced to five years in McAlester Penitentiary for forgery, a class C felony. The trial and sentencing were essentially bloodless, moot. Batson had signed an affidavit testifying to Booker's guilt; the two checks taken into evidence—they totaled $38.50, or, as Booker figured it, $7.70 for each year of his term—bore his fingerprints. There were other witnesses; he had little choice but to offer a guilty plea. His main concern was to leave his grandparents out of it. He stuck to this condition with an impenetrable obstinance, smiling politely as his court-appointed attorney dug through the pockets of his coat. "Here," he said. "Here is a man's name. He went to Howard University; he . . . don't you have any family? A loan you could get?"

"They told me you were free," Booker said.

120

"Yes, but"—the attorney checked his watch—"it's the sheriff's checkbook, kid. Don't you see? They're going to . . ." He looked at Booker's face. "All right," he said. "All right, then. I've got another case."

For his closest living relative, he gave his father's name.

He discovered that in fact, jail was the path of least resistance, and once he'd accepted that, civilian life held little for him to fear. Only once did he experience unmanageable pain. When the sergeant-at-arms led him out after his sentencing, he looked back at the gallery and recognized his grandmother sitting on a bench. Her hair was down, and he had a weird hallucination, the empty benches before her multiplying, tunnel-like, and her face receding like that of a passenger on a fair ride. When he blinked his eyes, he saw that it wasn't Maggie at all; the woman had come to see not him, but someone else.

This marked the third stage, then, of his relationship to the words *Mercury Chapman*. The idea did not come all at once. First there was prison to contend with: the guards, the pallid artificial light, the regulations, the language, the market for nearly any imaginable commodity, from cigarettes to flesh, and the sheer presence in one spot of so many minds dedicated to and familiar with violence, corruption, scam (there were times, looking into the prison's central vault, the tiered cells rising six stories high on all sides, when he imagined their gathered thoughts swirling like a vortex through the open space). The prison seemed as monolithic as a force of nature, as all-consuming as the sea, and six months passed before he surfaced for air. By then he had only eighteen months left, if his first parole application was accepted, and he began to consider what he would do next. It amused him, in a way. For more than a year Isaac's story about Hammonds and his absorption in the past had been things he had tried to avoid, erase. Now he seemed infected, too. He did not know what it meant, beyond the obvious parallels to his own betrayal and arrest. In the story, Mercury Chapman had arrested Hammonds himself, in the company of two MPs. He had been diffident, cold. A truck company allowed little room for airs; no officers' mess, no special PX, no jeeps with flags. Chapman represented a majority of one: the only captain, the only white. He had driven side by side with his men, slept under the same blankets, crapped in the same ditches. In Wales he'd organized a dance with the only black Anglican congregation in the British Isles: descendants of dockworkers imported from Africa and the West Indies. Seventy-five young women in the port town of Cardiff. When the two sides, men and women, had been too shy to mix, Mercury had ordered a corporal to choose a partner and dance.

There was another story Booker knew, however. Back in Mississippi, where the truck company had trained, a mob of black soldiers had once stormed the post theater on "white night," protesting their exclusion from the film. Somebody—Mercury, Isaac claimed in retrospect—had called the MPs, who'd dropped six of the mob by firing buckshot at their knees. So despite his familiarity with the men, despite their distance from the segregated States, Mercury had managed to draw a line. He had chosen to, Isaac said. Everybody remembered what had happened that first time with the MPs.

Okay, so Mercury had been an ass. He had marched into Isaac and Hammonds's tent with his big ears sticking out beneath his cap, wordlessly pointed Private Hammonds out to the white-helmeted MPs, and then just as wordlessly spun on his heel and left. He had no more needed to think about the incident again than Timpson had to about Booker's father, or the judge who'd put Booker away about him. The MPs cuffed Hammonds and transported him to Cherbourg in the back of their jeep, where he was placed under military arrest. Two months later he was tried and hanged, despite Mercury's specific assurances that this would not occur. Three other men were also hanged, for looting and/or rape, all of them black.

So what? It was hardly surprising that the men hanged as "examples" were black: most of McAlester's examples were, too. Booker was attracted to the story for a different reason, almost an aesthetic one. It was like a puzzle that he worked on without thinking, simply because the pieces had been left out. He discovered that those who did well in McAlester all kept up some similar mental game. Some followed football; others wrote letters to their congressmen, the *Tulsa Tribune*, even *Time* magazine, about politics. Some buried themselves in the minutiae of their appeals. Most of this activity was entirely illusory and had no discernible effect on the physical world, but illusion was the point. One evening he saw a war movie; more than that—rising suddenly in the viewing room's chair, focusing on the wall-bolted set—he realized that it involved the Battle of Bastogne. Patton's charge into Bastogne. The soldiers were dressed in white fatigues, like the suits worn to clean up toxic waste; they traipsed through snow-bent pine trees and over curving drifts. Winter. He had never imagined it in winter, and he looked around excitedly at the other watchers, some asleep, others bored, chewing gum. "My grandfather was there," he said. He jabbed a finger at the screen, where an avalanche had just engulfed four tanks. "He was there, right there. Drove a goddamn truck into Bastogne."

"Nigger," said a languid voice, "they filmed this picture in *Vail*."

"Belgium," Booker said. "Nineteen forty-four."

"Switch on over to *Miami Vice*, and I show you where my grand-daddy used to drive *his* trucks—"

"Looks Swiss to me."

"Nigger, get your finger off Mr. George C. Scott's face."

The discovery was a physical confirmation of something that had previously been only words, a dream. He didn't care that it was just a reenactment: the fact that so many actors, producers, stuntmen, and extras had considered the battle important enough to film somehow authenticated Isaac's stories. During the Battle of Bastogne, Isaac had saved Mercury Chapman's life.

He ordered a map of France. His cell was nine feet by eleven, with two poured-concrete bunks, a poured-concrete writing desk, and

123

a poured-concrete chair. His cellmate then was a young man who referred to himself as Check, a member of an Oklahoma City gang busted for armed robbery, his second offense. He lounged on the top bunk reading a copy of *Variety* while Booker patiently opened the mail-order tube and hung the enclosed map above his desk with chewing gum. Check's posters were of a stripper named Oral Slyck. "What haps, Buckwheat," Check said without looking up. "You planning on a trip?"

"Research," Booker said.

"I know a French word," Check said. He continued reading as he spoke, the magazine propped against his washboard stomach, his eyes peering over swollen weightlifter's pecs. "The French word I know's *merde*."

Isaac had told his stories without any continuity, at odd moments: while driving him home after a night out in town, over dinner, in a fleeting remark along a fence line. Now he rifled through these half-buried fragments like a magpie, searching for anything with a glint. The name Chartres returned to him several weeks after he bought the map. He repeated the word over franks and beans in the commissary, at first stupidly and then with increasing excitement, being forced to wait the remainder of the hour until the prisoners were returned to their cells, filing through the metal detectors and buzzing iron doors with an impatience that approached incontinence. He found it on the map, inland from Cherbourg (whose name had stuck in his mind, at least phonetically, from the start), not far from Paris. He did not know why he knew the word. It took several more weeks of helplessness before he remembered; this time it happened in the exercise yard. It was early spring. A cloud of starlings descended on one corner of the yard. A single prisoner stood among them, indistinct with distance, and when he bent to tie his shoe, Booker remembered Isaac's kneeling in a bare field. The memory involved no specific mention of Hammonds's arrest, and yet Booker felt certain the topic had been implied. Instead, Isaac had been explaining how his company had

124

once been camped in such a field and how, to the west, the sun would set behind a church.

A week later, his application for a library pass was approved, and he hunched over a 1950s copy of the *Britannica*, its pages tacky with age, peeling past "Cerebus," "Chalcedony," and "Chambers, Whittaker," to "Chartres"—not even certain there would be such an entry—and saw the cathedral for the first time. The photo had been shot across what he did not know was a field of rye, the cathedral's ribs and pinnate spires backlit, its portholes and buttresses encrusted by statuary. Carved reliefs (this in a closer photo) froze in howls of violence, barbaric, wielding spears. The library was extraordinarily bright. The walls had been painted with the primary-colored optimism of a pediatrician's waiting room, and when Booker shifted his head, the gleam of tube lights blotted out Chartres cathedral on the page. He found it nearly impossible to believe that Isaac and that structure had once existed in the same time and place. And yet that night he imagined Hammonds walking with the MPs through the grain, their silhouettes dark, and the cathedral looming like some bizarrely tethered airship in the beyond. At some point between dream and imagining, he entered the field himself. The furrows twisted beneath his ankles, and though he knew the cathedral was to his right, he kept his eyes forward, the grain parting and alive with the sound of sparrows, a man marching in front of him, a rifle slung across his back.

Other aspects of prison did not adapt so easily to dream. For Booker they inhabited the realm of antidream, things that he knew and stored someplace but whose presence cast no reflection, carried none of the hue and texture of actual memory. In the exercise yard, he'd seen a man separate listlessly from a knot of inmates, the dark slot of a knife wound in his back. He had seen a Cherokee—whether mad, stoned, or simply bored, he could not tell—hurl clots of feces from his cell until he was subdued with clubs. He had fought twice himself: once in the cafeteria when a man with a birthmark accused him

125

of spilling his juice; the second time when he exited the showers to find a prisoner called Trapper trying on his shoes. Trapper had named himself after a doctor in a war movie, whom—the doctor being Jewish with a walrus mustache and Trapper mulatto with a smooth, almost prehensile upper lip—he did not resemble in the least. Booker had found him sitting on a bench, a towel wrapped around his waist, privates showing between his open knees, and Booker's only pair of tennis shoes bulging around his larger, bony feet. "You suck?" the mulatto asked. Booker surprised his tormentor by attacking with the compressed violence of a cornered rat. Guards were called. He got his shoes back. But the incident refused to disappear into the realm of antidream. It disturbed him that he couldn't forget the scent left by Trapper's feet: peppery, foreign, and obscene.

"A fucker like that," Check said, "the closer you get to parole, the more he'll come after you."

"Why's that?"

"If you're going before the parole board, he knows you won't wanna fight."

They were sweeping out the shop. Check squatted with an iron dustpan before a heap of sawdust and spiral metal shavings while Booker handled the broom. "Trapper's scouting you same as you do that old guy," Check said. "I mean, you don't do all that studying just to get smart. You got some angle rigged."

" 'That old guy' . . . ?" Booker said.

"Captain What-the-fuck." Check lifted the dustpan and dumped it into a plastic bag. Half the contents sifted to the floor. "You're working up an angle on him, right? Rich white guy. Find his address, make up some kinda scouting report, blackmail, whatever you got in mind."

Booker had stopped sweeping.

"Everybody's got an angle." Check continued to push the dustpan through the pile, the shavings parting hopelessly before it, the small amount that he did capture deflecting off the folded lip of the

126

bag. "Scam or be scammed. Fuck or be fucked, you know what I'm saying?" He rose, eyes focused dully before his body, like a man adjusting the cuffs of his suit. He dropped the dustpan into the bag and it landed with a chuff. "I know a couple other brothers around here don't like that Trapper very much."

That same evening, Trapper—a convicted murderer, a sociopath, and a harasser of young men, but also someone whom Booker hardly knew—followed Booker back to the shop after he loudly mentioned that he'd be working there alone. The air had a mossy thickness, the scent of unseen rain. He watched Trapper's smooth upper lip flutter upward from his front teeth as Check and two friends flowed toward them past the drill presses and blunt vises, their cloth shirts pale and faded, their motions sure. "You done me, didn't you?" Trapper said to Booker. "You done me up real good."

With a broom handle, he cut the mulatto behind his knees, and then the others joined in, their blows mixing with the peep of sneakers as they struggled for leverage on the concrete floor. Trapper fell at some point, awkwardly, his eyes filled with glassy concentration, as if distracted by some important thought.

It was, Booker would realize much later, the same expression Mercury might have seen when Hammonds was led away.

The train rattled through good country all morning. The smaller rivers trickled between deep, mud-scalloped banks that seemed out of proportion to the water they held, like gutters for some giant ball. Driftwood. The V's of beavers. The country had no roads and thus possessed a pure quality of forgottenness, unseen save by the engineer and then only at sixty miles an hour, three times a month. Stands of oak and maple; citronella, boxthorn, larch. Booker saw a mansion that rivaled Isaac's, with a full porch wrapped about its waist and stained glass glinting fragmentary from beneath its eaves; a massive cottonwood ruptured its central cupola like an inverted spear. He stared intently at the grounds, making out a tank of heating oil beneath a flowering cap of sod, the unstrung traces of a paddock fence, but seeing nowhere any gravel, dirt road, rut, or even footpath that suggested how man had ever left that place. Beyond it came a swamp.

They approached towns from odd angles, the buildings flipping up suddenly trackside like paper targets and the train passing not through main streets or the outlying highway strips but among back-yards littered with deflated rubber balls and dolls abandoned in the mud. His lungs burned with the bitter loneliness of spring. He rose and walked beside the stacked tractor trailers on the flatbed he'd jumped, feeling the violence of sheer motion beneath his feet. They always returned to the woods, broken by muddy horizon-curving fields. The train seemed to voyage not so much through physical counties as through partitions in time. They were in southern Kansas—Quantrill's territory, as Isaac said—and he woke from dozing to see a man in a red riding jacket, posting through the trees. A bugle jounced around his neck, and when he brought his horse up stamping beside the tracks, he and Booker passed at eye level, each gaping as though the other were out of place. He made Kansas City by late afternoon, balling north through subdivisions and across interstates. It was rush hour, and taillights filled the concrete ribbons and cast a bloody glow against the sky. They crossed a river that seemed too small to be the Missouri, then another that he felt certain was. From the bridge he saw an airport, long tongues of tarmac flanked by flashing blue lights, a conning tower, and then he noticed that the train had slowed, approaching the yard. When the bridge ended, he jumped, rolling in the gravel until he found his balance on his knees. The train passed, cabooseless. Its noise expanded and then ebbed, and in the silence he could see the river and across it tall and canyoned buildings, some fashioned of glass and others of concrete, steel, in whose lighted windows the antlike shapes of people crept.

He'd been out on parole three months.

In the morning he entered the city by recrossing the same bridge.

128

The sky was overcast, the morning light white and thin through the bridge's iron latticework. He could see the bums he'd slept with filtering through the treeline and washing on the dirty river's beach. They'd given him directions to the bus, and he followed these through the switchyards, a solitary huntsman in a denim jacket and an orange, zip-collared shirt.

He lost track of distance on the bus. At first he oriented himself according to the river and by numbered streets, but then the river disappeared, and the numbers became random, senseless, the city swarming about him, unordered and immense. Then something changed. The bus groaned up a curving hill, and as if a painted backdrop had fallen into place, they appeared suddenly to enter a different city altogether: a long, flat thoroughfare whose median had been planted with peonies and whose houses on either side appeared in the unreal dimensions of a movie set, some made of brick with three-story columns in the front, others of finely cut stone, their doors and windows decorated by fluted ironwork.

"Fifty-ninth Street," the bus driver said. "In back there: this is it."

He walked for some time before he found the house. It was white with black shutters, two stories high, and it had an oddly rambling quality, seeming to drift backward from its simple front into more complex additions, passageways, vaults. On the brick walk, he stopped. Evergreens flanked the door, and beside the walk stood an old-time Negro lawn jockey, holding a ring. The iron statue was mounted on an iron post, its face repainted in pink flesh tones, hair yellow, eyes a bird's-egg blue.

What the fuck, he thought, *is that supposed to mean?*

He rang the doorbell. He had to guide his finger to the button, his hand seeming to care no more about his instructions than a struggling fish. The door opened with a vacuumed suck, and a woman's face appeared: her skin was cinnamon-colored, marked with the first livered spots of age. She wore a lavender pantsuit, and her hair was permed into an efficient wave. "Chapman residence?" he said.

129

The woman's expression made Booker feel like there was something nasty caught in his hair. "He's already got someone to do the lawn," she said.

Booker glanced involuntarily at the white jockey, then a second time, affectedly. "I'm not here to *do* the lawn, Ms. . . . Ms. . . ."

"It doesn't matter what my name is."

"Of course it doesn't, ma'am." Booker felt better now; the voice had come to him, slightly southern, slightly ass-kissing, but with patient violence in the back. "This is more like what you might call a family matter between myself and Mr. Chapman. A family matter"— he *liked* the sound of that—"which I'd rather not discuss with just anybody. So since I'm assuming that you're not exactly related to Mr. C."—he rose slightly on his toes—"I'd be glad to come in and wait." Here he grabbed, as casually as possible, the handle to the screen door.

The woman locked the screen door with a click. "You walked here," she said.

"My car is around the corner."

"Then pull it up in the driveway and wait there."

"I don't think Mr. Chapman will appreciate—"

"What he appreciates," the woman said—she enunciated very clearly—"what he appreciates, generally, is acting like a fool. So if you've got something foolish to sell him, or talk him into, or get him to donate to some fool club to which you probably don't belong, then everything will be fine. If you're here for something genuinely good, then he'll do that, too. Mix 'n' match. But, don't tell me you're here on *family* matters, 'cause I know all the families that have matters with Mercury in this town. So excuse me if I don't let in a young man who lies about why he's come and whether he's got a car, and looks like he slept last night in a ditch. He'll be back around three."

With that, she closed the door. Booker lingered, staring at the peepholes in its center, wondering if she was still spying on him. Just in case, he smiled, but his expression twisted unpleasantly. There had been, he observed, a certain lack of historic feeling in the exchange.

He had not eaten since the train. He felt lightheaded, almost euphoric, and when the rust-colored Volvo pulled up three hours later, he jumped too quickly to his feet. The car and driver appeared at the end of a tunnel that lengthened, then went completely black.

He was out only for the time it took to fall. But when he woke, he felt refreshed, as if he'd figured out something. Sprawled in the evergreens, he remembered the time Batson had been carried into the house with a fever and how his grandmother (who had previously refused to have hands indoors) had refused to allow him to leave. He heard a man's voice say, "All right, you grab his feet," and he relaxed all his muscles, lying in wait.

9

HE WOKE — or, rather, pretended to — on a tartan sofa. A man leafed through a catalog, seated at the sofa's foot. "I found you," the man said, "in my evergreens."

"Did you?" Booker said.

"Yes — hmmp! — as a matter of fact, I did." The man was dressed like a sportsman — khaki jacket open at the neck, pressed corduroy slacks, and Gore-tex boots (identical to those shown in his catalog) — but his hairless skull and hooded eyes, both sunburned, reminded Booker of a newborn bird's. His upper lip quivered like an egg tooth as he spoke: "Lilly Washington, who cooks for me — if it was up to her, by the way, we'd call the police — says you're here on family business. Hmmp! Which is a surprise. Hmmp! So I've been sitting here, trying to remember you. The problem is, I can't."

"I'm Isaac Bentham's grandson," Booker said.

The man sat strangely frozen, staring at him without seeing him, until Booker began to wonder if he'd gotten things horribly wrong. "Spackle!" the man shouted, starting from his reverie with such violence that Booker jumped.

"What?" he said.

"Sp-a-ck-le." The man scribbled on a scrap of paper, trying to make his ballpoint roll against the soft backing of his footstool. He said the word as he wrote. "I've got plaster falling over my desk up-

132

stairs," he said. "I never remember till I sit down, and then it's too late. Hmmp! It's the devil getting old, kid. If I think of something and don't make a note, it's gone. I've got pockets full of these." He turned out the pocket of his khaki jacket, empty save for the scrap he'd just put in. "Lilly," he said, adopting a tone of mock secrecy, "claims I need a note to pee—you know, so I remember what to do." His eyes flashed, and he returned to a regular voice: "Fortunately, I'm not as bad as all that. But I do have to write down spackle, haven't got a choice. Don't take it personally. Now, you were telling me something about somebody?"

Booker held the man carefully in his sights. "You *are* Mercury Chapman, aren't you?" he said. "Captain Mercury Chapman of Truck Company Four-nine-seven-one?"

"Yes." The sun had broken through the haze as it was setting. Its muddy rays caught Mercury sideways, like an optician's penlight, and deep within the slotted chambers of the old man's eyes, Booker saw a contraction of fear. Mercury shaded himself quickly with one hand. "Yes, of course I am, though nobody's called me that in almost fifty years. And your grandfather fought with me. Isaac. How embarrassing!" He stood, officiously. "Lilly!" he shouted. "It's more than embarrassing, it's . . . it's *very* embarrassing," he said to Booker. "And you sat all day on the stoop. Have you eaten anything?"

"Not exactly."

"Haven't eaten!" Mercury hurried to the broad, two-step entrance to the study, his bird's chin jerking, and shouted into the paneled hall. "Haven't eaten," he said, returning and gripping a chairback. "No wonder you were sick. A young kid like that. What are you, twenty? Twenty-one? Just a minute, and we'll get some food."

He closed the drawer of a lampstand at the sofa's foot, and Booker noticed, in the brief moment of its closing, a handgun's black butt.

"I remember your grandfather," Mercury said. "A good soldier. An Oklahoman, right?" They had sandwiches by then, a full plate of them, sliced neatly at the corners with lettuce and Swiss cheese. Lilly had fixed then. The entire process felt surreal, waiting amid the tartan opulence of the study, its stained cabinets filled with queer cups and plates, while a black woman dressed in a tailored suit fixed him sandwiches. A muted television glowed in the corner, stock quotes winding across the screen. Mercury had puttered in and out, advising Lilly: a diversion, Booker decided. An attempt at buying time.

"I talk a lot, around town, you know—" Mercury had poured himself a drink and fussed now with its ice. "Hunting, fishing trips, things like that. I tell war stories to my friends." He glanced up sheepishly. "But I never got back in touch much with the men. My men, the ones who were there. Oh, I wrote some letters off and on, but few. Not enough. Not to your grandfather, anyway."

It was a question: the moment, Booker understood, that they'd both been waiting for, and within which he had to make a choice. He was chewing, and his mouth tasted suddenly of salt. "My grandfather," he said when he had swallowed, "always spoke highly of you. He said you were a fine officer, a friend."

"He did?" Mercury examined his chair's arm, blinking. His eyes had clouded with release, an expression close to joy. "Well, that's the decent thing to say, but . . ."

"He meant it," Booker said.

"Well, we had some pretty decent times, kid," Mercury said. "I just never really knew . . . never had any way of . . ."

The old man's eyes looked wet, and disgust flooded Booker's throat: a cold, white string of bile. "My grandfather saved your life, Mr. Chapman," he said. "He told me I could come to you for help."

Three days later he found himself standing in the gravel drive outside old Pete Martin's A-frame and staring out at the unplanted bean field that fronted the property, as if he had, in the eight hundred and more days since he spent the night in a similar bean field, progressed exactly nowhere: or, rather, had circled and returned. Seven months later, his breath frosted a small, angry circle on the unglazed window of the hunting club's "renovated" shack as he watched Judge Sayers's tangerine sports car trail a white plume of dust up the drive.

It was late afternoon, the air taking on a fall chill; for the last two hours he had inspected the club's members (millionaires, he'd heard Stan Granger say) as they unloaded their staid Buicks and stretched, their legs curiously short and dainty beneath the outswell of their bellies. Clearly, the tangerine sports car caused a hitch. The biggest of the men (Remy Westbrook, though he didn't know his name then) hobbled around the corner of the A-frame with his pants front clutched in his fist. The others straightened up and removed—this in a gesture that amused him, familiar yet obsolete, like the ritual of some lost tribe—their hats. After the slight, boyish figure exited the sports car, they put them on again. He supposed it was a woman. That it did not look like a woman interested him. The figure was dressed in a miniaturized version of the canvas jacket, hat, and leather slippers favored by the men, and it immediately lifted the sports car's hatchback and began jointing up a gun. Through the shack's open door, he heard the light, aggressive metal clinks.

Booker had felt during that long summer the strange, hovering sensation of being tangled in something. It felt, as best he could describe it, like the tendrils of a spider's web: invisible, not restricting his motion, and yet always present, a soft, brief touch against his arm and face. At times during the summer's loneliness, this sensation had grown so strong, so pervasive, that a horrified violence had welled up in his throat, a desperation similar to that of a drowning man; one afternoon the sensation had seemed so completely real—coupled as it was with images of his youth: his father's jury-rigged studio, Isaac's starched socks, Batson (this with the distortion of a dream) hiding marijuana fronds amid the Bentham house's antiques—that he had swung his arms and torn his clothes off his body in an effort to get free. He had paced then naked, half wild, amid the time-capsule decorations of the A-frame—the bottle of Dr. Reymond's Hair Tonic that

135

sat alone inside the bathroom cabinet (since when? before his birth? before the war itself?), the antlers, the watercolors of flying ducks, the black-and-white photographs of Mercury Chapman in his youth, holding strings of ducks (again, before or after the war? did it matter?), the dead and musty mementos, the ribald bar signs—lunging and pawing at himself like an animal amid the decades of preserved good cheer. Luckily, the sound of Stan Granger's pickup had brought him to his senses, shame prodding him to put on pants.

So in an odd way he welcomed the arrival of the members, with their bourbon, their holiday shouts, their aura of cash. And when twilight fell and everyone went inside, he put on his Walkman (Mercury had bought it for him as partial payment for the summer's work) and headed for the A-frame's broad rear window to have a look.

The girl noticed him at once. She sat at one end of the long, wax-spattered table, the men in tableau behind the glass, her face canescent and smooth among the older men, whose satiny complexions were the product of bourbon and unfamiliarity with physical work. She wore an undershirt and suspenders, like a man, and he could see beneath the rust-stained fabric (it was her father's shirt, he would later discover), outlined faintly by the elastic straps, the precise curve of her breasts. She continued to eat, cutting her steak, forking green beans into her mouth, and watching him through the glass as she chewed, expressionless, as if he weren't there. Then she made a furtive gesture toward her ear.

He slipped his earphones off. He heard the hissing silence of the cold, the bleats of early geese, and, through the vented window, voices: ". . . attempting to improve the lot of our darker brothers," drawled the florid man who, earlier, had clutched his pants front in his fist; ". . . up from the ghetto and into the woods—better than playing midnight basketball with the mayor, I say."

". . . a protégé, hey, Merc?" he heard another say.

". . . a civil rights leader before they even had the word," the florid man continued, wiping his heavy, sensual lips. "Hell, he got along so

136

good with those fellas driving his jeeps and all—what was the name of that driver you had, Merc?"

"Gettysburg Jackson."

"That's right. Craziest old name. And there was the time they wouldn't let him into the whorehouse—excuse me, Judge—in Paris. . . . "

Booker listened to the ignorance of the black man's name and the coarseness of the men who spoke it, the smutty vibrato of their throats. For the first time he understood the impenetrable distance that separated Mercury Chapman, whom he saw now through the lighted window, dressed in a corduroy jacket and smiling nervously, from his grandfather, who lay, even at this moment, back in Oklahoma, in his bed. Against his cheeks, the earphones of his Walkman played a tinny refrain, its meaning and context entirely stripped away. A dog barked, and the men shifted in their chairs toward the window, forcing him to quickly back away. The mudroom door opened, and the girl came out.

"Do you want a beer?" she said.

"What?" he whispered. "What? Do I—what?"

"Want-a-beer, do-you?" she said. "Looks like you could use one, anyway. It's better than listening to those guys. Did you hear it? I wanted somebody else to listen so I wouldn't have to go completely nuts. Did you ever feel that way? Like if you're in traffic and you see a woman beating on her kid—you know, something so boring and gross that you look around hoping somebody else saw, too? It's because if somebody else sees it, then you don't feel nuts. That's what I think, anyway."

"If that's your dog," Booker said, "how 'bout you shut it up?"

"Oh," the girl said. She had been holding two beer bottles like a novice might hold ski poles, and now she thrust them into Booker's chest. When she returned from the car (where she'd touched her palm to the rear window and murmured through the door crack), she continued as though she'd never left. "What're you listening to?"

"Parliament," he said.

"Parliament," she repeated. He could tell she didn't recognize the name. "I saw them at the Uptown just last spring."

He got his first good look at her. The undershirt did not fit: the stretched part of the elbow bagged along her forearm, and she hiked the sleeves impatiently, the white thinness of her wrists and her face, the arc of neck beneath her short-cropped hair, seeming livid, almost feverish against the cold. Her eyes (he couldn't see their color) had the overlarge quality of an animal's in a greeting-card cartoon, only lightless, utterly dark.

"All right," she said. "If you don't have anything to say, I'm gonna go back in."

"What's so boring about them?" he said.

"Boring? A hundred things were boring. Are you telling me you thought that conversation was a blast?"

"I asked you."

"First of all"—she braced one fist on her hip and counted with her other hand—"it's not even the right war. I mean, we've had three wars since the one they all went to, so it's not exactly timely, if you ask me. Secondly, Mercury always tells the same stories about how he was in charge of a bunch of blacks. I guess you're black, right? So maybe it's interesting to you if you're a masochist or something, but in the real world—by that I definitely do *not* include Kansas City—in the real world, sometimes I feel like mentioning, you know, *things have changed.*"

"I'm certainly ready for a little of that," Booker said.

He unscrewed a beer and sidestepped quickly as its foam gurgled about his wrist, wetting the bare earth.

"You're not shitting," Clarissa Sayers said.

10

MERCURY CHAPMAN was afraid. Booker had felt it the first time they spoke in his tartan study, and he had felt it throughout the long, hot summer, as he and Mercury repaired his shack together. He discovered that the feeling gave him pleasure; it also represented—as Check had said—an angle for him to use. What the old man feared, in Booker's opinion, was exposure. He had done something he wasn't proud of during the war (Booker had a fair idea of what it was), and worse, he had spent his whole life telling lies about it to his friends, picturesque *Negro* stories featuring characters with names like Gettysburg Jackson rather than Isaac Bentham or Reggie Hammonds, and whose content could be summed up by the demand "Tell about the time they wouldn't let Gettysburg into the whorehouse."

Among this troupe of Sambos, Booker doubted he would find any soldiers like his grandfather (who could have whipped the fat asses of the club's entire membership), or any terrified buck privates who'd been led through rye fields to be hanged.

This fear was a weakness that Booker intended to exploit: not through confrontation, as Isaac would have done, but by complicity. His claim that Isaac had actually liked Mercury had been an intuitive lie, a reaction to something he sensed but hadn't yet defined, and it had worked perfectly. Once Mercury admitted that Isaac had been his friend, he couldn't refuse to help his grandson, could he? Especially if that grandson was "in some trouble with the law." With a foothold at the club, Booker had developed a system of lies—a system that they both agreed to accept. For instance, neither of them had told the other members who Booker really was. On the surface, this made little sense. If the members had all heard Mercury's war stories, why wouldn't he introduce the grandson of a man who'd fought with him? The answer was that Mercury didn't want to talk about Isaac, Hammonds, and the rest. And therein lay the crux of the con: without actually saying so, Booker agreed to leave the past alone, provided Mercury did what he asked.

It was blackmail, really—only by mutual consent.

Things had gone so well that by the time he met Clarissa Sayers, he'd decided to start pushing for a better job. Mercury had visited him later that same night, tromping down to his shack after the other members had fallen asleep. "Say, kiddo," the old man shouted, "how's it coming down here?" Mercury, who expressed guilt or uneasiness by doing chores, strode through the front door and started examining the floor moldings. "You got any rodent problems, kid?" he asked, wedging his head beneath Booker's cot.

Booker watched him from a metal folding chair, which was the only place to sit other than the cot. "Did you know," he asked, "that the citizens of Chapman County used to own about six thousand slaves?"

"What?" Mercury's head slammed the cot frame. "What the—"

"Remember how pissed off you got," Booker asked, "when I called this cabin a *nigger* shack?" He emphasized the slur, which had been common in prison, because it flustered the old man. "Well, I had Stan Granger drive me down to the library in Waterloo to check it out. I ask this lady a question, and—*boom*—she pulls out some slave census for eighteen sixty-three. They could've lived right in this very room, just like I said."

Amused, he waited for Mercury to extract himself from the cot.

140

"It's a real inneresting lib'ary, Merc," he said, slipping into dialect. "You oughta visit sometime."

Mercury strode to the front window and heaved against the frame. "It's caulked," Booker said.

"All right," Mercury said. He was breathing heavily now. "All right, it doesn't matter. That there is a sash-weight window. Do you think they had sash-weight windows a hundred and thirty years ago? Or propane gas lines? Or running water, for Chrissakes? That's the trouble with you people is that you won't admit history's made up of facts."

"Slavery's a fact," Booker observed.

Mercury clasped his temples, as if to keep some crucial substance from leaking out. "You passed out in my evergreen bushes," he said. "I gave you a place to stay, found you work. That's pretty decent, I think—maybe even more than decent. So my question is, what's it take for you to quit pestering me?"

"C'mon, Merc," Booker said, crossing his legs. "I'm looking for a career, not a caretaker's job. You're a businessman. You got all these rich friends, Rolodexes, Filofaxes, shit like that. And we both know that if my grandfather had been white—well, let's just say you wouldn't have stuck a *white* man in some shack."

Mercury opened his left hand sideways, as if it held a book. "Where," he cried, striking his palm, "is it written that I have to give you anything? I haven't read that part. Do you know why I haven't read that part? Because it isn't there!"

Mercury glowered. He had unknowingly addressed the boy in the same tone and cadence he'd once reserved for his troops.

"For Chrissakes," he shouted. "I don't even know if you're telling the truth!"

During this outburst, Booker sat with deliberate composure in his chair. When Mercury was finished, he reached inside the collars of his two borrowed sweaters and lifted a plain loop of chain over his head. Two metal plates dangled at the end of this chain, and he tossed them at Mercury's chest.

141

"Isaac Bentham's dog tags," he said.

The old man held them crookedly. He pulled a pair of reading glasses from his pocket and squinted through them.

"When did he die?" he asked.

"Know what I looked up once?" Booker said, avoiding the question. "That old church you guys camped out at—Chartres. You remember that? I can almost imagine you all sitting around the campfire, cutting up, the way you like to talk about." He leaned forward, whispering, palms spread. "That's *my* question: How much are all those nice memories worth to you, Merc? Five bucks? Ten bucks? A little squatter's shack in the woods?"

Mercury tossed the tags back. They fell short and landed on the floor. "Kiddo," he said, staring at Booker levelly, his eyes above the tortoiseshell reading frames a warlike, luminous blue. "I don't know what you're after, but you won't get it like this."

After Mercury left, Booker rose and examined the same window the old man had tried. He ran his fingers along its seams, wearing the same graven expression he'd once affected when selling pot out of Batson's truck. A dead hornets' nest hung in the window's upper corner, and he cradled it in his palm with curiosity and then amusement, chuckling.

He undressed after that and, crossing barefoot to his cot, stopped suddenly in the middle of the floor. "He's gonna do it," he told the empty cabin. "Yes, he is."

Within three weeks Mercury had found him a job in the city, starting that spring. "It's in contracting," he said. By then Booker had also convinced him to replace the cabin's heater (an expense that he suspected came out of Mercury's personal funds), and in daydreams he imagined for himself a slow, unfettered rise: first the contracting job, then a union card, a foreman's post, maybe even his own *company*— who knew?

142

The last thing he wanted, out of all these possibilities, was trouble with a girl.

She started bringing him clothes. It was dusk, her second visit to the camp. He was standing in the boat shed fixing a sheared propeller pin, and she came to the door, flushed, her usual indolence replaced by furtive excitement. She pulled a bundle of shirts from under her coat and spread them atop an oil drum, triumphantly.

"Get those out of here," he said. It was as if his mouth had spoken before he'd told it what to say. They both paused in astonishment, her eyes blinking like a cat's.

"You can't wear that same orange shirt every day," she said. Her tone was flat, almost scornful. "Not practically."

"Get those out of here," he repeated. He shut his mouth again, lips puckered. His anger surprised him, appearing in stubborn con-travention to his own stated philosophy and will, and when he real-ized that his hand had closed into a fist, he forced it to open, patiently, as if by a feat of telepathy. She gathered up the shirts with a precise and furious indignation, her eyes not leaving his even when she bent to pick up one she'd dropped. She stalked out, saying, "Well, fuck me for trying!" in her choirboy's voice.

Just like with Mercury, he should've been willing to take her for all she was worth (in this case, four freshly laundered flannel shirts and a cable sweater that he suspected had, and later would pretend hadn't, been stolen from her father's closet), and his failure to do so infuriated him. He hunted with Mercury and Eddie Coole the next day and returned to his cabin at dusk, opened the familiar door, and saw in the checkered moonlight the shirts stacked on his cot, per-fectly folded, together with a new pair of gloves. He carried them to the A-frame and left them on the dinner table with a note: *Somebody left these.*

It was a different kind of cold than he'd known down south. One morning he went to relieve himself in the cabin's bare, uninsulated toilet and found the water frozen in the bowl. This discovery came at the supreme moment of negotiation, and he was obliged to squat like a swimmer in the blocks, in order to finish what by then could not be stopped. He had two crewneck sweaters that Mercury had loaned him, two pairs of wool socks (Lilly Washington had sent these, though he didn't know it), and an utterly worthless pair of suede gloves lined with the same Styrofoam found in airplane seats. He wore the zip-collared shirt until it stank, then he wore the sweaters against his bare skin. When they became rank, he turned them inside out. He did his laundry once a month at Stan's trailer or, if he needed it more often, using dish detergent in the A-frame's sink, standing naked before the fire until the fabric got dry. He'd decided not to ask Mercury for clothes: request for such mundane necessities might dilute his effect.

A week later she drove down with her father. Booker ferried them to a blind, her face absurdly evocative beneath an oversize camouflage hat, the judge upright in the bow, vainly hatless, his clipped hair barely ruffled by the skiff's speed. Unlike the other members, he never invited Booker into the blind. "We'll need you after sundown but not before," he said, snapping and unsnapping his cases. "The best time is just before, and I don't like having it ruined by a boat. If we move, you'll hear us shoot."

As the judge took Clarissa's hand, Booker caught a glimpse of her profile: chin tilted upward toward her father, her expression every bit as vain as his.

They left for the city at seven o'clock that night, and when he returned to his cabin, he found the shirts stacked on his cot again, together with a down-lined coat. He ran onto the porch cursing, even though the judge's car had pulled out a full thirty minutes before. He carried the shirts back to the empty A-frame along with his original note, which she'd also returned. He walked back to his cabin, intending to eat. He filled a pot and placed it over the blue rosette of the tiny gas range and stood watching the torpid, unmoving water, the sound of his breathing steadily increasing. If anyone had glanced into that

144

totally unfurnished, uncarpeted, and undecorated room (some walls the sour yellow of old plaster, others the slate of new, unpainted sheetrock), they might have surmised that the pot held a gorgon's head. Without knowing it, he was on the frost-glazed path again. He charged through the A-frame's mudroom and the interior door and stripped off his jean jacket and Mercury's crewnecks with the harsh, furious motions of a man abandoning ship. He put on the first of the laundered flannels, stabbing his arms through the sleeves, then the new cable sweater. He folded the cleaner of his two crewnecks, slipped it into the cable sweater's place, and returned down the path to his stove.

The water was boiling by then, and he dumped his spaghetti in. He thought he'd finished with the clothes, but the minute the spaghetti hit the water, he was transfixed again, staring, beginning to pant. Then he found himself back on the path. He'd left the A-frame doors open as if expecting himself, and cursing, he removed the new cable sweater, the old crewneck, and the new flannel shirt he'd put on underneath, folded them, and donned the down coat instead.

After that it wasn't just shirts. She brought socks, toiletries, long underwear, even music tapes. He would discover anonymous parcels wrapped in newspaper and hidden in the boat shed. He had no idea how she managed to stash them there: during her trips, she never left the judge's sight except when in the field. He found the first parcel by accident, perhaps a week after it had been left, and from then on she always chose some new hiding place: behind gas cans, tucked against rafters, underneath an old hand-cranked broadcaster. He anticipated the moment of her departure almost as much as her arrival, because then he could go look. Sometimes he would fail to look in the right spot, and there would be an unexpected drop of sadness, even anger, that she hadn't done what he'd expressly forbidden her to do, and then he would find the parcel stuffed in a joint of PVC pipe with twice the pleasure and outrage as before. Once she included a pair of satin briefs like his father had worn, sweating in his jury-rigged studio,

145

and he held these up in the moted darkness like an artifact of someone else's life.

Another time she left him a bottle of Afro-Sheen, a product he would not have even known existed were it not for reruns of seventies detective movies. He didn't know whether to laugh or take mortal offense.

He would see her face, white, indolent, framed by a boy's haircut, appearing among the fattened bodies of the old men like the physical incarnation of some principle that their entire property and clubhouse had been designated to refute. She hunted from the sloughs and flooded trees along the creek, eschewing the wood blinds where the members sat listening to Kansas football games and eating daintily from tins of Spam, and he was silently pleased when he ferried members back from the fields empty-handed to find her sitting on a stool by the boat shed, lazily plucking her limit of drakes.

"What kind of woman," Remy Westbrook asked, querulously, "would want to kill things like that?"

He even liked her smell. She ate sourballs and smoked strong cigarettes, her very scent (a mixture of tree sap and ash) somehow antithetical to a place otherwise redolent of burlap and men's feet. She attended a Jesuit college in Kansas City, but mostly she talked about a school called Vassar, where she'd gone for just a year. "There were people from all over the world," she told him. "My roommate's dad worked at the United Nations. Can you believe that? He was a delegate from Morocco, and she was some kind of princess or duchess—whatever they have. Being a judge's daughter from Kansas City was completely bogus. Nobody cared. Personally, I thought it was a big relief."

They were hunting in timber, and she leaned against a trunk whose flood rings rose high above her head. "Oh, Booker," she said, "I really wish I hadn't left."

"Why did you, then?" he asked.

"Dad," she answered, shrugging. "He pretty much decided not to pay."

146

Despite this, she defended her father with a vehemence that he found difficult to comprehend. The other members treated the judge with thinly veiled contempt, refusing to sit with him in the blinds and mocking the expensive Labrador he used to retrieve his kills, and she railed at them for their provincialism, their meanness, their ignorance. Booker made the mistake of suggesting that the judge might improve things if he "just tried being nice."

"Don't make me puke," she said. "They don't like him because he went to Yale instead of drinking beer for four years at good ol' K.U. Nothing frightens people around here more than someone who *isn't* mediocre. I'm just surprised to hear it from you."

"So that must be why he took you out of school," Booker said. "To save you the trouble of getting smart."

"First off," she said, "he didn't take me out of college. We decided together that I could always go back." Her lips curled. "Secondly, where did *your* father send *you* to get a degree? I don't remember saying any rude things about that."

By Thanksgiving the freezes had begun to come with regularity, and in December he and Stan Granger—aided ineffectually by Mercury, Remy, and the rest—sledgehammered dark, rippling crescents around the otherwise frozen blinds. He wore the down-lined coat daily, and all the shirts he could find. As a last token of resistance, he avoided wearing any of the gifts around Clarissa's father, but eventually he forgot about this, too. Once, later in December, the judge came down alone, and Booker took him out in the skiff. The sloughs and deeper channels along the dikes hadn't frozen yet, and the judge rode upright in the bow as usual, hair as perfectly grained and coiffed as a sculpture made of wax. The temperature was twelve above, and Booker killed the engine as they glided to the blind. "I notice," the judge said, opening his gun case, "that you're wearing one of my shirts."

His voice paused hypnotically while the boat's keel grazed weeds.

"That's funny, since I almost never give away my personal belongings without obtaining a receipt. Without a receipt," Judge Sayers continued, "you can't write such things off as charity. Perhaps that's what you prefer to call it: charity, instead of theft."

Booker said nothing.

"They're really the same aren't they?" the judge observed. He had stepped onto the blind's raised platform and cracked his gun. "I believe in charity, just as I believe in the struggles of your race," he said. "So if you will please put that shirt in my car, along with any other of my belongings you've ferreted away, the matter will go no further than here."

Booker moved to start the engine, a high-pitched keening in his ears.

"Leave it," the judge said. "You have waders on: just follow the dikes."

To Thornton Sayers he returned a forest-green flannel shirt whose collar was flecked with slough mud. The rest he took to the consignment shop in Waterloo, ferrying bright fistfuls of fabric across the empty street while Stan Granger waited in his pickup, worrying. "All right, homey," Booker said, folding greenbacks into his pants. "Where's a guy go around these parts to *accessorize?*"

"Do you mean clothes?" Stan asked.

"What I mean," Booker said, slapping the dash, "is a brown-colored, no-wash, lie-in-the-mud insulated jumpsuit. The kind of jumpsuit my granddaddy used to like. The kind of suit"—he raised a finger— "you only take off when you crap."

Stan nodded, thoughtfully. "Them're at the co-op," he said.

When Clarissa showed up alone four days later, he walked off his cabin's porch and into the band of woods that surrounded the duck fields. Sitting on a downed log, he listened to a bad rap tape she'd given him (its case featured a black man who carried a machine gun and wore braids that jutted incongruously above his ears) and watched her hurry down the path to his cabin and pound soundlessly

148

on his windows, her efforts drowned out by chords loud as circular saws. By the time the tape ended, she had left.

He did not see her again for some time. He had become inured to winter by then, appearing against the dormant fields in a mud-brown stocking cap, leather gloves, and the ubiquitous canvas suit, a bony incarnation of the grandfather he'd sought to escape.

Judge Sayers owned a purebred Lab. It was young, male, and overly excitable, and it liked Clarissa better than him. The other members preferred to retrieve their own kills, the duck fields being shallow, easy wading even for septuagenarians, and as a result, the judge's dog (its name was Thurgood) rarely hunted at all. One morning Booker heard the judge calling his dog. He stepped from the boat shed and saw the Sayerses' twinned figures—the woman a reduced and thus more intensely focused version of the man—outlined against the A-frame's red apex. It had been two weeks since their split.

"Thurgood," the judge was calling. "Thurgood, come here now. Come here, Thurgood, now."

The dog bolted from them and ran downhill with a chumbling, vacuous gait, the drum of paw beats increasing until he rushed past Booker's knees, the boat shed, and the updrawn skiffs. He ran directly into the water, as if he hadn't expected the surface to give way. "Thurgood," the judge said. "Thurgood! Dammit! Booker, call him out of there."

The slough was no more than six feet wide. The dog's head bobbed in the middle like a bead, and Booker walked on dry land, directly at the swimming dog's side. "You wanna get out of there, dude?" he asked.

The dog nodded. A flea crossed his mucid, eager eye.

"If you come over here with me, you can walk," Booker advised.

The dog's muzzle lifted. He whistled yearningly through his nose and continued swimming dead ahead. Booker returned to the boat

149

shed. The Sayerses had come down, and he could hear Clarissa laughing while the judge tried to argue about something else. "If you want to hunt with somebody like Bert Gauss instead of with your own father, that's just fine. Perfectly fine. What you do with you own body is your business, but what I don't like is when a loser like Bert Gauss can sit at my own table and insinuate"—the judge struggled, as though his mouth had acquired a bad taste—"*leer* about the whole affair directly to my face, as if you'd given him permission. As if—"

"Do you think he'll swim clear to the creek?" Clarissa asked.

"What?"

"Thurgood," Clarissa said. "Do you think he can make it to the creek?"

"He—" The judge looked up. The dog's head, down the long, diminishing perspective of the slough, was no bigger than a tick. "I thought I told you to get him," he said to Booker.

Booker shrugged. "He wouldn't come."

"I'll tell you one thing about Bert Gauss," said Clarissa. "He has a really well trained dog."

Cursing, the judge crashed down the brambled finger of land that extended along the slough. Clarissa watched. Her jaw was clamped, and the muscles worked beneath it in tight bands. "It's been a long time since I've seen *you*," she said to Booker.

Booker was checking the skiff's plugs. "I've been around," he said.

The dog returned from an entirely different direction, dragging a dead snake that he dropped proudly at Clarissa's feet. "Hello, Goody," she said, kneeling and stroking his sleek head. Booker started the skiff, and they found the judge at the end of a promontory, shouting. Yellow paste coated the corners of his lips.

"'A well-trained dog,'" he said.

"It's not worth getting mad at him," said Clarissa. "He's just stupid."

"'Stupid,'" the judge said.

"Bert says Labradors are overbred."

"And what does Bert say to do in a case like that?"

150

"Start over," Clarissa said.

On their way across the duck fields, Thurgood abandoned the skiff twice. The first time he dove after two mud hens daubing in a flooded bush, and they nearly swamped the skiff hauling him back in. Clarissa laughed hilariously, and the judge's face turned increasingly white, like a knuckle being squeezed. Booker watched them from the stern. Just before the dog left the skiff a second time, whining and scrabbling, the judge's gaze crossed his. His hazel eyes appeared puzzled, as if begging for direction, and Booker noticed that his twelve-gauge, normally secure in its plastic case, lay across his knees.

The judge shot twice. The second report seemed louder, as if Booker's brain had caught up to what his eyes already knew. Clarissa lunged across the decoy bags and pushed down the barrel of her father's gun. The dog's body floated sideways, water seeping between his teeth, and Booker felt grotesque relief that he hadn't whimpered or tried to swim: the judge had shot him neatly in the head. Clarissa sat up slowly in her seat. She composed her face, the flesh smoothing over the bones like putty, then creasing again. "When I said 'start over,'" she said in a low voice, "that wasn't what I meant."

"I'm sorry, honey," the judge said. "I'm really sorry to do that in front of you, but you're right: it's dangerous to have a hunting dog that jumps out of boats like that."

It was incredibly quiet. The judge's voice had a strange, wheedling quality that made Booker twist uncomfortably in his seat.

"Hand me the anchor weight," he said. "I'll get rid of my own mess."

When he woke the next morning, Clarissa was sitting on his porch, drinking coffee from a Styrofoam cup. Sunlight slanted across her knees. "You were right," she said. "My father really isn't very nice."

"Okay," Booker said.

"If we're friends," she said, "you have to always remind me of that."

151

She took him for a drive. They went east along the river, among sparse bluff towns whose clinging roofs and bulbous water towers resembled coral beneath an inverted ocean of gray. Her father's mother had died of emphysema in a rented room. Ezra Sayers (Clarissa's grandfather) had met her during a business trip to Asbury Park, New Jersey, where she was "live-modeling" swimsuits on the boardwalk. First she had told him that she was a White Russian whose family had once attended tea parties with the czar "just like in the books" (a word she rhymed with *dukes*), and later that her uncle was the largest importer of plastics in Berlin. But Ezra cared about her past only insofar as she was smart enough to lie about it, a test she passed with flying colors from the start. Her handler assured Ezra that she was "a good clean goil from Queens." She was actually Ukrainian.

In Kansas City, Ezra introduced her as French.

Ezra's first wife had been a showgirl whose past was entirely too localized to be remade. But Clarissa's grandmother (her name in Asbury Park had been Bettina, which they changed to Josephine when she came west) could be manufactured conveniently from scratch. She arrived at Union Station in 1935. Ezra was twenty-seven by then and had opened the first of his drug palaces, at Thirty-third and the Paseo, in one of the oldest and most magnificent neighborhoods in town. Josephine joined the French Club, the Marseillaise Society, and the Appreciators of Impressionist Art. She did in fact speak French and substituted at the Pemberton Academy, where she taught a decade's worth of young men to pronounce their French vowels with an Odessan twang. She gave birth to Thornton four years into the marriage, Ezra's first and only son. Thirteen years after that, he divorced her following a party celebrating Charlie Sumner's appointment to the Italian consulate. Sumner had loaned Truman money back when he was selling hats; his wife was from New England and hated Kansas City: rare beef upset her stomach and the lack of salt air gave her hives. Mrs. Sumner had also spent her teenage summers in

Provence, and after listening to Josephine Sayers for five minutes, she pronounced loudly, "If that woman is French, I have a glass eye."

"Perhaps maybe that is correct," Josephine said, observing her accuser across a centerpiece of orange- and green-dyed tulips. "But a glass eye might be better than being so fat as you."

Ezra bawled with laughter when he heard this retort from his co-conspirator, and divorced her within the year. He'd been looking for an excuse: the war had recently ended and people were surprised to discover that it had been about Jews. French descent no longer carried the same currency (there had been, to everyone's amazement, entire city-fuls of Jews in France), and the women in Ezra Sayers's circle began dropping hints about Josephine. Not that they had anything against the Jewish faith per se, but it said something about a person if she could— supposing she was Jewish, of course—so easily repudiate her birth.

In Kansas City, no clique of any consequence admitted Jews, and when Ezra walked into the Blue Hills Country Club's dining room (he had not yet made his leap onto the Colonial Club's member rolls), he began to sense that questions about his wife's heritage were being whispered in his wake. As an outsider, Charlie Sumner's wife had merely had the guts to say these things to her face. Ezra was sad to see Josephine go: he had loved her hostile, fertile mouth, her will, her insolent deceit. When he told her of his decision, she said, "Okay, baby. I am weady to be around my own people, too. This part wasn't much better than model-showing swimsuits, but at least the pay was good. Promise you'll spend money on the kid, so he won't have the same ficking hard time as me." Then she cursed him in fluent Ukrainian, a language he could not even identify. "So," Clarissa said, "once the divorce went through, she pretty much disappeared."

"All right," Booker said. They were driving through the Missouri River's floodplain, her eyes intently focused on the narrow blacktop, her lips parted and slightly swollen, as if bruised. "So what's this got to do with you?"

She had always thought her grandmother was dead. Actually, that wasn't quite true: she had considered Ezra's third wife, whom she called Nanny, to be her grandmother, though she wasn't really her father's mom. "'Legally,'" she said. "That's what they always told me when I asked. I'd say, 'If Nanny is my grandmother, doesn't she have to be Daddy's mom?' And Nanny would start blowing her nose into her napkin, and Dad would smile at me and say, 'Legally, honey, that's correct.' But even I knew that legal was different from real, and since no one ever talked about his having a real mom, I figured she was dead. Besides, I didn't like Nanny that much: all she cared about was collecting stamps.

"But my real grandmother wasn't dead at all, and she hadn't even gone away, which was the other thing Daddy always said. I was thirteen. I remember it because Mother had been dead a year by then. I never liked her, either, because for as long as I could remember, she'd been sick. It isn't a nice thing to say about your mother, but it's true: all the time growing up, whenever my father didn't want me to play outside, or sleep over at a friend's house, or go to the skating rink, he always said I couldn't because my mother was sick. Now I know he'd think up any old reason, but then I thought it was true. She had cancer of the ovaries. It must've been a terrible thing to have everything cut out of her like she did, but I never thought of that. I just thought she spoiled things for me and Dad. And I knew he secretly felt that way, too—even if he pretended different in front of her. So maybe that's why all this stuff about Josephine dying is connected in my head because by thirteen I was starting to regret that I'd wished my mom was dead. I *had* wished she was dead. She'd never taken care of me, she'd always been sick or having treatments, and she'd had to wear this really ugly wig. And whenever I said something about her being dead to Father, he would hug me and say, 'But don't you love your dad?'"

Her expression was sardonic; her eyes lightless, dead. "When I turned thirteen," she said, "I realized there were things my mother and I should've discussed. Things women ought to talk about without

154

involving men. So I missed her. Or maybe not specifically her, but the idea of having a mom. And that was when the man took me to see Josephine."

It had been summer. She was playing alongside the front hedge. The baby-sitter had gone inside, and she remembered a sudden stillness, the prickling sensation of being observed, and she looked up into the branches of the elm trees overhead just as the wind moved through them restlessly. When she looked down again, a man stood beside the hedge. "I knew, technically, that he was the kind of man who should make me afraid," Clarissa said. "He was the kind of man you saw at the market stands downtown selling live chickens or iced squid. He wore white socks with his suit—I could see them under the hedge. 'Your grandmother is dying,' he says. 'I'd like you to see her, but you must come right away.' I could see he wasn't going to *make* me do anything, and so I thought about it and decided to go." They drove downtown in a station wagon with fake wood panels; the man didn't speak. "I never found him again," Clarissa said. "I went back a few years later to look, but he never told me his name. I suppose they were lovers, or she may even have been his wife. It's funny. I mean, it's funny that he chose to come get me, because it certainly wasn't her idea. I always wondered what he was trying to say."

The car had stopped in Columbus Park, northeast of downtown, where the Italians and other immigrants lived. "It looked like Brooklyn," Clarissa said. "Of course, I didn't know it looked like Brooklyn then, only when I remember it: little tenement buildings, door stoops, hills, iron railings painted black. We parked behind this one building and went up a fire escape to a door. There were only two rooms inside: the kitchen and the front room, where she was sitting. I remember very clearly that she was sitting, because I didn't see a bed. It must've folded down from the wall or something like that. She was wearing a green oxygen mask. She'd been a smoker all her life, I guess, and there were other people in there, and they all turned to look at me. It felt awkward, because I had on cutoff shorts and tennis

155

shoes and everyone else was wearing brown or black. The man sort of nudged me forward and said, 'She is here.' The woman took off her mask to look at me, and I could tell right away we were related, had the same blood: it was something I could just feel. She kind of chuckled and looked back out the window and then she said something in this raspy voice. '*Ça ne fait rien,*' she said."

"What's it mean?" Booker asked.

"Basically, 'That doesn't mean shit.'"

Clarissa had pulled the car into a dirt lot beside an open, shingle-roofed loggia, once a fruit stand or some other public place, now fallen into disuse. They walked from it to the riverbank. All about them were fields, both across the river and to their right and left, and the air held the compressed stillness of their vast expanse. The river itself seemed a final variation of the fields: ice cakes littered its surface, themselves filthy, strewn with dust and twigs, and as the river folded steadily inward on itself, sucking, rubbing, it possessed a bestial quality, sphinxlike yet alive.

"So," Booker said. "Your father quit seeing his mother for being a Jew."

"Not even because of that," Clarissa said. "There was a man in her room with a funny purple hat—I *thought* he was a rabbi because he didn't look like any pastor I'd ever seen. Years later, I saw someone dressed just like him on TV. He was a Russian Orthodox priest. My grandmother wasn't Jewish at all." She sat silently, musing on the river's flow. "That's when I started thinking maybe she'd been the one to escape."

"Escape *what*?" His tone was incredulous.

"Not telling the truth," Clarissa said. "My grandfather was a mean man. He was also a crook, a womanizer, and lost a ton of dough. My grandmother was a Ukrainian swimsuit model who died abandoned by her son in a rented room. Why? Don't ask Judge Thornton Sayers; he doesn't discuss dirty things like that, except when they involve people he's sending to jail. 'Judge Thornton Sayers is the most reputable man in the city': do you know how many women have said that to me? Women who were old enough to know exactly who his mother was. But bring *that* subject up, and they just say, 'Isn't it astonishing, given the circumstances, what he's achieved?'"

A riprap dike extended into the river from the lot. They were sitting among the stones on its tip, and for the first time he studied her openly, his eyes taking in the linen border of her cheek. "The truth is," Clarissa said, "my father's been pulling me out of schools my whole life. He always says the friends I meet are cheap, or from bad families, and that any men I like are just using me. The truth is, he fucking *shot* his dog yesterday because I went hunting with Bert Gauss over the weekend: maybe dog-shooting won't get you thrown out of the Colonial Club, but it's still a cruel, cruel thing to do."

It was dusk. Seagulls wheeled above the river, and in the half-light her face, above her father's hunting jacket, was a pale blur. He could see, out of the corner of his eye, her hands composed in a small knot, as if holding dice.

"Isn't that why you came to find Mercury?" she asked. "To make him tell the truth?"

"I just want money," Booker said.

"My mother had money," Clarissa said. "It didn't do her much good."

"Did I ever tell you about my lawyer?" His voice was not harsh, merely chiding, in the way men speak to women about sports. "He was a free lawyer, worked for the state, and he said flat out that I was going to jail if he took my case. But if I could pay for somebody better, I could just walk away. Money," he continued stubbornly, "is liquid. It lets you float past the shit."

"I've got money," Clarissa said.

"No, you don't," Booker said. "You've got a rich dad."

"I guess you're right about that." The sun had set by then, and her figure was a faint outline against the river's glowing ice. He could almost hear her thinking. "Maybe we could help each other out," she said.

"I doubt it," he said. They picked their way across the riprap to the car. Booker rubbed a piece of driftwood in his hands. "There was something else I meant to ask you," he said over the Stingray's roof. "About your father: How come he never got married again?"

"He always said"—Clarissa's voice was trancelike, vain—"that he just wanted to spend time with me."

11

HE TOLD HIMSELF that he didn't want to make love to Clarissa Sayers, and the more he told himself this, the more he thought of nothing else. The primary experiences in his life had been male. He might discuss combines, hunting, field hands, or the essentially masculine technicalities of court, but his experience in *courting* was nil. In high school, the goodwill of his classmates had rested on the premise that he wouldn't even *try* to bed their women, and so he'd never been on a date, exchanged a crush note, or slept with a woman for free. He told himself he didn't want to make love to Clarissa Sayers because he believed the opportunity didn't exist, and he remained in this state of agonizing constipation until early January. The duck fields were frozen solid by then, all hunting had been suspended, and she showed up with Stan Granger and three rented pairs of figure skates.

"You're joking," Booker said.

"Hey, buddy," Stan answered, his Adam's apple jogging beneath the collar of his coat. "Don't mess with tradition—me and Clarissa do this every year."

Booker had never skated in his life. Clarissa coached him, gliding backward with a sinuous and, from his point of view, entirely magical weaving of her hips and feet, while he followed in lock-jointed agony, his arms outstretched like Frankenstein's. It became a game. When

Booker fell, he pulled her down with him, and the two of them slid shrieking across the ice, their bodies intertwined and Clarissa's breath hot against his cheek. It was the first time he'd touched her, and he could sense—like any schoolboy—an excitement in her strivings, an invitation to the chase. They separated from Stan and skated through a grove of flooded timber, the trunks rising gauntly from the ice, mist-coated, and the wind tumbling leaves between the tree rows as if down some hallway in a dream. He could have kissed her then, her lips chapped and upward-turning, her cheeks burned by the wind, but his confidence failed, and instead he made a joke about his "busted ass." By the time Stan caught up to them, the moment had passed, and he skated back to the cabin with the rind of his own cowardice gnawing at his gut. Then it was dusk again, and time for her to leave.

Booker saw Stan off (Stan winking suggestively) and then returned to the mudroom, where Clarissa was packing up her skates. "So," he said. "You're going back."

"I have to at some point."

"You've got classes, probably."

"Thank God, no," Clarissa said. "They haven't started yet."

"Ah," Booker said. He waited, fists clenched in his pockets, while she gathered up her things. She was aware of his silence and moved with the exaggerated precision that women adopt when pretending that someone who irritates them isn't really there, marching between the A-frame and the mudroom, putting out lights. She looped her skates over her arm, waited for Booker to open the door, and when she reached to open it herself, he grabbed her above the bicep, where the bone pressed against her skin. He said nothing, his flexed arm trembling, his expression grave. Then he released her with a flick of his wrist.

She didn't flinch, but instead stood facing him. With the same arm he'd grabbed, she swept her bangs out of her face. "For Chris-sakes, Booker," she said with a half smile. "Why don't you try *inviting* me to stay?"

His anger was preemptive, fueled by the conviction that she would, somehow, reject him in the end. He heated three cans of Hy-Power Chili, this being the only food the members kept in stock (the cans towered eight high behind the sink, crammed the cupboards, and, for some unfathomable reason, lined the shelves of the freezer, too: he'd shown them to her, saying, "You want to stay for dinner? Fine—this is all I got to eat"), while Clarissa unlocked the liquor cabinet and poured drinks. They sat at the same wax-spattered table where he'd first seen her through the glass. After his second bourbon and soda, Booker set down his spoon and stared at her as she ate and then lit a cigarette, composing her gestures with the same exaggerated precision, as if she couldn't care less what he did. When she'd finished, he leaned across his plate until she met his gaze. "What would your father think?" he asked.

"About what?" Clarissa said.

Booker smiled aggressively. "About what?" he said. "Well, how about your having dinner with me, that's about what. See, I sort of remember him sitting in this very same chair, listening to those guys talk about Gettysburg Jackson and midnight basketball—all those funny stories about us amusing, ignorant blacks."

"My father would never tell a story like that."

"So you don't mind," Booker said, pointing to the darkened window, "that he's standing out there where I was, right now—"

Clarissa whirled suddenly toward the window, and he saw for one brief moment her stricken expression captured in the glass.

"See what I mean?" he asked.

But he felt embarrassed by his effect. Shaken, Clarissa smoked in silence, her face blank behind the haze of her cigarette. Her legs were crossed, and a small stretch of calf showed between her sock and jeans. "I'm sorry," he said, touching this with his fingertips. "That wasn't helping anything." She nodded without looking at him. He was certain it was hopeless then and embraced his failure with fierce vindication, thinking, *See? See? That's what would have happened anyway*, even as she stubbed her butt out and, leaning forward, placed her fingers gently on his chin.

"I'm willing to try this," she said. "Okay? Otherwise I wouldn't have stayed. But you have to promise you'll act decent—won't you?" She swallowed dryly. "Won't you please, please promise me that?"

He nodded in acceptance of that condition, and to his astonishment, her fingers slipped inside his mouth, tasting bitterly of cigarettes.

They made love in the loft, with Clarissa sitting atop him in Mercury's broken, narrow bed. She possessed an alluring blindness for the usual departments of human taboo and saw nothing odd in interrupting the proceedings to examine him, the blunt, unwhitened arcs of her fingers (she chewed her nails avidly) testing the weight of his prick, dropping it noisily against his belly, encircling it, tracing its hood and bevels. Once he woke from the far reaches of oblivion and found her squinting down it as if it were a telescope. He could not stand this for too long: once inside her he begged, in a language neither understood, that she grant him his release. With a half smile she reached behind herself and touched his balls with such fondness that tears streamed down his face.

"They feel like walnuts," she informed him afterward. "And they get all tight before you come."

She left that night, and he rose the next morning with a fever and a hallucinatory premonition of regret. His bones felt radioactive, and when he hobbled to his tiny unfinished toilet, the fierce stream of urine that he jetted among the ice chunks was hot as boiling tea. Later his flesh seemed to melt away. His shins ached with the drafts that seeped from the window across the room, and when he tucked his hands between his knees for warmth, they were cold as oyster shells.

In moments of clarity, he understood that his sickness was logically attributable to skating in wet clothes in near-zero temperatures, drinking booze, and then lying naked in saunalike heat (Mercury's

162

bunk was beside the chimney), but mostly he chose to blame it on Clarissa Sayers. She embodied everything that his life's experience and his conscious, rational mind told him to distrust. She was involved with the law (through her father), she was rich (like Mercury), and she wanted to be his friend (like Batson). His regret centered on her because, though he wouldn't have used the word himself, he was a romantic at heart. Wearing his grandfather's jumpsuit had not changed this, nor had the story of Hammonds's death, the absurdities of the courts, his betrayal by a Texan, or the persistent cynicism of the evening news. The truth was that—whether by genetic defect or a bolt of lightning hurled down from the stars—he was as doggedly and humorlessly romantic as the palest Frenchman who ever wrote a villanelle, as the most intrepid Englishman to swim the Hellespont on a bet, and in the face of this unalterable fact, the scam-or-be-scammed philosophy of prison (an attitude he still considered realistic, and thus *wanted* to believe) deflated like a paper bag.

He knew that he was capable of trusting Clarissa for the stupid and admittedly naive reason that she had taken him into her bed: that was why he blamed her for his sickness, and why he lay up in Stan Granger's trailer for a week.

When he returned, he discovered that she had been to the cabin at least twice, judging from the two Styrofoam coffee cups dumped in the oil drum outside, and had slipped a note under the door. A draft had blown the note into the backroom, so he didn't find it until his second day back. They'd already seen each other by then: she arrived with her father (never a good sign), and he was forced to wait shiftlessly for their skiff to return, contriving to hang around the boat shed as if by accident, and further contriving to act as if he didn't want to talk to her when, in fact, he did. Finally the judge went inside to polish his guns, and Clarissa sat alone on her usual stool, cleaning two Canadian geese. Their wings were wide as a man's outstretched arms, necks black as india ink, and Booker, pretending he needed a chain saw from the shed, found her with clumps of pearly feathers about her boots.

"So," he said, "did I miss anything while I was away?"

"I wish I could tell you," Clarissa said, smiling innocently, "but we only just came down. Was it a vacation?"

Booker shrugged. "Personal business," he said. "You know how it is."

"Definitely," Clarissa said.

He left the boat shed carrying a chain saw that he didn't need, and Clarissa merely widened her eyes in cheerful farewell as he passed, then continued demurely plucking her geese. Her stubbornness and her blatant lying (regardless of his own blatant lying) drove him to distraction, and he swore for the third time that he'd never speak to her again. That night he found the rat-gnawed note beneath his kitchen table, after an unbidden vision of Clarissa Sayers's translucent thighs caused him to spill a plateful of peas. The note was written on a paper napkin stenciled with the same convenience-store logo as the coffee cups, and both the salutation and the signature had been chewed away, leaving only the body of the text: *I won't be embarrassed about you if you won't be embarrassed about me. This means every-thing*—this word so heavily underscored that the paper had torn— *(and I've heard what happens to nice young men in jail). Ha, ha. That's only a joke, but sometimes I start thinking you're a joke when you disappear like this.*

He searched behind the crates, but nowhere could he find the scrap of paper that would tell him whether she had signed the note *sincerely, regards,* or *love.*

He convinced Stan to give him Judge Sayers's address (as a former caretaker, he had records of these things) and drive him into Waterloo, where he mailed her a postcard of Jesse James: *The shooting's been good in the country,* he wrote, and signed it simply with his initials. At the last moment he thought of her father and stuffed the card in an envelope, folded in half.

She showed up before the card had had time to arrive. This small and seemingly insignificant fact was, to him, as thrilling as the most

164

purple declaration of love, and he was waiting beside the A-frame when she pulled up, eager to embrace his fate. She rolled the window down amid swirls of white dust and said, "I just came to get this sweater I left."

"I got your note," he said.

"What note?"

"I hadn't gotten it when you were down here last," he explained, patiently prying her reluctant fingers from the wheel. "So I apologize for acting like an ass."

"I just want my sweater," Clarissa said irritably.

"I hid it," Booker said.

Her sexuality frightened him in many ways. Sometimes they would bathe in the members' tub, and as she watched him undress, her lean breasts just visible beneath the water and a faint line of perspiration shining on her upper lip, her eyes would have a strange, amoral glitter: a look not of wantonness, nor of opposition, but of pure, physical acquisitiveness, such as a child might give a rabbit or a sheet of foil. He'd seen this expression once before, on the face of the felon named Trapper whom he'd beaten up in jail. Its distance was so disconcerting that when he caught her observing him this way, in the middle of some acrobatic move, he'd stop and say, "This isn't a science experiment, Clarissa. We're supposed to be making love."

They would go on to make love in forgotten parks, hotel rooms, and coat closets, and (tangled in the Stingray's backseat) in the abandoned lots of war memorials all over Kansas City, but none of these places compared to the efferent pleasures of Mercury Chapman's bed. The psychological reasons for this were at once so obvious and so occult that they chose not to discuss them; the physical reasons were less obscene. The tin chimney of the fireplace (which they always stoked before making love) passed a yard from Mercury's bunk, and its corrugated cylinder gave off a dry and purging heat. Cramped in the narrow bed frame—"It's like a coffin," Clarissa once said, to

165

which Booker calmly responded, "A coffin doesn't have this kind of view"—they sweated like pilgrims in a Turkish bath, pores distended, bodies anointed from the follicles of their scalps to the soles of their feet with the glossy effluvia of their own flesh. Afterward they often trooped naked down the narrow stairs and sat beside the A-frame's floor-to-ceiling window to cool. Clarissa's skin would be a splotchy, lobster-colored red, particularly around her collarbones, while Booker's looked like leached tea. They sat in straight-backed wooden chairs so only their forearms touched, and gazed out across the hunting fields at dusk, feeling little need to communicate other than to listen to the other breathe. In late January the sky was filled with geese—snows, blues, Canadians—that appeared in squadrons against the horizon and veered like Mardi Gras parades overhead, and as they sat, feeling their skin prickle as it dried, they would begin to change color like negatives in a chemical bath, Clarissa's skin clearing to a marbled, blue-veined white while Booker's pared chest and slightly pouched stomach were burnished by the ocher sunset to a rich cherrywood.

Clarissa's explicit form of innocence made a shambles of taboos social as well as sexual: she said things about race that coming from other mouths, in other circumstances, would have driven him frantic with rage. Once, in the Waterloo grocery, she asked him what it felt like being black. Her tone and phrasing made it sound like she was asking how it felt to be a lion or an orangutan—a member of some species entirely different from her own—and he answered with irritation, "My guess is it feels the same as anything else."

"You're just saying that."

"Maybe you were expecting something *scientific*," he said, "like how we've got a natural sense of rhythm and our bodies don't float like whites.'"

"I didn't mean physically," she said. They were standing in the produce aisle, the dusty stacks of Cheerios and shelves of overalls entirely empty, hushed, so that the owner (posted at the store's single register) couldn't help but overhear. "I mean how people act around

166

you. Like that old geezer up front: when you walked in, I thought he was going to have a stroke."

"He wasn't staring at me," Booker said. "He was staring at *us*."

"Whatever he was doing," Clarissa continued loudly, "he better quit if he wants us to buy anything in this crummy place."

The owner rang up their purchases, bagged them, and returned the change without once looking Clarissa in the face. When they got back to the car, she asked him curiously, "So who was it said that, about black people not being able to float?"

"Jimmy the Greek," Booker said.

She took to bringing him articles from newspapers and magazines that discussed the subject of race, particularly interracial affairs. He used the *Kansas City Star* for toilet paper (always in short supply), but the magazines—copies of *The New Yorker*, *Fortune*, and *Newsweek* that still bore the white subscription tape printed with her father's name—interested him primarily for their financial news. He was surprised to discover that the economy of his country was engaged in a historic boom, a suspicion confirmed by the first copy of the *Wall Street Journal* that he'd ever seen. She had underlined an article about a black professor who'd quit his position at Harvard Law School because the university wouldn't hire female blacks. The grievance sounded esoteric to Booker, whose feelings about race had a more practical bent—"You're an idiot," he told the professor's ink-drawn face as it grinned at him across a bowl of chili—but a story in the "Marketplace" section broke over him like a wave. "It says here," he told Clarissa, tapping the paper with his nail, "that this guy made a million dollars last year, and he doesn't even have a job."

"What's he do?" Clarissa asked.

"He invests," Booker said. "He's *twenty-five*."

"I've got some stocks," Clarissa said. "I mean, I don't have them now, but I get them when my father dies."

Booker opened to the stock quotations. The unbroken columns of fractions and incomprehensible abbreviations—contrasted with

167

the A-frame's horsehair couch, its gas lamps and withered copies of *Field & Stream*—seemed infused with the strange and cabalistic power of the new.

Trying not to sound too eager, he asked her, "Do you know their names?"

On the subject of his own financial future, Booker felt optimistic. The job in Kansas City was a go, and Mercury had proved tractable in other ways: first agreeing to give him a salary as caretaker and then, under subtle, steady pressure, consenting to raise it from $150 to $300 a month. Clarissa provided him with the companionship he'd so often lacked, and since they both despised the idea of marriage, this came without practical strings. So in early February, as the goose season ended and the club prepared to close, he felt a sense of forward progress and began to dream, as was his habit, of even better things.

One day Stan brought his water truck by, and together Booker and Mercury set about filling the club's tank. Stan had gone down to the boat shed, and they stood alone, the hose—the thick, fireman's variety, sheathed with woven cloth—shuddering between their overlapped hands. "How about sending me to college?" Booker asked.

Mercury's hands slipped, and the hose exploded, uncoiling through the air.

"College?" he shouted through the spray. "Well, I'll be Jesus H. Christ. Isn't there anything you're ashamed to ask?"

They chased the hose down, hauled it back to the tank's upended pipe, and held it there, panting. "It'd probably be tax-deductible," Booker said.

An enormous drop of water hung dewlike from the old man's nose.

"I talked to Judge Sayers about that," he added.

"Just out of curiosity," Mercury said, "which college would this be?"

"Vassar."

Mercury sat down in a puddle to laugh. His jacket and pants were soaked, along with the handkerchief around his neck. He wrung this out and mopped his face, giggling tearfully. "Vassar," he cried. "Whoopee!"

"I'd study finance," Booker said. "Isn't that what you did to get rich?"

"You think that's what I did?" Mercury said, rising and tying his kerchief back around his neck. "Went off to college and presto, I was rich?"

"That's what all you people did."

"That's funny," Mercury said, "because I went to a community college on Locust Street, downtown. They had exactly three rooms, which they rented from Mercantile Insurance. The teachers were crooks." His face darkened, crossed by a shadow of lost time. Then he smiled. "Want to hear our fight song?" he asked.

Booker had no interest in their fight song, but Mercury sang it anyway:

> Hocus, pocus, dom-inocus
> We're the boys from Eleventh and Locust
> We don't smoke and we don't chew
> And we don't go with the girls that do!

"Me and Eddie Coole went there together," he said when he'd finished. "I got two years in before they sent me overseas. Do you know how much money I had when I came home from the war?"

"No," Booker said.

"I had five hundred dollars in back pay."

The water tank overflowed, and Mercury strode to the truck, shut the pump off, and came back. He looked at Booker reflectively, his head tilted to one side. "I wasn't all that much older than you," he said.

12

IN JUNE she invited him to hear her father speak. It was a Chamber of Commerce banquet, celebrating plans for a Negro Leagues baseball museum. Booker had no interest in baseball, Negro or otherwise, and suggested they break the news of their affair to her father more discreetly. "Trust me," she told him. "He'll appreciate your being there."

They arrived late. The judge had already started his speech, but Clarissa ignored Booker's suggestion that they sit in back and instead led him down the center aisle, her expression feverishly pleasant as they skirted tablefuls of the city's black elite—drugstore owners, physicians, restaurateurs, car dealers, the presidents of citizens' groups—seated in uncomfortable proximity to the Roman profiles and tufted eyebrows of the white bankers whose loans predicated the existence of their drugstores, practices, restaurants, dealerships, and groups. There were fifteen preachers there, along with a portion of the mayor's staff, which, being composed largely of young, unmarried women (the mayor was strongly committed to equality), bore an unintended resemblance to a choir waiting in the wings. The mayor himself, also a preacher, sat on the dais, and Clarissa waved to him. It was her best wave, as forward and unnerving as a mimed kiss, and the mayor plucked the judge's elbow to get him to look up. The judge shrugged him away, and the mayor, smiling, conscious of his audi-

170

ence, whispered in his ear. It became comic then, the judge reading mechanically, willfully, his knuckles whitening on the lectern, and the mayor raising his eyebrows for the crowd; only when Clarissa said "Hi, Daddy" did the judge consent to lift his gaze.

He wore what should have been a smile. But his lips were laminated into a rictal grin, and his face, framed in the camera lights, resembled the masks of demons that children buy for Halloween. The crowd went silent, and Booker felt a cold singing in his chest as the judge nodded to his daughter and read the remainder of his note cards ("This museum stands as a reminder of a time when men were judged not by their ability but by the color of their skin") through bared and gleaming teeth.

When the other speeches were over, Clarissa pushed her way to the dais and kissed her father on the cheek. "The speech was *primo*, Daddy," she said. "Booker and I especially liked the part about ability—you remember Booker, of course."

The judge nodded, pressing a napkin to his lips.

"He just moved here," Clarissa added.

"Clarissa has so many interesting friends," the judge said. "And now you're one of them, aren't you?" He studied Booker, the mute focus of his gaze extending until Booker inwardly writhed. "Yes," he said. "I see you are."

After that, Booker left. He waited for Clarissa in the hotel parking lot, watching her approach, still feverish, still excited, walking on the balls of her sandaled feet, as she did whenever she was in a good mood. "There was something wrong about that," he said.

"Well, I certainly felt terrible about being late," she said.

"Didn't you see his face?" Booker said. He had returned to the driver's side and sat examining the leather bindings of the steering wheel. "There's a difference between just knowing your father doesn't like something and rubbing his nose in it that way."

He looked at her, hoping for some tacit sign of agreement.

"If my father has a problem with our relationship," Clarissa said, flipping down the visor and pursing her lips, "then he shouldn't be making speeches like that."

He was in trouble then. He hadn't realized how much the hunt club reminded him of his own ancestral turf, or Mercury Chapman (this being the thought he resisted most strongly) of the grandfather who so detested him. Rather than bringing him closer to Mercury, his move to the city had the opposite effect. He lived in a cheap second-floor studio on Euclid Street, three blocks from the All Souls Unitarian Baptist Church, where Mercury had found him work. The job had no union and no prospects for advancement, and its location, deep within the city's black east side, seemed designed to keep Booker safely buried, in his place. More and more he depended on Clarissa for friendship and escape.

He led essentially a double life, working ten hours in the blazing sun, replacing gutters, framing porches, only to rush home and don one of the suits she had bought him so he could attend whatever function she had scheduled for that night. Together they crashed the city's most formal, straight-backed events: opera galas at the Bristol and political fund-raisers amid the tile floors and stained glass windows of the old Savoy. They went to art openings, Junior League picnics, concerts, and a birthday party for the daughter of a trucking magnate that featured two rented zebras and a giraffe. Clarissa was frank about the nature of their affair, despite the fact that at nearly every party they attended, Booker was the only black. She held his hand, kissed him, and used the pronoun *we*, but at the same time her explanations of who Booker was and what he actually did were outrageously fake. To doctors she introduced him as a broker, and to brokers she introduced him as "the first black recipient of the Hal Morris Scholarship at Johns Hopkins" (Hal Morris being the name of Booker's first-grade gym teacher, whom he'd happened to be telling a story about as they walked in). Of course, there were times when a doctor accidentally got mixed in with the brokers and sidled up to

Booker with a suspicious air, saying, "I know a thoracic man up at Hopkins, name of John Saunders. Ever heard of him?" Then Booker would have to guess whether John Saunders was real or whether the question was an attempt to trick him by getting him to claim acquaintance with a doctor who did not in fact exist.

In the hardest cases, he would take his questioners aside and explain, with winning honesty, that Clarissa's introductions were a terribly embarrassing joke. Then he'd offer an equally bogus, but consistent, version of himself, saying he was a graduate of Howard University, working in construction to earn some money before moving on to law school.

After her father's speech, Clarissa began to change. She developed an odd obsession with seeing her father—or, more important, it seemed to Booker (though she denied it), with her father's seeing *them*. Late in the tawdry, final hours of a party, when it had become clear that her father wouldn't show, she would grow aggressively, almost embarrassingly amorous and (particularly on nights when she had had too much to drink) would make sexual proposals that Booker hadn't heard of even in jail. If he rejected her, she flew into a rage. She accused him of ridiculous infidelities, of wanting another woman in her place, his murmured imprecations drifting outward from some private balcony or corner parlor while her voice rose above them, shrill, unreasonable, almost deranged: "I don't FEEL LIKE being quiet, Booker. Why should I care what these stupid people have to say?"

"Why do I get yelled at," he'd counter, "just because your father isn't here?"

"If you have problems with my father, I'm sorry," she would say, her eyes meeting his with a clear, untroubled openness that Booker had learned to fear. "But the real problem in this relationship involves your feelings about me—not him."

On other occasions she would debase herself in front of him, taking the blame for offenses that were purely imaginary and then offering—neck uplifted and back arched in poses stolen from cheap pornography—to make it up to him in some way. Often these discussions would continue from parties into bars, and from bars into the backseat of her car. Some mornings he awoke, still drunk, with the sense that some vague figure had been chasing him in a dream. Clarissa would be gone by then, and the ceiling of his apartment, lit by the blue tongue of a secondhand TV, seemed the very color of defeat.

Also troubling was her desire to make love at her father's house. He went there only twice, both times with a sense of impending dread. The house was Georgian, its lawn bisected perfectly by a weeded redbrick path, and the judge's presence seemed to fill its rooms as tonelessly as the scent of central air. It was as though he'd tried to erase the human signature of the place: the furniture, lampshades, pictures, bathrooms, even wastebaskets were all arranged with the calculated symmetry of a museum—or a crypt. Photos of Clarissa lined the stairwell, each in the same size frame. On his first visit, as an experiment, Booker switched two of them. When he came back a week later, they'd been returned to their original places. It was the presence of her father that, in the feverish and often mechanical disorder of their lovemaking, Clarissa intended to combat. She upset ashtrays, candlesticks, ice buckets; she threw sofa cushions on the floor. In the pallor of Judge Sayers's living room, its curtains drawn against the brilliance of July, Booker stood above her blindly writhing body like a bystander. Their copulating shadows loomed against the white plaster walls, forms that appeared to him not as human, but as monstrous and depraved.

In mid-August he escorted her to the annual Summer Symphony of Strings, a benefit for the Philharmonic League. The event was hosted by Cecelia Lofton, who lived in what once had been—and what Mission Hills residents still referred to as—the Sayers House. It was one of those rare evenings when the day's heat mysteriously disappears

174

and everyone speaks softly, as if afraid it will come back. "Oh, it's *you*," said Sally Lofton-Idlewidth, daughter of the hostess. "How very nice to see . . . *you*."

"Yeah?" Clarissa said, popping her gum. "Well, that's good, 'cause Booker and I don't have a ticket, but I'm pretty sure my father gives money to this thing. Is he here?"

"Your father," Mrs. Lofton-Idlewidth said, flushing and pretending to search her box of name tags. "There're so many people around, I'm afraid I can't—"

"Judge Sayers." Clarissa was on tiptoe, searching the crowd.

"Oh, *Thornton*," Mrs. Lofton-Idlewidth said, hands clasped and mouth puckered into a small button of good cheer. "Thornton; well, I have his name tag right here, and that would make you"—she thumbed discreetly a small book—"Clarissa. How very nice. And your friend should have a name tag, too. Your name is Bill?"

"Booker Short." Mrs. Lofton-Idlewidth's hand, when Booker shook it, had the chill of lunch meat. "Pleased to meet you," he said.

"He's a bond trader in Boca Raton," Clarissa informed their hostess, carelessly, as she picked up her father's tag. "So I guess this means he isn't here."

"Who?"

"*Thornton*," Clarissa said.

"Oh," said Mrs. Lofton-Idlewidth, "I'm sure he'll show up in a bit."

It was the largest house he'd ever seen. An immense mortar and pestle had been carved into the pediment above the door, the windows framed by sandstone arches, fish joints, and stained glass. They briefly inspected the pipe organ that Ezra has installed inside the foyer—"My family," Clarissa said, wrinkling her nose at its stained and useless ivories, "what a bunch of rubes"—and then adjourned to the back terrace, around the pool. Clarissa stepped away to see some friends, and Booker was watching her, speculating on the milling crowd, when a voice spoke amiably behind his back.

"I wonder if they did it here?"

Turning, he saw Bert Gauss. They'd met twice before: Gauss was of medium height, dark, with the heavy, cherubic air of a bachelor, but on this night an alcoholic pallor glowed beneath his tan, and he wobbled, a backward cigarette between his lips.

"Who's 'they'?" Booker asked.

"Clarissa and her daddy," Gauss said. He spoke conversationally, squinting at the incoherent form of the Sayers House, now awash in prowler lights. "For old times' sake, stuff like that. Used to worry about that all the time myself. Then I figured somebody better tell *you* about it—now that we've changed horses, so to speak."

"Tell me *what* about Clarissa and her father?" Booker said.

"Well, on a basic level," Gauss said, holding a brass-plated lighter to the filter of his cigarette, "tell you them two had a little affair."

"You're lying."

Gauss dragged and exhaled nothing.

"Who is, now?" he said.

The lawyer seamlessly nodded at other guests along the pool, smiling, as if their discussion had involved nothing more unpleasant than the economy, and Booker did the same, only with a different expression on his face. Clarissa was laughing near the bar, and when she saw him, she froze. Her hand fluttered to her throat. He turned to Gauss, saying, "Do you mean still? Do you mean they do it—" but the lawyer had disappeared.

Looking down, Booker saw his unsmoked cigarette floating in the pool.

He left the party on foot and didn't see her for three months. This separation was different from the earlier ones because during the earlier ones he had actually believed that he might leave. Now he watched himself rise in the mornings in his apartment, strap on the carpenter's belt he had purchased, and walk through the walnut-scented streets to the All Souls Church, where a pickup would be waiting to

176

drive him to whatever house he was to repair, understanding for the first time what Isaac Bentham must have known all along: that disgust could become so personal that a man could not leave it and still exist.

In early September he stood at a gas-station pay phone (his apartment didn't have a phone) and gave Mercury a call. "Booker," the old man shouted, in a voice that sounded surprisingly alert. "Goddammit, kid, I was starting to think you'd fallen off the earth."

"You still need a caretaker?" Booker asked.

There was a pause. Then, with a different kind of brightness, Mercury said, "I thought we'd already found you a new job."

"Yeah?" Booker said. "Well, they don't fix up poor folks' houses in the winter. Besides, you and me aren't finished yet."

Mercury was clearly unimpressed.

"I'll ask the members," he said. "The decision's up to them."

Two weeks later Stan came by in his pickup, his eyes goggling behind the dash as a cluster of young black figures blocked their passage on a narrow street. Booker opened the window and shouted, "Hey, Toby, tell these folks to let us by!" and as the crowd parted and the truck eased among their staring, twilit figures, he watched Stan's ashen face. "What's bugging?" he asked, chuckling. "Don't you feel comfortable about where I live?"

Eddie Coole had died in June. The members made their same ritual appearance on opening day, the Buicks and Oldsmobiles gathering in the gravel lot, the men emerging to stare at the pitched gray sky with cries of pleasure and relief, and yet it seemed to Booker—who now stood among them, cradling a paper cup of whiskey in his hand—that something pivotal had changed. A moment of silence marked the death. Mercury scuttled into the kitchen to hide his face, and Booker, head bowed, felt a hot jet of shame. The old man had mourned his friend all summer, he realized, and yet had never breathed a word of it to him.

177

On a more positive note, at least from the membership's position, Judge Sayers also wasn't there. "He quit," Remy Westbrook chortled, peeing luxuriantly in the grass. "He said it was him or you."

Booker considered this, astonished.

"Hell, don't worry 'bout it none," Remy said, waving his hand. "If I'd've known that little prick wouldn't hunt with black folks, I would've hired one years ago."

She returned on Thanksgiving Day. He and Stan were playing gin rummy in the A-frame when they heard her car pull up. They went to the mudroom door, and seeing the newly ruined profile of the Stingray, its front quarter panel crumpled, its headlight dangling like a gouged eye, Stan picked up his hat up and left without a word. When she exited the car and stepped toward him, he saw that she had aged. The gloss had left her cheeks, and as she brushed by him, he noticed that her lips were framed by oily seams. An accordion-shaped case rode against her hip. Opening it, she arranged sheaves of colored papers on the table, fumbling and apparently ashamed. He watched her with the remorse of a first-time hunter who, having believed his prey immortal, is shocked to find that it feels pain.

"I moved out," she said wearily.

"All right," Booker said.

"I figured that's what you wanted."

Booker didn't say anything to this.

"I figured you wouldn't leave like that unless Bert Gauss told you something, and if he was going to tell you something, I figured that's what it would be—" Her voice sped up hysterically, on the verge of becoming unhinged, and she calmed herself by force of will. She gave a brief smile, tried to speak, then sat quietly.

Booker studied a shelf of old French wine bottles that hung along the A-frame's slanted wall. "So this has been going on for a long time," he said.

"Yes," she said.

"When you first knew me."

178

She nodded.

"And when you were introducing me to all his friends, and taking me to parties, and asking me . . ." His mouth puckered. "In his house. In the same room."

"No," she said quickly. "I mean, I was trying then. I was trying—"

"To quit him by fucking a black man," Booker said.

"No," she said again.

"Yes," Booker spat. "Yes," he said. "That's what you did."

She began to cry then; he listened to this for a long while, watching the winter light refracted in the empty bottles: several had been filled during the same years that Isaac had been in France. "I moved out," she repeated. "I know you think I should've done it a long time ago, but it's not as easy as that. It's not so easy once you get started, because who else is there, then? He always promised that he'd take care of me, and that nothing would go wrong, and that I'd never have to worry about money; and then once you decide it *is* wrong, you have to decide that about everything, really everything. Who's going to take care of a person like that? Nobody, that's who." Her voice quickened again, hysterical and blank. "And who's going to pay for college, and going to the doctor, and car insurance, and clothes, and food, and all those stupid, stupid things, because I like those things, and now I've hurt him, really, really hurt him, and he won't ever—"

"If you didn't want to hurt him, why choose me?" Booker asked. Clarissa's head was bowed, and her hands hung in her lap. "Why not Gauss, someone like that?"

"If you want to hate me," Clarissa said, "that's something I accept."

"Hate you?"

Clarissa met his gaze. "I wanted to hurt him," she said. "I admit it, and it won't do any good to tell you that there were parts—parts about us, I mean—that didn't have anything to do with him. Because you wouldn't believe it even if it was true. I accept that. And I accept that you probably won't ever want to sleep with me again, or maybe even touch me, even though I miss that." Her face was ugly with tears, and hearing this, Booker shuddered inwardly. "I do miss that," she said. "And I'm glad for whatever we did, but that isn't why I came to see you. I came to make a deal."

Booker's lips curled. "To do what?" he asked.

"Make money," she said. "Isn't that how people float past the shit?"

The colored pieces of paper she had laid out on the table were dividend statements, and she spoke for thirty minutes, patiently explaining the minutiae of stock transfers, seasonal market fluctuations, and brokers' fees. "It's not a regular trust," she told him, "like when people talk about trust-fund kids."

He stared blankly.

"I don't get it now, even though I'm twenty-one," she explained. "I get it when he dies, instead. But he isn't *using* the money; he's got his own stocks and funds and stuff like that. The trust is just sitting here, and he promised it to me, so it's not like it would hurt him any if I—if we—took some out now. Rather than waiting, I mean."

Booker rubbed the last of the colored sheets between his fingers: even the paper felt lush. "There must be close to two hundred thousand dollars overall."

"How much do you need?" Clarissa asked. She tapped a pencil over a wide-rule spiral notebook, the kind used to keep attendance in school.

"What makes you think he—"

"Just take a guess," she said. "Like, I've got two more years of school left, and Vassar's tuition is eighteen grand, so I figured thirty-six plus a little cushion in case I don't get a job right away. Fifty, say." She tapped the paper, waiting. "Ten thousand. Twenty?"

Booker rolled his eyes, embarrassed by the absurdity of this game.

"How 'bout thirty, just in case?"

His fingers reached heavenward. "Why hold back?" he asked.

180

"Whatever it is," Clarissa said, bent over her figures, "it's more than you'll ever get from Mercury."

The basic outline of her plan had, in fact, been copied from his own dealings with Mercury. She explained it, again with the flat and sexless precision not of a student but—as if, in three months, her entire personality had been reversed—of a teacher describing the rational processes of math. "It's simple," she said. "We tell him that if he doesn't give us the money, I'm going to call the paper and tell the truth about him and me. See, nobody's tried that before—not my mother, not even Josephine. Oh, and I know him. He won't mind sacrificing some money, especially to keep people from thinking dirty about him."

"Why do you need me?" Booker asked.

Her eyes had a placid clarity that, given the subject matter, seemed to border on the insane. "Because he doesn't take me seriously," she said. "He'd try to call my bluff, and of course, I don't want to have a press conference. That's the last thing I need. But"—she lifted her finger—"like it or not, he'd believe it coming from you."

The similarities of the plans didn't shock Booker so much as their single, crucial difference: she asked him to blackmail Judge Sayers (a man he had no connection to, at least in terms of his past) *instead* of Mercury. It carried his idea of bargaining with truth to its final and most corrupt extreme: the truth one bargained with didn't even have to be personal, specific, but could be transferred with the anonymity of a credit-card bill. Or, as Clarissa put it, carrying her papers to the car: "What do you care if the money comes from Mercury or from my dad? They're pretty much both the same."

And yet, if he was willing to trade the truth about Isaac and Hammonds for a caretaker's job, why not trade Clarissa's truth for cash? It was, he decided, just a matter of degree, and this decision seemed to signal the end of his relationship with Mercury: that winter he became, like most white men, someone whom Booker had no reason to see.

· · ·

181

Whenever possible, he spent his off-hours with Clarissa. It was this final avatar of their relationship that people around them would most remember, particularly Stan. They seemed to have skipped over the middle regions of love, its dullness, its struggles, its arid oases of strife, and emerged immediately into the sexless, placid companionship of old age. It was as if, like old lovers, they had both realized they were short of time. They took long drives along the floodplain, stopping at junk stores and the barren placards that marked events in history, erected in forgotten fields. Eventually they were always drawn to the river itself, its speechless and ineffable bestiality. They could sit for hours at the foot of a leafless cottonwood and watch the ice cakes whirl on its snakeskin surface, their elbows touching almost insensibly through the sweaters and thick parkas they wore against the cold. They also liked to cook. Finally, with Clarissa's help, Booker prepared the feast he'd imagined for her nearly a year before, the night they'd first made love. They chose a Wednesday in late December, and Booker wrote a formal invitation on a Martin Luther King postcard and mailed it out to Stan. It read: *I have a dream about you coming to eat.*

Stan noticed that someone had colored in one of Dr. King's smiling teeth.

They shopped at the biggest supermarket in Kansas City and filled their cart according to a single rule: every purchase had to be something that one of them loved and the other hadn't tried. They bought artichokes and crawfish (Booker); kiwifruit and chevre cheese (Clarissa); and three immense and beautifully marbled rib-eye steaks that Booker personally selected. Stan arrived at six. They had spent nearly three hours in the A-frame's kitchen by then, grilling, paring, dicing, until the sink was piled with dirty dishes and not an inch of clear counter space remained. Clarissa tucked a bib beneath Stan Granger's chin, and they fed him like a king, constantly leaping up to check the oven and fussing over dishes in ways that would have irritated a less sanguine guest. At last Booker brought in the grilled steaks atop a pewter tray; they ate them at first with knives and forks, the meat sweet and soft as buttered bread, and then picked the bones up with their fingers, streaking their wineglasses with grease. Stan had bought the wine: it was, as Booker announced in perfect mimicry of Mercury, a fine example of Château *La Toor* and they placed the empty bottle among the others on the members' shelf.

But even this effort at exorcism seemed in its own way grotesque, and later that night, Booker held Clarissa's forehead as she vomited in the frozen grass. The violence of her convulsions frightened both of them, and afterward she began to cry. "Oh, I'm so, so sorry. It was such a beautiful dinner, and I tried to keep it, Booker. I really tried."

She had started to smell different. During her visits, the A-frame was haunted by the astringent odor of rotting salad greens, and Booker would hunt for a dead mouse or some forgotten bag of trash until he finally realized that the smell came from her. Once he found her in the members' toilet, staring with curiosity into the bowl. The urine there had an intense, orangish color, and the strength of its odor made him blink. "I'm spoiling," she told him simply. "If I can smell it, that means you must've noticed a long time ago."

That happened in late January; by March he'd returned to the city and was back working for the church. He'd left the hunt club without a single farewell, merely a terse note instructing that his last paycheck be forwarded to Stan. He took a taxi to her new address on Warwick Street, a bare, stucco compound with last fall's leaves piled in the corners of the empty pool, and when she opened the num- bered door, he stepped back involuntarily. The apartment behind her was foul with crumpled papers and smeared cartons of fast food, and she stood squinting like a mole in the fresh spring sunlight before she recognized him. "Oh, honey, you should've called before you came," she said. "I don't like you to see me living like this." Glossy pimples dotted her forehead and lined the seams along her nose. He asked to use her bathroom and returned to find her seated on the bare carpet, reading amid a haymow of books. She wore cat's-eye glasses fitted with the kind of beaded metal chain old women use, and tucked her chin against a linty sweater in what resembled a child's caricature of a spinster librarian.

"What the hell are you doing in here?" he said.

"Didn't I tell you?" she asked, peering nearsightedly through the black frames. "If I want to transfer back to Vassar, I've got to pass all my exams."

He had been glad that she had broken with her father, glad that she had chosen him, and yet this slow disintegration was something he felt powerless to stop. She'd been right: he could offer no substitute for her father's money, his authority, his class. He couldn't afford to give her a ring, a bracelet—anything—and it was out of frustration at this situation that he decided to give her Isaac's tags. She had liked to toy with them while, lying in bed, he told her his version of Isaac's tale, and during his first stay in the city, she'd asked for them as a present, a request he'd avoided instinctively. Now he went to a jeweler's shop and had them mounted in a small, silver-plated frame shaped like a butterfly. When she opened the satin box, she squealed with pleasure.

"The thing is," he said, embarrassed, "I mean, the thing I oughta tell you is, well—they're fake."

"What do you mean?"

"My grandfather wouldn't ever give me his tags," Booker admitted. "He didn't do stuff like that. The truth is, when I decided to come up here, I had a guy make them for me. In prison. They cost twenty packs of Carlton cigarettes."

Clarissa had already clasped the tags around her neck. "I think it's even better that you made them," she said. "They belong to you that way."

The last piece of clothing she bought him was a tux. It was late May by then. Her exams were over, but she had continued to lose weight, and when she picked him up in the ruined Stingray, he noticed for the first time since he'd known her that she'd powdered her

184

face. The base was nearly pure white, like cornstarch, and accentuated the startling pallor of her skin. She wore dark glasses, lipstick, and a black pantsuit and drove him to Jack Henry's on the Plaza, the finest men's store in town. There were stuffed pheasants on the shirt tables and real bookshelves filled with books. "Bruce," she said to the salesman, "I want a lightweight wool tuxedo for my friend. No polyester, no shawl collar—just black. French cuffs on the shirt. Put it on the Sayers charge."

He stood with amazement on the fitting stool while a bowlegged man in a rumpled tan suit scratched chalk marks on his ass. As they strode into the sunlight afterward, Clarissa lit a cigarette. "I've been thinking about that money," Booker said.

"What is it?"

"Is thirty thousand enough for me to go to school?" he asked.

Clarissa removed her cigarette from her mouth. She slid her hand behind his neck, pulled him close, and kissed him on the lips. "I wish I could tell you it was, baby," she said. "I swear there's no one in this city I'd rather tell that to. But the truth is, you can't go to college. Not until you've finished your parole." She brushed his lips with her free hand. "And even if you did finish, I can't promise they'd let you in."

She kissed him again on the street corner, and then he held her tightly in his arms, the crowd outside Jack Henry's parting politely for their embrace, and over her shoulder, he could see the people strolling toward the fountains of the Ritz-Carlton Hotel.

The plan was for Clarissa to find her father (whom, since moving out, she had neither spoken to nor seen) at the Founders Ball and pass him a note describing their demands. Booker would meet him in the parking lot afterward, carrying orders that would transfer eighty thousand dollars' worth of stock to Clarissa. The judge needed only to sign a release.

They chose the ball because it marked the high point of the city's social season, and the judge was certain to be there. Also (a condition more important to Booker than to her), it allowed Clarissa to meet her father in a public place and thus avoid any pleading, threats, or even violence he might attempt. There was only one thing Booker didn't like: Clarissa would attend the ball with Bert Gauss, while he waited outside.

"He asked me while you were gone," she explained. "Besides, tickets cost three hundred dollars, and my dad certainly won't give us any—not after he pays for your tux."

"So why buy the tux in the first place?"

"It's the coup de grace, baby," she said. "I think you ought to go right up to the front door and say you're Judge Thornton Sayers's guest. After all, he's been trying to get black people invited to that party for the last twenty years."

"He won't let me in," Booker said.

"Probably not, but at least he'll know you're there." Clarissa smiled: it was her old smile, insolent and alluring at once. "Plus," she said, "you look nice in a tux."

They had this conversation in a coffee shop on Forty-seventh Street, the afternoon before the ball. They were both already dressed, Booker in his tuxedo and flimsy patent-leather slippers, Clarissa in a short black dress and stockings, her face pallid with makeup, her lips a violent streak of red. She was taking a taxi to her dinner with Bert Gauss. As he walked her to the curb, she handed him the transfer order and the Stingray's keys.

"Good luck," he said.

"We don't need luck," she answered. "It's gonna be a breeze."

He showed up at the ball an hour and a half early to make sure he got a parking space. It was being held at the Nelson Gallery, an immense, winged stone museum with three-story-high columns in front, and from behind the Stingray's windshield, he watched the best of white Kansas City arriving at their most important, oldest event. The most obvious and striking thing about the guests was, in fact, their

186

whiteness, as if somewhere within the immense, columned museum, its pediment engraved with quotations by Goethe and Plotinus, lay the distilled essence of the race. He saw white children in buckled shoes and frocks; fecund white wives in white stockings, their hair pulled back beautifully from their curved, white necks; young white bachelors, their faces fiery from drink, who donned white gloves and greeted each other loudly across the grass. He saw white lawyers, white bankers, white brokers, and white members of the board of trade; he saw white rakes and white philanderers with their gaudily dressed white dates; he also saw what appeared to be sober, honest, and humble white husbands who stared at the fading beauty of their partners with tender regret. He saw old white widows, their skin as soft as cowslip, making their lonely and heroic odysseys up the museum's vast stone steps, and he saw two members of the hunt club—Remy Westbrook and Podge McGee—strolling arm in arm with their wives, the couples laughing and chatting with the natural ease of longtime friends. And he wondered, to his surprise, whether Mercury felt jealous of their happiness, and whom he went to the ball with now that he no longer had a wife. As the lone black face in the parking lot (even the valets were white), he received a fair amount of attention, secret glances of curiosity, if not of fear; when he met these gazes, most turned away, but several strangers greeted him with friendly waves.

At seven o'clock he walked up the steps himself and waited in the ticket line, sweating and uncomfortably conscious of his race. When he reached the front, he said, "Judge Sayers has my ticket," and immediately heard the hidden murmurs around him, the voice of one old woman who said, not with hatred or disapproval but with a carnivalgoer's glee, "Myrna, look at the young black man. They're not going to let him in." When the judge came, Booker looked directly into his eyes, both of them communicating wordlessly—Booker's expression being one, perhaps, of victory; the judge's perhaps one of fear—and when the judge shook his head and denied him, Booker walked quickly and calmly away. He had brought himself a sandwich, and he ate it standing before the Stingray's hood, being careful not to stain his clothes. The first guests began to leave at ten. They retired in small bunches that he watched from the car, and when the small bunches became a steady stream, he rose and stood in the shadows at the bottom corner of the steps. Clarissa's note had included instructions on where Booker would be, but when the judge appeared, he stopped and chatted for at least fifteen minutes at the doorway with other departing invitees. Everyone seemed to know him and to be attracted to him, even the men, his tall figure bowing among them, laughing, always careful to defer: the body language of a man who had been appointed to his job by someone no less important than the President himself, and who thus had no need to be politic with anyone, a fact that made his graciousness and his attention to formality seem all that much more genuine. He slowly angled down the steps to where Booker stood, and it was not until the judge passed him that Booker recognized the same jack-o'-lantern grimace he'd worn during his Chamber of Commerce speech. "Not here," he said through his teeth, still talking to those around him, and motioned Booker to follow with a short jerk of his hand. He trailed the judge at a distance (knowing this was exactly what the judge wanted, and at the same time hoping to avoid a scene) as he walked to his car. It was in a parking lot across the street. Here the crowd thinned. The judge opened his car door and, his back still turned to Booker, said, "I refuse to do this here."

"We can move," Booker said. "But I choose where."

"Do it, then," the judge said.

"The Scout, in twenty minutes."

The judge got into his car and rolled his window down. "All right," he said. "But I don't want to see her. If we talk, it's got to be just you and me."

The Scout was a statue of an Indian on horseback that stood atop a promontory overlooking downtown. The city had grown past it, highways ribboning its base, office towers springing up on its plateau, but the promontory itself remained impassable, its sides covered with steep woods and rock. When Booker arrived, the tangerine sports car was already idling in the lot, and he pulled up beside it, killing the Stingray's engine and lights.

"It's a sick world," the judge said through his darkened window, "when the man who comes to rob you is driving your own car."

"I'm not here to rob you," Booker said. "I'm here to make a deal."

Without looking back, he walked down the short grass incline that led from the asphalt to the statue's base. On the far side of the Scout, a drunken wedding party snapped pictures of the skyline, their white stretch limo purring in the lot. Booker continued past them, picking his way among crumbling ledges of limestone until he came to a patch of open grass. He was below the statue then, far enough from the wedding party that they could not hear his conversation but close enough that they could still hear him if he shouted. Staring out at the city, he waited for the judge. He could hear the older man's ragged breathing as he stumbled along the limestone, and when the judge was about ten yards away, Booker took a flashlight from his hip pocket and shone it in his face. Blinded, the judge stuck his hands out to shield his eyes, his wedding ring glinting in the pale electric light, and Booker kept him that way for a moment, feeling his helplessness and fear.

"Quit that, goddammit," the judge said.

Booker held the light up a few moments longer, then dropped it to the judge's chest. "You stand there," he said.

Booker swallowed, allowing the adrenaline to leave his arms and chest. The wedding party seemed untroubled by the flashlight. "I didn't come to talk about you," he said. "We both know there's nothing worse than a man like you, a man who fucks his own little girl" — Booker lifted the flashlight: the judge resisted his words frigidly, lips pressed — "so I'm going to talk about business instead. The deal is simple: if you don't sign these papers, then Clarissa goes to the TV people, and you'll be hearing about your habit all over the city. If you do sign them, we both walk away."

"What guarantee do I have of that?" the judge asked.

"Of what?"

"That Clarissa will just walk away."

"Her word," Booker said.

The judge sighed and shifted his feet. "I'd like to sit down now," he said.

Booker gestured to a rock, and the judge sat there, the light shining about his knees. His face was dark above the beam.

"You see, Booker," he said, "I don't make agreements without guarantees. It's not in my best interest. For instance, what's to keep Clarissa from getting money from me like this every year? You don't know Clarissa like I do, or you would've gotten some guarantees, too. After all, you're not the first person she's convinced to try a scam like this."

"That's a lie," Booker said.

The judge shrugged, his spotlit hands spread wide. "Do you really think a relationship like ours was entirely one-way?" he asked. "Sin is an insidious thing: I see it every day in court. Suppose that you have sinned once, suppose you've actually been to jail—yes, I know you've been to jail; I have access to records like that. Was that sin really completely your fault, or did someone offer you the opportunity to commit it? Did somebody push you a little bit? I'm not an innocent man—no, I'm not saying that. But let me ask you: When you went to bed with my daughter, was it your idea or hers?"

Booker retrieved the transfer forms from his pocket. "These are the deal, Judge," he said. "Either you sign them or you don't."

"I'm not going to ask whose name those forms are in," the judge said, "because I know it isn't yours. No, Booker, you and I are both in trouble, and that's why I'm going to offer you a deal. With you there's a guarantee. See, I know that after we finish this conversation, you're going to leave this city immediately because there is a federal warrant

190

out for your arrest, and if you don't, I'll have you thrown in jail. I'm even going to let you blackmail me, Booker. I'm going to reach inside my pocket"—he held his hands up as if asking permission—"take out my checkbook, and write you a check for five thousand dollars. It's probably not as much as Clarissa pretends she's going to give you, but given the weakness of your position, it's more than you have any right to ask for."

He opened the checkbook, uncapped his pen, and began to write. "Booker," he said. "I wonder if your parents knew what they were doing when they named you that?"

"Why?" Booker asked.

"Booker Washington was what I'd call a realist," the judge said, smiling. "We bought him off—just like you."

In one brief, violent movement, Booker swatted the checkbook from the judge's hands. "Don't be a fool!" the judge hissed. His bow tie had gone crooked from the force of the blow, and he groped blindly about his feet. "You are a black felon: you cannot vote, you cannot own a gun—the courts exist to *get rid* of people like you." He was on his hands and knees now, hunting among the rocks. "And if you think for one minute that anything you might say against me would stand up in a court of law, then I suggest you reconsider."

"I'm not the one who's in trouble," Booker said. "That's the difference between you and me—see, to be in trouble, you've got to have something to lose."

"Ah," the judge said. "So we reach the final refuge of every nigger"—he sat back on his hams, panting, his face cracked by a sardonic grin—"the belief that he is ruined and there's someone else to blame." He chuckled to himself, wiping his eyes with the back of his hand, but he didn't have time to finish because Booker was upon him then. He moved swiftly, without any extra movement, collaring the judge and pinning him in the grass. The judge was several inches taller, but Booker had the advantage in quickness, and with one hand around the older man's throat, he rammed his knee into his gut. The judge gasped, and Booker could smell the staleness of his breath. "Judge, I got just one thing to tell you," Booker said, hissing in Thornton Sayers's ear. "No matter what you want to say about your daughter—in my personal opinion, she was real, *real* good."

The judge bucked like an animal, heels flailing against the earth, but Booker held on. He looked down on the judge's face, twisted now, and spit-flecked. "Now don't go taking it dirty, Judge," he said. "See, that's not what good's supposed to mean."

Booker let go and sprang away, arms up, waiting for an attack. But the judge did not get up. He lay there quietly, tux shirt vibrant against the lush spring grass, and Booker shrugged his shoulders inside his jacket and slowly walked away.

He found her in a bar called the Newsroom, several doors down from the diner where they'd planned to meet. He was two hours late, and when he came in she was playing pool with a sedate, pickled-looking gentleman who spoke only Vietnamese. She sank a rail shot, chalked her cue, and said, "You shouldn't have let him get you alone."

"He didn't give me any choice," Booker said.

"I know," Clarissa said. She was still sinking balls, chalking and moving the cue rhythmically. Then she missed. "He didn't sign them, did he?" she asked.

"No," Booker said.

She did not seem upset, merely concentrating, thoughtful, and she was tender to him on the ride home, leaning across the Stingray's stick shift and rubbing her hands beneath the flap of his jacket, against his chest. "So what do we do?" he asked when they arrived at her apartment. "Shouldn't I stay with you, or something like that?"

"Let's not, tonight," she said, kissing his cheek. "Let's sleep on it. We're going to let my father sleep on it, and you're going to sleep on it—everybody's going to sleep."

"He's serious about turning me in," Booker said.

"I'm not going to let him," Clarissa said. "You'll have to trust me on that."

She left him with the Stingray's keys so he could drive home, and they kissed again at the door, warmly but not passionately—like old friends. He waved to her from the parking lot, her figure outlined in her evening dress against the cheap stucco walls and door, the empty pool, and she waved back. He never saw her again.

13

IN 1977, after the first desegregation order, the exodus began. For fifteen years whites fled the city south and west, their highways snaking out across the Kansas plains, shadeless, uniform, their shopping malls moored on parking lots vast as inland seas, their cities newly built and newly purchased and given names befitting pioneers—Santa Fe, Prairie Village, Overland Park—creating at State Line Road a far more imposing barrier than Troost Street had ever been. It was not that they disliked blacks per se: they appreciated their entertainers, and that wonderful running back, married to a white woman, who lived on Martha Belle Aiken's street—a handsome, dignified man. Their grandchildren usually had three or four of them in their grades. But these people were different from what they might have termed, if only privately, the *regular blacks*, who lived in the vast hills and dales of the city they had left, amid the mansions and old apartments that the whites' ancestors had constructed, and who attended the same high schools from which they themselves had received degrees. Even "open-minded" whites feared meeting such people on a dark street, and though some old-line residents clung to the safe pockets of Missouri that remained (Mercury even went so far as to refuse to move his company offices from the black Ward Parkway, Standard Avenue), most viewed life across the border as hostile territory. For them, Booker's appearance as a suspect in the Sayers murder meshed with

194

Missouri's rising murder rate, its crackhouses and driveby shootings, its schools that kept metal detectors at their gates. He had become what they imagined him to be.

Few witnessed this split as routinely as Detective Keegan and her team. They worked primarily in the old city—the third district and portions of the fifth, from Truman Road north to Sixty-third Street and from Troost east out to the highway—and they had seen people in these neighborhoods kill one another in nearly every imaginable way, had seen babies shot in their own cribs, the bullets fired from the back-seats of passing sedans. Keegan herself had last investigated the case of two sixteen-year-olds who had shot each other in the face, one with a Colt pistol, the other with a shotgun whose barrel had been sawed in half, the sole survivor's tongue so bored with lead he could not explain what had caused the argument in the first place. But she also knew that only a small percentage of blacks were responsible for such things. She knew the anticrime groups that met in church basements; the bereft mothers; the pastors and business owners horrified by their neighborhoods' violent change. And she knew the indifference of the whites who'd attended the Founders Ball and believed that such vio-lence had nothing to do with them personally, the housewives leaning out of their Saab windows to identify the sketch of Booker Short and saying yes, they'd seen him, but they knew only that he lived "over in Missouri."

Which, in their opinion, seemed to cover everything.

Mercury Chapman had been Keegan's only real lead. She found him trimming rhododendrons in the rain, an old man in dungarees whose hawklike face—as her boots pressed the grass beside him—glanced up with a sadness, a form of exhaustion, that she had not seen in any other witness yet. He led her around his tartan, wood-beamed study, showing off his business awards and plaques, apparently interested less in his business itself than in its address, 8516 Standard, which seemed to be the answer to some implicit criticism he wanted to deflect. "When I started out, Standard was a good street. Mixed-race. Middle-class," he said, staring at a yellowed photograph of the building. "Hell, somebody's got to stay, don't they, Detective? We employ a lot of people in that place." It took a long time before Keegan could get him to sit, the old man fiddling with the magazines atop the coffee table while she explained the situation, then lifting his head abruptly and asking, "Have you ever been in a situation, Detective—hmmp—where you knew a fact you'd prefer to leave out? Where right and wrong was different from the facts?"

"If you have something to report, I suggest you do that."

"What I know"—the old man peered at her over steepled fingers—"is that even if you'd filmed this murder, you wouldn't get people to agree."

"On what?" Keegan asked.

"Who to blame," Mercury said. "By the end of it, half of them would want to blame you for persecuting the blacks, just because you delivered the film. The other half would want to know why you were busy filming instead of putting that Negro away."

The word hung there, ugly. Rain drummed the windows, and Mercury sat with his head cocked, eyes focused at and beyond Keegan, as if listening for a distant sound.

"It's just an observation," he said.

Keegan knew enough about witnesses to sense a vulnerability, a raw nerve that might be tapped, and so she pushed him then, her gravel voice probing for the territory he wished to defend. But something had closed in the old man, and her questions, droning tirelessly over the minutiae of the case, died among the folds of plaid and circled lamps, the room lit with the dullness of a terrarium. Only when she asked, "Mr. Chapman, do you have any information on the suspect's whereabouts before the murder took place?" did Mercury's eyes flinch to the empty fireplace. "I already told you," he said, waving his hand. "The past two years, he'd work for me at the hunt club and when the season ended, he'd come and do repair work for the

196

church. Last year, he lived at a place on Euclid Street—but I lost touch with him this spring."

"I mean before," Keegan said. "How did you hire him?"

Mercury nodded toward the kitchen. "Lilly took him in—my cook."

Keegan leaned forward in her chair, pad and pen in hand. "Mr. Chapman," she asked, "are you trying to tell me that you have *no idea* why the suspect came here?"

"You see, that's what I've been trying to explain, Detective," he said. "Except for me and Lilly, see, black and white people don't talk to each other anymore around this place. You ought to have noticed that. Hell, her relatives are angry 'cause I got rich and didn't give them enough money—isn't that right, Lilly? Isn't that what Clyde thinks?"

In the kitchen, the disposal shuddered gastronomically.

"So you don't know anything about him," Keegan said.

"No," Mercury said. He mouthed his words above the noise, standing, his gaze still meeting hers, as if communicating a secret. "Nothing more than he knows about me."

They picked up the car the next day. A patrol officer had called it in: a tricked-out Stingray coupe cruising west along Southwest Boulevard, its plates belonging (as the dispatcher told him) to a Toyota Camry. A minor chase ensued. This took place at five o'clock on the West Side, a neighborhood whose stony hillsides and neat white houses lay hidden beneath the vaulted shadows of I-35, and whose residents, largely Mexican, were out enjoying their Saturday afternoon. Many of them had witnessed the stampede of polled Herefords—escapees from a cattle truck whose driver had failed to latch the gate—that had thundered down the middle of Southwest Boulevard two years earlier, and had urged the doomed cattle on to freedom, waving their jackets like capes. On this occasion, however, escape was not to be. The district encompassed a fairly small area, and after the first few minutes, the department's backup had closed the exits onto major arteries. The driver cut down a back alley behind the church of San Juan de la Cienega, only to have his escape route blocked by an unmarked Crown Victoria. A female detective stood behind it, her pistol braced against the hood, its barrel pointed with precision at the middle of the driver's face. There was something almost bored about her expression, deadpan, as if she lacked even the slightest appreciation of the chivalry of the chase, and after a brief attempt at chicken, the Stingray wobbled and then veered away.

Detective Keegan watched as the car burst through a hedge of boxthorn, clipped a whitewashed statue of Our Lady, and high-centered like a racing trophy, wheels spinning, impaled atop the fallen icon's base. Nothing stirred inside, and she walked toward the broken vehicle with the snout of her pistol raised. A young Mexican sat dazed behind the steering wheel, nose bleeding, and at his first gesture—a glib backhanded wave—she took three steps to the window and pointed her gun at his face. "Get out," she said.

He did so, smiling and slack-limbed, shaking his head at the foolish seriousness of the whole thing. As Keegan cuffed him, his chest flattened like a seal's against the churchyard dirt, he twisted his neck to look at her, his expression genial with secret threat.

"You're the one who did it, aren't you?" he said. When Keegan didn't answer, he smiled confidently and said, "Yes, I know. The lady cop who shoots the Mexicans when they run away. Yes? Carlos Ramirez's shooter—you and she are the same."

"Sí," Keegan whispered. "Yo maté a Carlos Ramirez."

Her voice was gravid, lush, the words exiting her lips with a bizarre and perfect accent, as if transported by a ventriloquist. "¿Y a quién mataste, joven?" she said.

A shadow crossed their figures then, dust faintly stirring in the orange-lit yard, while sixty miles away, in Chapman County, Stan Granger watched in helpless desperation as the Channel 5 newscopter swung away, the detective and her suspect shrinking to a single, glowing bead. Clyde Wilkins watched on the kitchen television at the Colonial Club, ignoring his patrons at the bar, and Wallace Evenrake watched from the back corner of the newsroom at the *Kansas City Star*. Lilly Washington watched, as did Henry Latham, the paper's president, and Morgan X. Pickering, founder of Commercial Bank, who stood in jodhpurs in his living room, listening gravely to the chopper pilot's *Seems like the officer's going to be all right* at the very same instant that Angel Diaz's mother (that was the Mexican's name) stood in her own living room in Rosedale, hand pressed against the electric aura of the screen. Everybody had a chance to watch, if not at six o'clock, then again at ten, when footage of the Stingray's twisted fuselage would be accompanied by a close-up of Detective Keegan. Hers was an unpleasant, unheroic face, sweaty, faintly mustached, appearing like a knot of wood against the upthrust mikes and hanging booms, and one had the impression that the reporters had been asking stupid questions—an impression that would be justified, since up until this prerecorded moment, no one had any idea what the car chase meant. Then Alvin Bailey shouted from offscreen.

"The last time anyone saw Clarissa Sayers," the reporter said, so loudly that the sound crews hidden in the news vans flinched, "she was in a 'sixty-five Stingray, same as that car over there. Is there a connection between this incident and the Sayers case?"

Keegan's lips were clenched, a stripe of dust smeared on her cheek.

"No comment at this time," she said.

So it was the car that people paid attention to, as if, lacking pictures of a body, the city had settled on it as a substitute, an apotheosis, whose chrome and curves and violated bumper possessed the same lewd clarity as the old statues of the Greeks. People cared less about the murder than they did about the violation, the rape. Some had already imagined it. They had seen the car last summer, its lurid redness, and the young, dead woman's hand fondling the black man's knee, and so the footage of the Stingray served as a vindication and an augury of all they secretly believed—*Yes, that's what happens with those people. Yes, we were right about them, don't you see?*—its doors splayed and the officers spreading white dust on the handles and probing with tweezers among the seats.

Mercury Chapman saw it, too, resting in the cool darkness of his tartan study, a damp washrag clamped against his face, his lips repeating now the same mantra, saying, *No, this time I am not to blame. I am not the one to blame.*

Thirty blocks away, Detective Keegan strode through the yellow mud of the San Juan de la Cienega yard to the paddy wagon that idled there. The Mexican sat inside, his wrists connected by long, loose chains to his manacled feet, and the whole apparatus anchored to an eye-weld in the wagon's steel floor. A detective sat nearby. He was an Oklahoman named Charlie Schiff, and he wore a two-piece suit whose color shifted from pale gray to buttercup, depending on the light. He also wore matching cowboy boots, which he uncrossed, making room for Keegan along the metal bench, and then he nodded at the suspect, saying: "Angel here is my main man." He smiled brilliantly, then allowed his smile to fade. "C'mon, Angel, can't you remember your line?"

"Fuck you," the Mexican said.

"That ain't it," Schiff said. He leaned forward, his expression so eager and intent that it was impossible to determine if he was playing a game. "After I say, 'Angel here is my main man,' you're supposed to say, 'And Charlie is my bro-therrr.'" He spoke these words with such a heavy accent that they sounded Scottish. Then he leaned back, smiling:

"Go on, try it—you'll sound so much more polite. Really."

"Fuck you," the Mexican said.

200

Schiff tapped one finger against his teeth. To Keegan he said, "He doesn't get that stuff from me."

Keegan nodded without the slightest interest. She wore blue serge slacks and shirt, the latter unmarked, unstudded, bisected by a blue serge tie. She'd been watching the Mexican since she entered the wagon, and when she spoke, her voice was husky, whispering.

"Mr. Diaz," she said. "Your car has illegally registered plates."

The Mexican did not respond.

"That indicates to us that it's stolen," Keegan said. "And what's more, we think it was stolen from a woman who is now deceased."

"I want a lawyer," the Mexican said.

Keegan studied her hands. "Does everybody at your home have papers, Mr. Diaz?" she asked. "Your mother? Your sister? An uncle? The choice is yours, Mr. Diaz. You can give me your friend, or we will find your family—either way, you have to rat."

He motioned for a pen and paper after that. She waited until he had finished writing, her face again stolid, inertial, lacking entirely in any visible expression of triumph and/or apology, her attention returning briefly to the paper the Mexican handed her and then disappearing again as she slipped it into the pocket of her shirt. Still she did not move, and after several seconds, the Mexican spoke of his own accord: "I don't have no address, lady. Name and phone number's all that dude give out, and I don't even know if the number's real." The detective stared at the wall of the police van. "He's a black dude," the Mexican said. "Stays at the Coronado sometimes, which is where I seen him." Keegan held him in her sights, chewing. "What *is* it, lady?" the Mexican asked.

"You've got my pen," she said.

She emerged from the police van with the pen clipped in the front pocket of her shirt and strolled forward to give instructions to the van's driver. It was almost evening then, the sun gorged above the highway overpass, the weekend traffic dead. The van departed, nos-ing among the onlookers while the camera crews took footage of its blank side, and Keegan crossed the pitted alley to Detective Schiff, whose boots were propped radiantly against the bumper of his own unmarked Grand Marquis. "I got a name," she said, taking out the piece of paper. "Reggie Hammonds. Twenty-year-old African American male."

Schiff squinted. "Sounds interesting," he said.

"Got a phone number, too," Keegan said.

"Let's call the little fucker."

"I don't think so," Keegan said. She held the paper up, her expression oddly discomfited, stiff. "You recognize that number?" she asked. Schiff shook his head, and Keegan continued to hold the paper, windblown, its edges dotted by a sudden gust of rain.

"It's Judge Sayers's private line," she said.

14

To Mercury the city has not always seemed so split. He remembers a time when the black race was generally familiar to him, a time when Eve Wilkins's touch and scent seemed vastly more important than his mother's own impatient caress, scented not of wool or chive like Eve's, but of cigarette smoke, perfume, and often gin. His parents were big drinkers then. Many Sundays he woke and dressed himself alone and went down to the kitchen, picking his way among the half-filled glasses, ashtrays, and forgotten ties and scarves that littered the parquet front hallway where his parents liked to dance—and that sometimes led, suggestively (though he did not know it then), up the risers of their front stairs. He would wait for Eve at the back gate. He did not question this, nor, it seemed, did she, a lanky, rawboned woman whose big toe protruded from the gap-end of her Sunday high-heeled shoes. She wore flowered skirts, a slip, a broad-brimmed hat, and beneath the hat a wig (which he had once seen her shockingly remove to reveal the strangely pleasant, tight-curled skull beneath), but he remembers the feet most clearly, gnarled, unladylike, with the specific weight and gravity of a man's. He realized in later years why he met her at the gate: it was her one demand, his one concession, that she not be asked to enter into her place of labor on her single day of rest. And he knew, this also in later years, what an effort this trip was for her: to ride crosstown and then uptown on the Sunday trolley, which left at 8:00 A.M., and then to walk five blocks among the bunkered hedges of Greenway Terrace in ill-fitting shoes to retrieve a young white boy whose parents did not attend church. But she was always there, slow-footed, in no particular hurry, her expression clouding as she paused along the rutted alley to stare up at his parents' rooms, and then she would reach out her hand and say, "All right, child—come with me," as the two of them paraded down the length of Greenway Terrace, solemn, hand in hand, until they reached the trolley's tracks.

The cars would be empty at that time of day, and he'd run along the empty aisle, reversing the swiveled wicker seat backs with a satisfying clap. Eve (who by law had to sit in back) would ignore him after this, saying, "I know a Chapman boy, but the one I know shows respect. The Chapmans are too familiar in my neighborhood for folks to believe in someone who don't act that way. Yes, and if I had a real Chapman with me, one who was trying to *represent* his family—why, I couldn't be more proud of someone like that."

"I'm a Chapman," Mercury would say.

"Is that right?" Eve answered, widening her eyes as if in surprise and looking at him for the first time directly. "Why, you do seem to resemble them in the face," she would say, levering his chin from side to side. "But it ain't the outside that defines a Chapman. No, the way I know one is by how he acts."

"You just watch me," Mercury said.

"All right," Eve would say, noncommittally. "I ain't opposed to that."

But it is the church that he remembers more than anything: a vast brick building, barnlike, wind-scoured, standing against a backdrop of twisted oaks and locusts atop the muddy precipice of Twentieth Street and the Paseo hill. They walked there from the streetcar, as did, it appeared, the entire congregation. The streets themselves were unpaved, puddled, some no more than winding, foot-beaten tracks, and

from the height of the church's front steps one could see entire families, uncles, cousins, filing upward like some strange and vagrant
army come to gather in that high place. There would be sisters
dressed in matching pink pinafores, their frilled panties showing high
atop their bony legs; businessmen in sharp blue pinstripes, gold fobs
dangling brilliant from their vests and their wives ranked just behind
them in taut-bowsed, ovoid hats; gamblers in mustard-colored jackets; single women in white high heels, their cotton blouses damp
against their chests; washerwomen, nurses, bellhops, grocers, and car
mechanics in brushed derbies: nearly all of them knew Miss Evie,
and more than half, to his surprise, would speak to him by name, a
sailor-suited white boy with a fresh scab upon his knee. He remembers the seriousness of these introductions, the extent to which—in
Eve's presence—he attempted to represent his family respectably.
But it was the singing that he cared for most of all.

    He did not talk about it publicly, and if he had, he would not
have known how to phrase it, what to say: kneeling in the wooden
booth, his palm clasped around a nickel Eve Wilkins had slipped him
for the plate, waiting for the slow and wavelike movement through
the congregation, building through the psalter, the announcements
by the preacher in his purple cape. It would begin soon after that, a
strange vibration that spread outward from the choir into the ranked
faces of the black women and black men. He did not know to be embarrassed yet. Or rather, he knew, but not so well that in the absence
of his schoolmates he could not be persuaded to forget. They would
be standing then. Eve Wilkins would have her hand atop his head,
the rhythm of the voices building, the songs' words still privately familiar to him at a distance of seventy years: old Negro hymns, the
words mythic, vibrant, speaking of Jordan, rising rivers, chariots, and
people who have gone to visit the promised land. But he waited not
so much for the words as for the moment when the room went beyond the words. He could feel it in Eve Wilkins, who stood beside

him singing in her clear, alto voice, and in those who had wandered into the aisle, shouting and raising up their prayerbooks—a terrifying feeling that lifted the hairs on his neck. Even now, at seventy-seven, he cannot define such a thing, but he remembers it with something deeper than mere nostalgia, a feeling closer to horror and disbelief at the destruction of that world, at how quickly it vanished from the city.

He sits forward now in his desk chair. He has already packed his bags, has already planned to leave, to visit his two children in California—having convinced himself, as they apparently already had, that the city does not need any more Chapmans. But he finds himself unable to get up so easily, the faces in the church connected somehow to the faces of Reggie Hammonds and Isaac Bentham, which have haunted him often in recent days, the web of memory tracing back nearly fifty years to the moment when, standing amid six rows of beaten cabbages outside Chartres, he picked the silk liner from Private Hammonds's helmet off a stick, its white corners fluttering with a meaning that he did not wish to see.

Or perhaps one could say that it had started two years earlier, at Camp Lee, Virginia, when he had been one of five officers chosen for a black command. Or in boot camp at Camp Brocklin, Mississippi; or, perhaps (had he listened to Isaac) in the 1850s, when his ancestors ran slaves in the county that now bore his name. At any rate, he has chosen this memory: the bright, cupreous European sky, the dreamlike rows of cabbages, and then, beyond a second field of rye, Chartres cathedral, the central window of its clerestory blazing like a giant golden eye. He held Hammonds's helmet liner for a minute, little more than that. All the soldiers' helmets had liners, soft and sweat-stained cuts of silk that padded the bowls of their steel helmets, and on which they had been required, in Basic Training, to write their names. Most used pen, some form of ink, but Hammonds had embroidered his with darning thread. It was not unheard-of—many of the men had learned to sew out of necessity—but the laborious loop-curls on the private's R, the slanted, optimistic M's seemed pathetic in comparison to the cathedral that loomed across the fields. And he noticed one further thing, one fleeting detail, just in the instant before the French police inspector turned and said to him, "Captain, what do you have there?" The helmet liner had not been torn from anything. Nor was it complete. Rather, the name had been cut from the surrounding fabric, its squared edges completely clean.

There was a feeling of relief upon the discovery of the helmet liner, a relaxation on the part of the French inspector and the American MPs who had, earlier that morning, told him of the Frenchwoman's rape. Each man was aware of the difficulties inherent in such allegations. Mercury himself knew that handing a man over without hard evidence would lead to certain mutiny, and so when the inspector took the scrap from him, read it, and held it out to the MPs, there was no real triumph in his face, only calm acceptance, relief, as he said, "Gentlemen, can we all now agree that this evidence will do?"

The MPs examined the embroidered name thoughtfully and then handed it back to Mercury, as if they all needed to touch it, the gesture ritualistic in some way.

"Captain," one said, "is this name familiar to you?"

"He is one of my men," Mercury answered.

"Can you identify this as his?"

There was a hesitation then, a break in their agreed-on certainty. And if Mercury had wished to change it, he could have spoken then, the doubt still unformed in his mind, its pieces uncoalesced. But he nodded instead, handing the fragment back.

"Of course, we will ask the woman to identify him," said the inspector. "Of course, we will attend to the usual formalities—the rights, as you Americans like to say."

He saw the helmet liner only once more after that. This, too, was in his tent, the same moldy and sunlight-pricked structure where the French inspector and the MPs had located him earlier to report the news of the alleged rape. The Frenchwoman was no longer there. Hammonds sat in her place, not yet in shackles but at the same time no longer free, his hands clasped between his thighs and an MP with a loaded rifle standing behind his back. Mercury found it difficult to look him in the face. It was a face that he knew well, having seen it nearly every day for the past eighteen months: the same stubbled skin, the same band of copper freckles across the nosebridge, the same crooked and faintly ironic smile, the same bad teeth. But there was a deadness to it now, Hammonds's cast eye gazing at a queer angle to his good one, as if he were trying to glimpse some unseen figure that hovered just behind his back.

"Private Hammonds," Mercury said. "Is there a reason why you don't have your helmet with you here today?"

"I lost it," Hammonds said.

Mercury watched him. There seemed to be a studied vagueness to his expression. "Did you lose it yourself?" he asked.

Hammonds smirked, his tongue pressed behind his lips' seam.

"What I mean, Private," Mercury said, "is to ask you whether anyone could have taken it without your permission, could have used it for some reason." He paused, giving Hammonds time to answer, but the private's expression had gone vacant again. Flies dropped from the overhanging canvas and buzzed about his head. "All right," Mercury continued, "perhaps you can tell us when the helmet was last in your possession."

For the first and last time during the interview, Hammonds looked Mercury in the eye. It was only a glance, brief, fragmentary, private, and yet Mercury felt convinced (for reasons he couldn't explain) that what Hammonds said next would be a necessary lie.

"Ten o'clock last night," said Hammonds. "I went out to take a shit."

The French inspector stepped in then. His suit pants were muddy, the lapel of his thin jacket spotted with grease, and when he spoke in

208

his thick Bourbonnais accent, his voice sounded apologetic. "Private," he asked, "where did you go for this?"

"The woods," Hammonds said.

The inspector flapped his hand. "I understand the woods," he said, "but this is where? Perhaps you mean the trees which go along the small pathway—"

Hammonds nodded.

"—over by the cabbage field."

Hammonds did not answer, and the inspector removed the square of silk from his pocket and held it to the soldier's face. In the dark room, its whiteness shone malignantly.

"We find this," the inspector said, "in a place where there is a Frenchwoman who says that she is raped. The ground and all the vegetables have been—how do you say?—*ravagé*. And we find this patch, too. How do you excuse this thing? Can you have an explanation for what you were doing? Does anybody see where you have been?"

"He means an alibi," the MP said, helpfully.

The tent went silent. Mercury could hear the adenoidal breathing of the French inspector and, through a flesh-colored wall of canvas, the chitter of sparrows in the field outside. Hammonds smiled at the patch of silk, as if it were a joke that only he could understand.

"No," he said, still smiling. "I cannot give you that."

He called Isaac Bentham last. It was noon by then, the tent sweltering, and after Mercury sent his corporal to fetch the witness, he sat down to shave. The tent that he had inhabited for the past year—in England, Wales, and now France—contained a collapsible table equipped with a worn enamel washbasin and a speckled mirror, and he looked at himself in it. He had not shaved in several days. The dust-caked growth (it was reddish then) conferred a faintly ridiculous authority on his face, and removing it, he felt an odd detachment, a clarity about the case. Of course he did not want Hammonds to go to jail unfairly; of course he would have fought for him if he'd proclaimed his innocence, but behind that was another fact: he would not always be the captain of a black company. No matter how unfair or wrong the treatment of his men might be, he himself would remain, in some essential way, always safe. The key, it seemed, was to keep his conscience clean, and he told himself, *Remember, this is just one more thing. Someday you'll be home and away from these people, and you can tell stories about it,* and as he was thinking this, the French inspector coughed, standing just inside the zip-flap of the tent.

"Captain," he said. "I understand your caution, but we can't wait here all day."

Mercury held up his razor. "You might be interested in this one, Inspector," he said, dipping the blade through the cold water. "We're gonna talk to his best friend."

The corporal had returned by then, and at Mercury's signal he brought Isaac Bentham in. The same two MPs accompanied the soldier: a tall, wasp-waisted black whose shoulders filled the tent crease, the canvas skimming his bent head. Mercury could see the lunate curve of his nails as he saluted, the gloss of his shaved cheeks. When he reached the stool, one of the MPs touched him, and he froze, the moment containing enough unspoken violence that the MPs hand moved to his sidearm, while his partner's rifle clicked. But Isaac ignored this, bending fluidly to brush off the stool top and then sitting down, smiling, and (Mercury noticed) unconsciously turning his wedding ring.

"What's with the muscle, Captain?" he said, crossing his legs at the ankles and stretching them out comfortably. "I didn't know I had turned into a criminal today."

"You haven't," Mercury said.

"Tell Huey and Louie about it, then." Isaac did not look at the French inspector or the MPs, his gaze directed between them, straight

210

at Mercury, his voice purring. "These gentlemen don't seem to appreciate that we are on the same team."

Mercury nodded to the MPs and they retreated to the corners of the tent as he paced forward himself, capless, his bangs and sideburns still wet.

"We need your help, Isaac," he said.

"Help?" Isaac said, arching his eyebrows and glancing around humorously.

"That's right," Mercury said.

He explained the situation, expecting the soldier to lie to protect his friend—hoping he would, in fact—and so he was surprised when Isaac said, "I'm sorry, gentlemen, but I can't *help* you arrest any black folks today. About that time, I was asleep—I'd been drinking, unfortunately."

When he looks up from the desk, the street is empty once again. The elms and locusts bow above it, thick with foliage; the stone and tile-roofed houses seem comfortable and well kept, and he stares out at the unshadowed light of the dead morning, retracing his thinking on the case. From the start he believed that Hammonds was covering for his friend. It would not have been an unheard-of sacrifice: the usual penalty for rape was a few years' labor, sentence to be commuted upon return to the States. And beyond that was the peculiarity of their friendship, what he referred to as Hammonds's Oklahoma dream.

The two of them had begun as bunkmates, mismatched in the classic army way: Hammonds in outlook and in practice less a soldier than a thief, while Isaac seemed to represent, in his pressed fatigues, his store-bought boots, and his grim demeanor, an example of Negro pride and even, perhaps, aristocracy. He had worked closely with both of them. Hammonds had arranged (with Mercury's implicit blessing) a picnic back at Camp Brocklin that had marked the high point of his command: two trucks loaded with "non-issue" rations—

spare ribs, fried chicken, and, most important, two kegs of beer—all smuggled to a secret forest road outside the camp. Isaac, by contrast, had taught his men to refuse the army's definition of them as second rate. True, there was a pridefulness in him, an air of injury, but he also had a soldier's eye for detail, and Mercury had given him control of his first platoon, replacing a white lieutenant who had preferred to read Strindberg in his tent.

Mercury often rode with them. The trucks of Isaac's convoy were always spotless, save for the cyclones with reddened, squinting eyes that Hammonds had painted on their canvas backs and the white legend on the bumpers that read THE OKIES. He had been there in open fields, at daybreak, to unload diesel canisters under mortar fire; he had been there in the eerie silence of the front, rolling through the plaster scree of villages and leafless forests, the trees smoking and cut off at their stumps. He had even spoken to them, at odd moments, stuck in the long convoys of the "Red Ball Express," about his past— a rarity for an officer, who was supposed to keep his feelings from his men—and they had done the same, especially Hammonds, who had talked compulsively about Georgia, about women, and, interestingly, about the Bentham family farm in Oklahoma, as if he took vicarious pride in his friend's establishment. "Do you realize this Okie here's got four thousand acres of *his own* land?" he would ask Mercury. "Four thousand acres. And he's got a wife crazy enough to stick with him and a new little baby—say, what was that kid's name again?"

"Illyria," Isaac would say, his profile still against the seat.

"See there, Cap?" Hammonds would say. "What he got going there is a dynasty. Ain't that right?" He would turn then, grinning at Isaac crazily. "So that's why I got to keep him safe, see, 'cause when the war's over, he's gonna give me a job out at his place."

"Am I?" Isaac would say.

"You got to," Hammonds would answer. "You just purely got to,

212

see, 'cause I ain't got no other chance." He would lean toward Mercury and say, confidentially, "You see, Cap, in Georgia, when we start getting land like white folks, they just come and take it back."

This was the first article of Hammonds's innocence. In a year and a half, Mercury knew, he had not received a letter or a package from a relative, relying instead on the letters that Isaac's wife sent every week, clutching the papers thin and translucent as Bible leaves between his grubby hands and saying, "All right, it's three o'clock here in Le Mans, and that puts it at eight o'clock in the morning back there. So, when a three-year-old girl eats breakfast at the Bentham estate, what she's gonna see?" And it was this passion, this intensity of imagination — the fact that he would force Isaac to tell him what birds would be in season and what flowers, how his wife and mother would be busy fixing sandwiches for the hands, and then say, "See, it sounds to me like you all need some help out at that place" — that had made Mercury believe he would be willing to cover Isaac's mistake.

The second article involved Isaac's pride. On more than one occasion Mercury had seen him provoked nearly to violence by the farm women who cursed his men for "trespassing" on their property, and had watched him arrive in towns with his black convoy to find the cafés all hung with *Fermé* signs despite the fact that patrons could be seen inside. These insults seemed to outrage Isaac more than anybody. It was as if he could stand being cursed by white soldiers, by the army, or even by the enemy, but not by civilians half a world away from home, and he would stand before the closed storefronts shaking, his gaze murderous, asking Mercury, "So, are these the people we're supposed to risk our lives to save?"

He thought of this, seated there in his tent sweltering, listening to Isaac's testimony. He did not know if the Frenchwoman had actually been raped or if she had instead complained about some imagined violation and goaded Isaac into striking her in some way. But he did know that it was Isaac, not Hammonds, who appeared to be ashamed.

213

And remembering Hammonds's admonition, he decided to let their testimony go unchallenged.

He thought they wanted it that way.

The final memory is of Hammonds's death. He attended it personally, driving nearly two hundred miles to Cherbourg in the jumpseat of an open jeep. It was November then, cold, the road buffeted by sharp gusts of rain, and he remembers his despair when Isaac Bentham (though not his regular driver, Isaac had insisted on escorting him) crested a hill above the city and they saw, beyond its dirty rooftops, the blackness of the winter sea. There was a nakedness to its presence, a relentless, mindless power that—lying in his hotel that night, listening to the booming of its breakers—he associated with the military. Even Hammonds's cell was on the waterfront, in what had once been a civilian jail, and its slotted window opened onto a horizon of ebony waves. Mercury spoke to him there, once in Isaac's presence and a second time with a black chaplain, on the execution's eve. By then, of course, it was too late. Hammonds had been sentenced not to prison time or to work duty (from which he could, when the war ended, be released) but to death, and the grotesque nature of this replacement dream—for it seemed that way—the dampness of his cell, its bleak vista, had sucked away all his jokes, the energy he'd had when free.

"I guess I was wrong, Cap," he told Mercury, his voice flat. "It looks like I ain't gonna get to see any of that Oklahoma green."

It was the sheer arbitrary nature of this death that reminded Mercury of the sea, its forcefulness, its mindlessness, its lack of reason or necessity. He had done what he could once the sentence came, had written letters, filed the required appeals, but at every level the answers had been the same: Brigadier General Ewart Plank wanted it this way. He was angry about supply drivers who sold their cargoes on the black market, reporting the trucks lost, and he was angry about civilian complaints of atrocities; the hangings were meant to be indelible

214

examples of his irritation, the final step in his campaign. But these answers failed to explain why Hammonds and the three soldiers who
would hang with him had been chosen as examples, aside from the
fact that they were unknown—and black.

In the end he was afraid not only for the condemned man and
for himself, but for Isaac, who, since the report of Hammonds's sentence, had gone silent. On his last visit, he tried to give Hammonds a
chance to recant, urging, "Tell the truth about what happened, Private. Tell me you're not covering for somebody," but the prisoner had
only smiled, gesturing at the cell walls, the slotted windows to the
north.

"What difference does it make?" he asked.

"There was a confession," Mercury prodded. "You said . . ."

"A confession?" Hammonds said.

"Yes," Mercury said. The cellblock was unnaturally still, and
shuffling through his briefcase, Mercury felt the chill of his own
sweat. "Here," he said, producing a sheaf of papers. "In the court
record—I mean, you told them you did it, don't you see?"

Hammonds took the papers, looked at them, and politely gave
them back.

"That ain't a confession, Captain," he said. "Sir."

"What?" Mercury said. "What—?"

But a murmuring sounded behind him then, and pivoting, he
saw prison guards and officers crowded into the corridor, listening.
Behind them the hands of inmates gripped the bars across the hall.
"Bentham," he said. "Get these men away."

By then it was too late. The obedience and perhaps the fear that
he was used to commanding as an officer had dissipated, and the
murmuring grew bolder, the voices of the soldiers blending into a
sound that was musical though indistinct. *What he means,* a voice
said, *is that it isn't a real confession when they tell you what to say.* A
second voice said, *Yes, you tell the man,* and searching for the first
speaker, Mercury found the hard, bright scowl of Isaac Bentham's

215

face. The voices spoke in a full chorus, each one individual but the whole completely fused: *They might be killing him for something, but let me tell you, it ain't rape,* and deeper, a bass accompaniment: *Three thousand miles. We come three thousand miles only to find out they can hang a black man just as easy here as in the States. Are you gonna be the one to say it, Captain? Are you gonna tell his momma and his kids?* A cigarette was cupped between Isaac's elongated fingers, and smiling, he struck a match.

"He'll be glad to answer your question, Captain," Isaac said, waiting until Mercury turned before standing himself. They were five years apart in age, but their faces seemed oddly similar—young, unmarked by time. "But first you answer one from me."

"All right," said Mercury.

Isaac tossed the dead match at his feet. "My friend was in this cell three months before they sentenced him," he said. "So how come you never once came to get him free?"

"I couldn't—" Mercury said, sputtering. "What was I . . . ?"

"You didn't," Isaac said. "You bailed out, forgot about it." His expression was rapt, almost childlike, his head tilted to one side. "You left that nasty trouble with the black folks for somebody else to fix. Am I right about that, Captain? Isn't that true?"

"It was in the courts," Mercury said. "I thought you both wanted—"

But the gallery overwhelmed him, their voices rhythmic, unrestricted, as if this were somehow an impromptu negative of Hammonds's trial, in which the defendant—Mercury, now—would not be allowed to speak: *Oh, the courts—that's good. Do you like that kind of justice, Captain? Are you a hanging kind of man?* Hammonds appeared to ignore them, his dead eye averted. But Isaac stared right at Mercury, the same rapt expression on his face.

"That's what I don't get," he said.

Mercury stared back, mute.

216

"How can one man," Isaac said, pointing through the bars, "decide that another one ain't even worth *trying* to save?" He paused, his lips curled into a smirk. "You tell me, Captain—what wrong did Reggie Hammonds do to deserve being treated that way?"

Now it is afternoon. He sits before the white and leaf-fringed window, rigid, priestlike, his dry lips moving silently. There is an odd hush, a suspended tension to the day, as if memory and knowing has stopped here, the suspended cables and gears of recollection taut against some unseen weight. He recalls the words perfectly. His first impulse was to protest, to fight—physically, if he must—to shake Hammonds by the collar and say, "You *know* me! Tell the truth—tell them that I'm not to blame." But in retrospect he sees an odd complicity in the scene, a static quality, as if all those present had spoken their lines with the stiff, preplanned intonation of the actors in a school play. It had already been decided that Mercury, like Hammonds, would not be allowed to speak in his own defense, but neither did Isaac want him to break down, to grovel or apologize in any way. Isaac wanted him to give them nothing, to be not Mercury Chapman but a white officer, an idol they had gathered there to hate. And he obliged them, willingly: not only then, turning, one hand on his sidearm as he elbowed his way through the mutinous assembly, but for the rest of the war and onward, for almost half a century.

It is here that memory pauses, waits.

He is not ready for it yet, the turning point, the change, and so he, too, waits, his thighs shifted forward in his desk chair, heels hooked on the lower rungs, hearing now the stillness of the men inside the jail cells, the hushed low brushings as their voices ceased. Their chorus was familiar to him, the voices similar in rhythm, style, and timbre to the choirs in the black church he'd visited with Eve Wilkins as a kid: one defiant, filled with hope; the other equally defiant and yet undercut with hate. Even Isaac Bentham's voice, raised in betrayal, contained an element of righteousness, of truth, descended from the older choir's vain lament, and so when he hears it now, fifty years later, he feels not only hatred and disgust but also an ecstatic and untouched longing, the knowledge of some bright sureness that he lacks. And it is here that memory begins again, the cables tightening imperceptibly, the pawl giving one more click, and he stares out his window at the Kendal-green lawn, the elm trees, the slickered children coming home from church. They hanged Hammonds in the rain. He remembers that, too: the gallows built atop the cobblestones, the grandstand that General Plank had constructed for the newsreel cameras and members of the press. He knew that Isaac was there. He could not see him, but he could sense and feel him watching over rank on rank of white, uplifted hands as the general instructed the troops to salute the flag, could feel his eyes upon the rows on rows of ducktailed necks (the black troops were mustered in the back), the hollow expressions of honor, discipline, and dignity chanted before the sergeant-at-arms led his friend onto the scaffolding. Hammonds came out with the three other men. All of them were black, and it was here, if anywhere, that the chorus of Isaac's betrayal made sense — how the lie had not been a lie at all but was connected to some older and more righteous complaint, the four black men forced to wait atop the scaffold, hands manacled, eyes staring straight forward into the ranks of their white countrymen. The sergeant-at-arms secured a bag over Hammonds's head. He knew that Isaac was watching, too, saw his friend's face disappear behind the canvas, saw the rope being fitted about his neck and the four black men standing with the coiled slipknots stiff and visible behind their heads, insectlike, captured in some grotesque and momentary apotheosis of all that they—he and Isaac—had fought about and of which he had declared himself to be innocent, and it was then that he began to curse, the words he spoke silent at first and then, as the door was pulled out from beneath the men with a bang, loud enough to be heard by the dignitaries in the stands, his lips repeating, *fuck you, fuck you, fuck you,* as Hammonds

218

fell and jerked, his tied hands and torso flexing in a backward C while Mercury shouted now *fuck you, fuck you* as if cursing the dead man.

Yes, he remembers that. Not only the betrayal, the anger, but also what had been shame, and he sits now before the tranquil houses of his youth, the dull, unshadowed lawns, knees bent, head bowed forward, repeating the same phrase: *I was not to blame.*

15

THEY HAVE KNOWN each other, off and on, for the better part of fifteen years, and yet they have never been acquainted intimately—have never revealed a weakness or spoken too transparently. The porch air that they breathe is fragrant and clean, and Stan leans forward above a glass of soda water in what was, just yesterday, his best white satin shirt and ironed Wrangler jeans (an outfit whose foolishness he knows Mercury will not mention, either), his voice working high and quick, as if he is afraid that his words will violate their agreement: "The minute she stepped out of that police car," he says, "it was like she smelled something, the way a dog might go over a couple of pups because they been someplace strange—or maybe I should've said wolf. You know what I'm saying? A female wolf. Didn't have no interest in what we had to say. She just started stripping the clothes off that dead girl, and the sheriff trying to put them back on just as quick, telling her the girl was drownt, as far as he could make out, and there wasn't nothing more for her to see." He snorts. The sound is at once rueful and admiring. "My guess is that wouldn't be the first time someone from Waterloo's accused you city folk of sending us pornography."

"So you found the body," Mercury says.

"Or maybe you could say it found me."

"I'm sorry you had to do that," Mercury says. "Terribly sorry." He

220

examines the riverman's face. "I mean, it's one thing to find a stranger, but someone you know, a woman. . . ." His voice fades here, his eyes shifting away.

"Oh," Stan says. "Yeah, that." It seems as if he has no real interest in the body itself, the physical corpus, except as a causation, a means of action. "It was more the lying bothered me," he says. "I had been trying to ease off to the side a little, clean my fish, you know, but she come and found me anyway. She wasn't mean about it, neither. She just come over with this little notebook, like she expected me to hide something, and asks, 'Is there anything else you want to tell me?' and there I am with Clarissa's necklace feeling about the size of a cue ball in my pocket, saying, "No, ma'am. You see what I seen.'"

"A necklace?" Mercury says.

"Yep," Stan says. "That's where it gets interesting."

He tells that part, too. It is Sunday night, cool, the rain increasingly steadily with darkness as it has done for the past week, and Mercury gets up twice as Stan speaks: once to close the rolled canvas awnings along the south side of the porch, to prevent the rain from blowing in, and then again to bring a plate of Lilly Washington's leftover brisket from the fridge. A hidden sadness runs beneath this account like a spring: the details vicarious, impotent, the two men discussing the dead woman and her young lover in the tones of archaeologists who are in some way envious of the passions of the dead. Mercury seems unconcerned, the topic safely distant, until the end, when Stan describes his decision to visit Keegan and turn the necklace in, his voice quicker now, suddenly embarrassed, telling about police headquarters, where he drove the night before, the smoke-stained blue paint and the pedaled water fountain and the three black doors marked *Homicide, Sex Crimes,* and *Robbery,* and how he waited for Keegan all night. He picks over the plate of brisket, saying, "The funny thing is, you know, I never imagined a fella could really go and see that kind of place. Shoot, all I ever did was watch police shows on TV."

221

"And so you have seen it now for real," Mercury says.

"I guess I did," Stan says. His mouth is full, sauce staining his chin, and he chews with (for him) the rare and prideful air of a young man who has done something risky and expects to be treated indulgently. "It sure was different from Waterloo."

"And I bet you surprised them," Mercury says. "A young man from the country who also happens to have information on the city's most famous murder case." His expression, too, has changed: gone is any semblance of welcome, of false joviality, replaced instead by the dryness of false agreement. "Yes," he says, "I bet you saved it for her, too. I bet you didn't breathe a word until she came back."

"Well," Stan says, "I figure it was something like that. I mean, she was glad to see me. Of course, on that first go-round, I didn't tell her everything. I'd already made up my mind about that."

"Of course," Mercury says. "Why give everything away?"

"That's what I thought," Stan says. "I figured we might as well start things off slowly, see if I could learn as much about her as she did from me. Anyway, she comes in this morning and calls me through this door—the secretary has to press a button to unlock it, see?—but I act like I'm not impressed. I act like it's nothing new to me, and that ain't too difficult because once we go in, all there is is desks. Just a bunch of desks and a map that don't look like it gets used much. And then she walks me down this aisle and points out her desk, which also ain't got nothing on it but a great big pile of papers, a fern plant, and a picture of an old woman and an old man. Her folks, I guess."

"No boyfriend?" Mercury says.

"What?" Stan says, blinking, confused. "What's that?"

"Never mind," says Mercury. His eyes glint, and he reaches to adjust a hurricane that has leaned too close to its flame. "Never mind. That's part of the lead-in, too, I'll bet."

Stan stops eating for a moment, watching him, fingers poised above his plate. Then he shakes his head like a dog who has unexpectedly gotten wet. "Anyway," he says, "we ain't done the interview

222

at her desk. They had a room in back with a big long table and a mirror and a window that faced City Hall, and we talked there—privately."

"Did you all talk about her visit here?" Mercury asks.

"She did, a little bit," Stan Granger says. In the candlelight, he looks like a corporal who expects to lose a battle and so has decided to get the fighting over with in a hurry. "Now," he says, "I understand why a man might have his reasons for not wanting to talk to the police—leave the river to the river, that's what my father always used to tell me. But when she told me what you said, it made me think. I mean, I never knew why Booker was there. I remember it sure *seemed* like you two was acquainted from someplace, I just never asked about where." He sucks air through his teeth. "I was just thinking that if we both went down to the station, then she—they—I mean Detective Keegan, might see the case differently. She said the same thing. She said, 'Well, Stan, I sure wish your friend would come down and try answering a couple more questions. It sounds like he might help us shed some real light on this case.'"

He pauses then. Mercury faces him, blinking. His skin is tight about his head, the full curve of his skull visible, moonlike, wrinkleless against the invading dark.

"'Questions,'" Mercury says. "What kind of questions, Stan?"

Stan has not moved during this exchange. He sits frozen, patient, but there is now the hint of a smile, suppressed, as he tucks his chin against his chest. "I had a feeling she ain't called you yet," he says. His voice is strangely triumphant. "And she could've, too. There wasn't any reason for her not to, unless—unless—" But he does not complete the sentence, thinking it instead, his face composed and inward-glowing: *Unless it was because she thought I was right about it. Because she trusted me.* And he reaches into his shirt pocket and retrieves a single sheet of green ruled paper, spiral-bound and torn across the top. "They got a couple things they can't figure out," he says. "Names, mostly. There's two of them. This first they got off the

223

Mexican who was in Clarissa's car, and the other one was printed on that necklace I gave back." He slides the piece of paper across the table to Mercury. "Marcy—er, Detective Keegan—thought it might be familiar to someone who knew Booker, his family."

Mercury unfolds the paper and holds it lightly between his fingers. It is written in a woman's script, clearly not Stan Granger's hand, the vowels and loops slanted backward, innocuous, so that the names themselves appear less like accusations, or murder suspects, than the articles on a grocery list:

> Reggie Hammonds?
> Isaac Bentham?

Mercury's cheeks twitch for a moment, lifting in the motion a man makes to adjust his glasses, except he isn't wearing any. He folds the paper and hands it back. "Stan," he says, "I am leaving town tomorrow. I've hired a lawyer to represent Booker if he's found; I've left money in an account, and I'd advise you to do the same: leave. Walk away. You're young. You can make new friends, new companions. You can still forget these."

"But what if he ain't done it?" Stan says. "What if—"

"Listen," Mercury says. His face looms lanternlike above the hurricanes. "You must listen to me, believe. It doesn't matter about that. It doesn't matter about the names. It doesn't even matter whether or not he did anything— Look," he says, seeing the expression of doubt, perhaps incomprehension, on Stan Granger's face. "Look here. I have known my housekeeper, Lilly Washington, for sixty years. There has never been anything between us that was broken, that needed to be fixed. Do you see? Do you see what I am saying? It's not a matter of white and black"—his voice is urgent, high-pitched—"it's that certain *people* in this world are broken. Those are the ones you have to be afraid of, because they will make you responsible for what happens. They will make you take the blame. And you can't help them,

224

either. Why? Because they . . . they don't . . . His voice sticks until his body discovers what to say. "Because they are broken," he repeats. "Booker and Clarissa. People like that. They are broken, and the only thing to do if you don't want to be broken with them is to leave, to run as fast as you can away."

He shrinks back in his chair then, his body seeming to implode, deflate.

"Go, Stan. Go," he says, waving his hand. "Get out of here. If you've got a confession to make, just tell it to the police. They're paid to deal with broken things."

"I can't do that," Stan says.

"Why not?" Mercury asks.

Stan considers for a moment, the two men silent, their figures framed against the hissing rain. "That's why I come to you," he says. "'Cause I ain't told her yet. I mean I could, I guess. I just don't know if it's legal not to—" But Mercury is already recoiling now, rising, his face white, as if bitten by a snake, saying, "If what is legal, Stan? What in God's name have you—" as Stan sits there with the candlelight spilling over his bony country face, his bulbous Adam's apple, his ridiculous white shirt with the black filigree.

"I found him," he says. "Booker. He left a message on my machine."

16

HE HAD WALKED downtown from Clarissa's Stingray, his duffel slung over one shoulder and beating against his back. It was noon. The rain had not yet started, but the air smelled sweet and wet, and as he passed among the old brick warehouses and machine shops in the lower Thirties, the seeds of cottonwoods swirled and darted toward him from the empty lots and jungled railroad sidings, like the stuffing from an exploded bed. He had decided nothing yet. It was as if his mind wanted to wait, knowing a decision must be made, knowing even what it would be, and yet saying to itself, *Yes, but you do not have to do it now. Not yet,* and for a moment he managed to escape into his memory. He saw again the image of his father's face, his bed on Beech Street, the alley down which he'd walked to school under a ripe persimmon tree. His desire for this fantasy, its closeness, sickened him. It seemed for a brief moment as if he might turn down an empty sidewalk and enter his own boyhood yet again, before so many mistakes had been made, and it was then that his mind started to work again, saying, *All right, now: you can think it now,* and he stopped in the middle of the sidewalk, the air humid, the cottonwood seeds spinning in tufts about his arms and feet, and he allowed himself to think about who had killed Clarissa Sayers, the certainty of what he had to do spilling over him cold, against his will, like a wave.

This certainty—or perhaps he would've called it madness—

226

lasted for about half a day. He had checked into the Coronado Hotel by then, crossing on foot under the interstate and its green palisade of signs and city names, TOPEKA and DENVER to the west, DES MOINES and ST. LOUIS to the north and east, and into downtown, the final circle of buildings caught between the river and the highway loop. He headed west on Tenth Street. He did not know where he was going, exactly, feeling instead as if he were being propelled by some force outside himself that, as long as he followed its directions, made him invincible — or beyond care. A cluster of one-night hotels lined Locust Street. He had glimpsed them once before, perhaps from the window of Clarissa's car as they drove to some reception downtown: the Schuyler, the Monroe, the Snyderhoff, the names themselves suggesting a burgherlike respectability that had long since drained away from their stained brick facades, their broken cornices, their sash-weight windows crammed with air conditioners' butt ends. The Coronado was the last of these. It faced onto Ninth, a rail-thin building with a neon sign that flashed slantwise on one end, and Booker entered it without question, as if he had, for all of his twenty-one years, been destined for this very place. The lobby was painted brown: not merely the woodwork and the walls, but the light fixtures, the banisters, the linoleum, even what had once been a gilded chandelier. The steps were brown, with heavy rubber treads and metal edge guards that had been painted, too (though not very convincingly), and as he climbed them from the anteroom, he came into a high-ceilinged, pictureless hall, its upper parts dark, its walls lit at head level by a series of wrought-iron lamps. A TV played behind a cage in back, set atop a coffee table and secured with a heavy chain; to his right was the front desk, enclosed in Plexiglas, its counter slick and glossy from repeated coats of paint, save for the slot through which the money passed. A television played there, too, chained to a metal stand, and he stood there watching as white letters rolled across the screen, promising more details on the Sayers case at six, until one of the men in the lounge noticed him and called out, "Hey, Eddie —

227

you got someone here," and a thick-shouldered man emerged from a room behind the desk. He wore slippers and pinstriped suit pants, his upper body covered by a tank-top undershirt, and his braces hanging against his hips. He had been in prison; Booker sensed this right away, just as he knew the man would sense the same thing about him, the two of them gauging each other across the painted counter, the man nodding briefly, a faint smile, almost imperceptible, touching his lips. It was then that Booker knew he would be safe here, that if he and this man had anything in common it would be a dislike of the police, a refusal to cooperate, the man saying: "How long you staying for?" and Booker answering, "Two days," and the man neither smiling nor frowning, just looking Booker directly in the face and saying, "If you ain't got a driver's license, it's twenty extra on the deposit, cash."

"All right," Booker said. "I'll pay tomorrow for the second day."

The man nodded as Booker removed his last eighty dollars from his wallet and set forty in the worn wood groove. He picked up a carbon tablet and a pen. "Name?" he said.

"Reggie Hammonds," Booker said.

The man wrote. He did so laboriously, the pen pressing deep into the carbon tablet, and then he pushed the pen and ticket through the slot to Booker.

"Sign it," he said.

The room was on the eighth floor. He had thought that he would stay in it until nightfall, that that was why he'd come, but once upstairs he saw that he'd been wrong again, smiling—perhaps maniacally, perhaps merely at fate—as he unlocked the dingy enclosure and found himself staring out a shotgun window at the stone walls of the Federal Judicial Building, just one block west of him, on Grand Avenue. He had intended to sleep. This had been his one conscious choice, his one attempt at logic, believing that he would be moving again by dark (thought he did not know what those movements would be), and yet five minutes after lying down in his underwear on the plastic sheet, he was sitting at the window again, searching for what he imagined would be the judge's private chambers, his pocketknife dangling between his knees. And at five o'clock he found himself outside the federal building itself, buoyed on the spring tide of secretaries and office clerks who poured forth from the city's cubicles with their eager punctuality, and gazing up at a bronze plaque that listed the amendments in the Bill of Rights. He walked back with a strange, wild sense of freedom, of invulnerability, as if the people about him were not real but had been filmed earlier and were being projected, as in old movies, onto a screen, so that he appeared as the only three-dimensional being among a mass of shades. He even strolled in front of police headquarters dressed in his best collared shirt and jeans, and ducked into the Total station down the street, where he bought four days' worth of soup, crackers, and tinned sardines. It was not until midnight that this madness broke, the rage passing like a fever while he slept, and he woke trembling, his sweat pooled on the plastic sheets, terrified at his own stupidity.

He stayed in his room that morning. He was thinking more calmly then, without the madness, and in his thinking he sorted out two things, the primary one being that he would rather die or quit a coward than go back to jail in Tulsa—a preference that in his opinion precluded any possibility of taking his own story down to the police.

His second conclusion was more complicated, though related: he did not want Judge Sayers dead. Aside from the fact that killing a man seemed fantastical, beyond his powers, it also defeated his purpose. He wanted Judge Sayers to *know* that he was there, to admit his presence, to be forced to deal with him in some way. He wanted him to realize that this time he would not run away. How this would translate into action, he could not clearly say, and in the end he had to laugh, seated in the bare and grit-covered chair, because having decided not to kill the judge, he could do nothing but wait—a prospect he did not relish in the least. The Coronado was generally depressing, filled with the steady, croupy coughs of pensioners, and so, when the occupant in the room next to him begin to sing along to salsa music,

Booker leaned out the window curiously. After a time, a thin-wristed young Mexican appeared in the window next to him, speaking in a mixture of Spanish and English, a cell phone clamped to his ear. The conversation seemed to be mostly about transportation, the boy repeating, *Yes, but I do not have the wheels,* the phrase drifting across the buildingtops to the courthouse on the hill. It was then that Booker had his idea.

"Hey, kid," he said to the Mexican. "How'd you like to do something interesting instead of sitting around this dump and singing hoochy songs all day?"

The Mexican finished his phone call and swiveled his head. "First," he said, "my name is Angel Diaz, not 'kid,' and if we are going to do business, it would be better for you to call me that. Second"— he listed these points on the fingers of his right hand—"this is not hoochy music that I listen to, but salsa, which has a name. Third, if this interesting thing involves money, I do not work for under one hundred dollars a day."

Their conversation continued in the younger boy's room, which, as he explained, he had "rented for the weekend" and which he, unlike Booker, had thoroughly scrubbed and cleaned, fitting the bed with his own pillows and sheets and hanging a discreet crucifix above the bed. Booker sat on a metal folding chair and told a story about Clarissa Sayers's Stingray designed to give the Mexican every reason to steal the thing. He kept the details vague: the car belonged to a friend who owed Booker money; the friend had gotten in some trouble and had left the car in Booker's hands. He needed someone to deliver it to the levee road that night, where some other friends would pick it up. "And pay you my fee," he added.

"What happens if these other friends don't come?" Angel asked.

Booker shrugged: he did not care. However, if Angel wanted, he would write down the number of the car's owner, just in case any problem should come up. The Mexican nodded, and Booker scribbled Judge Sayers's office number on an empty cigarette pack,

230

handing it to him with a mixture of elation and regret: elation at the message that he hoped would reach his enemy, regret because his messenger would know he'd been betrayed.

He left the hotel that afternoon. There were too many complications in staying after he had revealed himself to one of the residents— and besides, he could not afford to be there when and if Angel Diaz came back. It was raining, a fine drizzle, and he walked northward, toward the river, wearing a hooded sweatshirt, hands tucked into his pockets, a figure of indeterminate race wandering to the end of Grand Avenue, between the fruit sellers' warehouses and the power plant. The river swirled below, spanned by the steel scaffold of the train bridge that he had traversed more than two years earlier, when he first entered this strange city. The bridge beckoned him, the rails black and wet, running together on the far side of the span, but he resisted and headed instead eastward into a ragged stand of oak and elms along the river's bank, where he wandered for the remainder of the day. At some point, crashing through a willow thicket, he figured that he had already passed by Clarissa's dying place and toward nightfall he stopped among three men who'd built a fire where the foundation of a house had once been.

They were vagrants, partners. The two whites, he guessed, were brothers, their kinship stamped on their inward-cleaving foreheads, the matching fretwork of their hands' veins; the third was black, immense, and wore a huge orange poncho draped about his shoulders, like those used by football players or members of the mounted police. Booker sat with them to eat. The conversation was arcane, the men describing to him an unknown second world of politics and territorial disputes among the dispossessed, and when he asked them where he might stay, they suggested an abandoned building called the Hotel President. It was not more than fifteen blocks away, twelve stories of empty rooms—"if you don't mind sharing with pigeons," one brother said—and easy to get into, provided you could reach the fire escape in back. The brothers' voices were courtly, tinged with the

231

bent vowels of North Dakota, where they said they had been raised, but Booker was more interested in the black, who stared at the fire with his brooding, liver-colored face. He noticed a silence. The brothers had stopped talking, their eyes bright with feral curiosity. "Ain't you reckernize him?" one said, jerking his chin at the black. "Or feel like you did?"

Booker shook his head. The brothers seemed pleased with this.

"That there is Rosie Tucker," whispered the one on his left. "Played middle linebacker at Ohio State. Now, I ain't saying you're in trouble just 'cause you're out tramping in the rain"—he winked at Booker—"but if you was, he'd be one to considerate: a man who tackled like a one-man wrecking crew and got cheered by a hundred thousand folks every Saturday. Hell, Bart and I used to seen him on TV. And then one day we come up on the same old Rosie outside a railroad cut in Fort Wayne, Indiana. It's May. There he sits, a-blubbering and a-bawling under this old mulberry tree. From the smell of it, he hadn't moved in a couple days. You got to picture it: this big old black fella, strong enough to pick up a refrigerator, crying like a babe. Wits gone clear astray."

Across the fire, the black moaned in a low, plaintive tone, lips wet, boots shuffling. Booker gripped his duffel. "What happened to him?" he asked.

"He won't say," the brother said. "Maybe them Buckeye gals laid him so often, he just lost his head. Maybe all that being famous just went and rotted out his brain."

"—or he might've always been that way," the other brother said.

"A man who won't admit to his own troubles is a terrible thing," the brother said. The moaning deepened, ululant, and he rose and sidled toward the black, asking Booker, "You know what he's afraid of?" and then saying, "Tell the man, Rosie. Tell him what it is makes you upset," in a voice that might be used for someone deaf. He drew back the black's hood. Its owner whimpered and raised his hands to shield his head—revealing as he did so a rope that dangled like a horse hob-

232

ble, between his left ankle and wrist. "He's afraid of the goddamn rain," the brother said. "Imagine, a great big linebacker like that."

He turned for a reaction, but Booker was gone, sprinting through the trees, and as they listened to his footfalls, the black began to giggle, rocking before the flames.

"Hell," he said in a warped voice. "He got some speed, at least."

17

THERE IS ONE OTHER mourner on this Sunday night. He fills a glass with water from the tap and then seats himself at the kitchen table, where he has spread the briefs from his latest case. Each room in the house seems to hold the scent of every action that has happened there, the pungent ashes of his first marriage in the bedroom, his wife's cancer oozing in the commode upstairs. And so, looking up from his papers, he is not surprised to remember how, coming home from work fourteen years before, he found his wife squatting on kitchen floor, the scent of burning metal curling from an empty frying pan.

"She won't come to me," she said.

"Who?" he asked. "Who are you talking about—Clarissa?"

Crying, she bit her lip.

"This is no time for games," he said. He was frenzied then, shaking her—again by mere instinct, given how little he had, up to that point, been interested in the kid. "Is she in trouble? Is she hurt?" he asked. "Come on, you've got to talk to me."

"You bastard," she said.

"'Bastard'?" he said. "I just got home. What could I—"

"You bastard," she repeated. Her nose bubbled as she spoke. "It isn't fair. Do you have to ruin everything? Do you have to do it even when you aren't here?"

The judge found Clarissa in his third-floor office. The bolt had been thrown, and kneeling to the keyhole, he could see his daughter seated beneath his cherrywood table, surrounded by magazines. These were art journals, from a subscription to a vaguely European publication called *Réalités*, which he kept for their avant-garde cachet, their photographs of models in dresses constructed of tin cans and plastic sheets—very often nude beneath. He saw that Clarissa had been cutting pictures from the pages with her mother's wrapping shears. She wore shorts and sandals, and her hair, jet-black, fell about her face. Her cheeks still held their reservoirs of baby fat, but he noticed that her arms and legs had thinned, her ankles sinewed now when flexed, her arched feet almost womanly. There were other toys about, scattered marbles, a box of white-fuzzed wire cleaners and their accompanying hazelwood pipe, and when he knocked, she picked the pipe up and stuck it in the corner of her mouth, the bowl cupped in her left hand, which angled across her breast. He recognized the gesture as his, committed only in that same room, with the door locked for privacy (he did not smoke in any other place), and when she answered, without looking up, "I'm busy right now. Come back another day," a string tightened in his chest as if set to its peg: she'd been watching him in there, too, it seemed.

"Clarissa," he said. "What are you doing?"

"Playing," his daughter said. She was now self-consciously busy, holding the human-shaped cutouts from the magazines together like slips of shadow in her hands.

"I don't like people going in my office without permission," he said.

"I kno-o-w that," Clarissa said, as if she found this clarification exasperating.

"—or cutting up my magazines," Thornton said.

She looked directly at the keyhole then. Her face, he realized, was flushed with pleasure, and he felt the sudden pressure of his collar about his neck. "Daddy," she said, almost laughing, "are you spying on me?" His gaze met her dark eyes for one moment, exchanging a confidence whose meaning he could not then utter or explain, before he jolted upward to his feet, suddenly embarrassed, the blood rushing to his head.

"Open up this door," he said.

She did so. He could hear the reluctant slapping of her sandals, the turn of the bolt, and then the same feet scurrying hurriedly away. He entered slowly. The anger he felt had little to do with her transgressions, but rather centered on the impression of her solitary gaze: no child should be allowed to look at a grown man that way. Several of the photos she had cut out were, in fact, nudes: a photo essay on a nudist beach in which a balding man, his stomach rolled with fat, posed with his naked family; a topless pose struck by a dancer in a cabaret. He did not attempt to take these away. Instead he sat on the daybed just inside the door, where he sometimes lay to read. They were, father and daughter, aware of each other for the first time mutually, the evening sunlight pooling yellow on the oak floor, dust motes stirring lazily in her wake, and as he watched her thumb through his magazines, he felt dizzy at the presence of a life and mind whose complications he hadn't previously known to exist. "Clarissa," he said. "What's this about not letting people come up here to play? Why do you do that?"

"I let you in, didn't I?" Clarissa said.

"That's not what your mother said."

"Oh, really—?" She flipped a page with a slicing sound.

"Yes," Thornton said. He cradled his head between his hands then, bending slightly. His collar choked him, and he undid it. "Yes," he repeated. "Your mother is downstairs, and her feelings are hurt. She says you wouldn't let her in."

"My mo-o-ther," Clarissa said in the same bored drawl, "isn't very fun to play with." She looked up at Thornton. "She doesn't like things to be interesting."

"That's not nice," Thornton said.

Clarissa smiled at him as if he'd said something droll.

"But it's true," she said.

It was the beginning of his first and only friendship—the only one that ever mattered to him. They understood each other immediately, they possessed a common enemy, and so their relationship was one of secret partners, operating under the guise of Thornton's parental authority. He never disagreed with his wife's rulings, merely accepted them with a smile, his need to struggle with her having been adopted now by his daughter, who battled with her incessantly, was obstinate, disliked the ordered life of pool and store and women's luncheons, and watched too much TV. Clarissa understood the double nature of his role, and sitting in his empty kitchen, Thornton still remembers how, when he was sent to spank her for some grievous offense, Clarissa would cry in what seemed to be genuine fear until they reached her room, where she would flash a rogue's smile and howl with the conviction of a stage actress while he slapped his belt against his knee. At times he had to pin her, squirming, between his legs, hand covering her mouth so her laughter would not give them both away.

"Careful," he used to whisper. "You'll get me in trouble, too, honey."

18

IN FIFTEEN YEARS, Detective Marcy Keegan had rarely resorted to superstition in her work, the beat cop's shadow world of hunches and forebodings, and consequently she lacked the vocabulary to explain why she gritted her teeth each time her unmarked car glided among the clipped hedges and faux-English gardens that lined Mission Hills' broad streets. Or why, seated in the Mediterranean dining rooms of its residents, she worried that she'd chosen the wrong place and that her subjects had nothing to say—fears that weren't eased by her partner, who clearly believed that her instincts were off base.

"So what's it gonna be today?" asked Detective Charlie Schiff as they drove by the Sayers house on Fifty-ninth Street and entered the wealthy enclave. "We gonna talk to some more old ladies about their views on racial justice, or are we gonna do something important—like follow up on one of your boyfriend's tips?"

He smiled and took a bite of the apple he held in his left hand.

"To whom are you referring, Detective?" Keegan said.

"Mr. Granger, I guess that would be," Schiff said, straightening with mock formality in his seat. "Unless you got another one I ain't heard of yet."

"He has given us two good names," Keegan said.

"That's what's funny," Schiff said. He leaned forward, his arm

238

reaching out the cruiser's open window to pluck a bug from the windscreen. "Here you are one of the best damn trackers in the office, which is probably why they kept you on the case. And we also got a situation where there's somebody to be tracked, and where that somebody has gone and killed a judge's daughter, which nobody's happy about—least of all the chief. We've got the car, and the room that he was staying in, and yet here you are, driving around to golf courses talking about a couple of names, one of which we already asked this guy Chapman about and he didn't know anything." He wiped the green mess of the bug's body on the rubber window seal. "So," he said, "what do you think of that?"

"Not much," Keegan said.

"All right," Schiff said. "How about this idea: you can keep checking out your weird necklaces and the stories you get from some old-boy fisherman if you want to, but I ain't going down with the ship. There you've got it, fair and square."

Keegan's eyes fluttered between the road and the odometer, counting. "Charlie," she said, "I've been working with you long enough that you don't need to tell me that."

Schiff was right. Keegan had never previously been interested in the "story" of a homicide, but had preferred instead the simplicity of pursuit, her single theory being that once the missing parties were apprehended, the rest of the evidence would fall into place. Unfortunately, her instinct had failed her in this case. The desire wasn't there, the certainty that came from being on a suspect's trail, and she considered this—the superstitions of police officers, the fragility of reputation—as they climbed the Colonial Club's front drive. The clubhouse was pure white clapboard, multiwinged, and Keegan circled a shadowed carriage port where a white-haired woman dressed in lavender stepped from the backdoor of a Cadillac, patting her driver with one gloved hand. The scene flashed by, the woman's unheard chatter, her strangely youthful urbanity, suggesting in that moment an entire world and history that neither cop had ever seen. In the back lot, a child jogged past them carrying a tennis racket in a nylon case, and Schiff stared at her as she disappeared.

"Okay," he said. "So could you tell me why we're *here*, please?"

"Two reasons," Keegan said as they parked in a row of Lexuses and Mercedeses, all of which seemed to have been washed that day. "First, because the trail is dead."

"'Dead'?" Schiff said. "We just found the car."

"Dead," Keegan answered, "because we didn't find him." She stayed a half step in front of Schiff, her forehead lined, speaking to her partner more openly than usual, in part out of embarrassment. "We found his room," she said, "only he's not there. It's three blocks from the station. He signs in under this guy Hammonds's name. Same thing with the car: we find it right downtown, a week after the murder, and he gives the guy the judge's phone number and the same name. Now, what does that all mean to you?"

"It means he's too stupid to figure out another alias," Schiff said.

"To me," Keegan said, "it means he's not trying to run away. He had almost three days to leave before we even found the body—take the bus, hitchhike, whatever he wanted to do."

"So what's the second reason?" Schiff asked.

"Spikes," Keegan said. Despite his height, Schiff had to walk double time to keep up, skipping after Keegan in his pale-yellow jacket, the ankles of his cowboy boots visible beneath uncuffed pants. "Spikes," he whispered as they neared a path lined with maroon day lilies. "For Chrissakes, Marcy, the judge said she had them in her apartment. The kid probably just put 'em on her for the hell of it, to make her look different."

Keegan halted, facing Schiff along the flowered path.

"Don't you think," she said, "that sounds a little strange?"

A Mission Hills cop in full dress uniform stood at attention at the club's entrance. He was in his forties, sandy-haired, his scalp sunburned along a high widow's peak (he removed his cap as they came

240

in), and as Keegan reached for a door that led off the club's patio, the officer stopped her, saying, "I'm sorry, Detective, that's the men's grill. They don't let women in." They followed him to the far side of the building, Keegan's nostrils white about the edges as the officer waved them into a garage. Golf carts gleamed in ordered rows, their sides painted the same deep burgundy as the club's flag, and thick black cables coiled from a rack of metal boxes to each cart's battery. A boy hosed down the already clean floor, dressed in burgundy shorts and a white collared shirt stitched with the same insignia Clarissa Sayers had worn. "Now, Detective," said the Mission Hills cop, clapping his hands. "What exactly is it that we can do for you today?"

"I want to look around," Keegan said.

The officer bowed with condescending tolerance. "This is a private club, Detective," he said. "They may not have very many of these in Missouri, but I'm sure you know that you can't just go around examining the bathrooms and questioning the members—not without a warrant at least." He chuckled at the thought. "I'm sorry. It just doesn't work that way."

"She wants the pro," Schiff said.

"Excuse me?" said the officer.

"You heard what I said," Schiff answered. He was seated in a golf cart behind the officer, his boots up on the dash. "And if we can't get the pro, we'll try the manager. Hey, kid," he said to the caddie with the hose, "you got a phone line to the pro shop here?"

"Sure," the kid said.

"Well, let's buzz him up," Schiff said, wagging his thumb and pinky by his ear.

The pro arrived some twenty minutes later, strolling off the ninth green, a caddie trailing with his bag. Although nearing seventy, he maintained the athletic gait of a much younger man, his wrists cocked, his shirt hunched and sweat-stained about his shoulders. He wore an inverted sailor's hat, its formless brim offset by the brick-red definition of his face. "J. P. Lawton," he said, waving a putter. "Can I help anybody?"

"Mr. Lawton," she said, "I'm Detective Keegan with the KCPD. I was wondering if you could tell us who was working here the night of June twelfth."

"None of my boys," he said.

"Is there security?" Keegan said.

"Three men," Lawton said. "Not that it's worth anything."

"So at night people do sometimes get in," Keegan said.

Lawton shrugged. He gripped the putter he'd brought in, his fingers folding conchlike about the shaft. "Folks get drunk," he said, "carve bad words on the green. The usual stupid things—never very serious." He made a graceful practice stroke, smiling at Keegan from his follow-through. "But that's not what you came to talk about, Detective, is it? So how about if you tell me why you're interested in that date?"

"Because that was the last night Clarissa Sayers was seen alive," Keegan said.

"Ma'am?" Lawton said.

"Could I see your records, please?" Keegan asked.

Lawton seemed genuinely sad at this request. "Carrie," he said, calling to a caddie. "Get me the chart on last Sunday's greens repairs." The caddie brought a clipboard from a small office separated from the garage by a wire screen. Lawton thumbed through it, reading beneath his misshapen finger's end. "Moved the cup on numbers one, five, and eight," he said, skimming downward. Then he paused. "Replaced sod and trap lip on seventeen," he said. He looked up. "It's not unusual. Especially for a weekend."

But Keegan had already turned to leave the garage.

"I'd like to see it, please," she said.

They took a cart, Lawton driving, Keegan beside him, with Schiff and the caddie, who'd helped repair the damage, riding on the back grate. Lawton drove carefully. The course had been empty for the bet-

242

ter part of the week due to rain, he explained, and even now, during the morning's brief clearing, the carts had been kept in to prevent them from tearing up the fairways. The pro, for his part, stuck to the trees, jouncing over a root-ridden path that led them far from the clubhouse, far from anything, and that ended with Schiff's stepping down from the cart's back grate with mud spattered on his pant legs. "Sorry," Lawton said. But Schiff merely nodded, his jaw clenched as it had been since the start of Keegan's questioning. "Not your fault," he said. Keegan had left them already. She was crouching on the fringe, her fingers rubbing the bent grass, when the thump and roll of an approach shot landed ten yards to her left. Lawton removed her, his hand angrily gripping her bicep until the players finished, then guiding the detective forward again. "All right, go have your look," he said.

The green formed a standard saddle shape, with a high tier toward the back and a deep trap to the right front. The damage had occurred here. A ten-by-ten-foot section of the green had been re-placed by rolled strips of sod, their rectangular edges still visible, and—this according to the caddie; no visible evidence remained— the front lip of the trap had caved away, the sand divoted and mussed, as if "someone had been dancing in it." On her hands and knees, Keegan examined the new grass and lingered above the trap's pit. It had been raked that morning, the furrows circling outward from the center, geometrically.

Keegan beckoned to the caddie.

"Were there footprints in here?" she asked.

"Yeah," the caddie said. "There usually is—I mean, that's how people mess up traps, is walk in them. It could've been that the last player Saturday decided not to rake."

"You don't remember what they looked like?" Keegan said.

"Not really," the caddie said. "It could've been somebody fell or sat down or just hacked out of there a bunch. It seemed pretty ordinary."

Keegan turned back to the green and inspected the edges of the new turf. "And this part?" she asked. "What did this part look like?"

"Tore up," the caddie said.

"'Tore up' how?" Keegan said. "Like somebody had on spikes?"

The caddie shrugged. "I don't know. Just tore up," he said.

It had begun to rain. Lawton and Schiff stood some fifteen yards from the green, Schiff with his arms folded and his jaw still set. A second group of players leaned on their clubs in the fairway 150 yards away. The rain streamed down cool and thin, and a pale mist furled around the edges of the green. Oblivious, Keegan hunched over a set of small holes that showed incompletely on the edges of the new turf. She patted them with her fingers.

"C'mon, Marcy," Schiff said. "Fresh grass ain't gonna tell us anything."

Keegan rose. They had reached the clubhouse before she spoke again, still seated in the cart, after Lawton and Schiff had dismounted and walked away.

"Mr. Lawton," she said. "Could I see the bottoms of your shoes?"

"What?" Lawton said.

"Your shoes," Keegan said. "The bottoms of them."

Regretfully, almost like a child, Lawton picked up his heel. The bottom of his golf shoe had been fitted with small plastic knobs.

"Those aren't spikes," Keegan said.

"We call 'em soft spikes," Lawton replied. "We had the members change to them a couple years ago 'cause they don't hurt the greens. Nobody wears real spikes anymore."

"Nobody?" Keegan said.

"That's right, ma'am," Lawton said.

"Thank you," Keegan said.

Clyde Wilkins had been drying glasses behind the bar when Detective Keegan first crossed the club's terrace. His usual lunch crowd followed her with fascination: Mrs. Holloway with her snow-white hair,

244

her broadly wrinkled face; the Jones brothers, Clive and Harold, who though five years apart in age had grown so similar-looking that they were accepted as twins; Hattie Oldenbrook, Martha Wallace, and June Snifter, who sat at a nearby table, playing pitch. They were septuagenarians for the most part, widows and widowers, who used the club as people in Clyde's neighborhood might have used a church, and unlike most of the other members, they had been softened by the weakness of age, its fearful need of company. Clyde treated them indulgently—had grown to like them, even—and so was surprised when their interest in the policewoman irritated him so viscerally. He bristled as they squeezed together in front of the two windows on either side of the fireplace, their skirts and crisp suit pants in rows of red and teal, their aged and spotted heels lifting from the soles of sandals or polished two-toned shoes.

"That woman has a gun on her," Hattie Oldenbrook said.

"Does she? Where?"

"On the far side—that's how they wear them, isn't it? With a leather strap," Hattie said. "I bet that other man had one under his jacket. How do they call it?"

"A piece," Mrs. Holloway said.

"They're *packing*," Martha Wallace said.

"I bet I know what it is," said Hattie. "I bet they're here asking about Judge Sayers's daughter."

"Is that it, Clyde?" asked Martha.

Clyde shrugged.

"Come now, Clyde. Surely you must know *something*. . . ."

These questions only irritated him more intensely, and as he listened to his customers speculate on the detectives' motives ("HATTIE THINKS THEY'RE HERE LOOKING FOR THAT COLORED BOY," he could hear Clive Jones shouting to his deaf brother, "THE ONE THAT KILLED JUDGE SAYERS'S GIRL"), his ears burned with embarrassment. It was a sensation he usually felt when he interrupted a group of whites discussing race: an embarrassment at their embarrassment, at the way their voices dropped when he cleared their drinks. In this situation, however, the moral advantage had reversed. The woman's speculation had been innocent; they had asked him their questions directly, without assuming that he knew anything about the case. And later, after the detectives' car sped down the drive and Mrs. Holloway said, "I wonder what that poor boy has been doing, hiding out for a week in all this rain—" he felt an intense burst of shame.

The truth was that he didn't have the guts to say what he believed.

19

FOR THE REST of the city, the foremost concern on this Monday afternoon was the rain—a possible calamity that, like Clarissa Sayers's murder, kept fading irresolutely into gray. Henry Latham paced his third-floor corner office in the brick and terra-cotta confines of the Kansas City Star Building, irritated by these vagaries. Like everything in this city, the rain lacked power and clarity: it had no flash and thunder, felled no trees or power lines. It was instead a leak, a drip, a kind of rot that innumerable rainfall tables had failed to dramatize, and it did not help that now, at one o'clock, it had started up again. Latham returned to his desk. The light was poor in his office due to the wood paneling he'd installed to make it look different from everybody else's, and through his window he could see the dump of Grand Avenue: empty storefronts, bolts rusting in hieroglyphic patterns where their signs had been. In Dallas, where he was born, a developer would have demolished those buildings and put something decent there. The same went for Denver, or Cleveland, or Atlanta, or any of the other cities that Capital Cities (the company that owned the *Star* and for which he had worked since the age of twenty-three) might have sent him to. Nor would it have happened in Kansas, out at 115th and Metcalf, where he would've moved his office had the land not been so pitifully ugly and flat.

He felt, at such moments, like a colonialist: not an American one, but a Spaniard, or one from the south of France, a man who had been sent from a hot, dry climate to fester someplace wet. He had forgotten what power and clarity were supposed to be, and his crotch (he was a heavy man with a double chin, wearing cowboy boots that pinched his small feet) had developed an itch that no amount of medicated powder would ease. He leaned forward, retrieved a plastic transparency from his wastebasket, and set it on his blotter.

KANSAS CITY IN CRISIS

it said, over the logo of a house roof surrounded by water.

THE RAINS OF 199–

"I am doing," he said aloud to his office, "a series of articles on a crapping leak."

The word *leak* bothered him a bit. He knew perfectly well that in a world of power and clarity, the story he should have been following was Clarissa Sayers's death. His reporters had dug up no leads, in part because he had hidden several facts from them—most significantly that Booker Short, the suspect, had worked at a hunting club owned by Remy Westbrook, Mercury Chapman, and several other bigwigs. Henry had been invited there several times, had met the kid, even ridden in the skiff with him, and yet he had not told Alvin Bailey this because, in a jungle outpost like this, what one valued most—more than the truth or even a good story—was men of power and clarity. Remy Westbrook and Mercury Chapman resembled fellow colonialists, men who could remind one of one's own worth, of one's humanity. He did not care to print their names in relation to a murder, for the simple reason that he did not care to exile himself from their company. One dead white girl would not change anything. This thought caused Henry Latham to bark "Ha!" and jump up from his seat, worried that such reasoning proved he had gone native entirely.

"Margaret," he said into his intercom. "Get me McNeely."

• • •

By two o'clock the rain had settled in. It seemed not to fall so much as to drift, sometimes sideways, sometimes even upward, billowing away in spectacular, winglike buffets from the windscreens of the cars trundling south down Grand Avenue, outside Henry Latham's window. It swirled about the high glass walls of the American Phone Company Building downtown and dusted the backs of trucks in the deep canyons of the interstate, the drivers complacent in their high seats, eyeing the city's snarl of steel and concrete as they steered for the plains. It fell on road-crew workers and line trimmers and on city trash men who gazed up at the sky from beneath their yellow slickers and said, "Awright, Mr. Rainman, you can quit now. Don't wait on us for anything."

Behind the trash men, it fell on the roof of a Nissan 240 SX owned (or at least paid for monthly) by Bert Gauss, who also knew something about the Sayers case that he had not told anybody. He was sorry about it. He would've gladly done something heroic to save Clarissa's life, but for a young lawyer, testifying that a federal judge had committed incest had no upside. It was just a rumor; it would likely be excluded as hearsay in any trial, and his involvement would thus constitute a form of professional suicide. . . . Still, there was something nagging about the rain, the mucus-colored strings of trash juice that dripped from the worker's garbage bags, and he cursed it soundlessly from behind the Nissan's glass.

It rained on everybody equally. It rained on the shoppers scurrying between Brooks Brothers and Abercrombie and Fitch on the Plaza as Berg Gauss's car shot past; it rained on the doorman at the Ritz, and on the balconies of the lonely women who kept apartments in the Hemingway, the St. Martin, and the Sulgrave. It rained on Brush Creek, which on normal days flowed in a small trickle through the center of the Plaza, banked in a concrete ditch, but now ran in a thick black sheet some forty yards across, flecked with toilet paper and floating curls of shit. It rained down on Ninth Street, where Wallace Evenrake stood at the front door of the Coronado Hotel and attempted to imagine where, had he been a fugitive, he would've walked to on such a day. The building appeared to him as a sonorous and concrescent mystery, like an obelisk, its high brick walls and faded pediments dark against the sky, marred by the butts of air conditioners, the entire mixture so hermetic and so foreign with its Germanic fasciae, its murmuring black tenants, and its mythic Spanish name that it fed beyond any reason the curiosity of a reporter from the Kansas plains. He had no concept of what it would be like to stay in such a place, feared it, and yet desired to know the answer, watching as a woman exited through the glass front door in a yellow tubedress, her backside protuberant—and then he headed for the river, his imagination aflame, walking in the direction that he would have walked, it seemed, had he killed his lover on that same day.

Back in Henry Latham's office, the city editor, McNeely, had arrived from downstairs. He was the kind of editor Latham liked: pale, white-collared, bloated, his arm and belly flesh possessing the watery consistency of fresh crabmeat. "All right, goddammit," Latham said. "Tell me who the hell it is that we got on this Sayers case."

"Bailey," the editor answered. His lips resembled rosy strips of ginger. He scanned a clipboard. "And Evenrake."

"Who?" Latham shouted.

"Alvin Bailey—he's our cop reporter."

"No, no, not Bailey, I know him. The other one."

"Evenrake," McNeely said.

"Yes, Evenwrite," Latham said. "Who the hell is that?"

"Our intern," McNeely said.

Latham paused, his brows furrowed. He had strong opinions about reporters—namely, that good ones were dangerous and needed to be kept in check. McNeely, for instance, was a terrible reporter, which was why Latham had promoted him.

"All right," he said, cautiously. "What does Bailey think?"

"He's with the police."

250

"No racial conspiracy, et cetera?"

McNeely shook his head. "You know Bailey: he's got brains, he's stubborn, but he doesn't go for that stuff. Scientific journalism is his thing."

"And this kid, Evenhoff?"

McNeely stretched his immaculate fingers. "Well, I can't make any guarantees. Bailey seems to like him in a funny way." He spoke in the detached manner of an exterminator discussing a dead rat. "But as for his views—I'm afraid I can't say. He's *enthusiastic*, but he doesn't confide in me." McNeely smiled at his superior. "Editors don't seem to fit his image of what a news reporter should be."

"Well, get rid of him, then," Latham said.

"He's an intern," McNeely said. "We can't fire him till fall."

"All right, send him out to a bureau," Latham said. "This kind of story is too important for enthusiasm. I don't want it to blow up in our face."

And it rained on Fourteenth and Baltimore, in the center of the city, where the streets were overlooked—from deep within the shadows of the abandoned Hotel President—by Booker Short's solitary gaze. He sat there for several hours, high up on the twelfth floor, staring at the rain, as if by looking properly, he might catch the moment of a drop's formation and release. Then he backed away into the gloaming of the vacant building and descended the walnut staircase to the lobby, whose pay phone, ensconced in an old-fashioned cabinet, had never been disconnected. He dropped in his quarter and dialed from memory, the pulse of the call racing suddenly through the building's rotted wires to the phone poles out on Fourteenth Street. One could have followed it, in slow motion, as it hummed eastward and then turned right on Main, continuing south past Bert Gauss's Datsun and several beat police. It soared above the tile roofs of the Plaza and the swollen expanse of Brush Creek, then headed down Wornall Road (named, though the caller did not know it, for a slave-owning farmer whose house had been a hospital during the Civil

War), south to Fifty-ninth, where it hung a right and crossed Ward Parkway to Judge Sayers's house, one lot east of State Line Road. Nobody answered. The phone echoed through the house until the machine picked up, the message returning the way the call came. The voice was Clarissa Sayers's, recorded some months earlier and left there by her dad, her request for a clear message, date and time of the call followed by silence and then a click as Booker pressed the bracket and sat down to wait.

The rain ruined Mercury's plan to start driving to California that day. He had dreamed of the open road, the chalky, unspooling sky, only to come downstairs and find that a chunk of plaster the size of a serving plate had fallen on the sideboard. Its back bristled with horsehairs, its fragments still intact, like puzzle pieces that had just been put in place.

"Why, I'll be damned," he said, gazing upward. "It must be that upstairs leak."

"You don't need to tell *me* this house has a leak," Lilly said.

"It must've come down inside the wall."

"And did you think," Lilly said, slamming cabinets in the kitchen, "that if you let the ceiling fall down"—*whack!*—"it's not gonna *affect* us folks downstairs?" *Whack!* "Well, let me tell you something, Mr. Mercury Chapman: I can stand all kind of foolishness, all kind of ways to waste time. But I won't work for a man who don't have the smarts to look after his own roof. That's right. A man lets a leak like that go long enough"—*whack!*—"it's going to get the rats out of the basement, much less the people who like him around this place." *Whack! Whack!* "Are you listening to me?"

Mercury climbed onto a chair, its linen seat printed with the brown whorls of water stains, and traced his finger along the window frame. The paint crumbled like blue cheese.

"Amazing," he said. "Would you look at that."

"Are you listening to me?" Lilly said.

252

"I wonder if the studs are bad." Mercury whispered to himself. "I said, ARE YOU LISTENING TO ME?"

Lilly glowered in the doorway, clutching a packed valise, and Mercury two-stepped off the chair. "We had an appointment to fix that roof," Lilly said. "Three o'clock last Wednesday. And do you know what you were doing? Well, I know that at eight o'clock you were parked outside my nephew's house, scaring his wife half to death. Yes, I know that. And I wonder how happy you'd be if some fella started squawking about a murder during *your* dinnertime, when you hadn't even had time to take your shoes off yet or say hello to your kid, and when your wife has had to hold the food back on the stove for three hours, trying not to burn it—"

"They could've offered me something to eat," Mercury said.

"What's that?" Lilly said.

"I said," Mercury repeated defiantly, "they could have offered me something to eat." His mind wandered for a moment, bumbling across the wings of the burnished dining table, the vase of cut irises that Lilly had freshened just the other day. "It's not as though I was a stranger," he said.

She grunted, an appraising sound, like the one Mercury's doctor made after listening to his chest. "That's what you think?" she said.

"That's it," Mercury said.

"Well, I'm going to tell you something, Mr. Mercury R. Chapman," Lilly said. "I don't know why two good men who've known each other their whole lives can't say a civil word for twenty years—" As she spoke, Mercury studied her face, the dark mole on her left eyelid, imagining the room as it had been twenty years before, on Thanksgiving, his wife and both his children there, along with Remy Westbrook, perhaps, and his kids, Eddie Coole, and Lilly teasing him, arms folded, as he tried to carve the bird, and he thought: *She would've been past forty then, married. I don't even know if she was happy, what happened in that marriage, why they never had a kid.*

"And I don't know what's going on with that boy, either," Lilly

253

said, "that Booker boy you brought in here. I don't know if he killed that girl. They think so on TV, but *I* don't know nothing about that. Just like I don't know why on Wednesday you went over to pester Clyde about him, and now you got your bags packed and want to leave."

"I thought that was what you wanted me to do," Mercury said. "Forget about the case, not get involved. That's what Clyde wanted to do, anyway."

"I don't care what Clyde Wilkins done to you," Lilly said, ignoring him. "Or what you done to him. All I can tell you is what a good man is *supposed* to do: he's supposed to take care of his own house first." She snapped her valise. "Eve Wilkins would've told you that," she said, "so I can, too. She would've also spanked your butt, except I'm too old for that. Just remember this: stay, run off to California, whatever, but the first thing you better do is fix this roof, or this is the last you're gonna see of me."

Mercury scuffed his feet. "Hmmph," he said.

"It's dry out this morning," Lilly said, nodding to the window. "If I were you, I'd get started before I missed my opportunity."

And the rain worried Stan Granger, who stood at the end of Grand Avenue, examining the black crosshatches of a flood-stage marker and wondering if his trailer had been washed away. He had not, as Mercury had suggested, told Detective Keegan everything—had not told her, for instance, that Booker's message had included not only a claim of innocence ("Stan," his recorded voice had said, "I need your help. I think you know I didn't do this. Please, please just don't do anything until you talk to me") but also a number that Stan was supposed to call today. He lowered the binoculars, following a spiral of seagulls as it dipped past a train bridge but seeing instead Booker's half-naked figure, appearing like a riddle on the five hundred acres of dead land that had been Stan's to keep. He remembered the boy's silence and his waiting, which had caused his heart to quicken a beat, and he remembered, too, that Booker had come to take, returning after half a year's hiatus with the clothes and suits that Clarissa Sayers had bought for him, with stories of parties and of places that Stan himself had never even hoped to see. It was Booker who had invited him to the members' table, with a member's daughter, and uncorked extra wine from the members' locker, which Stan had never had the guts to drink, and he knew that he would never have attempted Keegan without Booker's example—or without his secrets to offer in trade.

Fifteen minutes later he dropped a quarter into a pay phone on Twelfth and Locust Street. The police department shaded a dirty courtyard there, its pavement littered with the trampled blossoms of a dogwood tree, and looking up, he saw Detective Keegan's black figure striding through them, at the same time as a voice answered on the line's other end.

"Booker?" Stan said. He said this loudly and then ducked his head, looking backward, but Keegan had continued past. "Son of a *bitch*," he whispered.

"Yeah, well, you're not the only one calling me that," Booker said.

"No, no, no," Stan said. He squeezed inside the metal shell that separated one phone from the next. "It's just that"—he glanced back—"well, I'm kind of . . ."

"Surprised," Booker said.

Stan nodded inaudibly. He switched the receiver to his other ear.

"You there?" Booker asked.

"Yes," Stan said. "Yes, I am."

"All right, look," Booker said. "Look." He sighed, it seemed to Stan, in an effort to compose his thoughts. "Before we start this, there's a couple things I got to explain. You help me, that's a felony. You even talk to me and don't tell the police, that's one, too—especially if I tell you where I am. You can get in serious trouble for this shit, so before we go any further, I wanna make sure that's something you understand—"

255

An officer bellied up to the phone bank next to Stan and put a quarter in.

"So, you wanna do this?" Booker asked.

"You bet, dear," Stan said. He smiled at the officer, fumbling first his paper, then his pen. "That sounds great. Just tell me where you are and what you need."

The sky was gnat-colored that afternoon, and the streetlights flicked on early, casting a griseous pall over the streets. Mercury Chapman tucked his hands into his pockets and followed the rails of an extension ladder to his roof's dark spine. Stan Granger gazed up at the smooth stone headquarters of the second-largest police force in four states, his Adam's apple bulging over a wet string tie. A mile of city separated their slouched figures, and yet their thoughts were twinned, each confronting at that hour a solitary journey he would have done anything to evade. Stan, for his part, mounted the worn steps of the police department's side entrance and entered the small, fluorescent-lit lobby where civilians came to pay their tickets, passing their chained queues, their downturned faces and rain-darkened backs, and proceeding to a second door, glassed with polyurethane, where a uniformed guard checked his pass. There was a small antechamber past that, undecorated, manned by an automatic camera, the floor scuffed black by the soles of all the cops who'd passed that way. It was like a staging area, and Stan stood with three officers, and then rode the elevator to the third floor and walked down a beaten hall to the office marked *Homicide*.

Keegan waited for him in back. She looked tired, pale. A fern wilted on her desk, and Stan examined one brown frond as she signed carbon forms, produced a photograph from a slumping mound of papers, and handed it across to him.

"My partner found this," she said. "Detective Schiff."

The photograph captured Booker Short at age sixteen. He was thin, his bones smaller, undeveloped, his faint mustache not yet

256

grown in. Nor did the image retain the normal complications of his face, the faint yellowing of his cheekbones, the orange, zip-front shirt that Stan had first seen him in. His skin registered simply as black against a white background and he looked lonely, staring over a numbered plaque that he held beneath his chin.

"Felony conviction for forgery," she said, watching Stan examine the picture. "Did he ever mention his record, Mr. Granger? Or did he leave you in the dark about that, too?"

"I knew about it," Stan said.

"That he'd jumped parole?"

"I knew he'd been to jail," Stan said. He tossed the photo onto Keegan's desk. "I knew it, but I didn't say. I didn't think it'd help very much."

"Help with what?" Keegan asked.

"Help get him free."

"Look, Mr. Granger," Keegan said. "I think you're an honest man, but the fact is, so far you haven't shown me a single scrap of evidence that would indicate Booker Short's innocence. Your locket seems only to connect him to the victim more directly."

"Wouldn't he have took it off?" Stan said stubbornly. "I mean, if he was the one that did it, then he would have took it off because he knew it belonged to him, and—"

"Let me finish," Keegan said. "My partner, Detective Schiff, has suggested that we arrest you. He thinks you know more than you've chosen to say. I'm not going to do that. But I will give you some advice." Her green eyes were flat, but her voice had a thick, ruptured quality. "It's no good holding back. It's no good because in the end I will find out about it. You should consider that when, and if, let's say, you get to talk to your friend." Stan tried to respond, but Keegan waved him off. "*If* you talk to him," she said, "which of course you haven't, because you know that to do that and not tell me would be a felony—"

Stan nodded vigorously at this.

"—but if you did, Stan," Keegan continued, her throat forming for the first time his given name, "you'd tell him to come to me. You'd know to do that, especially if he's clean."

"Of course I would," Stan said.

At the same hour, Mercury squatted atop his study's dormer, examining its open seams. He had not been on the roof since his wife's death, and somehow these subjects now became intertwined, Mercury seeing how the water had puddled on the dormer's flat surface, softened the asphalt, seeped through to the underlying tin, and then worked down to rot the insides of the walls, the studs, the ceiling joists, but thinking instead of his poor wife and Hammonds and what the rain had done to them over these many years. Even Clarissa Sayers's funeral had been invaded by the rain, the ground so sodden that the funeral director was forced to "evacuate" the grave, and Mercury remembered the gurgle of the diesel pump with a sharp twist of his neck, along with the image of Judge Sayers staring at the glossy divot where the gravewater coiled into the machine. Death had always been a subject that he'd avoided. The war had seen to that: the dead's presence and their stench, mixed among charred and broken pieces of machinery, or stacked like stovewood behind hospital tents, made the idea of heaven seem ridiculous. He could no more imagine the fields of dead soldiers drifting up (how? through what?) to meet and discuss the battle someplace than he could imagine speaking to his wife again. And it was this, he realized, that bothered him about the Sayers case: the emptiness of her death, its lack of meaning, reflected in the walleyed reaction of the mourners, who normally would've been talking up the whole business of the dead's attaining peace. There had been a wrongness to it (as he himself had felt after Hammonds's hanging), from which everyone had wanted to escape.

The rain increased, never a downpour but heavy enough that Mercury was forced to close up his sealant and quit. He climbed down his ladder at the same time as Stan Granger descended the police station's steps. It was a cool, fresh night. The west wind blew rain against the window screens, the air smelled of electricity, and as Mercury made plans to tear away the dining room's bad plaster, Stan drove south into the city. There was something instinctual about the latter's progress, wordless, choosing his turns and cutoffs with the same unconscious concentration he used to work a trot line. He did not know that Mercury had stayed behind, and yet when he rang the doorbell on Highland Drive and the older man's face appeared in a lemon wedge of light, neither man seemed surprised.

"Please," Stan said firmly. "I've got someone who you need to see."

20

THE HOUSE that Stan entered appeared to have been cauterized. The lamps were stripped of their shades, drop cloths covered the olive carpet, the dark oak table, and the sideboard, and Mercury stood atop a stepladder, whacking at the plaster ceiling like a stonecutter. From below, Stan told him Booker's story. No politeness this time, no decorum: he clenched his hat and summed up, bluntly, "I don't see how you can forget this kid just because it's risky." When he'd finished, Mercury sheathed his spackle blade, shuttled to the kitchen, and returned with a glass of bourbon in each fist.

"Old Red Mother Hen," he said.

"What?" Stan said, eyeing his glass.

"Mother Hen," Mercury said. He held the amber liquid up to the light and swirled it, smiling privately. "That's what they used to call me in the company."

"How come?" Stan said.

"'Cause I worried about risk," he said. "You would, too, if every morning you had to send twenty men inside German territory, sitting on enough live fuel to send them home in a cigarette case." Behind him a portable television played, the bright light of the distant outfield pulsing like the portal to a second universe. "A lot of them didn't understand what it meant to worry about risk. They weren't real appreciative of authority."

260

"Sure," Stan said. "I could see that."

"Didn't mean they weren't good soldiers," Mercury said. "I had one crew drop a transmission in the middle of a firefight. They went off into the woods, watched the panzers blow things up all night, and in the morning they got up and fixed the goddamn thing." He gazed at the television. The count was three and two on a veteran black outfielder, who tapped his bat impatiently on the plate. "That name you mentioned, Isaac Bentham—he was there," he said. "Hammonds, too. Both of them."

"And you?" Stan said.

"Hmmnh?" Mercury said absently, turning his head from the picture.

"You were there with the tanks," Stan said. "Weren't you?"

Mercury hobbled away. "Bentham," he said, "came from a farming family. Landowners. About six-two, uniform always pressed, fancy." Kneeling, he jerked cans from kitchen cabinets. "Saw him kill a man that night," he said. "Once the shooting started, we hunkered down in this stream. I see something moving to the right—German foot soldier. A flare goes off, I see his face, he's looking our way. When it's dark again, he starts circling toward the stream. We sit tight. I'm trying to figure out a way to get my pistol aimed quietly and suddenly Isaac's there. At first I don't know it's him. I don't know it's anything." He circled his arms. "It's like there's dark all around this guy, and then suddenly the dark seems to flinch, closes over him like a cape. Pretty soon Isaac's crawling toward us up the stream, carrying a German Mauser and four grenades. Broke the man's neck." Mercury rolled his wrist to check his watch. "Craziest thing I ever saw."

"And Hammonds," Stan said, entering the kitchen. "What about him?"

"Reggie Hammonds?" Mercury said. "Know what he used to say to me? The closer we got to the dump-off spot, the more nervous he would get, until one night he said, 'Captain, I don't mean nothing bad, but your face sticks out like a headlight. Makes everybody around you nervous as shit.' I had to cork my face just to get near the guy."

"So why'd you bring him?" Stan asked.

"He was a guy who could *arrange* things," Mercury said. He jerked two plastic water bags out of a broom closet and tossed them at Stan's feet. "Got booze when we needed it, eggs, milk, live chickens, truck parts—everything. Also discreet. No trouble for me. Sure he ran when the guns came out. But the next morning, there he is. He's got about five watches. A Mauser pistol. A sugar sack filled with sausages and old boots. But he's also found a ditched Kraut jeep whose transmission is intact. He convinces us to go get it. I mean, picture this: six guys, scared shitless, sneaking through a shell-holed bean field, tipping over a German jeep, taking the transmission out, and carrying it back. And Hammonds just smiling, shrugging his shoulders, saying, 'Don't worry, fellas, I got an idea.'" The old man took a breath. Something had appeared in his face, the structure of his bones beneath his aging skin: a second self, younger, in some crucial way undamaged, brought forward by the concentration of memory. "And he did it, too—he lay under that truck, Isaac handing him the wrenches, parts falling out into the mud. An hour later he stood up and we all climbed in and Isaac fired her up and Hammonds looked at us and said, 'All right, no stopping, now—we only got one gear.' And so we left the fuel for whoever wanted it and drove back to Chartres in first only."

It was silent in the room then. The story was unlike the war stories Stan had heard the old man tell before, not comedic, not spiced with pratfalls, but infused instead with the cadence of forgotten pride. Somewhere within the house, a clock chimed the half hour.

"So what happened to him?" Stan asked. "To Hammonds?"

"He died," Mercury said.

"Oh," Stan said. "I'm sorry. I—"

"The army hung him for attempted rape. Or successful rape, depending on who you asked." Mercury filled the water bags at the sink.

262

"Isaac Bentham blamed me for it. Because he believed I didn't care. Even after two years overseas, another eight months of training. Almost three years of my life, my best efforts. Even then."

"And that's why . . . ?" Stan asked.

"That's why Booker came to find me," Mercury said. "Because Isaac was his granddad. He thought I owed him for that. So, let me ask you this: I did my time with that black company. I built my plant at Eighty-fifth and Standard. Half my payroll goes to blacks. I give four hundred dollars a year to a black church. So when is the payment period over with? What gives that boy the right to come and demand such things from me?"

"I don't know," Stan said. "I guess if you done all you could for this Hammonds fella, then you don't owe him anything."

Mercury's eyelids fluttered.

"The hanging was wrong," he said. "It was wrong, terribly wrong. The army would have commuted his sentence if he had been a white man."

Stan nodded. "Well," he said. "This one might be wrong, too."

But the old man's focus was gone. "I don't think you understand," he said. "These crimes—such crimes as this—what right do they have to ask for payment? Hammonds, you know, was also a friend to me."

"What if *I* asked you to do it?" Stan showed his teeth. "'Cause Booker was my friend, like you and Hammonds—only I ain't planning for it to turn out the same way."

Mercury thought. He plucked the cork from an empty wine bottle on the drainboard.

"Where is it?" he asked. "This hiding place?"

"The Hotel President," Stan said.

"How do you get in?"

"The fire escape in back," Stan said.

"All right," Mercury said. He gestured at the cans stacked on the counter, the two water bags. "There's the supplies. I'll give them to you and I'll get you down there, but that's it. No more phone calls, no requests. I don't have to *infiltrate* anyplace."

"Deal," Stan said.

"There's one more stipulation," Mercury said. He took a lighter from his pocket and applied it to the cork's end, squinting as the ember faded into ash. "We do it the Old Hen's way. Which means that if you're gonna try to save a man like Hammonds, you might as well learn from what he does better. Like, for instance, being hard to see."

21

THE HOTEL PRESIDENT had belonged to a famous concatenation of hotels, clip joints, pools halls, opera houses, casinos, ballrooms, and speakeasies—both low and high society—that once filled Kansas City's downtown. Cowboys had strolled the streets fresh from cattle trains; Charlie Parker and Count Basie had visited from the great black clubs on Vine Street; bankers had overlooked it from the steam-room at the Kansas City Club, towels wrapped around their waists: a world that by the time Booker reached it had become a junkie's paradise, the President's squat brick stump rising, soot- and weather-stained, above a plain of parking lots, each with its bulletproof attendant's cage.

He spent his first few days checking the rooms for things he might need. Some had walls destroyed by water damage, the carpets marled with pigeon shit, but others, when their doors were pushed inward, would gasp as if releasing air sealed there since the hotel closed in 1980. He found checkbooks, bills of sale, receipts made out to guests whose bedding still remained unchanged. Strangest were the radios that each room contained, which pulled out from the wall in walnut consoles: no treble, no bass, simply a central speaker overstitched with nylon threads of red and tan, offering three stations by name, KCMO, KMBZ, and WHB. Fortunately he had some business to conduct that kept him sane: the collecting, for instance, of cool and

heavily evaporated water from the backs of toilet tanks, which even after he boiled it (in a steel bowl stolen from the kitchen) left a gritty
film on his teeth. He also netted pigeons in a pillowcase. But mostly
he had to wait, stopping in the endless, cloistered rooms, staring
downward at the city from different angles, trapped—as he had been
at Isaac's farm—in someone else's past. This past, though Booker did
not know it, was in part Mercury's. He had spent a good portion of his
childhood in the company of the hotel's owner and founder, Frank
Stanton, for whom his father had acted as lead attorney, and crouching now in the darkness of the north parking lot, the old man gazed
up at the ruined building tenderly. He could remember playing tag in
the servants' passage outside the Aztec Room. He could remember
the doorman and the head chambermaid by their first names (Harold
and Minnie), and seeing Harry Truman strolling to his hat shop, and
Pendergast goons wandering the hallways when the boss came to stay:
all that, his childhood, his city, his blood now washing away from him
in the rain. "All right," he whispered to Stan. "Where's your man?"

Stan shrugged, staring at a broken windowpane.

"Ain't it typical," Mercury said. "You wait up all night to help
these guys. You stand out in the rain. And then they don't even bother
to help you help them."

"What're you gonna do?" Stan said.

"Me?" Mercury said. His eyes flashed strangely.

"I mean, you can go if you want. I don't mind."

"I'll tell you what I'm going to do," Mercury said. "I'm going in
and get an explanation." He lifted a canvas rucksack stuffed with chili
cans and threaded his arms through its straps. "It's not gonna work for
one guy to carry all this stuff anyway."

He had replayed the argument a thousand times. Outside of his wife's
memory, it loomed as his most vivid fantasy, and as such he had spent
hours re-creating what he *should have* said to Isaac Bentham on that
last day in Cherbourg, both his assertions and his evidence ringing

266

hollow because he had no witness to convince. This was also what motivated him, as he clung to an electrical conduit twenty feet above the pavement, to close his eyes and jump: not heroism, not valor, but the hardened memory of Isaac Bentham cursing him before a cell block of black soldiers while he, Mercury Chapman, failed to defend himself. He experienced a moment of suspension, silent and clean, and then belly-flopped onto the fire escape, blood blossoming between his teeth. The broken window was only two floors above him now, and after hauling up the rucksacks, he crawled into a corridor whose smell of rot bore a strong resemblance to the atmosphere of Cherbourg prison—the difference being that this time he had come to speak his peace.

"Booker," Stan said behind him. "It's me, Stan Granger. Come out, please."

No one answered. The corridor opened onto a wider, more open space—the balustrade above the vaulted lobby where Mercury had once played. He toed his way along a balding carpet covered with broken glass and plaster chips, the banister gone now, burned by vagrants, until he teetered above the lobby's black pit.

"Hold still," a voice said.

He stiffened.

"You didn't say anything about a second man."

"It's Mercury," Stan said.

"It's what?" Mercury recognized the voice, along with the acidic scent of sweat and Afro. He felt a jab against his tailbone, just beneath his pack—no gun, but something larger, rounded—and he spun his arms for balance. "Mercury Chapman?" Booker continued, his finger probing the burned cork that Mercury had used to coat his cheeks. "No, no. That can't be it—Mercury Chapman can't be related to a spook like this."

A beat passed. Mercury stood still, his arms outspread.

"We're camouflaged," he said.

"Oh," Booker said. "Is *that* what it is?" Strange squeaks and chirps of laughter reached Mercury's ears, as if his assailant could not breathe. "Nigger camouflage!"

"Either push me or get away," Mercury said.

His voice carried all the authority that his old captain's bray could muster and Booker's giggling stopped, the mop handle's pressure renewed against his back—though a bit more uncertainly. He noticed that Stan had retreated from the landing's edge. "Wait a minute. Wait a minute," Booker insisted, still holding the mop in place. "I think the captain's got something to say. Maybe he don't like standing at attention, the way old Isaac and Reggie Hammonds used to do for him. Is that it? Or maybe he thinks I should be more thankful for his help. Maybe I ought to get down and grovel for his generosity."

"Did you kill that girl?" Mercury asked, staring at the void beyond his feet.

"No," Booker said. "Did you kill Reggie Hammonds?"

"No," he answered.

"You see," Booker said, his voice mirthless now, serious, "that's where we got a problem. 'Cause I heard about you differently."

"Then let's settle it," he said.

The back stairwell of the Hotel President was inhabited largely by rats. Mercury followed Booker toward it, the clicking sound of small feet scrabbling ahead of them, accompanied by urgent squeaks. Their conversation had been left unfinished, the lobby seeming the wrong place for such a thing, too open and too echoing, and so he waited, following. After several flights, he drew a flashlight from his pocket and switched it on, the beam's pale circle bending over the concrete stairs. "The light's okay in the staircase," Booker told him. "No windows. That's why everybody makes their fires here. But the hallways stay dark, so nobody outside can see." It was true. The landing's walls were charred with smoke, the concrete floors scattered with dead ashes, shards of half-burned chairs and paneling. At times they skirted nestlike piles of bedding, broken whiskey pints. On the twelfth floor the smell of woodsmoke was fresher, more intense, and their boots stirred soft clouds of pigeon feathers, iridescent in the flashlight's beam. "My cookout spot," Booker said. As he opened the steel fire door, Mercury killed his light.

"If you didn't do it," he said, "why not turn yourself in?" He gestured to the bleak stairwell, the feathers. "Be done with this craziness."

"You ever been to prison, Cap?" Booker asked.

"I've visited," Mercury said.

"Did it make you want to stay?"

He had an answer, but he was distracted by the fleeting image of Hammonds in his Cherbourg cell, staring out across a winter sea. By the time he recovered, Booker had flowed past him down the hall, opened a door at the far end, and stood waiting in a cube of jaundiced light—the glow of streetlamps, Mercury realized, drifting upward through the rain. "All right," Booker demanded when he arrived. "What about you? If you didn't kill Hammonds, how come you never mentioned him to anybody?"

"Because I wanted to forget it," he said. It was the truth, at least.

"Yeah? Well, that right there is exactly what's wrong with a black man turning himself in. First he gets forgotten. Next he's up for the lynch committee."

This time he was ready. *Lynching,* he was going to say, rising on the balls of his feet, *is hardly what I would call an honest description,* but Stan Granger's callused hand pawed his chest. "Now, Captain," Stan told him, "let's see if we can't get the kid some food before we argue with him just yet," and he allowed himself to be led inside the open room and seated on the mattress of a king-sized bed. The room resembled a honeymoon suite: windows opened to the north and east in sturdy, sash-weighted banks, the bed, which commanded almost half of the space, guarded by a tarnished champagne stand whose matching flute Booker had adopted as a water glass. Stan chatted, filling the awkward silence that came when Booker ripped open the rucksack that Mercury had carefully packed, lifted one can to the window light, and said "Chili" as another man might have said "Shit." Mercury noticed that he ate it anyway, his spoon (which Mercury had also thought to pack) protruding at right angles from his fist, as one might hold the handle of a crank. He had to calm himself by force of will, fifty years of arguments buzzing in his brain, while Booker slurped water from the champagne flute and then from a five-gallon water bag, which he held trembling above his head. Only when the boy had finished two chili cans and started on a third did Mercury trust himself to speak.

"Who told you that it happened that way?" he asked.

Satiated, Booker lounged with his back against the writing desk. He dandled the champagne flute on his knee. "What happened what way?" he said.

"The war," Mercury insisted. "You keep saying I killed Reggie Hammonds, but you weren't there. So I'm asking, who told you that?"

"Isaac did—back when I was living with him."

"No parents?"

"They left off," Booker said.

The finality of this threw him. He walked to the side window and pressed his palm against the glass. "Is Isaac alive?" he asked.

"I don't know," Booker said.

The answer made Mercury feel dizzy, as if the floor had dropped from beneath his feet. The window was cold against his skin, and staring over the brownish acres of the city, he realized that he had never imagined that Isaac might die—or that there might be no one left to hear his case.

"The army hung Hammonds," he said, quietly. "Not me. I did not sit on his court-martial. I did not charge him or hand down his sentence. I filed every possible appeal. I did not control the army: the army controlled me."

"But it was wrong," Booker said.

270

"What was wrong?" Mercury said. "Was it wrong to file appeals?"

"They hung those men because they were black," Booker said. "That's the way I heard it—that if Hammonds had been a white man, even if he *had* done it, they wouldn't have hung him for a thing like that. Are you gonna tell me that isn't true?"

"No," Mercury said. "No, I can't."

"Are you gonna tell me that they didn't hang three other blacks that day?"

Mercury expelled a breath.

"Or that those trials were fair?"

"What," he answered testily, "am I supposed to do about that?"

Booker shrugged. "I ain't a captain," he said.

That was the moment when he knew it would be okay. From his position at the window, he could see Booker's face, rutilant, shadow-flecked, sneering at him with the same pompous confidence that his grandfather had displayed, as if those lost years had not in fact passed but had merely been misplaced, locked up like the vitiated air of this hotel room, these dead and mundane walls and paint, and he felt almost grateful—grateful because not only the words came back now, but the memory of days when it mattered what he had to say. "Well, think like one, kiddo," he suggested. "It's war, right? I got one hundred and forty men. No guns, no ammunition. What do you want me to do, pack everybody up and invade Cherbourg to bust one guy out of jail? Resign my commission?" And when Booker shrugged and said "Why not?" the answer came easily. "Why not?" he said. "Why not? Do you know what happens to an officer who resigns his commission in the middle of a war? That's avoiding duty, desertion—unless that's exactly what you want, eh? If a black man gets destroyed then I should destroy myself in protest, is that it? That makes a helluva lot of sense. Besides, my resignation wouldn't have stopped them from executing Hammonds, anyway."

"Neither did you staying in," Booker said, standing and removing his shirt. "The way I see it, if you're part of something wrong, you're wrong. Unless you quit."

"Quit?" Mercury gazed heavenward, hat in hand.

"You heard me," Booker said.

"Then how come Isaac didn't quit?" he asked.

"'Cause he didn't do anything wrong," Booker said.

"You know, I'm getting a little tired of this word 'wrong,'" Mercury said. He hoisted a water bag, following Booker to the bathroom. "How 'bout we have *it* quit?"

The bathroom was windowless, papered in the style of Piet Mondrian. He sat there for twenty minutes, watching Booker bathe in his flashlight's beam, rising every so often to fill the sink basin from the water bag (a process familiar to him from his army days) and then retiring to the toilet cover, wondering why their argument had lost its heat. "All right, look: some things *were* wrong," he admitted. "The men didn't have decent clothes, terrible barracks, had to eat at a separate mess—hell yes! Anybody in his right mind could see that. But if the army isn't ready to change, what am I supposed to do? Quit? On principle? Let somebody run the outfit who thinks it's *right* to do things this way?" He wagged his finger at Booker's reflection. "A lot more people died in that war than Reggie Hammonds. And if I quit, I felt some of them would be my responsibility."

In the mirror, a plastic razor revealed Booker's face in strips: umber cheekbone, coal-stubbled jaw, parched lip. "Well," he said, "I guess that's the question."

"What's the question?" Mercury asked.

"Now that the war is over," Booker said, "when's it going to be time to quit? Take that Colonial Club of yours, for instance. Ain't you never in forty years thought about letting black folks in? 'Cause if you been trying to fix that place up from the inside, like you did with Hammonds and the army, then I *do* think it's time to quit."

272

A silence followed, but this time Mercury was not afraid of it. He knew he had enough to finish then, enough rancor at least to get the words out, and so he said nothing as Booker splashed water against his cheeks, snuffed the candle, and stepped back into the half-light of the main room, where Stan handed him a towel that, again, Mercury had packed. This, too, he endured silently, hands in pockets, watching as Booker dried himself without a word of thanks, his mind saying *fuck you, fuck you,* until at last the boy finished and he allowed his mouth to speak. "It wasn't that simple, kid," he said.

"No?" Booker said laconically, slipping on his jeans. "What wasn't?"

"M-maybe your grandfather didn't rape that Frenchwoman"—he stuttered, the words themselves rusty, dried out from disuse—"maybe he just scared her, cuffed her around, but the fact is that he lied. He lied and he let Hammonds cover for him."

Booker stopped in the act of dressing, one pant leg on, one off. "My grandfather did what?"

"Your grandfather committed that crime," Mercury said. At this, Booker's grin faded and he saw in him, at last, the sneering avatar of those black soldiers in the Cherbourg prison whom he had come to hate. "They didn't expect it," he said. "The hanging, I mean. They figured Hammonds would do time, get out, and go to work for your granddad. And I let them get away with it"—he surged forward, fists clenched—"I let them do it because I thought Hammonds wanted it that way, and then when it went bad, your grandfather blamed it on me—on me, you understand?"

It was not a particularly athletic fight. Even in the middle of it, he noticed that the entire exercise seemed to consist of a series of grapples, of headlocks broken and released, and of wrist- and elbow-twisting—never once during the entire process could he get his arms completely free. The flashlight fell from his pocket and switched on accidentally, its beam skidding and flaring beneath their feet, and occasionally when it pointed the right way, he recognized a face: Booker's tongue pinched between his lips in earnest concentration; Stan Granger sweating, his hat pulled down over one eye. It took a while for him to comprehend that Stan was not actually on his side. They'd tumbled on the bed by then, the metal frame catching the back of his knee, and all at once even the flashlight's glow disappeared and he heard voices talking about him, Booker saying, "Dude, you've got to grab his feet," and Stan responding, "Just a minute now; I can't get hold of anything." His arms and face seemed suffocated by a soft, padded weight, and he thrashed in a final effort, clawing and scratching, until at last he heard a tearing sound and a cool substance sifted around his neck, like snowflakes. Looking up, he saw Booker kneeling atop his chest, clutching the torn edges of a pillowcase.

"Settle down, Cap," he was saying. "Whoa now man—"

"I hated him for that," Mercury said, the words coming now whether he asked them to or not. "Do you understand? All those soldiers, everything I'd worked for, ruined just because I was a white captain, because he knew I'd be easy to blame."

"Did Isaac ever admit to it?" Booker said.

"No," Mercury said. "Not to me."

"So why should I believe you, then?"

"Because I was fucking *there*," Mercury said.

Booker didn't respond. His neck was bowed beneath the flurry of snowflakes (feathers, Mercury realized) and suddenly his shoulders began to shake—though whether from tears or laughter Mercury couldn't say. "You knew him," Mercury prodded.

"Oh, yes, I did," Booker said.

"So perhaps"—he meant to say this seriously, but something about Booker's tone caused him to grin—"you might admit the possibility?"

Booker sat back on his haunches, knees still pressed against Mercury's chest, and sucked in a breath. His eyes were wet, and when he shook his head as if in disbelief, tufts of feathers swirled whimsically about his ears. But his voice was determined when he spoke. Mercury, studying his face, was surprised to find an echo not of Isaac or of Hammonds, but of himself, his wife, and thought, *Yes, that is the difference. He has lost somebody, too.*

"All right, Cap," Booker said. "I admit a possibility, and you do the same."

"Deal," Mercury said.

"I did not kill Clarissa Sayers," Booker said. "I would never have done such a thing. What's more, I know who did it and I'm gonna need your help to make it right."

"Who?" Mercury asked.

"Her father," Booker said.

Mercury lurched upward. "Wait," he said. "You can't—"

But Booker shoved him back.

"No," he said. "The deal is you believe."

22

AT TEN O'CLOCK ON Tuesday morning, Mercury rang Judge Sayers's doorbell and then paced across the doorstep, his face washed and pale against the misting rain. He rang the bell a second time, and when no one answered, he circled to the side yard and climbed over the judge's padlocked gate. His age caught up with him then. He was not used to staying up all night, or to drinking on an empty stomach, and the nausea he felt was accompanied by a terrible, undefined fear—a feeling of complicity—as he landed on his knees, his face buried in the lush and well-trimmed mattress of the judge's zoysia grass. He continued on, wobbling. The backyard was entirely vacant, weeded, hedged, and divided from the surrounding yards by a six-foot-high cedar fence. The grass itself appeared untrodden, the geometric pathways of a lawn mower still visible through the dew, and as Mercury sidestepped the ashless barbecue, he discovered that he did not want the yard to look this way: he wanted it to look normal, with scattered rakes and garden tools, with hoses coiled unevenly in the flower bed. He pounded on the locked door. "Thornton," he shouted, "it's Mercury Chapman. I've got to talk to you about something." The alcohol came up again then, and he leaned his cheek against the door's glass storm. When he recovered, Thornton Sayers's face was inches from his own, his breath so close it fogged the pane. "I'm working," the judge said. "Can't you see?"

276

His voice sounded as if it came from inside an aquarium, there being a short delay between the movement of his lips and the emergence of his words through the pane.

"I understand that, Thornton," Mercury said. "It's just about the boy—there's something I wanted to tell you, something I haven't—" He reached for the storm's handle, but it was still bolted. The judge tilted his head, smiling uncertainly.

"Please, Thornton, listen to me," Mercury said. He pressed his palms against the storm. "I knew that boy, Booker. His grandfather fought with me. And I knew he'd been in trouble, too. I knew it and I didn't say anything. I never thought—I mean, if I'd have known—"

The two were quite close together, separated only by a reflected fragment of the sky, but at the mention of Booker's name, the judge's face whitened. "Wait," Mercury shouted as the judge vanished down the hall. Several minutes later, he reappeared, carrying a tape machine. It was of the sort that had been popular twenty years before, black, rectangular, with a single red recording button, and as Mercury watched him unroll the cord and plug it in, he discovered that his legs were shaking. "Do you know what the major problem is with over ninety percent of the cases I see?" the judge asked. He was on his knees, working intently over the machine.

"Thornton—" Mercury said.

But the judge held a finger to his lips. As Mercury said his name, he had pushed the record button, and now he rewound the tape and played it back, lifting the speaker against his ear. "Documentation," he said, smiling. "Clear, precise documentation is the key."

"Thornton," Mercury said, kneeling. "Just open the door, please."

"My counsel says that anyone who was a danger to Clarissa might be a danger to me."

"I'm not dangerous to you."

"Aren't you?" the judge said.

An image, half remembered, slithered quickly through Mercury's brain. "Thornton," he whispered. "What happened to Clarissa?"

277

The judge tucked his chin against his neck. For several minutes it appeared as though he'd forgotten Mercury; then he leaned forward, confidentially, against the pane.

"My daughter," he said, trembling, "did filthy things."

"I can understand why you might—"

"Oh, no," the judge said. "Oh, no, I don't think you understand. I don't think you know what that's like—the stink of it. The filthy things she said. That filth coming out of her own mouth, and then to have her tell you what she did with it"—the judge's throat flexed— "her *mouth*. Her fingers. Her ass." He closed his eyes, prayerfully. "Oh, no," he said. "She did not spare me the filthiness of that."

Mercury backed away. Five feet from the door, he heard only the soft hissing of the rain, and yet he could still see the judge's figure in the lighted doorway, his shoulders rocking, his lips moving feverishly. As soon as he reached the side yard, he ran. His footsteps were muffled then, and he scaled the side gate clumsily, hurtled the front lawn, and loped down the sidewalk in a broken, back-glaring trot. The image that the judge had conjured finned after him, and even after he had lost sight of the house, he hurried, heels tapping from one maple-shrouded street to the next, the houses comfortable and open, their dining rooms and silver candelabras visible from the street, until it caught up with him. The sensation was physical, as if something oily had curled around his neck, and he saw Judge Sayers and his daughter together in the years before her death, saw the flowers left in vases in the hunting lodge, the inane birthday cards, the ticking on Judge Sayers's bunk with its faint, sweet smell of sweat; he saw Clarissa's mouth, small, adolescent, her lips ruby-colored, chapped, and he stepped into a copse of cedars in Fred Abercrombie's side yard and let himself be sick.

By early morning the rain had a chill to it, the drops heavier and harder, the sky divided in thick reefs. An optimist might have seen this

278

as news of a real storm that would blow the front away, but the beat cops who assembled at 6:00 A.M. in the roll call rooms of the patrol divisions—central, east, and metro—moaned when their duty sergeants handed out lists of traffic checkpoints. The purpose of the checkpoints, the central division captain explained—waving a Xeroxed drawing of Booker Short, alias Reggie Hammonds—was to find this fugitive, a parole violator and a suspect in the Sayers murder case. "What that means," he said, "is stop anyone who looks like this. Don't sweat the drunks, for once: we want this kid instead."

The fix, in other words, was in.

Detective Keegan was perfectly aware of this. That same morning she sat in the investigation room reserved for the Sayers case—a room she rarely visited since she did not generally believe that murder cases could be solved by reading files, or by discussing them with people who had not been there. Two file boxes full of coroner's reports, witness depositions, and other paperwork (most of which she had typed up herself and thus did not care to look at again) bulged beside an unplugged coffee urn. She noticed, however, that since she had last been here, Detective Schiff had brightened up the decor. An aerial map of the city hung on the swivel-jointed cork board, and colored pins highlighted the places where Booker Short had been—Clarissa Sayers's apartment on Warwick Street; the parking lot on Troost where Angel Diaz found the Stingray; and the Coronado Hotel (whose façade was repeated, life-size, in the room's window)—with a bull's-eye around the Newsroom bar, where the victim had last been seen, playing pool with a black between the ages of eighteen and twenty-three. On this morning, other detectives also filled the room: members of the homicide squad, several uniformed officers, the homicide captain, and the major in charge of violent crimes. Schiff lounged in a corner beside the window, tilting a Styrofoam coffee cup back and forth in his hands as if studying its dregs. He wore a darker suit than usual, reddish-brown—the color of a Lincoln Log—with

279

one pale boot pushed through the back of a wooden chair, and when his eyes trailed vaguely past Keegan's, his thumb wiping the corner of his lip, she knew he'd made good on his threat.

The captain stood up. "All right," he said. "The way I understand our situation is that we can pretty much trace this kid's movement, on the day the story broke, from the Forty-seventh Street McDonald's, to the Coronado right down here, where the Mexican kid saw him at"— he flipped through a typed timeline that Detective Schiff had prepared—"at around one o'clock on Friday. Have I got that right, Charlie?"

Schiff nodded toward Keegan. "Marcy's the lead on this," he said. "I just do the paperwork."

"Detective Keegan?" the captain said.

"That's right," Keegan said.

"Fine." The captain tongued a blond wing of mustache. "So he's down here, three blocks from our back window." He smiled tersely at his audience. "Got no car, no way to travel, and he drops off the radar screen. Blip." He held up the pages of the timeline. "So, my question is this: What have we done since then?"

"Anybody check the stolen-car reports?" a uniformed officer asked.

"Five," Keegan said, "in a twenty-block radius between Thursday and last night. Two got picked up. Of the three outstanding, two happened during daylight, which makes them seem unlikely." She nodded at the file boxes. "If you want it, all the stuff's in there."

"Make it forty blocks," the captain said. "Detective, you get your stuff typed up and give it to him." He pointed to the uniform. "We're done waiting for reports."

"What about the bus?" another officer said.

"The Greyhound station is on Tenth and Troost," Keegan said. "We interviewed ticket takers on Friday, Saturday, and Sunday. Sent a query to drivers—so far, no hits."

"All right," the captain said. "What's left?"

280

"The river," Schiff said, "crack houses"—he had opened the window beside him and now slung the dregs of his coffee into the air—"or hopping a train."

"You done anything on that?" the captain said to Keegan.

"No," Keegan said.

"Why not?"

"Because I don't think we'd get anywhere," Keegan said.

"Matthews," the captain said. "Take a squad of uniforms down to tent city tomorrow morning and roust the bums, see if they've got anything to say. Do it early, before everybody's gone for the day. Do we have someone from Narcotics in here now?"

An officer in aerodynamic sunglasses raised his hand.

"How many active sites do you have in the area?" the captain asked.

"Four," the officer said. "Two are setups—run by our own men."

"You got any reason to go into them?"

"Well, of course, we'd have to get approval."

"You'll get it," the captain said. He kept Keegan in his sights during this exchange. "The way I understand it, this case looks pretty clean. We've got a black kid out of McAlester jumps parole, meets a white girl. According to one witness, a Mr. Granger"—he thumbed sheets—"they had an affair. Great. So he's got motive and he's got means. He's the last person anybody sees her with: at the bar"—he whacked the map's bull's-eye—"and at her apartment. The coroner estimates time of death as later that same night. So if somebody will tell me why we shouldn't be looking—"

"No one saw him at the apartment," Keegan put in.

"Excuse me?" the captain said.

"The woman next door," Keegan said. "That's not what she testified. I interviewed her. She only said she heard the car arrive, heard voices at the victim's door—talking, not fighting—then heard the car drive away. That doesn't mean the victim was in it."

The captain stared at her.

281

"There's phone records, too," Keegan said. "She called her father at one forty-five, ten minutes after the car left. No answer. And then there's the clothes." Keegan cleared her throat amid the scent of cigarettes and alcohol-tinted aftershave, her face adunc, eyes gazing blandly ahead. "At the bar she had on an evening dress, same one as at the ball. But when we found her she was, as you know, wearing golf clothes—one shoe, a skirt, and top. She put those on herself," Keegan said. "Somebody else did not do it for her."

"How do you know that?" the captain asked.

"The bra matched," Keegan said.

There was laughter, the sudden exhalation of male air.

"It was a white one, solid, like you use for sports," Keegan said, ignoring this. "Not the black lace one she wore with the dress. A man wouldn't think of that."

The captain smiled into his mustache.

"Are you saying, Marcy," he asked, "that after the suspect left, the victim changed her clothes and then went out to go golfing at two A.M.?"

"Possibly," Keegan said.

"And if that happened," the captain said, "if, in fact, that's why you've been conducting your investigation at the Colonial Country Club, then how did she get there?"

"I'm checking taxis," Keegan said.

"If she did get there, who killed her? Do you have another suspect?"

"Not at this time," Keegan said.

The captain did not smile at this. He had been bending forward across the table that ran down the center of the room, and now he straightened, turning slightly so Keegan could see the small, unfastened buckle on the back of his vest, and opened a briefcase on the chair behind him. He closed it after slipping Schiff's report back in.

"All right," he said. "This case is under my custody. Everybody in

282

this room works double shifts until we find this kid." He left without looking at Keegan again.

On the night of the ball, Judge Sayers had returned home after his meeting with Booker Short and headed to the golf course for a walk. Detective Keegan did not know this, of course, nor could she have guessed—during a day spent shuttling between roadblocks and the excruciatingly scripted ballet of tactical officers taking down a drug house run by undercover cops—why the judge had decided to take a five-iron, a putter, and a wedge and set off for the Colonial Club's moonlit greens. The anger at his daughter's betrayal still remained. He could feel it: a second self aping his familiar, almost forcibly casual movements, the opening of the back gate, the caress of the Marquands' retriever, in a way that mocked their normalcy. At the golf course, however, this sensation eased. The moon was full, the ball's trajectory visible for a hundred yards before it vanished into the night, and though he'd never been more than a weekend duffer, his swing had the unrefined simplicity of a teenager's—its power aided by his height. He played up the long, par-four tenth in two perfectly shaped and entirely unconscious shots, the ball appearing in the fairway just where he expected it (another pleasure that Keegan would not have anticipated, having never played the game), and then arcing off again with a faint whiff of grass, his club without vibration in his hands, as if he had not hit anything. In between, the reality of his daylight life would visit him, intolerable, enough to make him heave and sweat. There were pictures: vivid images of Clarissa, the scallop of her white instep, the vantage point not his own, exactly, but from a position just behind his back. He saw images of her with Booker, too, her face contorted as if with pain, fragments of conversation, the smugness of the young black's face, all of that present, horrid, like a grotesque reflection in a mirror, and yet disappearing when he addressed the ball. He bogeyed ten only because his wedge shot, *too* well struck, flew impossibly behind the green; then he continued on to eleven. He parred this and then birdied, unexpectedly, number twelve, whose green, shaded by a thick curtain of locust trees, sat at the bottom of a steep ravine, so that his tee shot vanished into a black pit whose bottom he could not see. He searched for his ball in the traps and rough before discovering it two feet from the pin.

He began to play in earnest then. The more he concentrated, the more the intervening years slipped away, until, sweating now, quietly exultant, he felt each shot as a redemption that returned him, as his present self, to the boy he once had been. He bogeyed thirteen, his mind slipping to an image of himself and Booker struggling in the grass—an image he proceeded calmly to erase. Fourteen and fifteen were pars, the latter after a miraculous bunker save. He felt optimistic, even happy then: he had never broken forty on the back nine, and yet now he stood at just one over, with four more holes to play. The air was cool, the fairways silver-green, and he felt like a man who had awakened from a long illness, tranquil and at peace: if Clarissa and her boyfriend wanted money, perhaps he *could* arrange something; it would be enough for him just to stay here in this place, and as he reached this resolution, he noticed a shrouded figure shadowing him down sixteen.

He attempted to ignore it, hitting a decent tee shot, mind focused, eyes straight ahead, and then hacking his way down the long dogleg for a bogey. But as he labored through the rough to seventeen, his daughter's voice echoed to him from a grove of walnut trees.

"Daddy," she said. "You've got to talk to me."

Clarissa had often accompanied him to the golf course in the high days of their affair, and so he could understand how she might have found him here. But there was also something threatening about the way her fleck of shirt flitted in and out among the trees. She resembled a figure in a dream, a siren, come to distract him now that his mind was finally at peace, and he chose to take her in this way, striding up to his ball as if no one were there. He struck it perfectly, seeing the ball rise with mathematic progression until he looked down at his feet and realized that he'd aimed left, away from his daughter and toward an overhanging cottonwood that guarded the seventeenth green. He waited, hands high, until he heard the icy report of ball on bark, and then Clarissa's voice surrounded him, back and front, issuing from the bell-shaped shadows of the trees. "You can't ignore me this time," she said. "It's not like before: this time you're going to have to listen to what I have to say."

Beneath the cottonwood, he searched for his ball on hands and knees. He knew he had little chance of finding it: the shot could have bounced anywhere, the tree too far off for him to see it come down, but he hunted anyway. Clarissa was closer then. He could see, in his peripheral vision, her form drifting on the edge of a small copse of oaks, the patch of her white shirt, one hand trailing against the trunk of the nearest tree, as if for safety. She wore the white-flapped spikes he had once bought her at a garage sale, which, with their sewn uppers and tees stuck through their laces, had looked so compelling on her in her younger days. "Please," he said, avoiding her. "Please—just leave me alone."

"I want to make a deal," Clarissa said. "A fair deal, that's all I'm asking for. Except this time I'm making the offer to you, instead of you making it to me."

He staggered in the opposite direction, tripping on his five-iron.

"There's a ball back here," Clarissa added. "By the way."

One of the same white-flapped spikes, checked out from Evidence, now accompanied Detective Keegan as she drove south into the night. News of the manhunt had calmed the city's inhabitants, and they sat at their dinner tables as Keegan's Escort passed, men like Remy Westbrook, Podge McGee, gazing at the female anchor, who herself was black, as she said, "Police today began the first phase in what they say will be a citywide search for Clarissa Sayers's killer, operating checkpoints on most major highways. . . ." But Keegan didn't

285

hear this. Nor did she hear the usual radio traffic, her civilian car lacking police band, and so she headed up the Colonial Club's front drive in silence, her mind filled with an image not of Booker Short, but of a white-shirted figure on the seventeenth green.

The night of the murder, Judge Sayers had gathered up his clubs and walked back toward his daughter—noticing, as he did so, that she continued to retreat. His ball had bounced some seventy yards backward directly along its original line of flight, and he felt a pungent despair, standing only one and a half holes from perfection and yet aware that he must fail, that he was too old to succeed now, and that he would never be young again. He stepped to the ball and swung, but it was the swing of an old man, abbreviated, pinched, and the ball shot forward in a slicing curve, skipping past the green.

"I had a chance to shoot forty," he said.

"What?" Clarissa said.

"To shoot forty," he repeated. "I was one over when you came."

"For God's sake," she begged, "this isn't about a golf score—it's about *me*." He could hear her sobbing as he walked forward, in the kind of display the old Clarissa had never indulged in. "I know you're angry," she went on. "I know I haven't always done what you thought was best. But if you could just this once listen to what I have to say. . . ." For a moment he thought the old Clarissa might reappear: outrageous, corrupt, aware somehow of the comedy in what she said. But the voice that returned to him was pleading and aggrieved: "I just wanted to be independent. I wanted to be able to do something, and I was afraid you wouldn't let me. Now, maybe that wasn't the right way to go about it, but I wasn't trying to hurt you personally—please, can't you try to understand that, at least?"

"I have no opinion," the judge said.

"Why not?" Clarissa said.

"Because," the judge said as he swung, "you've tried to steal my money and then dressed it up in other reasons. That's the real truth of it, it seems to me."

286

"'The truth'?" Clarissa said. They walked almost together then, Clarissa cursing, quietly at first and then louder, her mood changing with the velocity of the woman he loved and knew. "What kind of nutcase are you to want to talk about the truth? You've never told the truth to anyone in this whole city."

"I have always said I would be loyal to you," the judge said.

"That's a crack-up," Clarissa said. "That's a real knee-slapper, Daddy. I'm not really very interested in 'loyal'—I'm more interested in facts. You want to hear some facts? How about statutory rape? That's a fact. How about corruption of a minor? That is, you know, actually illegal. I looked it up, right there in your law books."

"Are you saying," the judge asked calmly, "that you had no part in that?"

"Or how about this one?" Clarissa said. "The fact that what really upsets you, Mr. Federal Judge, friend to all minorities, is that your daughter is sleeping with a black."

The judge broke stride so abruptly that Clarissa nearly ran in to him.

"I thought I asked you not to speak of that," he said.

"I protect my friends, Daddy," Clarissa said. She was almost within reach, leaning forward, the words vaulting from her pale, round face. "You can forget about the money if you want to, but if you do anything to Booker, I will make you pay."

They had approached the seventeenth green together, their figures like the tinted etchings for some lost allegory: the father caliginous, indistinct, striding off into the darkness, while the daughter trails behind in bridal white, her lips stained the color of pomegranate seeds. It was a scene that Keegan struggled to re-create as she crouched on the same darkened fairway, carrying a flashlight and Clarissa Sayers's golf shoe in a yellow plastic bag. She had parked her car in the Colonial Club's back lot and sneaked onto the course between the tennis courts and the club's north wing, the cut grass fanning around her like an unlined football field, curving, undulant, surrounded like a hallway by dark stands of trees. It was very quiet. She could hear the rain hiss into the short grass, could hear its drops cascade among windblown leaves. The seventeenth green lay ahead, and (though she did not know it) she stood beside the patch of fairway where the judge had hit his fourth shot, leaving a divot that, if she'd crouched and turned on her flashlight, she could have put her fingers in. It had been a fairly simple pitch, the pin in the front center, and he'd hit it gently, the ball popping high in the air and landing short along the fringe.

"You won't leave with him," the judge told Clarissa, grabbing his putter and strolling toward the silvery green. "You can imagine as well as I the life you'd lead: living in a trailer near the penitentiary? working in a convenience store? You don't even have your degree." He removed the pin and returned to squat behind his putt. "Besides," the judge said, "once he sees that you don't have the money, your friend will leave. No, I don't see why I should throw good money away for that."

"You forgot one thing," Clarissa said.

"Oh?" the judge said, bent over his line. "What's that?"

Clarissa stepped forward then, the ball of her right foot pressing the exact spot where Marcy Keegan now knelt quietly, unwrapping the two-toned spike from its bag.

"You have always," Clarissa said, enunciating slowly, "disgusted me. Fucking you is like fucking something rotten, a dirty, sick old man."

The judge stroked his putt. He hit it far too hard, though right on line, the ball shooting straight across the cup without stopping, and he whirled, as if on his follow-through, and swung the putter like a baseball bat, the toe of it punching through the soft bone of his daughter's temple, just above her ear. Her neck jerked and she dropped suddenly to her knees, the force of the club like a railroad spike, directed perfectly. One hand clutched her temple, then brought the blood down before her face, her hand darkened, color-less, and to his astonishment, her tongue flicked out to taste it.

"Shit," she said.

This, of course, was the moment that Detective Keegan wished she could see more than anything: the moment at which, as with any murder, she found herself in the presence of the central act. It was no ordinary murder scene. She had no witnesses, no ballistics experts, no blood or even a body to inspect: merely a waterlogged spike print sur-rounded by darkness and rain. And yet as she set Clarissa's shoe atop the print and tapped it with her fingers, she could feel the tremor of the victim's presence, as if her bare heel were still inside it. She picked the shoe up and, cheek pressed against the green, set the spikes down more directly on the print until, with no pressure from above, they sank a fraction of an inch. When she tapped the shoe, it would not slide, and she pushed down with her palm, driving the spikes in.

When she lifted the shoe, she saw the same unchanged print, and she sat back on her heels. The next questions followed logically. How, for instance, could a killer have moved the body unseen? Lawton had told her that the back nine was protected by a fence and a creek. The seventeenth green overlooked the back side of the course, and as she stared in that direction, a car's headlights circled an unlit cul-de-sac; she stumbled down a brambled hillside until she could see an un-marked road on the far side of the club property, across both fence and creek. A killer could have hidden a car there discreetly, particu-larly if he knew the layout of the course, and following the creek, she found a bridge that spanned it upstream. The top was fenced, but a tunnel opened underneath, the water running fast atop a limestone shelf, mudless and—she guessed, ten days earlier, before all this rain—easy to wade. She shone her light down into it, the water black, foam-flecked. By now she imagined the sequence like this: the killer knocked the body into the trap on seventeen, picked it up there (thus the struggle marks—like "someone had been dancing in it," the caddie had said), and carried it down the hill to the creek. He left the club's property underneath the bridge, pulled a car up to the cul-de-sac, and dumped the body in—all with very little likelihood of discovery, since, in the hour Keegan had been on the course, she'd seen only one car pass.

She was right about all this, unfortunately.

But there were several other things she could not explain. For instance, she did not know why Clarissa Sayers would have come here in the middle of the night, or why she would have put on her golf clothes voluntarily. Most important, she could not yet imagine who the killer might be: could not, for instance, see the sick, rachitic smile on Judge Sayers's face as he emerged with his daughter's body on the far side of the creek. Or hear the oddly high pitched humming noise he made as he heaved her tarp-rolled body into the trunk, checked for witnesses, and lit out for the river, breath seething through bared teeth.

But she figured that she would, eventually.

By the time Keegan got back to the parking lot, most of the other cars were gone. Their absence highlighted her trespass, and she walked nervously through the bare lot amid the humming of theft-protection lights. A figure was waiting by her car. She had seen it as she came off the eighteenth green and had since then tried to ignore it, fearing it was a member of the club's security staff. He—or at least it seemed to be a he—was black, the face an indistinct knob above a beige overcoat, shoulders towering above the few small cars in back. As she reached her car, the man took several hesitant steps toward the rear bumper and said, "I need to talk to you." Keegan fumbled mutely with her keys. "Please," the man said, glancing back at the clubhouse. "Miss, I saw you out here at the club yesterday, looking for that girl. I know you two's the same."

290

"How did you know it was me?" she asked.

"Saw your car pull up but nobody came in," Clyde said. "Ain't nobody else gonna drive to a country club and then stand out in the rain, excepting the police."

His name was Clyde Wilkins. He offered this information half an hour later, sitting in Keegan's Escort outside the club's back gate. His face recoiled from each oncoming headlight, then followed the car as it receded. "So you say you knew this boy, Booker Short," Keegan said. "You got a job for him at the request of Mercury Chapman, whom you've known since you were a kid. All right, I appreciate that, Mr. Wilkins, but that's not the kind of information that would make a man come to the police—unless, of course, there's something else you'd like to say." The bartender had ducked his head to fit beneath the small car's ceiling, and he stared at the dashboard fixedly.

"You right about that," he said.

"All right," Keegan said. "Let's talk about it, then."

Clyde Wilkins pursed his lips. "How 'bout if I ask you a question first," he said. "Like maybe I could ask you what you were looking for out on that golf course tonight?"

"I think a girl died here," Keegan said.

"Is that right?" Clyde said. He did not look surprised.

"And I'm not sure that boy did it," Keegan said.

"Yep," Clyde said. "That's where it gets complicated, don't it?" He shifted his bulk to face Keegan, the car's springs twanging underneath them. "You ever thought of something you ain't supposed to? Something you know your boss don't want you to say?"

"Yes," Keegan said.

"I heard a couple things," Clyde said.

"All right," Keegan said.

"They might mean something, and they might not," Clyde said, "but once you started poking around that golf course, I got to wondering a little bit." He gazed out the passenger window. "I got me to wondering what time of day you thought she might've been there."

"It would've had to be at night," Keegan said.

"Yep," Clyde said. "Seems funny, doesn't it?"

"It does," Keegan agreed.

"And then I got to wondering if any of those security folks said anything to you about the judge—you know, the girl's dad."

"No," Keegan said.

"I figured that," Clyde said. He rubbed his thumbnail on his cheek.

"Do you know something about Judge Sayers?" Keegan asked.

"I seen him on that course sometimes at night," Clyde said. "Once or twice. Buddy Acheson's the only other fella does that, and he's seen them, too. Both of them."

"You mean the judge and Buddy?"

"I mean the judge and his little girl," Clyde said.

Keegan froze. In her head she heard the roaring of the creek.

"What's the other thing?" she asked.

"That they were a couple," Clyde said. "You hear things as a bartender that you don't want to hear." He looked at Keegan. "That was one of them, I guess."

"Would anyone else corroborate this?" Keegan said.

Clyde Wilkins had already eased out of the car, his body plugging the door frame. "One of my patrons, do you mean?" he said. "You can ask them if you want to, Detective. But I doubt it. Not if there's a black man they can blame."

He closed the door, the sound of the rain disappearing as it sealed.

23

MERCURY CHAPMAN had fallen asleep that night around eight. He had intended merely to rest, exiting his now-plaster-coated office and lying down for a brief moment atop his bedspread, but instead he lost consciousness and descended deeply into dream. The dream was of his wife. He was sitting on the porch of a white clapboard house that resembled a country sanatorium, an old hotel, of the sort one found down south in Missouri, near the river, where the hot-springs spas used to be. The toilets had elevated tanks, and the trees about the house were gnarled and silent, and he knew that other friends were there, that Eddie Coole sat alone in an upstairs room, whittling a pencil for a sketch, that the Barton twins were there, and Phil Samuels, whom he had played dice with as a kid. He went out then to meet his wife, unlocking the veranda screen. Dusk was, as he well knew, her favorite time of day, and she had been out cutting chives, her fingers muddy, a pair of rusty scissors hanging from a string about her neck. She seemed as real as she had ever been. He could smell her skin, spiced, like hickory. He could hear her humming lightly, see the slight flush that lit her cheeks when she was happy and wished to talk to him, and he cried for all that he had missed. His wife seemed unconcerned by this, continuing toward him smiling, and when she dropped the cut chives into his hand, they turned to mint, the fragrance sharp and pungent between his fingers. She touched his elbow encouragingly, saying, "It's always sad to see the last of spring," and he woke with his face wet, knowing more certainly than ever that he would never see his wife again.

By midnight he was outside the Hotel President. First he left a message on the judge's machine, apologizing for that morning and then suggesting that they meet at the hunt club the next morning at eight—"I've got some information on the boy," he said. "You might be interested in it." After that he rose and rummaged through fifty years' worth of tie tacks atop his dresser until he found the handheld tape recorder he'd been given upon his retirement. He replaced its batteries, left a note for Lilly saying *Thanks for the advice*, and drove downtown, parking his Volvo beneath the hotel's fire escape.

He clambered to the bottom platform from the Volvo's roof and, after ducking through the open window, mounted the back steps. He suddenly feared that his decision to help had come too late, and he hurried to the twelfth-floor landing, its door propped open with a toilet lid. "Booker," he said. "Come on out—it's me." No one answered. The reek of guano oozed beneath the doors; paper peeled off the walls in strips, fibrous along their ends. He imagined his safe bed, the plaster ceiling he would have enjoyed replacing that day, and then shuffled into the hall. Booker was waiting at the far end. His form materialized by degrees, his eye whites, the neck of his T-shirt, and instead of anger at his silence, Mercury felt a flush of relief. "I talked to the judge," he said.

Booker nodded cautiously. "Where's Stan?" he asked.

"He went back to the police," Mercury said.

Booker barked at this, cursing dryly and with some amusement at the stripped wallpaper. "For what," he said, "to turn himself in?"

"I don't know." Mercury stepped forward. "Look," he said. "I'm afraid we made a terrible mistake—all of us. Because if it happened

294

the way you said, then we . . . we . . ." He stumbled here, swallowing. "I'm sorry," he said. "I'm sorry. I made an appointment to meet the judge at the hunt club tomorrow morning. I want you to come."

Booker glanced at him, motionless, cheeks glossed with sweat.

"You sure you want to do that?" he asked.

"No," Mercury said. He cracked a salesman's smile. "No, I don't want to do that at all. But I'm willing to try on two conditions, only."

"All right," Booker said.

"First, no violence," Mercury unfolded a finger. "And second, if this fails, if he doesn't show up, we go to the police."

"Deal," Booker said.

They drove east, through the center of the city: past the old banks and federal buildings, the solitary department store with its wooden-slat elevator that Mercury had ridden on as a teen, the law offices where for forty years his father's desk had sat and to which the Chapman family still lent its name. He checked the streetlights in his rearview mirror nervously, stopping far too abruptly at an intersection as yet another police cruiser nosed in front of him—a clean blue lozenge of force. He felt particularly aware that evening of the city's force. Its presence slid over them like a dark, membranous wing, brooding from west to east, its dark veins hidden just beyond the rain. Booker's presence on the rear floorboard increased this sense: he imagined what it must be like for a fugitive to walk through these streets, the wastewater pouring into the sewers, the empty doorways and vagrantless bus stops, the rigid thrust of the Commerce Tower, the false-marble front of United Missouri Bank. Their doorways and their atriums were chromed and monumental, while beside them crouched defunct hat shops and lunch counters, their plywood fronts stamped with the legend SECURED BY INMATE LABOR OF THE STATE. Those aspects of the city that had once seemed innocent now struck him as sinister, alien, halogen-lit. Even the statue of Harry Truman leered from the median on Eighth Street, and stopping at a light on Grand Avenue, he found himself looking up at the federal courthouse's carved, iconic face. Rain sluiced down the steps, and he stared through his windshield at the wrought-brass eagles that appeared above its door in frieze, their wings outspread above the darkness, arrows clutched in their clawed feet. Here he felt the centerpoint of his foreboding, the stirring of something too large to see.

Once they got outside of town, Booker crawled up to the front seat. He fiddled with the Volvo's radio, the stations flashing from country music back to reports of flooding along the Missouri River, and then he switched it off and rested his forehead against the glass as, so many years earlier, he had done in the cab that delivered him to the Bentham place.

"I mean, are you saying you disagree with everything my grandfather said about the war," he asked, "not just Hammonds but everything, the truth of it?"

"I don't know," Mercury answered. "It depends on what he said."

"Did he kill any Germans?" Booker said.

"One," Mercury said. "At least that I saw, anyway."

"One?" Booker said. He seemed confused, a finger rubbing his ear. "I'm not for killing people, but that doesn't seem like much for a guy who was there a year."

"We weren't supposed to," Mercury said.

"Excuse me?" Booker said.

"We were a supply company," Mercury said. He peered at Booker long enough that the car began to drift. "Didn't he tell you that?" he asked, glancing up to correct his course. "We drove trucks. Took fuel and ammunition to the front lines and then came back again. We didn't fight anybody. It wasn't that we wouldn't have, it was that the army wouldn't let us." He puffed his cheeks with air. "The truth is, the army didn't like giving guns to blacks. It had nothing to do with bravery."

The car's tires hummed against the road.

"So it was all a bunch of crap," Booker said.

"What was?"

"All those guns and knives he had," Booker said. "All those little German hats. Coming off like he was some kind of war hero, shooting up the Krauts, when all he really did was drive a truck around in back. Shit, man—" His voice rose, oddly strangled. "You don't know how often I had to listen to that, to that hero fucking crap—"

It was the first time Mercury had ever heard him express anything like regret.

"Wait a minute," he said.

"Never mind," Booker said. "It's just another fucking waste. Don't seem like any of you were much interested in telling the truth."

"No," Mercury said.

"The big war," Booker said. "What a crock of shit."

"Listen," Mercury said. He stepped on the brakes, the highway running at that point between two unlighted, mud-slick fields. "Your grandfather was a good soldier," he said. "What he did was not picturesque. He led no charges. He did not invade anything. But he, they—all those men—did their job. They did not quit. Even after Hammonds got hung, he did not quit." He shoved the car back into gear. "He blamed Hammonds's death on me. I don't accept that. But that doesn't mean he had no reason to be bitter, or that he wasn't brave. Sometimes it's easier to lie than to admit you're fighting for the wrong thing."

"He always said he saved your life," Booker said. "Is that true, or did he make that one up, too?"

"Yes," Mercury said.

"Yes what?"

Mercury drove in silence for a time, as if no question had been asked.

"Yes, your grandfather saved my life," he said eventually. "He did."

297

"Tell me about it," Booker said.

He did. It was a story he had known and remembered for almost fifty years and yet one that he had told infrequently, sensing that—unlike his comic stories—its events were somehow cheapened when told for entertainment, to an audience that had not been there. It began in December 1944, a month that found his company snowbound in a marble-floored château near the Belgian line. Hammonds had been dead three weeks, and Mercury had felt, in his wake, the first tremors of rebellion in his men: a sullenness, a certain resistance to order that they had never previously displayed. When the château's furniture began to disappear—chairs, tables, bureaus, all burned for firewood—he found himself unable to punish anyone directly. The same went for the women in scarves with shaved gray heads, who had just a few weeks earlier been consorts for the German officers and now lived with his men. As fellow outcasts, the Americans sympathized with them, and so when, during a feast with the château's owner and his wife, one of the shaved French serving girls shrieked and tried to hide herself from the couple's gaze, the men had turned on their hosts immediately. The owner's toast to *"nos libérateurs nègres"* was met with silence until Isaac rose at the table's end and said, "Let's make a toast to Reggie Hammonds. I know he's just a Negro, not a general, but I would rather drink to him." The other men stood in unison, the sound they made less like a toast than like a jeer.

The next morning he descended a winged staircase into bedlam: dirty plates and bits of chicken carcasses in the great hall, fed on by the château's cats, the ripe scent of the potato-peel "whiskey" his men liked to make. A room opened to the left of the staircase. Isaac lounged there on an upholstered love seat, cradling a gilt-framed portrait of M. La Vaux's great-*grandpère*, whose pale index finger extended along the buttons of a red velvet vest. As Mercury entered, Isaac held it up. "What do you figure?" he said. "Eighteen seventy? Eighty?" He reversed the picture, studying it. "I wonder if anybody painted a picture of what my granddad looked like back then. Or yours," he said, smiling again. "Don't you come from Missouri, Cap? From folks who maybe owned some property?"

Mercury scanned the room. It, too, was a mess, the curtains ripped down from their rods and blanketing the sleeping men.

"You sober enough to move," he asked, "or just to talk?"

"Move where now, Cap?"

"North," Mercury said. "I'm going to take two trucks north, try to find the line, some communications." He touched his sidearm. "I figure if you have some problems with my actions, as I do with yours, this might give us a chance to settle them more personally."

Isaac was standing then, several inches taller than Mercury, the picture dangling from his left hand. "Why, Cap," he said, "I think that's a fine idea."

"Good," Mercury had said. "Ten minutes. I'll meet you outside."

"So he forced you out of there," Booker said. The road had flattened, bearing northward to the river and thus the hunting club. The rain had broken momentarily, and through a patch of open sky ahead, the moon glowed paper-colored, rolled on its back.

"In a manner of speaking, yes," Mercury said. "You could say that."

"Like it was his idea," Booker said.

"Probably," Mercury said. "But you know, if it hadn't've been that, it would've been some other reason—to find the war. That was what we both really wanted, I think."

They had driven into town through snowdrifts, the tires wrapped with chains, dismounting at times to clear the road by hand. The day was bright and clear, and they rumbled through open fields, glittering curves and humps of white, broken only by the black tracery of streams. He did not tell Booker everything. He did not tell how, despite his outward cheerfulness, he feared that he had lost command, or how, when they stopped in the empty village, he had suggested that they head south to Verdun—the city farthest from the front—and

299

Isaac had countermanded him, tapping Belgium on the map and saying, "Our last drop was there. Me and the men think it would be quicker to go back."

Nor did he tell about his private thoughts, his musings: how he had wondered whether Isaac's hurry was due to guilt over Hammonds's death, or if he saw the confusion of the war zone as a good place to ambush his captain, to silence him for good. He merely said, "And you know, the funny thing about it was, by the time we reached the village, we were feeling pretty happy. I mean, no one had expected us to get that far, that early in the day."

"What did it look like?" Booker said.

"Excuse me?"

"The village—what did it look like?" Booker repeated, and Mercury noticed that he'd closed his eyes, as if in an attempt to imagine it.

"Well, hell, it didn't look like much of anything."

"Did it look like Waterloo?" Booker asked.

"Oh, hell no. Jesus, no—um, let's see here," Mercury said, leaning forward above the wheel. "I mean, it was the same size as Waterloo, about. The same kind of town, you know. But as for looks, it was completely different." His mind rifled backward to find the fragment of a town he'd seen nearly fifty years before, in December, at the beginning of the German defeat. "I mean, it wasn't spread out," he said. "And the buildings were made of stone, not clapboard or brick. Gray fieldstone with big wood shutters and little balconies. And the streets were real, real narrow. No light poles, no parking places or stuff like that. They had the shops along the street and the apartments over them. All these little shops with beat-up painted wooden signs—*Patisserie*, and the butcher, which was *Char . . . Char*-something. There was light in some of the upstairs windows, but there was no one on the street. Nobody. No gas stations or convenience stores. No people anyplace. Although I suppose that wasn't all that unusual when our soldiers came into a place. I doubt anybody there had ever seen three blacks in their main street."

"That's like Waterloo," Booker said.

"Sure it is, yeah," Mercury said, but he was not listening. "The funny thing about a war is that you can be right there in the middle of it and not know anything. The places that had been burned or had their windows busted out were covered up by snow. You couldn't hear any shooting. All you could hear was wind and the roofs dripping and then . . ." He seemed to wake up now, squinting forward at the road and then into his mirror. "And then, eight hours later, we *were* right in the middle of it."

"The middle of what?" Booker asked.

"The Battle of the Bulge," Mercury said. "Bastogne. That was where we went."

They had come down from a pass into a valley and found them there, the tanks white-painted, sheets of canvas strapped across their turrets, and the infantry, too, in white ponchos—a ghost army fanned in a pale chevron across the plain. They did not make a sound. The troops, in fact, did not seem to move at all, focused in a long, brecciated stain that seethed and folded on itself but never changed length. But it was the tanks that most fascinated them. They spread in a rough wedge about the men, gliding silently, a faint plume of white and a gouge line following each, so that they appeared from a distance like the small balls of snow that precede an avalanche, and yet much slower than that, inexorable, churning directly through and over the dark spots of pines. They had heard tanks firing in the night, had seen them at rest, awaiting fuel, but never had they seen them deployed—a full division—in the field, and it was as if in this bleak formation they confronted the war's true face. Coming out around a ridge, they found them ranged to their right, approaching with hypnotic slowness, the 76mm barrels—so long and elegant from far away—now foreshortened, snubbed. Mercury had frozen, eyes fixed on the nearest tank's central bore, until Isaac shook the gearshift, saying, "Go man—go!" and he stamped on the gas, pulling out of the tank's path and watching as it breached the roadbed, the frozen earth buckling, the treads squealing around a wall of metal wheels.

The troops surrounded them next. He was not sure how he and Isaac had gotten there: one moment they had been on a spur road, and the next they were in the middle of the column, the troops parting around the truck's bumper and banging its hood and wheel wells, someone shouting, "Hey, lookit, Johnson. The general's sent us a fucking ice cream truck. Hey, ice cream man, you got a bomb pop in there?" and the men laughing and yelling, with snow caked about their boots. They were going to die. That was the first thought that occurred to Mercury, and to Isaac, too: their cheeks gaunt, unshaved, their lips blistered with the cold. A jeep pulled even with them, the driver standing as he drove. Peering into Isaac's window, he shouted, "It's a Negro unit, sir," and then looked again and said, "No, I'm sorry, sir—the driver's white," and, listening to instructions, waved them off to the side.

The armored unit's commander stood on the jeep's passenger seat, a tattered ensign flapping atop the dash. "What the hell are you doing here, Captain?" he shouted. He had his hat off, and the wind whipped his hair.

"Looking for the war, sir," Mercury said.

The commander paused. He held an orange in his hand, the one spot of color in the entire valley, and it seemed to Mercury that at another time he might have made a joke "Well, you've found it," he said, lifting the truck's canopy. "What've you got, diesel?"

Mercury nodded.

"All right, dump it, then," the commander said. "On the ground, so the Germans can't use it if they come here. I need a medical unit, not fuel. Can you transport that?"

"Where is it?" Mercury said.

302

"Down the road three hours," the commander said. "We'll give you the coordinates. Call in your other trucks if you can find em. Then turn around and catch up."

"Where are you going?" Mercury asked.

"Bastogne," the commander said.

They returned after dark. The column had snaked into the mountains by then, and they eased into its rear guard, the truck's headlights out, the troops faceless now and stumbling, their heads down as they trudged toward a narrow pass. The first shells fell ahead: the soft flutterings of mortar rounds, the crump when they came down, the truck shaking just perceptibly beneath their feet. Mercury sped up, driving paradoxically toward the shellfire—and thus toward the troops, thinking that if he was going to be shot, he would prefer that it be in the company of whites rather than with this black man who disliked him. He remembered Isaac's opening the door to peer ahead and then looking back at him, not smiling but somehow satisfied, communicant, as if Mercury's fear had somehow proved his case. "I guess if you're gonna be a white officer, you owe it to your men to get shot at in the white way," Isaac said, chuckling. "You know, be brave and all that crap."

"I don't owe you anything," Mercury said.

"Is that right?" Isaac said. "Well, how come you're here, then?"

"Because I'm sick of your crap."

As he spoke, a shell landed on the hillside just above them, spattering the windshield with snow, mud, the webbed branches of a tree. Mercury tried to accelerate—"Cut it back! Cut it back!" Isaac shouted—but instead the truck lurched sideways no matter how he spun the wheel, the back fishtailing, the tires engulfed by now in a sliding wave of white debris. For a moment the truck balanced in empty space. He saw Isaac leap from the passenger door, feet kicking as if swimming in the air, and then the truck began to roll, his vision disappearing like a picture jerked away.

When he woke, the cab was filled with snow, the grains packed tight against his face. He drifted in and out of consciousness. His right arm was pinned behind his back, but when he tried to straighten it, two bones knocked together in his shoulder, their touch so painful and electric that he retched—the snow plugging his mouth like a gag. He could, however, move his left arm and his head, and he worked to loosen both, scratching with his fingers and twisting his chin from side to side until he heard the rasp of metal hitting snow. It came from straight above, and he whimpered, afraid a shovel blade would split his skull. Then the digging stopped, followed by a scrabbling sound and the astringent brush of oxygen, as cold as the water from a stream. He looked up passively. The edges of the hole were jet black. Then a match was struck, the snow flooded with a golden light, quite beautiful, that refracted and glittered off Isaac Bentham's sweat-stained face.

"So he did come back," Booker said.

"Oh, yes," Mercury said. "He most definitely did."

They had reached the hunt club by then, the two of them seated in the now-quiet car, the grass in front of them columned with fireflies.

"And that was it?" Booker said.

"No," Mercury said. "No, it wasn't."

"Did you talk about Hammonds?" Booker asked.

Mercury's eyes slipped away from the younger man's. "Yes," he said. "Yes, we talked about him."

He had been trapped: he remembered that sensation more than anything, the horror of being buried alive, entombed in white, unable to move his limbs or speak. And he remembered, too, that Isaac had stopped digging and rolled over on his stomach, as if noticing the same thing. "Well, well, well, looky here," he had said, brushing ice crystals off Mercury's eyelashes with an oppressive tenderness. "Aren't you gonna give me an order, Cap?" he asked. His lips bobbed inches from Mercury's pupil. When the match burned down, Isaac struck another, his face foreshortened, peering down from the hole's edge as a child might look at a goldfish in a bowl. "That's the funny thing about orders, ain't it, Cap? Once folks get used to who's taking them, they can't imagine it any other way."

Mercury had twisted his neck again. He could feel Isaac's weight pressing down on his chest, suffocating him.

"You want to learn what it's like to be a nigger, Cap?" Isaac asked.

Snow blocked Mercury's mouth. He did not, in any case, want to learn.

"I mean to be a nigger and a man," Isaac said. "To know. You understand what I'm saying, Captain? To *know*"—he whispered this, the words invested with an emotion that Mercury had never before encountered—"*that you ain't?* Do you know what happens to a man like that? You white folks wait until he hits back: maybe it's an officer, or a cop. Maybe it's a woman who comes up and cusses him for no reason in a field." He dipped closer to Mercury. "How'd you like to wake up every morning *worrying* that the minute you slip up and act like a man—bang, they gonna put you away? How'd you feel about justice then? Your *legality*. How'd you like to know that a judge could decide to *take your life*, and all the while he's only thinking, Well, it don't matter, he ain't no different from the rest of those damn niggers anyway." Mercury shivered, and Isaac dug for a few moments, scooping the snow from around his jaw. Then he sat on his haunches, as if unsure whether to proceed.

"You did it," Mercury said. "That woman. You let Hammonds take your place."

Isaac stayed silent for a time, rocking, staring up into the air.

"Do you know what I told him?" he asked.

"Isaac," Mercury said, "I'm getting cold." His lips were numb, and he formed the words slowly. "I'm going to die if you don't get me out of here."

"You know what I told him?" Isaac repeated. He had leaned back on his elbows, with his helmet—which he had used to dig the hole—

305

propped between his knees. "I said we ought to trust you. I said you wouldn't let the army hang him if he didn't do it. I said you owed us that. Ain't it funny?" He rolled over then, picking up the helmet and jamming it in the snow beneath Mercury's chin. "Ain't it funny I said that? And do you know, that's why I came to save your ass: because of Hammonds. Because I want you to always remember that there was at least *one* black man better than you will ever be."

They sat side by side, the air chilling, cooler, their breath fogging the windshield, a curved patina of blue, as if that marked the final deposition of what had been said. Booker touched it. "So what was the difference?" he asked.

"The difference of what?" Mercury said, opening his door.

"Between the three of you?" He followed Mercury to the car's trunk. "I mean, Hammonds was a thief, right? He doesn't sound like the kind of guy my grandfather would like. So why would he say that Hammonds was a better man than you—or him?"

Mercury unloaded his shotgun case and handed it to Booker.

"I guess," he said, "because he gave up something."

"You mean he let himself get killed?"

Mercury did not answer. He picked up the bedroll and his canvas jacket, draped his waders over his shoulder, and headed for the cabin. Booker trailed after him, stepping into the musty, rubber funk of the mudroom with its hanging rows of waders, its gun rack, and remembering with a shock Clarissa standing here. Inside, Mercury had begun to light the gas lamps, removing the glass globes and touching a match flame to the ashen mantels. Shadows leapt about the two men.

"The question is what your grandfather and I made of it—of getting a second chance." Mercury smiled at him. "It doesn't sound like much, according to what you say."

"I'm not sure that's what I meant," Booker said.

"Well, it's what I heard," Mercury said.

306

They went to bed not long after that, Booker on the horsehair couch downstairs and Mercury in his usual bunk, up the rickety loft stairs, where some eighteen months earlier his companion and Clarissa Sayers had first consummated their affair. Before parting, they had hidden Mercury's tape recorder behind the shelf of wine bottles on the far wall of the A-frame. The plan was to tape the judge for evidence, and having tested the machine, Mercury lay awake, his mind contentedly busy, filled with new projects, as it often was when he came to the end of something. He felt particularly excited about the tape recorder. It had been sitting in his dresser at home, unused, since his retirement, but now, hearing it replay his voice during the test (he'd told the story of Pete Martin's cabin), he was enamored of its possibilities. How many stories had he told here? How many nights had he lain awake here in this very bunk, thinking pleasantly of long-gone things: of the towns he'd canvassed as a salesman, of the deals he'd cut and the fields he'd slept in; of the funny ways people used to speak; and even his memories of playing in the Hotel President, which he'd thought about so recently. It seemed to him a shame that all of this had not been recorded for posterity. It seemed to him, even, that recording his own stories might, in some small fashion, help him avoid the silence of dying, which had always frightened him: maybe if he'd just recorded his wife, she might not seem so far away.

He felt—as people often do on the verge of sleep—as if he'd discovered some great thing, and his mind drifted back by logical progression to the last story he'd told Booker. It seemed a natural for inclusion on his tape, and yet he felt a nagging worry. It had been more difficult than he'd expected to remember what Isaac had said that night some fifty years before. His own words, his own memory of other words, kept getting in the way. In the end he could not be certain he had told the whole thing truthfully. It seemed that Isaac might have said, "*I* am a better man than you will ever be"—meaning Isaac himself, not Hammonds. The story, of course, would have been quite

307

different that way, and he lay still for a time, considering the change. Isaac's saying "Hammonds" was better, of course, and Mercury argued back and forth with himself until he realized that it didn't matter anymore what, exactly, Isaac had said.

The point was that he'd decided to tell it that way.

24

WHEN STAN HAD RETURNED to police headquarters on Tuesday, an unfamiliar detective had arrested him. He waited in a small holding cell until Detective Schiff stuck his head in and said, "Looks like you been out all night again, Mr. Granger. You care to tell us where you been?" To which Stan responded, "I'd like to see Detective Keegan, please." He remained optimistic as he sat on the bare concrete slab, counting seams in the white-painted brick and thinking, *She will come as soon as she gets in,* and then later, *She will come on her lunch break.* By six o'clock she still had not appeared. Only then did he begin to fret, remembering how Booker had sat in the ruined hotel room and said he wanted to see the judge personally, and how Mercury had said, "You're gonna have to let me think on it"; and by the time he convinced someone to let him use the phone, the number at Mercury's house kept ringing until the answering machine picked up.

He had tried it every hour since. He made the last call at seven o'clock Wednesday morning, an unfamiliar detective peering at him through the glassed door of the interrogation room, Stan's right hand cuffed to the table leg. The phone rang for several seconds, followed by Mercury's booming, recorded voice, and then, unexpectedly, a smaller voice under that, saying, "Hello? Hello there?"

and then addressing the message directly as it played, saying, "Oh, you be quiet now. They ain't paying no attention if you ain't even here."

"Hello?" Stan said.

"I ain't going anywhere," the voice said. It was a woman's. "You just wait a minute until he decides to quit." The message ended, followed by a squeal of feedback.

"Turn it off," Stan said. "Turn off the machine." He held the phone a foot from his ear, hearing a jumble of amplified noises, then silence.

"I unplugged it," the woman said.

"All right," Stan said. They both waited for a time, in case the noise returned. Then he continued, "This is Stan Granger, and I work down at the hunting camp. Now, I don't know if you've heard him talk about me, but if you called Mr. Westbrook or Mr. McGee—"

"Where are you?" the woman asked.

"Excuse me?" Stan said.

"Mr. Granger," the woman said, "my name is Lilly Washington. I run this place, and I want you to listen to me." Her voice was calm, authoritative. "Mr. Chapman ain't here. His hunting jacket's gone, and so is his shotgun. Now, you tell me where you are."

"Gone," Stan said.

"I've got no time for foolishness," the woman said.

"I'm in jail," Stan said.

"Aw-huh," Lilly said. The sound was neither positive nor negative but rather skeptical, as if surprised it wasn't worse. "And which one do they got you at?" she asked.

"Downtown," Stan said.

When he returned to his holding cell, it was seven-fifteen. Lilly Washington's final words echoed in his head: "Honey, do you think in sixty-some years of living in this city I haven't learned how to get a man out of jail?" He turned as the detective uncuffed him.

310

"Could you get Detective Schiff?" he said. "I've got a statement to make."

Schiff barged in two minutes later. He wore a suit that resembled both in color and in texture the nickel plating of a gum machine, and his tie bloomed with flower petals that had been applied by airbrush directly to the fabric. He frowned at the toilet, then sat next to Stan atop the concrete slab. "Shit, partner," he said, "you're confusing me." He tilted his head back beneath the fluorescent dome mounted in the cell's ceiling as if he intended to sun himself in it. "One minute we got to arrest you 'cause you won't say where you been. And then—bing!— you make one phone call and decide to give us a statement. That's funny, don't you think?"

Stan paced in a small half circle until he stood in front of Schiff. Schiff observed him across his boot tips.

"Now you listen," Stan said. "It's right that that boy was a friend to me. Maybe I wanted to protect him a little bit, but that river's coming up, and I got a trailer on it. I got two skiffs. So you can decide right now whether you do or don't want to deal."

"If you were so worried about that trailer," Schiff said, "why not go there?"

"I did," Stan said. "That's where I heard it."

"Heard what?"

"Heard what my statement's gonna be."

"He called you?" Schiff said, incredulous.

"That's right," Stan said. "He said he needed food and water." A patrolman ducked in and when Schiff nodded, he led Stan to a room where a video camera blinked atop a metal stand. "You get this on tape," Stan said. "I got a phone message from Booker *after* I talked to Detective Keegan. She never heard about it 'cause she ain't had no chance to ask me." He waited, staring at the camera, then addressed Schiff again. "Are you gonna set my bail and let me go," he said, "or are we gonna keep trading these stories?"

"You don't need any bail," Schiff said. "Yet."

Stan nodded to the patrolman who was hunched behind the recorder's eyepiece.

"All right, fellas," he said. "Now, I ain't never seen this place, but on the message, the boy you want asked if I could meet him at the Hotel President."

Mercury Chapman had woken that morning at six. He had always been an eager riser, and today—boots gathered in one hand, hair extended like an airfoil at his temples—he tramped down the loft stairs and went outside to pee. He did this every morning he was at the camp, eschewing both the regular bathroom *and* the special outdoor latrine (which, two years earlier, Booker had helped to dig) and continuing downhill to the dike that jutted past the decoy shed. The grounds looked more like a Caribbean jungle than a hunting place, the blue water packed with fans of waxen-flowered lily pads, the trees festooned with leis of clematis and muscadine. He marveled at this, his pants unzipped, watching the mist waft up off the water as if it were heated from underneath. Then he returned to the cabin through stands of burdock and goldenrod, their blossoms not yet gone to seed, and stamped into the mudroom, calling, "Hey, kiddo. What about something to eat?"

They breakfasted at the front table. Booker had showered and sat in a fresh flannel T-shirt and some Brooks Brothers underwear that Mercury had slipped inside the bathroom door. It was dawn by then. The cabin smelled of coffee and woodsmoke, and the mist lifted off the trees through the broad picture window that covered its far end. Mercury served the food, sat, and then quickly rose again, trotting outside to the shed in his apron and shutting down the generator. Booker watched him through the window: a spare and spry old man in leather boots and an apron, jerking and flaring over the machine, and he felt, for the first time ever, protective of his energy.

"It's good," he said when Mercury sat down. "The food."

312

Mercury nodded, burping, his fork held sideways in his hand. They ate in silence for a time, the calls of mockingbirds drifting in from the fields.

"How much time we got?" Booker asked.

The entire station house reacted to Stan's news. Although Schiff had at first received it noncommittally, saying, "Okay, we'll check up on that," Stan had watched him sprint down the hallway as soon as he left the room, his flowered tie streaming back. He heard shouts, the musical sound of men running with their pockets full of keys, followed by silence, as if the building had been evacuated by a bomb scare. Stan stepped back from the cell door's peephole. He checked his reflection in the dull gleam of the stainless-steel toilet seat, and then clasped his hands behind his back, waiting, until the door handle clicked and Marcy Keegan came in. "Mr. Granger," she said. "There's someone here to pick you up."

She read from the clipboard as if she did not know his name. "I lied to you," he said.

Keegan set her clipboard down. "Turn around, please, Mr. Granger," she said.

"Wait a minute," Stan said.

"Around," Keegan said. She twirled her finger in the air. "C'mon, Mr. Granger—we're all busy. Don't make me call somebody."

"Five minutes," Stan said. "That's all I ask."

Keegan put her hands on her hips. Her face had the beaten and faintly savage look of a stray, one cheek pillow-creased and her lips still bruised with sleep. She fixed her eyes on Stan's belt buckle rather than his face, and he squatted to intercept her gaze. "Close the door," he said. Keegan rose, shot the bolt home, and then pivoted halfway, so he saw her profile.

"What if I told you I knew where that boy is?" Stan said.

"Then I'd say you were in trouble," Keegan said. She brushed her hand across her lips. "Especially if he isn't where you told Schiff."

"Well, he ain't," Stan said.

Keegan nodded. Her jawline tightened below her ear.

"And why should I believe that?" she asked.

"You don't got to," Stan said. "You just purely don't got to, that's all there is to it. I'd understand that. But I was wondering if maybe you'd started to think different about this case." He screwed up his face, as if tasting something bitter. "You see, 'cause I talked to him, Booker. Me and Mercury Chapman went down and seen him at the Hotel President. Now I know," he said as Keegan jerked upright, her mouth agape, "I know I done wrong. I know I should've told you about that, but here's the thing: I told Schiff about it 'cause he ain't there—Booker, I mean. I told him that 'cause I wanted to talk to you privately. And I also did it 'cause I thought they might be in trouble."

"How in trouble?" Keegan said. "Other than you telling me where he hid?"

"'Cause I think"—Stan stood, kneading his hands and strolling away from Keegan to the corner of the room—"well, that's just it, I think those two went to meet the judge. Down at the hunt club." He cracked his knuckles. "That's what worries me."

"Why would Judge Sayers agree to—" But then Keegan stopped.

"I was wondering what you might say to that," Stan said quietly.

Keegan kept her eyes on him. It was as if she were seeing him for the first time, as if he had, at that moment, shifted from the casual, the unimportant, to the real, standing there before her gangly, his hair matted Caesarlike against his forehead and his Adam's apple jutting above his trimmed silk shirt. "How far is it?" she asked.

"About an hour," Stan said. "Depending on where the river is."

"All right," Keegan said. "Let's get you out of here."

Clyde Wilkins was waiting for them at the front desk. Stan, of course, did not recognize him, but Keegan did, glancing with astonishment at the big man's face, his bartender's livery replaced by a generous herringbone suit, a fedora, a tie with a gold pin. He was flanked

314

by two other men, blacks, one a bail bondsman whom Keegan knew, the other a lawyer, she guessed. They seemed submissive to him, responsive, and she was saddened by the difference between his bearing in this world and in the other she had seen him in.

"My name is Clyde Wilkins, ma'am," he said. His eyes acknowledged her covertly. "I'd like to know why—if there *is* a reason—Mr. Granger's been detained."

"I can't find one," Keegan said.

She stepped away. The bondsman and the desk secretary had been chatting when she arrived, and now the lawyer stepped into the bondsman's place, unlocking his briefcase. "What exactly *was* the charge?" she heard the lawyer ask. "Or did you keep him just for kicks?" She left Stan waiting in the hallway and headed back to the office to get his things. There was still danger for her in this, less so now that Schiff had authorized Stan's release, but danger nonetheless, and she felt profoundly grateful for Clyde Wilkins's solid presence just outside the cage, his glance of recognition. It seemed an omen, a reminder that she was not chasing ghosts, entirely. She returned Stan's wallet, belt, and tobacco in their plastic bag.

"You know where the garage is?" she asked.

He nodded.

"All right, then, you walk on past it going east," she said. "I'll pick you up."

"Fine," Stan said.

The other men had finished by then. Clyde Wilkins stood apart from them, immense in his pressed suit, Stan gazing at him curiously until Keegan guided him to the window and the secretary. She approached Wilkins alone.

"I wanted to thank you," she said.

"I came here for my aunt," Clyde said, as though this embarrassed him.

"I see," Keegan said. "Still, at any rate . . ." She was about to leave, the conversation dying, awkward, when Clyde Wilkins touched her arm, and she saw a glimmer of the same fear, his eyes oddly passionate beneath his white hair.

"What you're looking for is real," he said.

25

THEY FINISHED BREAKFAST at seven, washed the dishes, dried them, and returned the plates and silverware to the cabinets. Mercury shuffled through the main room adjusting the candlesticks and ash-trays, the stacks of magazines—as if each, in his mind's eye, had its proper place—and then pushed a ladder-back chair against the far wall, next to the shelf that held the tape machine. "The way I see it is that I'll sit here," he said. "It might look funny, but it's the only way I'm going to be able to see everything." He blocked the scene like a director, positioning his chair between the dining table and the sofa, opposite the mudroom door. Then he pointed to the loft above the fireplace. "And when the judge comes in, I want you to be up there, out of sight. It's important that you stay hidden until I say."

"How do I know when that is?" Booker asked.

"Just, just work with me a minute," Mercury said. "The idea is what? To try to get him to say something incriminating, right? Fine. So let's see how this is going to look. You play the judge for a minute—go outside and pretend you're coming in."

Booker opened the door and slammed it.

"All right," Mercury said. He closed his eyes, massaging his fore-head. "I talk to you a little bit, the tape is running—"

Booker looked at him. "You got your gun?" he asked.

"Oh, hell." Mercury waved his hand as if this was a minor concern.

"Listen," Booker said. He squatted before the older man, grabbing his plaid sleeve. "Let me talk to him alone. It's the only way it will work."

"That's crazy," Mercury said. I—"

"You know it isn't," Booker said. "He'll admit it to me and not to you, and do you know why?" He counted on his fingers. "He'll say it to me because I'm black. Because he thinks it doesn't matter if I know. And he probably wants to tell me anyway."

Mercury scuffed the linoleum floor.

"He won't say it in front of you," Booker said.

"No," Mercury said. "I made a mistake with your granddad and Hammonds, right? Well, this time I'm going to stay and see it through." He smiled at Booker briefly, pleased with the precision of his argument. "Hell, I've known Thornton Sayers since he was a kid," he said. "You got to figure a man like that, brought up by your own people, he's got to have *some* shame. No, we're gonna do it straight. I'll tell him the charge and let him try to explain it. That's the only way."

Booker shrugged and stood. "It might work," he said.

"A man like that . . . ," Mercury said. His voice trailed off.

"A man like that will kill you," Booker said.

At seven forty-five, Mercury stood in the cabin's picture window. It was full daylight. The sun's rays fell direct and unimpeded on the earth, not hot but following a long and graceful curve so that they gathered in soft piles atop the flats of pin-oak leaves, his car roof, and Booker's tin-roofed shack, spilling off the edges of everything. A pitchfork leaned against the shack, its rusted tines ablaze in white, its shadow pure, cool black bent by the shack's edge. He admired this. The light seemed to carry in its journey both the heat and the dark of space, and as he scanned the horizon, he saw rills of sunshine flooding the furrowed earth, distant phone lines, sheets of water that flick-

318

ered through the trees, and he had the illusion that he saw these things not by their names but as movements of pure light. He was still standing there when the judge's car pulled up at 8:05, and he watched as his solitary figure trotted through the glade of jack pines that lined the path to the shack. The figure seemed improper, out of place. It wore an out-of-season pea coat, the blue wool buttoned tight against its chest, and Mercury viewed its progress with the taste of ashes on his lips, watching as the judge paused on the shack's porch before entering through the screen. Mercury had no interest in such a figure on this day, and only when the judge reemerged from the shack and headed for the cabin did he finally step back from the window, unseen.

By contrast, the inside of the cabin seemed dank. His eyes did not adjust immediately, and he hovered for a moment beside the table, blind, fighting the urge to go back to the window. His service revolver's holster was strapped against his right hip, and he fingered it gingerly. "Booker?" he said, calling to the loft.

"I'm ready," Booker said.

Mercury switched on the recorder and sat down. He drew his shotgun from its case and disjointed it, giving himself the appearance of industry. The pieces lay on a towel at his feet. He picked up the butt and, removing a rag and a can of oil from the club's cleaning kit, polished it. "I ever tell you about my factory?" he said, loud enough to reach the loft. Booker didn't answer, and he peered at the shotgun's bore, his hands shaking visibly. "Pharmco was the name of it," he said. "Founded it at Eighty-fifth and Standard. Right in the middle of the ghetto—kind of place where Hammonds maybe lived."

"You paying attention to where he is?" Booker asked.

"I used to think that if I hired enough people from that neighborhood—I had fifty-two employees overall—somewhere in there Hammonds would get paid."

"Cap," Booker said. He had scooted to the railing.

"What's that?" Mercury said.

"Listen to me," Booker said. "You don't have to explain that any-more. You came here to help out—that's gonna be enough for me."

"Really?" Mercury said.

"Really," Booker said. "Now pay attention."

"All right, then," Mercury said. He glanced up at Booker and then outside. The sun shone beyond the picture window—beyond, not in, the window itself being in the shade—as if in mockery, the new-leafed trees gladelike, flickering, a rip of blue sky just visible above their peaks. The blue looked unreal to him, a dream.

"I'll do that," he said. "Thanks."

The judge entered the mudroom soon after that. He resembled a ru-ined priest: a swatch of black hair, his fine-boned jaw angled side-ways, lingeringly effeminate, a pair of leather driving gloves snapped about his wrists. Booker had scurried back to his hiding place, and Mercury watched the judge open the inner door alone, seeing at the same time the boy Thornton had been forty years before, seeing also his father, his bombast, his absurd house, the daydream of a mother he had lost: all this, the pale lines of family, present in his face.

"Hello, Thornton," he said.

"Ah," the judge said. He thrust his chin toward Mercury, his hazel eyes scrutinizing the room. "There you are," he said.

"Have a seat," Mercury said, nodding to an empty chair.

The younger man slumped in it awkwardly. His boots were muddy, and he carried with him a duffel bag and a shotgun case that he balanced across his knees, his face wearing the fretful expression of a man who has smelled something he cannot identify. Mercury did not look at him directly. He continued to polish the shotgun's brace piece, dabbing oil upon a rag. For a time it seemed as if they might stay this way indefinitely, the hum of the country surrounding them, and then Mercury sat forward, tossing the brace piece between his feet. "You know what I was just thinking about?" he asked. "I was try-

320

ing to remember the first time you came down here with your dad. You were what, seven then?"

"Thirteen," the judge said.

"Thirteen?" Mercury said. "I would've put you at younger than that." He shifted in his chair, hands folded in the rag. "Look, Thornton, the truth is, I've been thinking about you a lot—since your wife died, really. I've got some idea what that's like, you know, being alone too much, nobody to talk to. Having the bedroom empty—"

The judge raked his fingers through his hair. "I'm sorry," he said, "but I was under the impression that you had something important to say—about the boy."

"Why, sure," Mercury said. "Sure, sure—of course I did."

"Then why are you asking me about my daughter?" the judge said.

Mercury paused. His face had not moved: the grin was still there, the sunburned crow's-feet. "I'm not," he said. "I am asking about your wife." He raised his eyebrows, mouth open as he waited for the judge to catch this, and then patted him on the knee. "But what the hell, right?" he said. "A man gets protective of the women in his life. I got a daughter. I know that. That's why I brought you down here, Thornton, instead of going to the police. Because this is a private matter, a family thing. The fact is I've heard some rumors about you and your daughter—some very unpleasant things. And what you told me yesterday didn't help anything. Do you remember it?"

The judge made a clicking sound with his teeth.

"It seemed funny that a father would talk that way," Mercury said. "Like you didn't mind her dying so much as you minded the idea that she and this black boy had—had—" But he broke off, realizing that the judge was trying to speak.

"What was that?" he asked.

"*Lectin*," the judge said.

"What does that mean, Thornton?"

"It's an ingredient," the judge said. He was smiling in a way that

321

frightened Mercury, fully confident, mocking. "And now I'll like to ask a question, if I may."

"Of course," Mercury began. "Of course—" But the judge leaned toward him, serpentine, louche, his pale lips slightly wet.

"Are you suggesting my daughter and I had an affair?" he asked.

"Well, I don't know, Thornton," Mercury said. "I was—"

The judge watched, reclining now in his chair, his head tipped sideways coquettishly. Mercury's face was frozen, reddening; he felt sweat trickle along his ribs. "Can you even say it?" the judge asked.

"You—" Mercury said, halting. "You—"

The judge set his shotgun case on the table so the tapered end pointed at Mercury, and strolled to the window, his hands clasped behind his back. "I hope you understand," he said, "the reality of what you are attempting, let's say, to *intimate*." A blue jay had landed on the grass outside and the judge tapped his fingernail against the glass. "Imagine a trial, for instance. Imagine that you were called up to the stand, what with reporters there, television cameras, and imagine that you were asked to testify that I had done this thing. Would it make sense to ask why you hadn't mentioned it before today—why, after all these years of my daughter and I hunting here, you never thought to call attention to what you'd call our inappropriate relationship?"

"You," Mercury said, gutterally, "are a coward."

"Not really," the judge said. "I am a member here, and so are you. We like it. And in order to be members, we agree not to see certain things. Wanting to change that rule now is what strikes me as cowardly." In the window, Mercury could see his reflection superimposed upon the trees. His teeth were bared, like a skull's.

"I agreed to no such thing," Mercury said.

"Didn't you?" the judge asked. "What about that boy? Clarissa told me a little bit about him. How come, if you were so interested in helping him, you didn't offer him a job in that factory of yours? How

322

come you didn't let him stay at your house, introduce him around town? You didn't expect us to ask you any questions about that." Mercury saw the judge's eyes shift upward in the glass, and turning, he glimpsed the almond oval of Booker's face at the top of the loft's railing. "You're no accuser," the judge said. He had reached the gun case atop the table, feeling behind him with his hand. "Why not leave a situation like this to its principles? It would seem to me that you ought to appreciate its complications—" As he spoke, he drew the gun slowly from the sheepskin case. It was a twenty-two, the barrel long and thin, slightly rusted, almost harmless-looking, and Mercury realized that it was not the judge's own gun, but Booker's, which he had stolen from the shack.

"Put that away, Thornton," Mercury said, standing.

"Oh, come on, Mercury," the judge said. "You and I both know that I won't hurt him. I just want to take him to the police."

The two men reached a stalemate, Mercury with his revolver at his waist, not aiming yet, and the judge smiling, clearing the rifle's barrel from its case. Footsteps sounded on the loft timbers above him. "No," Mercury said, and glancing at the loft, he saw Booker's eyes white against the gloom, his mouth open, and his finger pointing back in the judge's direction.

"Watch out—" the boy said.

The first shot hit the old man in the chest. Booker saw it from the loft railing, the report cracking like the slap of wood on wood and the old man's jacket puffing open like a flower petal, the air behind him tufted with the floating remnants of his red plaid shirt. He started running then. For a time he felt as if he were doing both things simultaneously: running and standing at the ledge aghast, watching the two men, their figures slanted, foreshortened by his vantage point, and their clothes oddly beautiful, each fold and color crisply rendered as though in wax. The old man was still walking toward his shooter when Booker hit the bottom of the stairs, Mercury not pleading, not afraid, not even visibly injured but merely hectoring, impatient, saying, "All right, Thornton, put that thing away," and Booker had just vaulted around the facing of the staircase when he heard the second report, echoless, like the snap of a dried stick, and saw the old man's hand drop like that of the starter for a sprint. He dove in front of the fireplace. The logs were still there from the previous night's fire, tilted in their own ashes, and he could hear Mercury's voice, somewhat out of breath, saying, "Son, now look here. You listen to me." The old man stood between Booker and the judge, two dark patches of blood on his back, and Booker glimpsed the judge's harassed gaze around his shoulder before he started running again, heading for the front room of the cabin so Mercury's body would stay between the two of them. He got there. He was somewhat surprised at that, at hearing no shooting at his back as he tore through the cramped and musty-smelling bedroom, past the two white-sheeted cots, a square of sunlight falling on the left. It was the same bedroom that Clarissa had first slept in with her father—she had, months earlier, told him so—but he did not stop to think of this. Nor did he pause to check the window, instead lifting a chair from beside the bureau and throwing it straight through the pane and in one jump following it.

The judge set the rifle down on the table, pulled out a chair beside the old man, and waited until he ceased to breathe. He removed his gloves and lit a cigarette, alone now, gazing at the photographs of dead men nailed on the walls, their images suffused in saffron light. It was then that he heard the click. The sound was almost negligible, unrepeated, and yet he rose, an odd smile on his face, and hunted around the chair where Mercury had sat, examining everything: the gun-cleaning case, the chair, the shotgun parts. All at once he reached with satisfaction behind the row of wine bottles on the shelf and grabbed the tape recorder. He rewound the tape and listened to it, the air alive again suddenly with his own voice saying, "You're no ac-

324

cuser," and then he rewound it to the beginning, pressing the record button and the fast forward so it would erase. Then he carried the machine to the outhouse and dropped it through the wooden hole that Mercury had cut out for a seat.

He slipped his gloves on after that. He packed up Mercury's shotgun-cleaning kit and replaced it carefully in the club locker. After some thought, he assembled the old man's shotgun, zipped it in its case, lugged this to Mercury's car, and then brought out his own empty shotgun case, fitted his twelve-gauge inside, and left it on the MG's backseat. He checked upstairs, found Booker's bag, which he ignored, and climbed down instead with Mercury's bedroll, which he tied up, and carried outside. After that he returned and, stepping carefully to avoid the bloodstains, picked Booker's twenty-two up off the table, put one foot on an arm of the horsehair sofa, balanced the rifle, and pointed its muzzle at his thigh.

26

STAN GRANGER and Marcy Keegan got to the turnoff at nine-fifteen. They had been driving since eight, Keegan's black Crown Victoria swooping down from the bluffs and across the jungled floodplain, the barns and flooded fields and fenceposts whipping by telegraphically. At times the river crossed the road, seething and buckling, as if pouring over the spillway to a dam. Other times the road itself simply disappeared, its asphalt twisted and upended, embedded sculpturally in the silt of nearby fields. As they reached these obstacles the car would already be braced into a skid, Stan pointing in the direction their new course should be, and now, as they shifted from the paved road to gravel, he thumbed the window button and gestured at the cabin across rows of sprouting beans.

"That's both of them," he said.

"Both of what?" Keegan asked as the car fishtailed beneath them.

"Both cars," Stan said. "The judge's and Mercury's." He looked at Keegan, her face expressionless behind the wheel. "What do we do when we get there?" he asked.

"You don't do anything," Keegan said.

The unmarked car rolled up behind the judge's tangerine MG, burdocks and thistle tinkling against its undercarriage. Keegan removed a shotgun from the trunk. The front window of the cabin had been broken out, and she walked up to it, finding a chair and a twenty-two-caliber rifle amid the splintered glass and weeds. She went inside then. Stepping into the darkness of the mudroom, she waited, the cool and oddly fleshlike legs of rubber waders dangling against her cheek. There was a second door ahead, and she approached this one indirectly, flattening her back against the doorjamb and peering in. The room was partly sunlit. A buzzing sound came from inside, and as she opened the door with her foot, she saw a body seated by the window, its head tipped back, the face unrecognizable, blackened by iridescent wings.

"Who's here?" she said.

The cabin remained silent. She released the safety of her shotgun, her gaze swinging from the loft to the kitchen area, the front bedroom, and the bath. This last door was closed, and ducking quickly underneath the loft, she approached it, checking the bedroom on her way. It was empty, though she could see bloody footprints leading there—and blood on the floor generally, in a tracked, repeated pattern, dried to the color of resin. She tried the doorknob of the bathroom and then jerked the door open, darting back behind the jamb as she did. Slowly, she looked in. Judge Sayers was sitting in the stand-up shower, a dishtowel wrapped about his thigh, his face distorted by the plastic curtain that he had pulled closed around him.

"Get up," Keegan said. She opened the curtain with her shotgun muzzle and aimed it at him. "Get up, Judge Sayers. You'd be best off doing exactly as I say."

The judge's chin wobbled dreamily.

"I've been shot," he said.

"Get up," Keegan said. "You weren't shot in there."

"I was hiding," the judge said. "From the killer."

"Were you," Keegan said.

They went outside fifteen minutes later, the judge first, his legs bare, whey-colored, protruding from beneath the edges of his canvas hunting coat, dried blood streaked along his shin. Stan hardly recognized him; it was as if he, Thornton Sayers, did not exist without pants. The judge turned to Keegan at the doorstep, saying in an undertone, "At least let me be decent. Don't make me go outside like this," but Keegan's face was inflexible, blank, as she tapped the rolled khakis that she had stuffed into a plastic bag and said, "Sorry, Judge. These are evidence." Stan was standing on the far side of the Crown Victoria, as he had been since Keegan entered the A-frame, afraid to go in but at the same time unable to sit. The gravel about his feet was speckled with brown spit, and he glanced twice at the judge before he recognized him and demurely averted his gaze.

Keegan put the judge into the car, her small hand protecting his head, and then she circled to the driver's side and radioed the highway patrol. The dispatcher's voice crackled. "I've got two gunshot victims," she said. "Chapman County, east of the city on highway four-two-two. You turn on section road—" She clicked the microphone off and nodded at Stan.

"One twenty-eight," he said.

"Section road one-two-eight," Keegan said. "I'll need at least a couple of patrol cars and the coroner. I'll need you to patch me through to the county sheriff, too."

She clicked the microphone off as the dispatcher repeated this.

"That's right," she said. "Section one-two-eight."

She dropped the mike on the seat.

"So we were too late," Stan said.

Keegan nodded. An amber line of hair was plastered against her cheek.

"You said two victims," Stan said. His stomach felt light, as if he'd forgotten to eat. "Does that mean both . . . ?"

"No," Keegan said. She frowned at the judge's hunched figure. "He's one of them. The other was the old man. He's dead."

Stan did not answer, his eyes open, brown, the color of a beagle's.

"And the boy?" he asked.

"You did a good job, Stan," Keegan said. For the first time since she'd left the cabin, she met his gaze. "Your instinct was right—everything you said. You can't be blamed for being late."

"Go on and tell me," Stan said.

Keegan shrugged. She was still looking at him.

"The judge says Booker ran away," she said. "He says he shot Mr. Chapman, and shot him, and then ran away. So what does your instinct tell you about that?"

"You gonna look for him?" Stan said.

They both turned then, staring down past the cabin and the scrub pine, the outhouse, and the sun-creamed trees along the duck fields.

"Eventually," Keegan said. "But if he hurries, he's got a chance."

As it turned out, he had better odds than that. The highway patrol's tactical unit did not arrive until twelve-fifteen, most of them having been called away to help with a room-by-room search of the Hotel President—a search that Detective Schiff had refused to end—while other officers had been farmed out to roadblocks, assignments that took new orders to countermand. There wasn't much to chase. Few patrolmen traveled with hip waders, or johnboats, and though party after party followed Booker's footprints down to the boat shed and stared regretfully at the flooded channel, only one went so far as to commandeer a hunt-club skiff and motor, which it piloted fifty yards before running out of gas.

A similar lack of direction afflicted the media, whose delegates—thanks to "private" tips from Detective Schiff—spent the day outside the Hotel President, reporting live from the scene of the raid. Wallace Evenrake, however, was not one of these. His most recent story, which claimed that two vagrants had spotted Booker near the river, had been rejected. A transfer to the Olathe bureau sat on his desk. And, as a consequence, he found himself alone, writing letters in the newsroom (*As far as fall goes, tell Mom not to worry—it looks like I'll be coming back*), when Keegan's voice broke over the scanner, giving the hunt club's address. No cop reporters remained to field the call—or to say he could not leave—and so he headed for the country in his sky-blue Chevrolet Caprice. He arrived before the highway patrol had time to secure the scene, jogged up the gravel drive, and stopped beside Keegan's Crown Victoria, where he addressed the smoky outline of Judge Sayers's face. "Hey, wait a minute, I know you—Judge Sayers, right?" he said. "What are you doing here?" The judge scooted away from the glass, his shoulders pivoting so Wallace saw the cuffed wrists behind his back and then—his gaze traveling down—the naked legs beneath his shirttail, a bloody bandage wrapped about the left. Wallace's eyes widened. He looked up at the cabin, the black-shirted members of the tactical unit, the ballistics experts carrying out small plastic bags, and his hands began to shake. "Wait a minute," he said, fumbling with his notebook. "Wait a minute, you there. Hey, don't you walk away from me. I need some answers here, mister. I'm a *member of the press.*"

For his part, Stan spent the morning as far away from the cabin as he could get, wandering unobtrusively down to the boat shed as the lawmen photographed the A-frame, measured it, marked the resting places of shell casings, and carted his old friend's body away. He knew that Mercury had always disliked funerals, and so he decided to remember him alive instead of dead. There were also some people whom he hoped to avoid, including Detective Schiff (who never appeared) and Sheriff Crapple, who showed up at midday, looked at the broken window and the twenty-two Remington lying in the grass, and proceeded down the gentle sloping field to the water, passing Stan in his shortstop's gait and pausing where Booker had put the skiff in.

"Well," he said, staring out across the flooded channel, "I guess you didn't tell me everything that first day, did you, old buddy?"

"I apologize for that," Stan said.

With his boot-toe, the sheriff levered a pebble from the dirt.

"There's footprints here," he said.

Stan nodded.

"I don't suppose you mentioned to anyone about that."

"I think they're on top of it," Stan said.

Crapple punted the pebble into the shallows, where it sank.

"Well, hell," he said. "A fella's got to kinda wonder about just how on top of it they is, seeing as how don't nobody else here want to talk to me. They gonna go get him, or ain't that the kind of thing city cops do—something where they might dirty their feet."

"Once the water goes down," Stan said, "they think he'll be easier to trace."

The sheriff snorted, staring at the water.

"Unless you want to take a boat yourself?" Stan said.

"Hell, no," Crapple said. "I'll just read about it like everybody else."

Stan went back to the city with Keegan later that day. There were forms to fill out, statements to be made, and it was four o'clock before the department decided he could go, Keegan releasing him absently from behind a paper-covered desk, as if she did not want to know where he was going, nor ask any questions yet. He drove home then. It was a beautiful June night, the air soft and buoyant, the sun in his rearview mirror fading to pink behind a blackened line of trees. People emerged from their houses now, after the rain. Along the winding river road, Father Mortensen strode in rolled shirtsleeves from the Baptist rectory, a brush saw in his hand. Stan waved to him. He saw the widow Everett in a denim apron, pruning her rose bushes. He saw teenaged women in their side yards, dressed for evening prayers, a young boy suspended above a trampoline. There was a fecundity to everything, a brightness to the salad shoots of grass, the lips of daisies, even a brightness to the dirt, the smoky curves of sand and silt that the retreating flood had laid atop the fields, and he felt glad to be returning home just then, as if he were seeing that countryside for the first time in several years. In downtown Waterloo he bought a gallon of milk, a case of corned-beef hash, and a saucepan and charged it to the hunt club's account. He loaded the food into the truck's bed but carried the milk with him to the cab, opening and drinking it, as he drove to where his home used to be.

He bounced down a rutted drive, stopped in a muddy clearing, and got out. The paving stones he'd laid to his front door still remained, along with the vague litter of human use: the oil drums that stored his trash, dangling phone and power lines, his propane tank. But the trailer itself had vanished, and as he perused this scene—the scratch marks of fifteen years—Booker Short's thin form unfolded from the branches of a nearby linden tree. Stan lifted his milk jug to his lips and then handed it to the boy, who accepted it awkwardly.

"I did it," Booker said. "I come to tell you that."

Stan closed one eye. "Did what?" he asked.

"Lost you your trailer," Booker said.

Stan broke a chunk off the jagged lip of earth where his trailer once had stood. He watched the current swallow it and then plucked the milk jug from Booker's hands and drank, breathing through his nose audibly. When he finished, he spat, the last mouthful falling bluish on the dead leaves. "I hope to never spend another night alone in a goddamn place like that," he said, staring out at the river. "And I am serious about that."

Booker thrust his hands in his pockets, shivering.

"And how did you get here?" Stan asked.

"I took a skiff from the hunt club," Booker said. "The water was so high I just rowed the creek." He rubbed his toe through the dirt. "You been out there yet today?"

"Yessir," Stan said, "I have." He ambled downriver to check on where Booker had tied up the skiff, collecting dried sticks as he went. When he returned, they started a fire with the sticks, lighting it with scraps of paper from Stan's grocery bag and feeding in the whitened driftwood. Booker retrieved two lichen-chined logs from Stan's former woodpile and dragged them over, and the two men sat facing each other across the flames. It was a cool night. They built the fire

332

outward from the center, drying the larger, wetter logs beside the flames, each rising wordlessly in alternation to walk off into the brush and gather fuel again. The river stretched beyond them, and they had a clear view upstream, where the roots of fallen cottonwoods swerved and spun like saw wheels, and they could see how the stands of loose-strife and horsetail that grew along the bank had all been bent back-ward by the water, each twig festooned with a mantle of drying leaves.

"You ain't never gonna see a thing like that," Stan said. "Not in my lifetime, anyways. You know what I'd do if I had time for it? I'd put some food in that damn skiff of yours and float it, see what she looked like busted loose this way."

"Would you?" Booker said.

"Yes, I would," Stan said. "Something to tell my kids about some-day."

The conversation was not over yet, Booker's face still brooding, his lips compressed, but Stan seemed not to notice this. He walked to the truck bed and removed two cans of corned-beef hash and the saucepan and returned to the fire. He opened the cans laboriously, punching triangles around their lips with the churchkey on his pocket-knife, and he then poured the hash into the pan and held it above the flames.

"I could've saved him," Booker said.

"Who?" Stan said. "Mercury?"

Booker nodded. "Both him and Clarissa," he said. "If I hadn't've come out here, neither one of them would be dead. I got a bad effect."

Stan shrugged. "I never felt that way," he said.

"I thought he owed me something," Booker said.

The hash was hot by then. It smelled of cloves and sizzled in the pan, and they ate it from Stan's knife blade, their mouths open, breathing to cool the food. "So now you think he didn't owe you?" Stan asked. "Or are you just embarrassed by the way he paid?"

"'Embarrassed'?" Booker said.

"That's right," Stan said. The steam from the pan swirled about

333

his face. "You didn't shoot nobody, did you? You didn't force Mr. Chapman to go out to that cabin and . . . and . . ." He swallowed. "What was it that happened out there, anyway?" he asked.

"The judge got a gun," Booker said. "And Mercury stood in the way."

"All right, then," Stan said. He was quiet for a minute, as if surprised. "The question is what you gonna do about it now, seeing as he saw something there to save."

They slept in the truck's front seat, blanketless, their hands tucked in their front pockets to keep them warm. Before they got in, Booker thanked Stan, shook his hand, and clapped him on the back, and now they sat awake for a time, staring out the windshield from their cold, right-angled seats. It reminded Booker of all the other pickups he had been in, of his grandfather's and of Batson's—of his night out in the bean field, the night when he and Batson had tried to escape. "Tell me about how you'd travel on that river," he said, and Stan did, explaining about the currents and the buoy markers, about which channels would be used for freight. "But in a flood like this, there wouldn't be no one out," he said. "That's the beauty of it. A guy could run all night and maybe all day and never see anything. With the current like it is, he could make St. Louis in a couple weeks."

"You think a guy could really do it, then?" Booker said.

"If he didn't have anyone he was in a big hurry to see."

After this exchange, Stan Granger pretended to fall asleep. He reclined his seat and rolled onto his side, away from Booker, his knees balled up to his chest. He could hear the night and the river; he could hear locusts calling from the trees. After about a half hour he heard Booker say his name and he did not answer, breathing steadily and listening to the creak of the pickup's door and Booker's footsteps on the grass. The door closed slowly, quietly. He felt a lift in the truck's springs as Booker pulled the case of corned beef from the bed, and then he waited several minutes more before peeking up through the windshield cautiously, in time to see the boy wandering downstream

334

toward the skiff, his silhouette as mysterious as ever, ducking beneath the branches of the linden tree.

In the morning he found a note under the wiper blade that read: *I owe you one case of corned beef. Thanks for everything—Booker Short.*

27

IT WAS AUGUST before the trial began. Despite efforts by the judge's counsel to speed things up—and, conversely, efforts by the prosecutor to delay them—much of the summer bled away, the visceral memory of the murder dissolving in its turquoise haze.

Two things happened against this backdrop, the steady ebb and flow of life that Clyde Wilkins (and other blacks old enough to have seen the repeal of the Jim Crow laws) had ceased to believe meant change. The first was Mercury Chapman's funeral. Clyde brought his son, despite the fact that he was well aware of the obscene—in his opinion—pleasure this would give the white descendants who, though they might feign surprise, nevertheless expected their father's servants to appear. He felt intimidated by the stone walls of Grace Cathedral (imported, a sign said, from Lancashire), by the grave banners and polished organ pipes played by a man he could not see. And yet he noticed that the priest's face bore the yellow stain of gout, that the choirboys were pimpled in their flowing robes, and that during communion the acolytes chewed gum and stared at the women on the rail wolfishly. This reassured him in some way. His son, he realized, had never been at an event with this many whites, except perhaps at a baseball game, and the boy stood transfixed, absorbing the scene as, though he did not know it, Mercury Chapman himself had done as a child seventy years earlier, visiting Eve Wilkins's church on Twentieth Street.

Lilly, of course, was there. She had been present, as an infant, when Mercury Chapman attended All Souls Unitarian in his Sunday blazer—and she had chaperoned Clyde Wilkins as he wore the same jacket, years later, when she was in her twenties. She stood in the family's pew erect, perfectly coiffed, with a matching handbag and suit of lavender, a gardenia cut from the dead man's own garden pinned to her chest. She sang. It was an old hymn, one that she knew by heart and that she also knew Mercury had first heard at her own church, the choice of it like a message, an acknowledgment, and her voice rose to meet the tune clearly, firmly:

> Every time I feel the spirit
> Moving in my heart, I will pray.

Clyde Wilkins held the hymnal out for his son, who read the words, eyes magnified by his glasses, and he heard the alto of his wife beside him, rhythmic, sensuous, and he sang, too, their voices mixing with those of the other parishioners: a full crowd was packed to the remotest reaches of the vast church. He noticed that farther back there were other blacks, employees of Mercury's factory and even the deacon of All Souls Unitarian, to which for so many years the old man had sent his money, and Clyde felt a full-throated tenderness and pride for his family—three generations of it—and how good they all looked standing there, his wife's voice clean and free of regret, and his son's stumbling, slightly off key. For them the past had already been erased. They knew nothing of the Chapmans because he had never spoken of them, and the thought struck him with a strange combination of joy and sadness, an odd purgation that shuddered through his bowels, the knowledge that with Mercury's death a large portion of his life and his mother's and his grandmother's would disappear as well. The city would have no more Chapmans left, except in memory.

Jordan River, chilly and cold
Chills the body but not the soul

They drove then to the gravesite, at Seventieth and Troost, practically the length of the entire city, his son perched atop his thigh in the middle of the Lincoln's front seat, sitting trim and proper like a young gentleman, and his wife beside him, and Lilly in her veil. Again he thought how glad he was to have them seen. They walked out across the soft spring grass together, to the newly dug grave, and he recognized Stan Granger there, and Remy Westbrook and Podge McGee, whose faces he remembered from his childhood. They were old, he saw: old and about to die. Suddenly he realized he wanted them to meet and touch his son—their replacement—and he stepped forward to Remy Westbrook and said, "Remy, I'd like you to meet my son, Carter Wilkins," and the old man said, "Why, fine," and stooped to take the boy's hand, saying, "I knew your great-grandmother, kid, if you can imagine that. Evie Wilkins. And I've known your dad since he was no bigger than you." He clapped the boy on the shoulder and grinned at Clyde's wife, then said to Clyde, "That's a fine-looking woman there." Clyde felt strangely ebullient. As the priest spoke, he hoisted his son onto his shoulders so he could see, and as the dirt rained down on the casket, the boy whispered a question in his ear.

"Daddy, who is this person, anyway?"

"Who?" Clyde asked. "Do you mean Mercury?"

"Is he the one who came over to the house the other day?"

"That's right," Clyde said. "He was a businessperson, someone your great-grandma knew. I guess you could say he was a family friend."

For two months Detective Keegan worked ferociously on the case, sending a team of print experts to the Colonial Club's seventeenth green (which, to the irritation of the membership, remained roped off for three weeks). Casts were made of the spike prints, along with photographs and careful measurements matching them to the single spike Clarissa had been found in. A residue of blood was also discovered, and a few strands of hair separated meticulously from the trap's sand, attached to bits of scalp so contaminated that the experts could not be certain of their DNA. To this evidence Keegan added the phone records, the "coordinated" brassiere, and a deposition from a cabbie who had taken a fare from Clarissa's apartment house to State Line Road at 2:05 A.M.

It was enough, perhaps, to exonerate Booker Short; enough, even, to convince the department that Keegan had the right man. But it was not enough to convict. She lacked a motive, someone who would testify to a direct knowledge of the affair between the judge and his daughter. Here the trouble began. People did not want to believe in such a thing: "Who said that?" Sally Lofton-Idlewidth asked. "Did she? Well, for goodness' sakes, I would never want to be murdered, but what do you expect when you go around accusing your own father of such things?" Bert Gauss, on advice of counsel, signed an affidavit that he had "no direct knowledge" of the victim's relationship with her dad, while Remy Westbrook led the detective in among the thick wood beams of his Cape Cod cottage on Greenway Terrace (he had moved years before out of the Westbrook family home, an Italianate palazzo on Fifty-fifth that he described as drafty), poured her a scotch and water, and then burst unashamedly into tears. He, like most of the members, seemed to blame the judge implicitly, but when Keegan tried to pin down his testimony, Remy paced away from her, saying, "Goddammit, it's not that I wouldn't want to testify, it's just that I don't have anything to say. I don't honestly see how I'd help your case. Who killed whom? I don't know. I can't imagine the kid doing it, but . . . hell, I wish no one had done it."

The closest thing Keegan got to a break was Buddy Acheson, the night golfer whose name Clyde Wilkins had given her. She found him trotting briskly down the first hole at dusk, wearing knickers and argyle kneesocks, and when she called to him from a clump of pines, he hushed her and pointed to the silhouette of a red fox, its tail raised in the air. Keegan ignored this and strode across the fairway toward her witness, who was hissing, "Go on, git," as the fox gazed at him insolently. "Do you see?" he said as Keegan arrived. "That's what I've been calling you people about. I want that fox off this property."

"Calling who?" Keegan said.

"Animal control," Buddy Acheson said. His tongue clicked like a finch's beak.

"I'm a detective," Keegan said.

"That's even better," the small man said. He was fairly open when Keegan began her questioning, outlining the club's history as to break-ins, telling the story of the time Charlie Flivver set up his pup tent in the ravine on number six and lay there reading comic books all day—this was the summer of 1973, after he came home from the war. He told stories of sledding parties that had torn up the greens ("'Cause they grow in wintertime; they're not like a tabletop, you know, something that can be easily replaced") and even, at Keegan's prompting, spoke of the judge himself, explaining, "But it isn't him you got to worry about. I mean, the judge—at least he comes to play. He and his daughter. They don't tear up anything." But when she asked about the specific night of the murder, he quieted.

"I thought they already had somebody for that," he said.

"Yes," Keegan said. "Well, I mean, no—that is, we think she may have been here. Over on seventeen. And since you said you'd seen the judge out here . . ."

"Did I say that?" Buddy Acheson asked.

He had stopped even picking up his balls by then and was limping quickly across the course, Keegan following him. He looked back at her occasionally, his pace redoubling, until the two of them traversed the course in an odd duck walk, neither willing to run just yet, waddling through high groves of elms and across fairways, until the golfer reached a garden gate and stood fiddling with its lock near the fifth tee.

340

"No, I'm sorry," he said. "I can't help you. It's not possible. Nobody likes a spy, you know. Not here. Besides, I only play the front nine anyway."

It got to the point where she began to understand, in some small way, something the judge had said in the days immediately after his arrest. It happened in one of the interrogation rooms, during a break in what Keegan found to be easily the most unpleasant part of any arrest: the discussion and negotiation with a suspect whom she knew to be guilty and yet who, by his very inclusion in them, seemed to normalize the events. The lawyers had stepped out for a drink, and the judge loitered before the window, surveying the city to the east: Independence, Truman Road, and (though Keegan did not know it) the clump of forest where he had dumped his daughter's body, just beneath the Chouteau Bridge. "Of course you know that none of this is going to matter to any of them," he said, as lunchtime traffic streamed by below. "Not even if you told them. It doesn't fit into the dream." Keegan responded in spite of herself, asking, "What?" and the judge smirked at her: "Or maybe you don't understand that yet," he said.

"I don't believe the city is a dream," Keegan said.

"Look at it," the judge said. He gestured like a carnival barker at the city. "Is this Paris? Athens? Rome? Constantinople before the Crusades? Has anything ever happened in this city that anyone would ever care about? No. There is absolutely no difference between this city and the most obscure village on the Congo River that Conrad once went past. Not even one he wrote about," the judge said, smiling. "Just one he passed. And that, then, is the dream, isn't it? It's a permanent dream—that we are not, in fact, so obscure as savages, eh? That we have some reason not to kill and rape? And having had that dream for so long, we find it easy, don't we, not to see the things that do not fit?"

He picked up a glass of water from the table and sipped it.

"Sometimes I think it's the criminals who have the clearest understanding of all this," he said. "They at least understand something about insignificance. But for my constituents, what you accuse me of doing simply does not fit. They will never believe it, no matter what you say, unless . . ." He shrugged. "No, probably not even if you proved it."

The trial played out flawlessly, at least from the judge's point of view. He needed only to appear clean, complacent, and aggrieved, a man who not only had lost his wife and daughter but now had to go on trial for the latter's death. There was, as Keegan herself would've admitted, a shrillness to the prosecution's case, a desire somehow to remind the jury that there was a killer in their midst, one who dressed well, had gone on record as an advocate for integration, but had committed murder anyway. The prosecutor produced a chart not unlike Schiff's, showing Clarissa's and Booker Short's progress through the city, providing evidence from bar patrons that they had not argued that night, and from her neighbor that Booker had left Clarissa's apartment ten minutes before she called her father. They could put her at Fifty-ninth and State Line, could even put her on the golf course with their forensics, but they could not prove the judge had been there, or give him a motive for the deed. Clyde Wilkins gravely took the stand to testify that he had seen the judge walk on the golf course at night, though not on the night of the murder specifically; that he had heard comments about his and Clarissa's affair but had seen no evidence firsthand. Stan's testimony was awkward, halting, the caretaker being forced to admit that in fifteen years of service at the hunt club he had seen no direct evidence of this supposed "relationship." It went mostly like that, the surrounding facts all in place, ominous, yet the centerpoint still hidden behind the judge's well-shaved face.

In a way it was the verdict that finished him, not with the jury (which, on a Thursday evening, the city's asphalt and brick still holding the heat of a 105-degree noon, had voted to acquit) but with the

342

membership, the denizens of the great houses of Mission Hills and the Colonial Country Club, the boards of the ballet and the symphony, whose protection and whose dream of propriety—though blindly given, ratified by laws they did not question—he had failed to understand was also mandatory, impossible to escape.

In short, they pitied him. A delegation headed by Cecelia Lofton arrived at his house immediately after the verdict, the women perfumed, stockinged, standing on his redbrick front stoop with their Mulebach's bags of casserole and brisket dishes—all the food necessary for a wake. After watching them enter with a startled expression on his face, the judge backed slowly from the living room to the den, then finally to the kitchen. The house was, as they had hoped, a mess, the living room filled with dirty plates, papers, overturned ashtrays, the judge himself in an undershirt, smoking a cigarette. The women went to work at once, washing and drying, flushed and pleased with their own efficacy, their delicacy, Mrs. Cecelia Lofton saying (without looking at him directly, so as not to embarrass him in any way), "Thornton, you just don't know how sorry we are about this whole thing, these rumors. And I just want you to know that the girls and I don't believe a word of this. I mean, how hard must it have been—" and then looking up from her dishtowel to see the backdoor ajar and the judge's car swerving down the drive and into the street.

So they just watched him after that. They did not judge him; that would have been too easy, and besides, they knew in the end he would have to accept their pity more certainly than any sentence that the court could adjudicate. They followed his career. It seemed the one thing he had not been prepared for, the dream that he had counted on to save him being also that which he most detested, the same pity and tolerance, the same desire by sheer force of will to create normality that his wife had possessed, and he rebelled against them in the same fashion, except this time his opponents were ready. This time they knew how to act. It was almost a continuation of their old battle with his father, the women different now but the principles the same, the elder Sayers having been victorious only because he had provoked them, had convinced them to attack. This time they knew better. And so when he fled from them in his own house, they simply ignored it. And when he snubbed their invitations to their parties and their benefits, when he responded to Cecelia Lofton's symphony fund drive by mailing in a one-dollar bill with curses scribbled on it, they kept inviting him anyway, grimly now, their lips tight and their consciences clean. They were almost like nurses then, or like the asylum keepers of former days who had been in their own way mad: willing, in white frocks and with pursed lips, to endure almost any insult, and willing to comfort him even as he screamed profanities or wallowed in his own shit, not out of concern for the patient per se but because his profanity represented a principle they were determined to erase simply by denying it. Judge Sayers showed them his worst, and to his utter astonishment, it did not change a thing. He retired from the bench, and started up his own practice. He was finished then, though he did not know it yet. He put on weight. For a time he would appear drunk in public, even at church, wandering about unsteadily. No one said anything. In the spring he made his final attempt. He had a secretary then, a tall mulatto woman by the name of Constantine who arrived at his house at eight o'clock each weekday morning and left again at six. That was what they called her, anyway—his secretary—as if this, too, were part of the game. They even felt sorry for her, partially, having to clean up after him, given the condition of the house, and professed to be glad that he had someone to talk to, someone with whom to spend his day. And so when he brought her to the Colonial Country Club's dining room on the anniversary of his daughter's death, even then they did not say anything. In fact they did not even let the tenor of their conversation change: Cecelia Lofton was there, along with Hattie Oldenbrook and Holly Seifert, the women acknowledging the judge and the woman as they

344

came in and then continuing their discussion without a hitch, the room completely silent, calm, and vast, save for the chatter of their voices and that of the judge, who seemed to be arguing vehemently with his secretary. The argument persisted, modulating, rising, the women carefully but politely ignoring it until, toward the end of the first course, they heard a crash and turned suddenly to find the judge standing with his napkin tucked in his shirt and his chair upset, glowering at the room. His eyes were glassy. "I will not have you staring at me," he said. "I will not have you staring at me during dinner. Eh? I am a member of this club, and I can bring whoever I want—"

"But Thornton," the secretary said, "there's no one—"

"Don't 'but' me," the judge said. "I know these people. If I'm doing something they don't like, they can come and talk to me. I don't owe them anything, and I will be damned if I will stand this treatment—being yammered at by those bitches over there."

He kept at it full steam, his voice echoing, high-pitched, against the ceiling of the room, as if he were waiting for someone to stop him or say something, but no one did. Instead they all rose from their places, one by one, and left. Bob Minor went to call the police. And when the secretary stumbled out, crying, awkward in her high-heeled shoes, Hattie and Cecelia intercepted her. They led her to the ladies' room, which was the size of a parlor, complete with a card table and white wicker chaises done in lace. They sat her down on one of these, the judge's profanity reverberating down the varnished hallway until Hattie closed the door on it, the secretary saying, "Oh, I'm so sorry, I'm so embarrassed. It's almost impossible to talk to him when he gets like this."

Hattie handed her a handkerchief that she had dipped in lavender water.

"That's all right, honey," she said. "It's not your fault. The poor man just needs professional help, and we'll see that he gets it. You don't have to worry about a thing."

345

28

HE STAYED ON the river for about a week. It was easier than one might think: once he was out on it and no longer committed, as it were, to any point along the bank, the river seemed utterly placid, the skiff drifting slowly in an unchanging relationship to all that moved on it. He ate and slept in the mornings, on islands or along unflooded portions of the riverbank, boiled water in the saucepan he'd stolen from Stan, poured it into a series of liquor bottles he had found floating in the shallows, and then hung them over the skiff's side to cool with scavenged bits of string. He put back in in the afternoon, before the bugs came out. It would still be light then. After Lexington, which he passed on the first night, its high, spiderwebbed bridge clear against the small town's streetlights, he drifted into a section of the river that seemed abandoned, a long stretch of meandering bends and oxbows, with the bluffs cut high, like canyon walls, above the river on one side and fading into hardwood forest opposite. He saw no people. Even in Oklahoma he had never seen country unmarked by human progress in some way, by telephone lines, fences—anything—and yet here the river snaked on and on this way, and he began to ride it even in the day, forging deeper into what seemed like the heart of the country, before the people came.

It was Mercury Chapman's skiff. He had ridden in it with him and with Clarissa, and inevitably, when his mind wandered, he

346

would think back to them. At first the thoughts embarrassed him. He would see scenes with sudden, unexpected accuracy—Clarissa seated atop him with his prick folded in her hands, or Mercury confronting the judge, the cotton fragments of his shirt floating gently behind him in the air—and he would have to hoot to dispel these things, call out to the river, startling rafts of seagulls from the big logs they rode. "Fuck you!" he would say. "Fuck you motherfuckaaahs!" the words addressed not to the dead, or to the river, but to something indistinct, perhaps simply the strength of memory.

Over time the urgency of these visions ebbed, and he could recall the dead without embarrassment. He thought about them most often at dusk, when he took his bath, naked, treading water beside the skiff. Behind him the sun dipped into the smoking river, which at eye level looked like a vast ocean he had set out across, leaving those whom he remembered on a different continent. "All right, you white folks—" he often said, in preface to some argument he wished to carry out with Clarissa or Mercury. "I know it bugs you to hafta listen to me, but pay attention anyway." At times their presence during these conversations made him laugh, so pure were the expressions of their personality: Clarissa with her small fist clenched, cussing something that irritated her; Mercury hacking his way through a bit of forest with his machete, talking constantly, while the trail lay only a few yards to the left. On the fifth night he sat naked in the skiff, facing upstream. "I'm sorry," he said. "I'm sorry about pulling out on you folks. . . . Well, fuck it. I'm sorry, is all, but I just got to keep on moving. I mean, don't you worry about me." He did not know what he was saying; his throat burned and his eyes were wet. "I got her whupped pretty much, I think. I'm lucky. That's right, I'm lucky. I'm gonna go off here for a few years and come back so rich you all ain't gonna recognize me. Ain't that right? And then I'll take you all out to dinner then. . . . He kept raving like this until he fell asleep. When he woke, it was raining, and he paddled the boat ashore and wandered inland through cornfields.

He reached Flora, Oklahoma, in three days. He hitchhiked from the river to the nearest town, a place called Dalton, on a seed truck and used the hundred dollars Mercury had given him to buy a ticket at the local Greyhound station, which was really a Sinclair station on the town square. The bus came at eight. The station manager had to phone the company directly to inform them of the actual existence of a passenger, and in the meantime Booker strolled across the square to a small store with begonias hung along its eaves and dresses displayed in its front window, called Kenna Kaye's Repeat Boutique. He had forty dollars left, and he bought a pair of industrial-green chino pants and an electric-blue shirt with a flared collar and a tag that said ON SALE. He changed in the filling station's bathroom, stuffing his old zip-collared shirt and pants into the trash can and then carrying the trash can out back to the Dumpster and emptying it personally. Outside, the sky softened from rain clouds to simple gray. Gladiolas bloomed at the courthouse steps, and secretaries gazed out the stone building's windows beneath cracking window shades, and he felt the yearnings of his childhood welling up in the softness of the dusk and in the shouts of children through the dusty street. Perhaps the station manager noticed this: he paused beside the bench, an oil rag in his hand, and said, "So you look to have done some traveling."

"I've been out on the river," Booker said.

"Ah," the man said. He did not seem surprised at this, one dirty thumbnail picking at the rag. "I see. And where are you gonna go to next?"

"I'm heading home now," Booker said.

The first bus went to Jefferson City, where he made a transfer that got him to Tulsa the next evening. He bargained with the woman at the ticket window to let him board a bus to Flora on the same ticket, and the next morning he crossed the Verdigris River and stopped by the Whitmore Hotel, whose windows he and Batson Putz had spied through one winter night more than five years before and which was now entirely boarded up.

He was still a wanted man, technically, and so left the town by way of residential streets, hoofing it past the tidy yards and asbestos-shingled houses of retired farmers and maiden aunts, retracing the route he had followed as a boy, after a night out with Batson, when Isaac would pick him up at school. The rest of the journey took all day. Outside town he traveled roads where cars, much less pedestrians, were rare things. The houses rose toward him out of the ridged red earth, silos first, then roofs, then barns, and finally the whole homesteads visible, with their tractors, woodpiles, cattle pens. The dogs would wake up and he would have to trudge by them in the dirt, the grandson of the man who had been the biggest farmer in the county now chased by the curs of men his ancestors had spent their lives trying to defeat. Only one man spoke to him, an older farmer and handyman out digging a posthole, who set his tools down at Booker's approach. He wore overalls, a quilted jacket, and thick glasses with black frames, his eyes magnified and pale behind them.

"I know you, boy," he said. "Don't I? You're the one what went to prison."

Booker smiled at him as if he'd not heard of such a thing.

"Issac's boy. Isaac Bentham," the man said. Booker shuffled on, head down. "Well, you better keep on walking," the man said, "'Cause you'll not find him here."

He hit the main road after that, the road that led down to the Bentham place. The fields had been planted in soybeans and corn, and in one a tractor churned along the rows, piloted by a white man he had never seen. He saw the house not long after that, looming into view as it had done nearly fifteen years earlier from a taxi window in the rain. The letters on the roof were more obliterated—B ⁺ N I I / M, they said—and the walk and side pens were overgrown with weeds. In the back, the shiny gray lumber of the old homestead had caved in on itself like a cavity. It no longer seemed a living place, and for a moment he stopped before the gate wondering what he had come here to see, and proceeded then through the side yard, past the osage orange trees

349

and the driveway where Isaac's truck used to be. A dog was barking, chained to a tree. He had not noticed it at first, his mind awash with other things, but then he recognized it as the same beagle he had trained, her coat overgrown and matted, her bones visible beneath. He crouched and stuck his hand out to her, the dog still barking, until she smelled him and mewled uncertainly. "C'mon, girl," he said, "you remember me," and as he did so, he heard his grandmother's voice call through the screen. "Alice," she said (for that was the dog's name), "now cut out all that racket. There ain't no one here except you and me. You hear that, okay?"

"Wait a minute," Booker said.

"Who's that?" The screen opened a crack. "Is somebody there?"

Booker did not say anything, and his grandmother came out on the porch, older than he remembered her, in a peach housecoat and unlaced boots. Her arms were bare, with an old sweater buttoned around her neck, her face lined, frail. When she saw him, her hands twisted into the hem of her housecoat, and Booker approached her, smiling. He circled behind her and touched her all-white braid, her body relaxing suddenly against his, and he cupped her cheek. "Oh," she said. "But I thought—" but he shushed her, his chin atop her head, staring at the ruins of the place.

"Let's go inside," he said. "You want to do that?"

His grandmother nodded, pressing one finger against her lip.

"Good," he said. "That's good. You know, I figure it's been about five years since I had a decent meal to eat—five years at least."

He was sorry he'd asked to eat. The kitchen was furnished with the same oilcloth curtains, the same steamed windows, the same counter space, her pallet set up in the side room as it had always been—dustier, if anything, grimmer, as if she were slowly losing control of the place or had ceased to see it properly anymore—but its bounty had disappeared, the stacks of butcher-papered meat, the netted bags of oranges, the potatoes in their burlap sacks, the loaves of bread along the counter and the joints of ham: all the food that she

350

had kept around for the hands' lunches was gone, despite the fact that it was planting time. She managed somehow, without complaining, to conjure up a plate of beans, some unbuttered rice, and two biscuits that, clearly, she had meant to eat herself. Although he knew this embarrassed her terribly, almost to the point of tears, he knew also that she would never make excuses for the meal, it being one of Isaac's pet peeves to hear a cook complain, a point he used to make by saying, "If it ain't good enough, why bring it? Words ain't gonna change the way it tastes," always adding, later, "Besides, there has never been anything to apologize about on your cooking, Maggie, believe you me."

And so neither of them said anything, Booker just accepting the plate from his grandmother, its contents so meager that both avoided looking at it. As a substitute, he stared out the window at the backyard, where he could almost see Isaac's drop-forged figure returning from the fields.

"He's dead, isn't he?" he said. "Isaac."

"Yes, he is," Maggie said.

Booker picked up his fork, watching her. She stood with her back to him, washing dishes in the sink, the water steaming up about her bare elbows.

"Come away from there," he said, "and tell me how it went."

She did so, sitting across from Booker while he ate. He had died of a heart attack, she said. It was harvest time, and she heard a call over the radio from one of the Dominicans that the boss had fallen down and was "looking sick." She drove there immediately. The field she found him in had been half harvested, and she could see at the far end Isaac's pickup truck, and the combine stopped at an odd angle where it had become—by accident—tangled in the field's fence, and the grain buggy beside it tipped over, spilling a fan of soybeans. Isaac's body lay facedown there. His hat was gone, thrown she guessed, and she knew he was dead before she even touched him because of the strange angle at which his body lay. As she described this, Booker stared out the window at the copse of pines where he and Batson used to meet, and when he spoke he was smiling, rueful: "Must have been one helluva ruckus when he saw that combine had gone through that fence."

"I thought of that," Maggie said.

When he looked at her, she, too, was smiling, but her eyes were wet. "He had so many disappointments," she said.

"I know it," Booker said.

"It was worse after you went away," she said. "You may not have known it, or noticed it, but he was glad to have you. With you here it seemed like there was a chance of keeping things going. And then after it went bad with you and him, he didn't know how to go back."

"What's happened to the land?" Booker asked.

"Debt," Maggie said, fretfully. "He borrowed so much to expand. . . ."

"No," Booker said. "That's fine. You did the right thing."

But it was not until evening that he told her why he'd come. Perhaps he didn't even know it himself before that. The two of them spent several hours apart after he ate, Booker exploring the now entirely dust-laden front rooms—which he knew Maggie did not enter, and whose collections she had never liked—while his grandmother drove to town to buy food. Isaac's chair was still there, his lamp, his ordered files. So, too, was Booker's own old room, up the front stairs, the rocking chair he had broken five years earlier stored in pieces in the closet, the rest unchanged. He took only his mother's farewell letter from the front drawer of his desk, an unboxed tape of his father's voice that he had kept since his Tulsa days, and the still-clean underwear and socks from his bureau's top drawer, washed, folded, and heavily redolent of mothballs, as if Maggie had somehow known he would be standing there again. He left all the other things—rulers, slingshots, school boxes, small plastic soldiers, his basketball uniform—all the detritus of childhood, which, like Isaac's trinkets, oppressed him in some way. He went downstairs after that, carrying his belongings folded in a paper grocery bag, crossed into Isaac's front rooms again,

352

and, after some searching through stacks of picture frames, found the photograph of his grandfather and Mercury standing in Belgium with their company and tucked it in the bag. He felt unaccountably happy after that, free. It was nearly evening by then, and he sat with his grandmother in the kitchen as she prepared the meal, chiding her about how she had first greeted him and his mother with a claw hammer in her hand. When dark fell and dinner was ready, they sat across from each other at the kitchen table, the candles lit, and he leaned over his plate to study his grandmother's face. She was well past seventy, he guessed, but on close inspection still retained a flicker of youth, an air of girlishness, her hair tied back in a ribbon and the muscles in her shoulders still firm and trim.

"I'm not going to be able to stay here," he said.

Maggie nodded at this, as if she had expected it but wished he had not chosen to talk about it right away. Her glance dropped to her plate.

"I did my jail time, but they still want me for parole—at least in this state. So," he said, sighing, "I want you to come with me."

Maggie jerked upright, startled.

"Where?" she said.

"I don't know," Booker said. "I was thinking about going west—Washington? Oregon? Someplace with space."

"But he's here—Isaac. We buried him," Maggie said.

Booker spread a stroke of butter across his bread.

"He's also dead," he said. "We can remember him without having to join him." He took a bite. "Don't you think?"

Epilogue

AFTER MUCH CONSIDERATION, Stan asked Marcy Keegan to go boating. It took him all summer to work up to it, renting a room in the Coronado Hotel downtown and walking to police headquarters nearly every day to prepare his testimony—or to do whatever else seemed to be at hand—and returning then to his solitary room to stare out across the tar-roofed city, the empty summer avenues and chain-link parking lots, and curse himself for not having said anything. He did this until the trial ended. He had been waiting for a moment when such a question would not seem out of place and arrived instead at the moment when it could not help but be: he caught sight of the detective as the gallery recessed, the television cameras there, the reporters shouting questions that she refused to answer, and followed her at a distance of ten paces to her parking space. She noticed him as she was getting out her keys, the city massed behind his lonely, hatless figure, the great curve of buildings, glass, and street. "Hello, Stan," she said. "Is there something I can do for you?"

"Yes," he said. "You could."

She let the car door close, so apparent was the gravity in his voice. "All right, then," she said. "Shoot."

"I was wondering," Stan said. "I mean, this ain't really the time or place to ask, but I was wondering if you'd like to get out on the river someday."

"With you?" she asked.

Stan shuffled his feet. "I was thinking that way," he said.

"Why, sure, Stan," she said. "That sounds real good."

And so he had no choice after that. They had agreed to meet on Labor Day, out at the Waterloo boat ramp, and Stan pulled up in his new skiff, wearing a suit and tie, a picnic basket balanced on the center seat, to find the entire town collected there for the church's potluck lunch beneath a checkered tent. He stared at them, aghast. But there was nothing for him to do but wait, seated there in full sunlight, sweating, his eyes fixed on the far bank, enduring the comments of casual observers curious as to what wedding he was boating to that day. For the first time since he'd known her, she was late, and fifteen minutes past their arranged starting time he walked gravely forward to the bollard, jumped onto the ramp, and continued toward the parking lot, eyes forward, back erect. The lot was filled with the cars of picnickers. He searched among them for the dark shape of Keegan's unmarked car, his eyes browsing among the sun-glossed trunks and windows until he saw a silver Escort, late-model, from whose open driver's door protruded a bare and sandaled leg. It was Keegan's. He knew it instinctively despite the fact that he had never seen her out of her work clothes, much less in a navy sundress, its hem hiked above her knee. The leg was of absolutely pure formation, pale and muscled like a jockey's, the foot arched and pink, and he felt a stab deep in his bowels as she set the hand brake, got out, and padded toward him smiling, a pair of sunglasses perched atop her head. She misread his expression as amazement at her car, which she shrugged at matter-of-factly.

"It gets good mileage," she said.

"Uh-huh," Stan said.

"Well, are we gonna go or aren't we?" Keegan said, squinting at the moving river beyond the lot. "I brought my best bug spray."

All of the town's women watched them, high school sweethearts and local matrons, women who had spent their lives feeling sorry for men like Stan, watching as the two processed down to the sun-pierced river, Stan in his dark-blue suit and absurd peach tie, the woman in her fresh sundress—hard-looking, not particularly pretty, but alive in some important way. They watched Stan help her into the skiff, prancing about the edges of the water in his strange dress flats, the woman ignoring him completely, first tossing her bag in and then gathering up her skirt in one hand and wading to the boat's bow and calmly stepping in. And they saw Stan, confused, plunge in after her, wading up to the calves of his dark suit pants and clambering into the stern, the woman rising to steady him as he slipped. It was an unprecedented sight. To them the river—and, by definition, the boats of the men who worked it—was profoundly unfemale, dirty, trash-strewn, dangerous, the place where dead bodies lurked. And yet they found themselves feeling obscurely jealous as Stan fired the engine, a puff of smoke licking the water just behind, and the woman removed the painter and whooped as Stan throttled up the motor, facing forward with one hand atop her wide-brimmed hat, then glancing back with what seemed to be mute approval as the bow lifted and Stan opened up the engine, speeding out ahead.

It was evening before the town heard from them again. Bessie Taylor had decided to walk along the river then: she had gone first out of duty, fearing that the church picnic (which she had organized) had not been cleaned up properly. But she had been seduced, like so many others, by the river's unending seethe, its oddly beckoning quality, and was standing there with a paper plate and two crushed beer cans in her fists, the river's vague, unbordered distance swaying before her like a black sheet. She was fifty-three. Her children had grown up and gone away, and her husband was at home watching TV, not so much a victim as a helpless observer of the intense busy-ness of his wife's middle years—her store, her prayer group, and her committees, her involvement in which, since the changing of her body, had relentlessly increased. And yet when Bessie first heard the voices talking across the water, she found herself transfixed, mouth open, listening. They were a couple, a man and woman. They were out someplace on the river, motorless, drifting by unseen, and yet she could hear their voices and the squeak of oarlocks as if they had been no more than fifteen feet away. The man was apologizing for having run out of gas, saying, "Well, I just wasn't thinking. I just wasn't paying attention to the doggone thing. Hell, in twenty years, I ain't never—" and then the woman hushed him, saying, "Stan Granger, I'm going to jump right out of this boat if you apologize again. I've had a wonderful afternoon." A silence followed. The boat was nearly abreast of her, and Bessie Taylor could hear the hollow bong and clank of someone moving in it, the man saying, "Well, I could probably row us in right quick." The woman did not answer, and she heard more bonging, the clatter of spilled cutlery, the man saying, "Well, dagnabbit, there went that—" and the woman spoke then in a tone that Bessie Taylor remembered intimately, her voice thick and smoke-filled, only slightly chiding, saying, "Mr. Granger, if the problem is in the back of the boat, why are you up here?"

It was a line that weeks later, after she (to her own amazement) told this story, would become her husband's favorite, but at the moment she just stood there pleading with an old, forgotten lust and passion for the man to do something. For a time she heard nothing but the water lapping as if the boat itself had disappeared, and then suddenly the man began to apologize again, the boat farther off downstream now, saying, "Dagnabbit, I shouldn't've done that. Here, now, I'll just row her in," and the creak of oarlocks starting frantically. The woman's voice spoke up after a while, languid, saying, "You can row all you want, Mr. Granger, but what I like is a man who can finish what he starts."

And Bessie Taylor listened to the slow cessation of the oars, the bong as they were shipped, and then she dropped her trash into the river and turned home in the heavy summer air.

Acknowledgments

The School of Professional Studies and the English Department at Rockhurst University, the James A. Michener–Copernicus Society Award, and the Iowa Writers' Workshop have all generously helped to keep this writer off the streets.

I would be nowhere without my mother and father, proprietors of the "Crestwood Bar & Grill." I thank my teachers—John McPhee, James Alan McPherson, Margot Livesey, and Ed Quigley—for their inspiration and friendship. And I thank my friends, family, and colleagues, all of whom contributed to the making of this book: Rick Harsch (and fellow Brutalists), Starr Terrell, Paige Terrell, Gayle Levy, Hamilton Cain, Dorothy Straight, Kate Griggs, Susi Cohen, Ann Davis, Mary Bunten, Alissa Taylor, Jerry Vegder, Dr. Charles Kovich, Dr. Patricia Cleary Miller, Jeannette Nichols, Libby Snyder, and most especially Bebo and her golf game.

I am blessed with a tenacious agent, Warren Frazier, and an editor, Ray Roberts, who has enough patience for the both of us. Major Rachel H. Whipple graciously advised me on police work; any exaggerations are my doing. I'd also like to remember Redman Callaway and my grandfather, Dick Sloan—two friends who taught me how to hunt.